# Praise for
## *No Comfort for the Lost*

"You'll be transported back to old San Francisco as you walk those dangerous streets with Celia Davies, who has dedicated herself to saving lives but ends up seeking justice for the helpless."

—Victoria Thompson, national bestselling author of
the Gaslight Mysteries

"Herriman's historical details provide a rich framework for a gripping mystery and engaging characters."

—Alyssa Maxwell, author of the Gilded Newport Mysteries

"Weaving together an intriguing mystery and a fascinating clash of cultures, *No Comfort for the Lost* will keep readers turning the pages long into the night."

—Anna Lee Huber, national bestselling author of
the Lady Darby Mysteries

"Herriman crafts a finely detailed series debut with a sympathetic protagonist and impeccable, colorful depictions of 1860s San Francisco—from Chinatown slums to the violent docks of the Barbary Coast. This atmospheric mystery is just the ticket for anyone who misses Dianne Day's Fremont Jones series as well as readers of Rhys Bowen's Molly Murphy historicals."    —*Library Journal* (starred review)

"Entertaining. . . . Readers who like independent heroines should welcome this historical series."    —*Publishers Weekly*

"Very finely written and highly recommended reading."

—The Best Reviews

Also by Nancy Herriman

*No Comfort for the Lost*

# No Pity for the Dead

*A Mystery of Old San Francisco*

# NANCY HERRIMAN

AN OBSIDIAN MYSTERY

OBSIDIAN
Published by New American Library,
an imprint of Penguin Random House LLC
375 Hudson Street, New York, New York 10014

This book is an original publication of New American Library.

First Printing, August 2016

LIBRARY OF CONGRESS CATALOGING-IN-PUBLICATION DATA:

Names: Herriman, Nancy, author.
Title: No pity for the dead/Nancy Herriman.
Description: New York: New American Library, [2016] | Series: A mystery of old San Francisco |
"An Obsidian mystery."
Identifiers: LCCN 2016000400 (print) | LCCN 2016004533 (ebook) | ISBN 9780451474902
(softcover) | ISBN 9780698192270 (ebook)
Subjects: LCSH: Nurses—Fiction. | Murder—Investigation—Fiction. | San Francisco (Calif.)—
History—19th century—Fiction. | BISAC: FICTION/Mystery & Detective/Historical. | FICTION/
Mystery & Detective/Women Sleuths. | FICTION/Medical. | GSAFD: Mystery fiction. | Historical
fiction.
Classification: LCC PS3608.E7753 N63 2016 (print) | LCC PS3608.E7753 (ebook) | DDC
813/.6—dc23
LC record available at http://lccn.loc.gov/2016000400

Printed in the United States of America
10  9  8  7  6  5  4  3  2  1

Penguin
Random
House

To my grandparents,
whose immigrant story endlessly inspires me

# NO PITY
## *for the* DEAD

# CHAPTER 1

*San Francisco, June 1867*

*I'm in for it for sure. Dan and his buried treasure. Dang it all.*

Owen Cassidy glanced over at Dan, the lantern dancing the man's shadow over the cellar wall. He didn't know how long they'd been digging, but they were both down to their sweat-soaked shirtsleeves, and Dan had been cursing under his breath for at least the past quarter hour.

Dan Matthews swore again as another hole revealed only sand and rocks and bits of broken construction rubble that had been used to level the building lot. "Anything there yet, Cassidy?"

"Nope," Owen said.

Soon. Dan would give up soon, and they could stop and pretend they'd never been looking for gold. It *had* to be soon. Owen was tired of breathing in the dust they'd stirred up, most of it from the coal heaped in the corner, and his left palm had an ugly blister that was sure to burst. Plus, he was scared Mr. Martin would discover that two of the workers he'd hired to refurbish his offices had been down in the cellar poking around. They'd lose their jobs for sure.

Worse still, if Mrs. Davies found out what he was doing, she'd scold the skin plumb off him. And Owen never wanted her mad at him. She was the closest thing to a parent that he had, since his real ones had gone and vanished.

"You sure Mr. Martin would bury gold down here?" Owen asked. "I mean, beneath his offices and all?"

"Where better? His house, where some nosy maid might find it?" Dan replied. "Who'd ever come looking down here? And why do you think he's in an all-fired hurry to have this cellar bricked over when it's been fine as it is for so long, huh? 'Cuz he wants his money covered over for safekeeping and none the wiser, that's why."

Dan sealed his commentary with a nod. It did make sense. Sorta.

And then it happened. If only Owen hadn't shifted to his right and begun a new hole.

The sound his shovel made was suddenly very different from the clang of metal on stone. "Dan?"

Dan almost fell in his haste to reach Owen's side. "You've found it!" he crowed. "It's old Jasper Martin's bag of gold!"

He dropped to his hands and knees and started clawing at the ground, forgetting about his own shovel in his haste to reach the wealth he was certain they'd found.

"What the . . ." Dan drew back, his face turned the color of a lady's fine handkerchief. "Shit!" he shouted, jumping to his feet. "Why won't he leave me be?"

"Who, Dan? What?" Owen asked, trying to get a look past the man's broad shoulders. He couldn't believe what he saw peeking around the peeled-back edge of a length of oilcloth.

Owen felt his stomach churn, and he clapped a hand to his mouth. Because what he saw sure did look like part of a blackened, rotting arm.

"*M*rs. Kelly, you must stay off your feet if you do not want this baby to come prematurely."

Celia Davies sat down, the cane-seated chair creaking beneath her, and clasped the hand of the woman grimacing on the bed. Maryanne Kelly's skin was clammy and her pulse rapid. In the adjacent room, the Kellys' young daughter bawled, adding to the tension. Fourteen months since that child had been born and already another was on the way, more quickly than it should have been.

"But I've nobody to help, Mrs. Davies." Maryanne pressed her lips together as beads of sweat popped on her upper lip. She'd been experiencing night pains off and on for the past week, and Celia worried for her and the baby. From what Celia's examinations had revealed, the fetus was small and not particularly energetic; an early birth might threaten the child's survival. Worse, it had yet to turn head-down.

Maryanne exhaled as the current pain passed. "John leaves early and gets home so late from his work, especially lately," she said. "He can't help with the baby. And he can't help with the cooking and the cleaning, either."

If Celia had a penny for every time she'd heard the like from her patients, she would have been wealthy by now.

"And don't tell me to hire a nurse," Maryanne added. "You know we haven't any money to spare."

That truth was easily observed by a quick scan of the cramped bedroom where Maryanne lay. The meager contents consisted of a rope-strung bed topped by a straw mattress, the chair Celia occupied, and one chest of drawers that looked as though it had been rescued from a rubbish pile. The linens were clean, however, and the damp air coming through the window was fresh and smelled faintly of the ocean. Celia had seen worse lodgings. Far worse.

"Yes, I know." Celia released Maryanne's hand and stood. She folded away her stethoscope, returning it to the portmanteau that served as her medical bag. "But you must spend more time resting. Ask a neighbor to help. Surely there is someone nearby who can stop in for an hour or two."

"To help a Mick and his wife?" Maryanne asked. "We should've stayed among the Irish rather than live near the Italians and the Spanish and their endless guitar playing. But no, John had to move up here, after we'd had that nice set of rooms off Market and I'd thought we'd finally stay put someplace."

Her daughter's bawling increased in pitch and volume, and Maryanne looked toward the door. "And that one with the colic. What am I to do? Some days I think you're a lucky one with no children, ma'am."

Celia would not call it luck. And she expected she never would have children, especially given her singular lack of a husband residing with her.

"You will feel more cheerful after the baby is born, Mrs. Kelly."

"That's what John says, too."

"Take some sage tea to ease your pains or a teaspoon of paregoric if the tea does not work." Celia snapped shut the portmanteau and tossed her mantle over her shoulders. "For your daughter's colic, you can try some ginger tea, if she'll have it. Otherwise, a warm compress on her belly might help."

"I just wish John could be here more often," the other woman said. "I'm worried he won't be with me when the baby finally does come. But I wouldn't want him to lose his job because he's tending to me. He had such poor luck at work before we came to San Francisco."

"Do ask a neighbor for help, Mrs. Kelly. You might be surprised who is willing to assist a woman in labor." It was a common enough condition among the women who lived in the lodgings that spilled down the hills toward the Golden Gate, and many would be sympathetic.

"I *would* be surprised," said Maryanne, hauling herself to her feet, a hand on her protruding belly.

"There's no need to show me out," said Celia.

"Do you need a candle to light your way home? The fog's coming in thick tonight."

"I've only a few blocks to walk, Mrs. Kelly." Celia fastened her blue wool mantle atop her garibaldi and grabbed her bag. "I will be fine."

"You've more courage than I do to walk these streets alone at night, ma'am."

"They are not so bad." Which was what she always told her housekeeper as well. Addie Ferguson tended not to believe Celia, either.

Maryanne thanked her, and Celia let herself out the front door. The fog was indeed thick, thick as the fogs she'd experienced in London, the corner gaslight a fuzzy spot of yellow in the distance. Mist swirled around a horse and rider passing on the intersecting street, a shadow moving through the blanketing white like a specter. After an anxious inhalation, Celia descended to the street, clutching her portmanteau close.

It was only a few blocks to reach home, she reminded herself. She was well-known in the area and would be perfectly safe.

Better still, she was a very fast walker.

Aside from a cat startling her as it darted across her path, Celia turned the corner onto Vallejo Street without incident. Up ahead, the lights of the houses on Telegraph Hill winked through the mist. Beyond, a cliff plunged to the shore below, and Celia wondered anew at the tenacity of the homes that clung to the hill's sides like barnacles on a boat, some perilously close to the rocky edge; one good shake and they might tumble into the sea. But the homes were much like their inhabitants—strong-willed. Unyielding. And Celia was proud to count herself among their number.

She climbed the steep road, nearing home. The wind was such that she could hear the ding of the fog bell moored off Alcatraz Island, clanging in time to the rhythm of the swells. Next door to her house, the sound of her neighbor scolding one of her children in a burst of Italian echoed along the street, and a nearby dog found something to bark at. Life was normal, safe and sound.

Celia ascended the stairs to the comfortable brick home she shared with her cousin and their housekeeper. She passed beneath the sign that read FEMALES' FREE CLINIC just as the front door swung open.

"You've missed supper, ma'am," said Addie, her hands fisting on her hips.

"I trust you have a bowl of mulligatawny at the ready for me." Celia stepped around her housekeeper into the warmth of the entry hall.

"I ought to let you starve if you canna keep normal hours like other doctors."

An idle threat, coming from a woman who enjoyed mothering Celia, even though she was three years younger and, moreover, a servant. "I am not a doctor, Addie, only a nurse, as you well know. And as my patients do not keep normal hours, neither can I."

"I can dream."

Celia dropped onto the chair in the entry hall in order to remove her boots and slip her feet into the soft leather mules she kept near the door. Surrounded by the bits and pieces of her everyday life—the umbrella stand and the patterned rug on the floor, the case clock, and the tiny painting of a rolling green landscape that her husband had purchased on a whim, saying it had reminded him of his home in Ireland—she felt the tension leave her shoulders. It was always good to be home, the scent of Addie's cooking in the air and the sound of her housekeeper tutting over her.

"Any news from the Chinese quarter while I was out today?" she asked.

"None, ma'am," said Addie, gathering up Celia's boots.

"Ah well."

It had been several months since one of her Chinese patients had died while under Celia's care; she'd hoped that by now she would be welcomed back. But the anti-coolie movement continued to stir up hatred in the city, and Celia reminded herself it was too soon to expect the members of the Chinese community to welcome an outsider's ministrations.

"They'll return, ma'am. Dinna fret."

"I hope you are correct, Addie."

Piano music drifted through the closed doors to the parlor off to her left, followed by peals of girlish laughter. Despite Celia's fears that her half-Chinese cousin would never have friends, Barbara was entertaining that evening.

"Have the girls eaten?" Celia asked.

"Aye," said Addie. "And that Grace Hutchinson, for all she's as slender as a thread, has a healthy appetite. Maybe they dinna feed her at that fancy house of theirs."

"I am certain Jane feeds her stepdaughter. You know she dotes on the girl." Jane had become as dear a friend to Celia as Grace was to Barbara. She'd also become an ardent patron of Celia's clinic, going so far as to gain others' financial support. *We are both fortunate, Barbara and I.*

"But who else makes a mulligatawny like you do?" Celia added.

Another burst of giggling erupted in the parlor.

"Och, those two! They're like as not still laughing over their little joke about Mr. Knowles from the butcher shop." Celia's mantle joined the boots in Addie's hands. "Asking me if we're to get our meat delivered for free if I marry him."

"It is a reasonable question. I hope we do," teased Celia.

"Me, marry that galoot? What a thought. Even if he is . . . Och, nae you mind that."

Before Celia could ask what Addie had meant by her curious comment, her housekeeper hung the mantle on a wall peg and marched with the boots into the kitchen at the end of the hallway. Celia slid open the parlor doors and went through to where the girls, both seated at the rented piano, had their heads bent close together.

Barbara heard Celia's arrival. "Cousin, you're finally back."

Grace Hutchinson rose to her feet. "How is your patient, Mrs. Davies?"

Barbara followed her friend's example and stood, too, wavering on her disfigured left foot before she regained her balance. The girls could not be more different. Barbara was black haired and dark eyed, her features an echo of her deceased mother's Chinese heritage; Grace, a pale blonde with eyes a snapping hazel, was willowy and already taller than Barbara though she was a year younger. She was a polite, cheerful girl, and anyone who could make Barbara laugh was welcome in their house.

"She is well enough. Thank you for asking, Grace." Celia consulted the Ellery watch pinned at the waist of her holland skirt. Nearly nine. How had it gotten to be so late? "I did not expect to see you two still up at this hour, however."

"We were both hoping to sit with you by the fire and read before we retired," said Barbara, Grace nodding in agreement. Grace was staying the night; Celia expected there would be more giggling and whispering before they finally fell asleep.

"If you are exhausted tomorrow, Grace, your stepmother will not be happy with me."

"She would never be unhappy with you, Mrs. Davies. She thinks you're so strong and brave, and I can't tell you how much she admires you," Grace insisted. "I mean, who else would've been so daring as to discover her friend's killer?"

Addie, setting the bowl of stew on the table in the adjoining dining room, cleared her throat in disapproval. The story had been in every newspaper, for all reporters loved to write about the sensational or the merely strange. A nurse helping to find the killer of a Chinese prostitute had apparently fit both categories.

"Yes, that," said Celia sternly, dissuading any further conversation on the topic. It was best left buried in the past, since her success had truly only garnered Celia whispers and gossip.

"Can we stay up for a little while longer, Cousin?" pleaded Barbara.

"You may," said Celia, conceding. "But not too late."

"Should I bring in some milk and shortbread?" Addie asked.

The girls grinned.

"Please do, Addie," answered Celia, and went to sit at the dining room table.

Barbara and Grace ran back to the piano and plopped onto the bench, Grace singing to Barbara's tentative accompaniment. The scene brought to mind a quote: *Two friends, two bodies with one soul inspired.*

*An apt observation by Homer,* she thought.

She'd barely dipped her spoon into the mulligatawny when someone pounded on the front door.

"Not another patient at this hour!" Addie called out from the kitchen before hurrying through the dining room on her way to the foyer. "I'm turning them away, ma'am. You're closed."

It wasn't a few seconds before she heard Addie scream. Celia jumped up and rushed through the parlor.

"Stay there, girls," she told Barbara and Grace, shutting the parlor doors on their startled expressions.

Owen Cassidy stumbled across the threshold, gasping for breath. He was covered in coal dust and dirt from head to toe; the only pale parts on him were the whites of his wide green eyes.

"Och, lad," chastised Addie. "Dinna even think of coming inside—"

"Ma'am! He's dead!" he cried, gaping at Celia. "He's dead!"

"What nonsense are you blathering?" asked Addie.

"The fellow in the cellar! He's dead!"

"*Y*ou are quite certain of what you saw, Owen?" said Celia, once the initial excitement had died down and the girls had gone upstairs despite Grace's attempts to linger in the parlor and hear what else Owen had to declare.

They were seated at the table in the kitchen, Owen munching a biscuit Addie had given him.

"Yes, ma'am. Sure as I'm sitting here!" Owen declared, and wiped crumbs off the lapels of his filthy jacket. "We were digging for—we were digging in the cellar to, um, level it, me and Dan."

"Truly?" asked Celia. "And do you mean Dan Matthews? Maryanne Kelly's brother?"

"Och," Addie muttered, shaking her head.

"I forgot Dan's sister is married to Mr. Kelly," said Owen. Mr. Kelly supervised the crew working at Martin and Company, the crew that Owen belonged to. The crew that Grace Hutchinson's father had hired to level the cellar floor, along with other tasks.

"She is indeed," said Celia. "And neither she nor her husband shall be happy to hear this piece of news about him."

"Wonder if Dan'll have a job with Mr. Kelly much longer." Owen paled and swallowed. "Wonder if *I'll* have a job with Mr. Kelly much longer."

So did Celia. "So you and Dan Matthews were digging in the cellar . . . ," she prompted.

"And then my shovel hit something soft. It was some oilcloth.

Dan pulled it back to see what it was covering, and when we bent down to look closer, I could see an arm sticking out." He furrowed his brow. "I'm pretty sure it was an arm. Only it wasn't a whole one. Some of it was chopped off, and it was all oozy and sorta blackish . . ."

Addie gasped and collapsed onto the other chair. Pulling a handkerchief from her pocket, she pressed it to her mouth and breathed deeply, the linen fluttering against her chin with each exhalation.

"Perhaps you are mistaken," said Celia. There had to be an explanation for what Owen had seen. Because there simply couldn't be a dead body buried in Martin and Company's cellar. "Even if it was decaying flesh, it might not belong to a person."

"Now you're suggesting someone's burying animals in the basement?" asked Addie. "I dinna think that's much better than a dead man, if I might say so, ma'am."

"Shh, Addie, keep your voice down. I do not want Grace to hear. This is her father's business we are talking about, and the site of a potential crime, which is sure to raise a horrid scandal."

They could only protect Grace from the news for so long, however. And poor Jane. How might she react on hearing that a body had been found at her husband's offices?

"Maybe I am wrong, ma'am," said Owen. "I mean, I ain't had cause to see many dead folks, you know? Could be wrong."

"It is possible you are simply tired from your day's labors, Owen, and mistook what you saw. But I think it best that I go and see for myself," Celia said, and rose from her chair.

"You're doing what?" Addie screeched. "You need to tell Detective Greaves. Have the police look into it. It's not your affair, ma'am."

"I will inform Mr. Greaves should the need arise," said Celia, aware that she sounded cross. She'd convinced herself that it did not matter that the last time they'd spoken, Nicholas Greaves had softly touched her cheek and claimed they would see each other again. She had also convinced herself it did not matter that she had actually believed him.

"Now, ma'am, just because you havna heard from him since March—"

"My reluctance has nothing to do with that," she said even more crossly.

"So you say."

"It is simply that, if this is an error, I would prefer not to alert the newspaper reporters. They seem to have eyes and ears in the walls of the police station," said Celia. "I will go with Owen and see what we have."

"I canna say I like this, ma'am." Addie hadn't given up. "Wandering about at this hour. With the saloons open."

"I have been out on the streets at this hour before. Besides, Owen will keep me safe."

Owen puffed his chest and scrambled to his feet. "You bet I will, ma'am!" He patted Addie's shoulder. "Don't you worry. I'll protect Mrs. Davies!"

Addie looked dubious. "You, a skinny fourteen-year-old boy, will protect her? Now you've both lost your minds!"

The building where Owen worked was located on Montgomery Street among the finest of the city's establishments. With ornamented pediments and high arched windows, they were all towering structures of brick and granite and limestone, lining both sides of the roadway. Their awnings were furled for the night, shutters and blinds closed against the shadowed darkness, asleep like a tidy group of children tucked into bed. Martin and Company itself occupied a sedate two-story building that, despite its modest size, managed to evoke the soberness of the business contained within its walls. Here, Mr. Jasper Martin offered only the most desirable parcels in the most promising of neighborhoods, sure to return good money on a person's investment. Here, the architectural design created by Mr. Abram Russell would be the envy of one's fellows. Here, Mr. Frank Hutchinson would provide the best building crew available, true craftsmen.

A dead body in the cellar did not in any way fit into the calculations of these men. Of that, Celia was certain.

"How are we to get inside?" she asked Owen. Standing beneath the flaring gas of a streetlamp, the light it cast dimmed by the fog settling between the buildings, they gathered curious looks from the passengers of the first-class carriages that traveled along this road, bound for a sumptuous meal at Etienne's or the evening's entertainment at the Metropolitan Theatre. A woman in workaday clothes and a raggedy teenaged boy staring at the front door of a business across the way had to look suspicious. Any second now, they would hear the tromp of a police officer's boots coming in their direction.

She smiled sweetly at a man in a frock coat and top hat who slowed to stare at them.

"Good evening, sir," she said, her proper English accent reassuring him that she, at least, was not a typical criminal.

Owen tipped his cap at the fellow, and the man moved on.

"Dan didn't stop to lock up, ma'am. We were in a mighty

hurry," Owen murmured, and dashed across the road after a horse and rider had clopped past.

Celia hiked her skirts and ran after him before she could change her mind about the folly they were pursuing. By the time she reached the building, Owen had already disappeared inside. Closing the front door behind her, Celia paused to let her eyes adjust to the dimness, the streetlamp's already diminished glow muted further by the shades pulled over the large windows.

"Owen?" she called out. Where had he gotten to so rapidly?

Gingerly, she moved forward. The room was large, the back half partitioned into small offices by cut glass–topped dividers. Planks were stacked against the walls along with a quantity of gas fixtures. An orange glow from warm coals peeped around the gaps in the door of the box stove situated in the nearest corner. Construction debris, ladders, and holland drop cloths were everywhere, and the air smelled of fresh paint and sawed wood. The space was not at all sinister in appearance, but then she hadn't been downstairs as yet.

"Owen, where are you?" She took another step, evading a scattering of tenpenny nails spilled on the floor. "Owen!"

"Here I am, Mrs. Davies." Owen's head popped around one of the dividers. "I thought I heard something when I came in, and I was just checking."

"You heard a noise," she said, wishing her pulse would cease dancing a jig. Perhaps they should have stopped at the police station after all. Or at least contacted the neighborhood beat officer, even though the fellow would've asked uncomfortable questions about why they wanted to investigate the basement of Martin and Company.

Owen gestured toward an open door at the rear of the room. "Here, ma'am. These are the steps to the cellar."

The door led into a small vestibule. One set of stairs descended into the cellar. She presumed that behind the closed door to their right a second set led to the upper floor. Owen had halted at the head of the cellar stairs, and she peered over his shoulder. A lantern glowed in the depths, and a sour smell filtered through the air. She'd encountered enough death in the army hospitals to know what that smell signified.

"Dang! What is that stink?" Owen asked, digging around in his trouser pockets and locating a scrap of checked cotton. He covered his nose with it.

"Didn't you notice the smell before?" she asked, retrieving the handkerchief she'd thought to bring along and holding it to her face. Perhaps the body had not released its stench until the oilcloth had been peeled away.

"I was choking on coal dust, ma'am. Guess I didn't." He scrunched his nose. "But I do now."

"Let us make this quick, then. I do not doubt I shall confirm what you saw earlier."

Celia drew in a quick breath and descended the stairs behind him. There were mounds of dirt everywhere, two discarded shovels, a lantern teetering on the uneven ground . . . and a large gaping hole with a man-sized bundle exposed in its cavity. The dark discolorations of putrefaction had set in. Additionally, she could see the reddish blue stains of pooled blood on the underside of the torso, partly twisted out of the grave.

"I thought you only saw an arm," she said.

"Dan and me didn't leave it like this," said Owen, his voice muffled by the scrap of cloth.

The stench was overpowering, and Owen retched.

"If you didn't leave it like this, then someone else—" Celia paused and listened. Was that a noise overhead? It had sounded like footsteps. "Does anyone live upstairs in this building?"

Owen shook his head and wiped his mouth with the back of his sleeve. "The bosses' offices are up there. That's it."

Celia heard the noise again, the rap of heels against wood, moving quickly. Her heart pounded. She was trapped in a cellar with a mere boy, while overhead someone who might not want them to know about a buried body could be blocking their only safe exit.

"Whoever attempted to dig up this body is still here," she whispered.

"He's trying to get away!" Owen reached into his right boot, pulled out a knife, and ran up the stairs. "I'll catch him!"

"No, Owen!"

Celia grabbed the lantern and chased after him, tripping over her skirts. She reached the vestibule just as he raced out the rear door. "Owen, stop!"

She stumbled through a small courtyard and into the narrow dirt alleyway behind the buildings. It was dark and cloaked in fog. And Owen had disappeared from sight.

"Bloody . . ." Clutching her shawl, Celia leaned against the doorframe. "Now what?"

She wasn't about to run out into the alleyway herself, with only a lantern as a weapon and no idea what sort of dangerous maniac she might encounter.

It wasn't long, however, before she heard the sound of running feet. She straightened and prepared to dash inside and bolt the door if the feet belonged to someone more menacing than Owen.

"I lost him," a voice called out, and Owen materialized through the mist.

Celia released a breath. "Thank goodness you're safe."

"Couldn't see who it was, though." Owen folded his knife and returned it to the safekeeping of his boot. "We've got to tell the police now, don't we?"

"Most certainly we do. There is a dead body downstairs."

"Just don't tell 'em what I was doing down there, ma'am."

"I thought you and Dan Matthews were leveling the floor," she said. He evaded her gaze, suddenly finding a spot on the ground very interesting. "That was not what you were doing, was it?"

He glanced up, a sheepish look on his face. "You won't yell if I say, will you, ma'am?"

"I won't yell."

"We were digging for gold."

"Owen!" she yelled. "Mr. Hutchinson shall be furious!" *Gad.*

"I know, I know! It wasn't right! But Dan told me I had to help and if I told him no, he was gonna tell Mr. Martin it was all my idea and then I'd be in trouble!"

"You have gotten yourself into trouble one way or the other, Owen," she said.

"Mr. Greaves is gonna throw me in the calaboose, ain't he?" he asked, squinting down the alleyway as if debating whether to make a run for it.

"I have no idea what he shall decide to do," she said, wondering how she would extract both Owen and Maryanne's brother from this mess. Of the two, she certainly cared more about saving Owen.

"Ask him to take it easy on me, okay? He'll listen to you," said Owen. "He's sweet on you, ma'am."

"I very much doubt that those are his sentiments, Owen," she said, suppressing the desire to ask him why he thought so. *Foolish, Celia. Don't be foolish.* "Might the person you chased have been Mr. Matthews? Perhaps he returned to remove the body."

But that was not logical. After all, he had invited Owen to dig up the cellar.

"Don't think so, given how scared he was when we found it. Don't think he'll ever come back here."

"Do you have any idea who the buried person might be? Has anyone you know of gone missing?"

"Nope," he said, and then his eyes lit with an idea. "Hey! I wonder if it's that fella Mr. Hutchinson was having a shouting match with a few weeks ago. Ain't seen him around lately. Thought they'd come to blows that afternoon. But that wouldn't have been fair. The other man was missing part of an arm. Oh!" He locked eyes with Celia.

Just like the body downstairs.

*Bloody* . . . More than Owen and Dan Matthews were in trouble now. "We *are* going to have to inform the police."

"Durn."

"Indeed."

*B*lood. There was so much blood and pain. Hot. Burning. His *left arm on fire.*

*He heard his name called. "Nick!"*

*The kid in the gray coat hadn't moved. Just stared. Like he couldn't believe what he'd done. And then all of a sudden there was an explosion, and half of the kid's head was gone, blown apart like a melon hit with a hammer. A giant red melon.*

*The ground rushed up, felt cold and hard beneath his knees.*

He looked over at Jack, running toward him, his gun still smoking. Ah. So that was what had happened to the kid.

And then came another explosion, from out of the woods, and Jack flew backward as easily as a doll tossed by a child. He fumbled for his gun with his right hand, his good hand, raised it just as the reb soldier broke through the cover of the underbrush and aimed.

He screamed. He knew he screamed as he pulled the trigger on his Colt. Pulled again. Again until there wasn't a reb soldier and the click of the hammer meant the chamber was empty.

"Jack. Hold on. I'll be right there."

He crawled to where Jack lay on the ground, squirmed over rocks and tree roots and broken branches, the musky damp of churned-up earth mixing with the acrid smell of gunpowder.

"Jack. I said I'd be right there. See?"

Jack's gaze shifted to his face. There was blood seeping from his mouth. "Dang, Frank'll be mad."

"The hell with your cousin, Jack."

Jack chuckled. Tried to chuckle. A gush of blood choked off the sound, and he drowned in a gurgle.

"Jack!"

He shook his friend, his best friend. The only real friend he'd ever had. Shook him like he could stop him from dying, his startled eyes staring through shattered branches at the darkening sky overhead, the clouds turning pink from the setting sun. Red sky at night, sailor's delight . . . "Damn it."

But it was too late for Jack.

Too damned late . . .

"Mr. Greaves." He heard pounding. It echoed in his head. "Mr. Greaves."

Nick sat bolt upright in the chair he'd fallen asleep in, the glass of whiskey that had been resting on his lap rolling off onto the floor.

"Mr. Greaves! Are you in there?" His landlady pounded on the door to his rooms, setting Riley to barking. "You're wanted at the station right now."

He scrubbed his hands over his face, a spasm of pain shooting through his left arm, down from the wound that never let him forget that day.

"Mr. Greaves!"

"Yes, yes, Mrs. Jewett. I'm in here," he said over his dog's barking. "That's enough out of you, Riley."

The dog, half greyhound, half setter, retreated from the door and came to Nick's side.

"Should I tell them you'll be at the station right away?" Mrs. Jewett asked through the closed door. There was no mistaking the concern in her voice, and he could picture the look on her face at that moment, the lopsided furrow she'd get in her forehead. She'd lost her only son at Shiloh and had transferred all of her motherly worries to Nick, the replacement for the boy who'd never come home.

*What a replacement.*

"Yes. Tell them I'll be right there," he answered. "Right there."

# CHAPTER 2

For the third or fourth time, Celia offered a smile to the booking sergeant leaning against his desk in the corner of the main police station, located in the bowels of city hall. Down here, the air was stagnant and reeked of cigar smoke and the stench that drifted from the jail cells accessed through a barred door. The smells were enough to upset a person's stomach, which might explain why the sergeant didn't return her smiles. Instead, he turned to watch Owen, who had found entertainment while they waited for Nicholas Greaves by rifling through the papers atop the desk belonging to the detective's assistant, Officer Taylor.

"Hey, kid!" yelled the sergeant. "Get outta that stuff. It's none of your business."

"Mr. Taylor won't mind," Owen had the temerity to claim. "He knows me."

"Owen, perhaps you should—," Celia began just as the door that led to the side alley banged open and Nicholas Greaves stomped down the short flight of stairs and into the room.

His eyes met hers. They were bloodshot, and he looked very tired. Or inebriated. Or both.

But he was still handsome. And she still wanted to sweep the errant strand of dark hair off his face and see welcome in his gaze. But there was no welcome; in fact, he looked rather angry. Had she honestly expected he would be happy to see her, or repentant for not having contacted her for weeks and weeks even though he had asserted that he would?

*Yes, Celia, you had.*

"Why am I not surprised it's you, Mrs. Davies?" he said.

Owen bounded up from Mr. Taylor's chair. "Hey there, Mr. Greaves!"

"And you, Cassidy," said the detective. "The two of you have managed to get into trouble again, haven't you? Just wish you could do it at a more reasonable time of day."

"It is only ten," said Celia, taking a look at the clock ticking on the wall. "Is this an unreasonable time for a police detective?"

"It is today."

"Then pardon the lateness of the hour, but it could not be helped." She twisted her hands in her lap; she would ask what she'd been promising herself she would not. "Have you been well? It has been so long, I'd begun to fear you had come to mortal harm."

He reached for his left arm and the old war wound that pained him when he was anxious.

*Good. At least he is anxious and perhaps a trifle guilty.*

"No harm, ma'am. I've just been busy."

"Busy, then. I see."

"Since I suspect this isn't a social call," said Nicholas Greaves, his expression darkening, "can I ask why you sent an officer to my rooms to drag me here?"

"I found a dead body, Mr. Greaves!" exclaimed Owen.

"I wouldn't sound so proud of that if I were you, Cassidy," said Mr. Greaves. "Does this have anything to do with your clinic, ma'am?"

"Nope," Owen replied for her. "I found the body at the place where I work. But you're not gonna lock me in the calaboose, are you, Mr. Greaves?"

"Why would I do that?"

"Because of what he was doing when he found the body," responded Celia. "Owen, you need to explain everything to the detective. From the beginning. And do not worry. Mr. Greaves will not be so crass as to throw you in the calaboose."

She slid Mr. Greaves a glance that indicated just how much she doubted that he would not be crass, then gestured for Owen to begin his story.

"*I*'m guessing this Jasper Martin won't be so happy to learn that you and"—Nick consulted the notebook he'd borrowed from atop Taylor's desk—"Dan Matthews were digging around looking for gold."

Cassidy's shoulders sagged, and he glanced over at Mrs. Davies, whose posture had maintained an uprightness that owed only part of its rigidity to a corset. "He *is* gonna arrest me, ain't he?"

"Mr. Greaves, it is clear that Dan Matthews coerced Owen into participating in this escapade," she said. "I know Mr. Matthews' sister—Mrs. Kelly is a patient of mine—and she has often despaired of her brother's impetuousness. But it seems unlikely he would wish to risk his employment at Martin and Company by murdering a man and then burying him—"

"Wait, wait, wait. You're claiming this was all some sort of escapade?" Nick interrupted. He understood why she wanted to protect the scruffy Irish kid she'd taken under her wing, but some fellow who was the brother of a patient, too? Was she hoping to act as a guardian angel for the entire blasted city?

The way she was staring at him with her icy pale eyes suggested precisely that. Things never changed with her.

"Dan Matthews was excited by the possibility of finding gold, nothing more," she replied. "And as I said, he gained Owen's cooperation through coercion. I wish to be certain that Owen does not take any blame for another man's impetuousness."

When she was on edge, her accent always did take to sounding like what Nick imagined Queen Victoria's might be. "I'd guess that's up to Mr. Martin, whether or not he wants to press charges on Mr. Matthews or Mr. Cassidy."

"However, you could influence his decision in that regard?" she asked. "Unless that is something else that inconveniences you."

And sarcastic. Celia Davies was really good at sounding sarcastic.

Okay, so she blamed him for not keeping in touch these past three months and one week. He'd thought about contacting her, though, lots of times. Had trailed her as she moved about the city, watched her house, trying to work up the nerve to climb the steps and knock on the door, listened for any news on her. Did all that even though Nick had decided that a woman who continued to search for her missing husband, despite the man's having abandoned her, wanted the fellow back.

She was waiting for his response. Meanwhile, the station room had settled into an uncomfortable quiet, which was broken by a drunk in the adjoining cell bellowing for a lawyer and the warden shouting at the man to be quiet.

"See her safely back home, Mr. Cassidy." Nick tucked Taylor's notebook into a coat pocket. "I'll contact the coroner and see what there is to discover at Martin and Company."

Mrs. Davies opened her mouth, but he cut her off. "And I'll relay your concerns about Owen Cassidy's role in this little 'escapade' to Mr. Martin."

"Promise, Mr. Greaves?" asked Owen.

"I promise," he said, and shot Celia a glance. Her mouth quirked over the irony of his making—and keeping—promises to anybody. But in her eyes, he saw that she still trusted in his abilities. Believed in him.

*She's made me realize how much I've missed her.*

Celia Davies was really good at that, too.

"What am I to do now, Uncle?" asked Celia, looking up at the portrait of Barbara's father that hung above the parlor settee. "I can hardly step aside in this affair when Owen and Frank Hutchinson and Maryanne's brother are involved."

Uncle Walford's image grinned down at her. He'd been deceased two years now, and with each passing day, Celia believed she missed him more.

"And to have needed to encounter Nicholas Greaves again . . ."

There. That was what troubled her nearly as much as the thought that Maryanne's brother had encouraged Owen to dig for gold and that Frank Hutchinson had been seen fighting with a man who might have ended up dead and buried in a cellar. She was troubled by the fact that she had encouraged Detective Greaves to investigate, and there would be no avoiding him while he did so.

"Heavens, Celia, be honest with yourself. You are looking forward to this."

The painted image did not chuckle over her quandary, but if Uncle Walford had been there in the flesh, he would have done.

Celia hugged her mother's shawl around her shoulders, the consoling softness of the crimson cashmere brushing against her chin, and heaved a great sigh. She was talking to a painting. Surely, she had cracked. Thank goodness Addie had gone to bed soon after Celia had returned from the police station. If she observed her mistress conversing with the artwork, she'd likely take the next ship back to Scotland.

*This is what Nicholas Greaves does to you, Celia. He makes you stark staring mad.*

However, there were questions that required answers. Such as who *was* buried in that cellar? The man Owen had witnessed fighting with Frank Hutchinson?

Celia felt a pang of guilt for not pressing Owen to inform Mr. Greaves of the argument he'd witnessed. The detective would eventually find out about it, and she had gained little by withholding information simply because she wished to protect Jane and Frank from scandal for as long as possible.

She had once told Nicholas Greaves that she wanted to see justice served, proper justice. Perhaps when it came to the Hutchinsons, her dedication to that cause rested upon shaky ground.

With another sigh, Celia turned away from Uncle Walford's portrait and fetched the empty teacup and saucer she'd left on one of the side tables. The figure in the parlor doorway startled her, the cup rattling against the saucer.

"Barbara! I did not hear you come down."

Her cousin had thrown her cotton wrapper over her night-gown and was tightly clutching the ties trailing down its front. "What did Owen mean by 'He's dead'?"

"Please do not worry yourself about that," said Celia, heading for the kitchen. Barbara hobbled after her.

"I heard you go out with him, though," said her cousin. "Did you go to see the body in the cellar?"

"Barbara, I really do not want you fretting over this." Celia deposited the teacup in the wet sink in the corner of the room. "Please go back to bed before Grace notices that you're missing and gets alarmed."

"She's snoring away. She'll never notice." Barbara snagged Celia's sleeve. "You promised me you'd never get involved in another murder."

*I did?* "Who said anything about murder?"

Barbara released her grip on Celia's blouse. "Owen wouldn't have come to you about a dead body for any other reason. He thinks you work miracles. Since you cleared your brother-in-law of murder charges, Owen believes you're better than the police."

"Mr. Greaves was responsible for clearing my brother-in-law," said Celia, heading into the dining room.

Barbara followed her. "That's not how Owen sees it."

Celia tugged the chain on the overhead chandelier, shutting off the gas and snuffing the mantle's flame. "But that is the way it is."

"Does the dead man have anything to do with Mr. Hutchinson's business?"

Celia stopped and faced her cousin. "What did you hear? And did Grace hear as well?"

"We didn't hear much. But I figured, since Owen is working at Mr. Hutchinson's office, that has to be where the cellar with the dead body is." Barbara peered at her. "I'm right, aren't I?"

"We do not know that this has anything to do with Mr. Hutchinson," said Celia, though she herself already suspected him.

"But if Owen found a body at Martin and Company, it will involve Mr. Hutchinson," said Barbara. "His name and the names of the other men he works with will probably be in every newspaper in town."

"I am aware of that eventuality," said Celia. "But please do not speak to Grace about this matter until I've had an opportunity to talk to Jane. She is the proper person to break the news to her stepdaughter. Not either of us."

"I can't keep a secret from Grace!"

"I assure you, you shan't have to for long."

Barbara rolled her lips between her teeth. "I don't like this. The last time you got involved in a murder investigation, Owen nearly got killed."

"I have hardly forgotten, Barbara," Celia responded. She would *never* forget Owen's blood splattered across the kitchen floor, seeping into her gown. Never. "And I do not intend to become involved, unless Jane requests my help."

"Do you think she's going to ask?"

Yes, she did. Once the police came to question Frank. "We shall see tomorrow."

"I hope she doesn't."

"So do I," said Celia.

*Well, well. Frank.*

The silver-plated plaque hanging next to the front door of Martin and Company reflected the streetlamp's muted glow, which picked out the names engraved upon its surface—JASPER MARTIN; ABRAM RUSSELL; FRANK HUTCHINSON.

Neither Owen nor Celia Davies had mentioned that Frank was one of the partners. Would he have decided against taking the case if he'd known? No. Not in the least.

But he had hoped like hell to never see Frank's face again.

"Mr. Greaves," shouted his assistant, J. E. Taylor, running up the street through the fog. "Sorry I'm late. Just got your message."

He'd put on his gray policeman's coat in a hurry, the black buttons misaligned with their proper buttonholes. Beneath his hat, his hair was slicked into place, and he'd recently received a close shave. Nick sniffed the air. Definitely shaving lotion. Lime, to be exact.

"Did I interrupt your evening plans, Taylor?" Nick asked him.

Taylor, pale and freckled, flushed. "I was at Maguire's with a lady friend. The Martinetti Troupe was there along with some female gymnasts doing the Niagara Leap. It was a lot of fun."

"My apologies, in that case."

"What're we doing here?" Taylor looked over at the front door of Martin and Company. The local cop, whom the property owners along this stretch of Montgomery paid to patrol, was making a show of guarding the door and stared back at Taylor. An effort coming a little too late for this particular property. Nick had asked the man if he'd seen anyone suspicious fleeing the store, and he'd fumbled for an answer, explaining that he patrolled this stretch of road only at the top of the hour. Nick decided the property owners paying the man weren't getting their money's worth. At least the local had known how to reach Martin to tell him to get here as quickly as possible.

"We're here, Taylor, because earlier this evening Owen Cassidy discovered a body in the cellar of this building."

Taylor whistled, his breath misting in the damp air. "The Irish kid who hangs around Mrs. Davies' house?"

"The same."

"Who's the dead person?" Taylor asked, stepping over to the front windows to try to get a look around the closed shades. The local glared at him. "Sheesh, I'm with the detective there. I'm not going to disturb anything." Taylor flashed his badge, and the man relaxed.

Inside the main floor office area, a light bobbed. The coroner, who'd arrived a few minutes earlier, had brought a beat cop with him to poke around.

Taylor returned to where Nick stood at the edge of the sidewalk. "No idea who it is," said Nick. "Let's go in and see what Dr. Harris has learned so far."

"Um . . ." Taylor swallowed. "You need me to go see the body with you, sir?"

Taylor had a weak stomach; a corpse buried in a cellar wouldn't be all that fresh, and it would be far more than Taylor could handle.

"I can manage on my own."

"What do you need me to do, then, sir?" Taylor felt his coat pockets, looking perplexed. "Shoot. I left my notebook at the station."

"Here. I brought it with me," said Nick, handing it over. He recounted what Cassidy and Mrs. Davies had told him.

"They interrupted a man trying to dig up the body?" asked Taylor.

"Yes," said Nick, "and in the morning, I need you to locate the fellow who'd been working with Cassidy. A laborer named Dan Matthews. Bring him into the station and see what he has to say. He convinced Cassidy to help him look for gold in the basement, and I want to know who gave him that idea. As well as who he thinks the dead body belongs to, because it seems he recognized the man. He might also have some ideas about who might've wanted the man dead."

"Searching for gold in somebody's basement? Ain't heard that one in a while." Taylor chuckled, licked the tip of the pencil, and jotted down details.

"Next, I'd like you to learn everything you can about the partners at Martin and Company. Details about their business dealings. Who their enemies might be. Especially Frank Hutchinson's enemies."

"Who's he?"

"A man I used to know very well," Nick said, massaging his old battle wound. "I haven't seen Frank since I returned to San Francisco after the war, but I doubt he's changed."

"Sir, should you be investigating a crime that involves a friend of yours?"

"He's not a friend." *Not anymore.* "And I'll be impartial, Taylor. Don't worry."

Which was a whopper of a lie. Because Nick hadn't any doubt he'd be happy to prove that bastard Frank Hutchinson had been mixed up in murder.

"I'll see you in the morning, Taylor," said Nick, going inside the building. The beat cop had gone to do his poking around someplace else, taking the lantern he'd been using with him and leaving the room in shadows. Nick hunted around for matches and had just lit a kerosene lamp on one of the desks when Dr. Harris came up from the cellar.

"There you are, Greaves," he said, wiping his hands on the dark cloth he carried everywhere with him.

The coroner was an immaculately groomed man with graying whiskers and clear eyes, but his clothes carried the sickly sweet stink of death. Nick wondered how a man ever got used to that smell; it always reminded him of the battlefield.

"What have you learned so far?" asked Nick.

"From my examination of what's left of the body, the victim was a middle-aged man of average build," said Harris. "In addition, the corpse is missing part of his right arm, just below the elbow. Should help identify him."

"Old cut? New?"

"It looks to be an old cut. Maybe from the war. Like so many others." Harris glanced at Nick's left arm. The doctor knew about Nick's wound, the one that had nearly cost *Nick* an arm. "Our victim appears to have been killed by a deep penetrating wound to his abdomen. Likely made by a knife, but the opening has deteriorated to the point I can't be sure. The implement probably nicked his aorta, if the blood vessel wasn't severed completely. I'll know more after my autopsy tomorrow. But I expect he bled to death pretty quickly."

"There must be stains around from all the spilled blood."

"Not that I've noticed. The murderer must have spent time cleaning up." Harris finished wiping his hands, folded his cloth, and tucked it into a coat pocket. "I also think the corpse has been there a little while. Can't be positive, but I'd estimate a week or two, possibly longer, given how chilly it is in the cellar. The coolness slows the decay, just like storing meat in an icehouse. I wouldn't want to swear to it in court, though. Just telling you that to help you with your investigation."

"Thanks, Harris."

The coroner nodded. "I've covered the corpse and am going to leave him here overnight. No point in calling for the wagon at this hour when it's just as cold down there as it is at the undertaker's. I'll have a jury look at the body first thing in the morning. A technicality, since it's obvious the man was murdered," he said, crossing the room to retrieve his hat from where he'd left it hung on a nail stuck in the wall. "You've got another good one here, Greaves. Rich businessmen and a rotting corpse on the premises. Ought to be interesting."

"Glad I can always count on your sympathy."

"What are friends for?" Harris asked, chuckling as he took his leave.

Collecting the lamp, Nick went down into the cellar. He was hit by the smell and lifted a sleeve to his nose. Taking shallow breaths, he raised the lamp. Its light flickered across the uneven surface of the walls, the piles of coal and stacked bricks, mounds of dirt, and a pair of shovels.

Harris had re-covered the corpse with a length of oilcloth. The killer must have used it, rather like a shroud. Nick wondered why he'd even bothered. To help mask the stink of a decaying body, maybe? On the edge of the material was a smear of dried blood, perhaps from the murderer's hand, caked with sandy dirt that had clung to it when it had still been fresh and wet. There didn't look to be much more blood on the cloth, though, which suggested to Nick that he'd stopped bleeding long before he'd been wrapped up like one of those Egyptian mummies traveling professors liked to talk about.

Nick swung the lamp, illuminating the corners of the room. The workers had finished bricking only a small section of the cellar, and as Harris had said, there weren't any dark stains from spilled blood on the ground. Killed elsewhere, then, and brought down here to be buried.

*But killed where and why and by whom?*

He stared at the bundle dragged partway out of the hole in the ground. "Well, mister, guess that's what I'm here to find out."

"Mrs. Davies, may I ask you a question?" asked Grace the next morning, seated across from Celia in the hired hack.

Grace had never before requested permission to ask a question, her boldness either refreshing or shocking, depending upon one's definition of propriety. Celia had an idea what Grace's question would be. *Gad.*

"Of course you may," said Celia, steeling herself against the inevitable. "What is it?"

"Something bad has happened, hasn't it?"

"Why do you say that?" Celia asked lightly, as if Grace's question were quite the silliest thing to ask.

"Because you wouldn't have rushed me through breakfast if you weren't anxious to get me out of the house," she replied. "And we heard what Owen said last night. The parlor doors aren't really all that thick," she added, rather mischievously.

"Yes, Grace, something bad has happened," said Celia as the

hack slowed. They had arrived at the Hutchinsons' home on Stockton, a simple house compared to some of its neighbors' but possessing lovely filigree work trimming the center gable, a pair of fine bay windows, and a large garden. The property emanated refinement and tranquility; the latter would soon be horribly disrupted. "But I will let your stepmother explain, once I have spoken to her."

Grace appeared triumphant. "I was right! I told Bee that Owen's discovery meant the body was at my father's office. She wouldn't say so, but of course that's what it means! Owen's working there, isn't he? And you'd want my stepmother to explain to me because that's where the body was, and our name will be in every newspaper . . . Holy mackerel!"

*Oh dear.* "Jane will explain what has happened. That is all I shall say for now."

"She never tells me anything, though."

"It would be improper of me to do otherwise."

The driver opened the carriage door. "Then I'll ask Papa. He'll tell me," Grace announced, and clambered down to hurry through the gate in the white fence fronting the street.

Celia stared after her. Would Frank be any more forthcoming than Jane, when he'd possibly fought with the dead man? He would be a suspect and would need to be circumspect.

*Now, Celia, you are leaping to conclusions about Frank's culpability.* If arguments naturally led a man to murder, San Francisco would be a town devoid of males. The two incidents were likely not connected in any fashion.

"Ma'am, are you gettin' out or what?" the driver asked her.

"My apologies." Celia climbed down and fumbled through her reticule for the fare. After she paid the driver, she noticed a

man walking along the street toward downtown, intently scribbling in a notebook. He had to step quickly to avoid colliding
with a clutch of young boys kneeling on the pavement, engrossed
in a game of jacks. The lads jeered him as he passed, their cries
not nearly as angry as the look on Jane Hutchinson's face. She
stood in the front doorway of the house, glaring at the man's
back. Grace had disappeared inside.

Celia went through the gate and up the front steps. "Who
was that?"

"A journalist. From the *Elevator*." Jane Hutchinson was younger
than Celia, with a lively demeanor that had attracted Celia from
the moment they'd met. Right now, however, she was far from lively,
instead fretfully clinging to the ruffles of her peach-colored morning gown. "He was asking the most ridiculous questions about
Frank's work. I sent him away . . . after I gave him a piece of my
mind for spreading gossip."

"What did he say?" Celia asked, though she knew the reason a journalist would have come here. It was only surprising
how soon he'd arrived.

"That there's a dead body at Martin and Company. Which
is the ugliest gossip—"

"It is not gossip, Jane," said Celia, taking her friend's elbow.
"Come inside. We need to talk."

"*Merciful* heavens," said Jane, crumpling the embroidered
linen handkerchief she held in her lap. Celia had convinced her friend to sit in her parlor, rather than immediately
rush off to find her husband. "It can't be true."

"It is true, Jane. I saw the body myself."

"What does Grace know?"

"That Owen Cassidy found a dead body. I did not admit to her where he found it, though," said Celia. "I thought it best she hear the news from you or her father."

"Perhaps I shouldn't say anything to her," said Jane. "Grace is only fifteen. She'll be upset."

In the hack, Grace had not appeared upset in the least by the prospect of a dead body in the basement of her father's office building. "You must, Jane, before she hears the news from an acquaintance who might not be tactful."

"Especially some of *our* acquaintances. They might relish the scandal a bit too much."

Despite their modest home on Stockton, the Hutchinsons were wealthy. Enviably wealthy. They would draw gossip to them like a lodestone attracted iron shavings.

"So what happens now?" Jane asked.

Last night, the exceedingly busy Mr. Greaves had detailed to Celia what the next steps would be. He would request that a police officer guard the offices of Martin and Company; then the coroner would come with his jury to assess the cause of death, and the body would be taken away for further examination. Celia didn't envy Dr. Harris the task ahead of him; the body would be quite putrid.

"The coroner will do an autopsy. The police will look for clues," said Celia. "And they will question all the partners. Including Frank."

"But what could Frank know about some stranger buried in the cellar of his office? It's ridiculous to think he'll have any information."

"We must consider that the dead man might not be a stranger," Celia pointed out. "Furthermore, Detective Greaves will be thorough. In fact, he might even come here to speak with you."

"Here?" Jane surveyed the contents of her parlor, as if trying to envision a policeman standing on her Brussels carpet or rummaging through the porcelain statuary and Chinese urns on display.

"There's no need for them to come here." Agitated, she stood and began pacing. "Grace and I don't know anything about this event. They shouldn't waste their time."

"I merely wish to prepare you for the possibility, Jane."

"We don't even know who this person was," she said. "Besides, the body might've been there a long time, since before Frank took his father's position at Martin and Company."

"I am no expert, but I know enough about decay to be quite certain that the body has not been buried in that cellar for several years. Ample flesh remained on the bones."

Jane halted. "How gruesome."

"Death can be an ugly business." And murder more so. "There's something else," Celia went on. "When I went with Owen to see the body, we interrupted a person attempting to disinter it. In order to remove the corpse from the premises, I surmise. This individual seems to have heard our arrival and was hiding upstairs. When he made to flee, Owen chased him, but he managed to get away without Owen seeing his face. It was too foggy."

Jane retook her seat on the mahogany sofa. "Do you think it was the murderer, returning to the scene of his crime? You could've been killed."

"Possibly, but how would the murderer have learned so quickly that the body had been found?"

"That is a good question." Jane considered her. "Do you intend to investigate?"

"I am not a detective, Jane. I shall leave the case in the hands of the police."

"The women at the Ladies' Society of Christian Aide discussed your part in finding the person who killed your Chinese patient, you know."

"With revulsion, no doubt, over my unladylike behavior." Celia was finding it difficult to forgive the ladies' hurtful treatment of her cousin. She hadn't anticipated that an organization, its primary purpose to help poor women, would turn against the Chinese along with so many others in the city, since before they had only been generous.

"They admire you more than you realize, Celia, and many of them regret that Barbara felt unwelcome the last time you spoke at their meeting," said Jane. "Your voice is missed there. I miss having you there."

Celia sighed. "For you, Jane, I shall return. Someday soon."

"Good," said Jane, crisply nodding. "This man's death will undoubtedly be the main topic of conversation at the party Mr. Martin is hosting on Sunday. What a way to celebrate ten years since the establishment of Martin and Company—the discovery of a corpse on the premises."

"Perhaps he shall cancel," said Celia.

"Not him. Once Jasper Martin decides on a course of action, he charges forward like an angry bull." She scooted to the edge of the sofa and tapped Celia's knee. "You should come with us.

We're going to Cliff House, and I know you love it there. Besides, everyone will be talking about the crime, and I'd like you with me for support. And to prevent me from fainting."

"I cannot attend without an invitation."

"Jasper won't mind. He'd love the addition of a beautiful woman to the list of guests. He was very taken with you at my party, by the way."

*How wonderful. A potential swain.* "If that is what you wish."

Jane settled against the sofa back. "I do. I'll send a note telling him to expect you in our group."

Celia chewed the inside of her bottom lip. She had to ask about Frank's movements last night but was uncertain how to proceed without upsetting Jane.

However, nothing ventured, nothing gained, as her uncle Walford used to say.

"Jane, I've told you all this because I must know the answer to a question," she said. "Shall you be able to account for Frank's whereabouts last evening?"

"I can't believe you asked me that."

"It needs to be asked. If the police are not satisfied by what they learn this morning, *they* will ask."

"Good heavens, Celia." Jane stood again and resumed pacing.

"Jane . . ."

She paused at the mantel and straightened a figurine of a dog that hadn't been askew. "Last night was one of the nights that Jasper closes the business early. On Tuesdays and Thursdays, around six or so, in order for the men to spend more time with their families during the week." She moved the dog again, back to its original placement. "Frank usually takes the opportunity to spend

those evenings with Abram Russell, however. He's the third partner at Martin and Company. A civil engineer and architect."

Jane's voice was taut, and she pushed the porcelain dog
around with more force.

"What time did Frank come home after his evening out
with Mr. Russell?" Celia asked quietly.

Jane looked over, tension in every line of her face. "I don't
know. I haven't been able to sleep lately, and I took a soporific
last night. At eight, I think. Hetty might remember. She brought
a glass of water to my bedroom for me right before I went to
sleep."

Hetty was Jane's maid of all work. Celia would stop to speak
with her before she left.

"So you cannot say when Frank returned home last evening. Because you were asleep."

"No, I can't say, Celia. I can't, and I wish I could."

Abruptly, Jane raised her hand to her throat, in the process
snagging the porcelain dog with her sleeve. It tumbled from the
mantel and crashed to the floor, shattering into pieces.

The sight of a pair of police officers carrying a fabric-draped
body through the rear door of Martin and Company had
assembled a crowd of onlookers out in the alleyway, where a
wagon waited to haul the corpse to the morgue Harris had set
up in the basement of an undertaker's establishment. The carpenters and painters employed to refurbish the offices all stood
around gawking, too. Inside and off to Nick's left, the gaunt
Jasper Martin watched as well, his dark eyes staring down his
beaklike nose. He had taken his gold timepiece from its vest

pocket and was snapping the lid open and closed. The sound was setting Nick's nerves on edge.

Taylor trotted over from where he'd been talking to one of the painters. "The cops who've had a look around haven't found any clues as to who might've killed the fella, sir," he said. "And none of this bunch claims to know anything about anything. Don't know who the dead guy is. Don't recall seeing anything funny going on. Can't figure who could've ever gotten in the building. Guess Martin's a stickler for making sure the offices are locked at night. Oh, and Mr. Kelly, the supervisor"—he nodded toward the Irishman lounging outside of one of the glass-partitioned office spaces—"claims he can't recall any time that the locks have looked like they'd been forced."

"Maybe they weren't forced. Which means we need to find out who all has a key." Or maybe the offices actually weren't locked the evening a paunchy middle-aged man missing part of an arm was murdered and buried in the cellar. Martin might be a stickler for insisting the place was secured at night, but with all these men coming and going, it would be easy to overlook an unlocked window or door.

"Will do," said Taylor. "And Mullahey's gone to bring Matthews into the station. I'm headed back there now to talk to the fellow."

"Thanks, Taylor."

His assistant tapped his fingertips to the brim of his hat and hurried off.

"Get back to work, gentlemen." Jasper Martin's voice boomed, echoing off the fancy plaster on the ceiling. "Mr. Kelly, see that your workers do what Mr. Hutchinson and I pay them for."

Kelly straightened and strode out into the main room. "You heard Mr. Martin. It's back to work with you lot."

The laborers scattered. Kelly gave Nick a sideways glance before going to inspect the gas fixtures being installed.

Jasper Martin turned his gaze on Nick. "It's Virgil Nash."

"Do you mean the dead man?" Well, that was quick. "What makes you think so?"

"After I got here last night, I took a look at the body. The face . . . was somewhat recognizable, and Virgil Nash was also missing the bottom portion of his right arm," answered Martin. "From a mining accident up at the Comstock Lode, is my understanding."

"There are other fellows in town missing parts of their arms." There wasn't a day Nick didn't notice ex-soldiers with missing limbs. The war had done more than just kill men.

"Most of those men are not former clients of mine."

"And Mr. Nash was, I gather."

Martin scanned the people in the room. They were all doing a good job pretending not to be listening. But the sound of hammering wasn't nearly as loud as when Nick had arrived that morning.

"Let's come back here and talk," the other man said.

Nick followed him to an office in the far corner. Martin stepped inside. It wasn't much quieter. "I don't have any secrets to keep. I would simply prefer this remain between you and me."

*That* wasn't going to happen. On his way into the building earlier, Nick had shoved past a reporter from the *Elevator*.

"I'm all ears, Mr. Martin," said Nick, leaning against the partition. Martin took a seat at the desk, not seeming to mind that the chair was covered in construction dust. "Virgil Nash was a client whom somebody hated enough to stab in the stomach and bury in your cellar."

"A *former* client," Martin clarified.

He rested his elbows on the chair arms and steepled his fingers. The undersides of his coat sleeves were shiny from wear. It wasn't because the man couldn't afford new clothes; Jasper Martin was simply a skinflint. Taylor had done his research and told Nick what he'd learned. Martin was one of the wealthiest men in town, having tried his hand at just about everything—panning for gold, investing in railroads, purchasing shares of Nevada silver mines, buying and selling real estate. Plenty of money for fancy clothes if he wanted them. The question remained, though, whether all that wealth had made Jasper Martin enemies, and whether Virgil Nash had been one of them.

"What sort of business did you do with this former client?" Nick asked.

A muscle ticked in the man's bony jaw. He was as hollow cheeked as the old miners reliving their glory days in every cheap saloon in the city or chewing over their miseries in the square across from the police station. The grizzled old miners, however, were scrawny because they'd gambled away their riches and couldn't afford a bite to eat. Jasper Martin was scrawny because he must not believe in spending money on food any more than in spending it on clothing.

"Our dealings are a private matter, Detective Greaves," said Martin. "But let me reassure you that the transactions with Mr. Nash were thoroughly legal."

"But you no longer did business with him."

"It was mutually decided that we would cease working together on a recent project."

"Maybe you can tell me about the fellow who found the body. Dan Matthews," said Nick, omitting any mention of Owen. "What was his job?"

"Not digging in my cellar looking for buried treasure." Martin reached for his infernal watch again. "He was employed to level and brick over the cellar, among other things. I should say formerly employed."

"Do you intend to press charges?"

"I expect depriving him of a job will be punishment enough."

"Do you think he might've killed Nash?" Nick asked as Martin began snapping the watch lid again.

"And then tried to dig him up again?" asked Martin, sounding incredulous. "I doubt they even knew each other."

*That wasn't what Cassidy thought, though.* "What about anybody else who works here?"

"I have no idea. Nash was a rich man, and everyone knew it," he said. "The man was a fool and liked to carry money on him, show off his cash. Did you find any on him?"

"I didn't check the man's pockets, Mr. Martin. The coroner will make a full inventory of what was on the body."

"Anyway, I wouldn't be surprised if you find that Nash was robbed, and the killer decided to implicate us. Simple as that."

"That's a thought." It might even be correct. But in Nick's experience, most thieves didn't go to the trouble of burying their victims. They just let them lie where they fell. "So you're thinking this was a robbery. That doesn't explain what he was doing here in the first place, though."

"I think the reason Virgil Nash was killed and buried here is your job to uncover, Detective."

"That it is, Mr. Martin. That it is," said Nick. "I'd like to speak to your partners about the man. Where are they?"

"Mr. Hutchinson is overseeing a project of ours near the Second Street wharf. I expect Mr. Russell is with him as well."

"Would either of them have reason to kill Virgil Nash?" Nick asked.

"You'll need to speak with them."

"Which I plan to do." Nick shifted his weight and stared at the man. "Last night, somebody tried to remove the body after Mr. Matthews and Mr. Cassidy found it. Can you tell me where you were last evening?"

"I'm going to cooperate, Detective, despite that insulting question," said Martin, spots of red appearing on his neck. "I was eating at Jean-Pierre's, as I usually do on Tuesdays and Thursdays. The proprietor can tell you I was there."

Nick located a scrap of paper in a pocket along with a pencil and made note of the information. "Can anybody speak for what time you got home from Jean-Pierre's?"

"I live alone. The woman who cleans my house and cooks for me doesn't live at my residence, either. And on Tuesdays and Thursdays she leaves early, since I always go out to dine."

"I see." Nick returned the paper to the inside pocket of his coat. "I'll probably have more questions for you, Mr. Martin, so don't go leaving town."

Martin hoisted himself to his feet. "I have no intention of leaving town, Detective. Because I want to make sure you do your job."

# CHAPTER 3

"So you are positive, Hetty, that you gave Mrs. Hutchinson her glass of water shortly after eight," Celia asked the maid, keeping her voice low. After sweeping up the shattered remains of the figurine, Jane had gone to Grace's bedchamber, but Celia did not want either of them to overhear.

"I'm sure, ma'am." Hetty nodded briskly. "I am."

"Did you hear Mr. Hutchinson come in last night?"

She nodded again. Celia worried for the muslin cap pinned to her hair, which looked in danger of becoming dislodged. "I did, ma'am. I'd finished in the kitchen and gone up to my attic room when I heard him at the front door."

"He does not expect you to wait up for him?"

"No, ma'am."

*Late nights must be a common occurrence, then. Poor Jane.*

They had not been married two years yet, and already he was spending evenings away from her. Not unlike Patrick, who'd invented numerous reasons to delay returning home at night in the years after they'd wed. His decision to take to the sea—and then to disappear after his ship's boiler exploded—had turned into a rather permanent absence. Although, if Celia truly believed her husband was dead, why did she continue to pay her investigator, Mr. Smith, to search for him? Did she think his reported death in a Mazatlán saloon was a terrible mistake, or a lie? *I never did trust Patrick, did I?* How easily charmed she'd been. But then, her husband had been extremely charming.

"Ma'am?" asked Hetty, breaking into Celia's thoughts. "If you're finished, I've got work to do."

"Pardon my woolgathering. I have one more question," said Celia. "Do you know what time it was that you heard Mr. Hutchinson?"

Hetty screwed up her face in thought. "Ten? Yes, ten, I think."

Which left a gap of at least four hours between when he'd left work at six—if Jane was correct about his habits—and when he finally returned home. Sufficient time to dine and return to Martin and Company and attempt to dig up a body. But how would he have learned about Owen's discovery so quickly? And why would he have wanted to remove the man buried in the cellar rather than alert the police? The only reason would be that he did not want the police to recover the body. If there was no body, there would be no arrest for murder.

*I cannot suspect Frank like this; it is simply not possible he is a murderer.*

"Thank you, Hetty. You have been very helpful." The girl held out Celia's wrap, and Celia draped it over her shoulders.

The front knocker sounded and Hetty went to answer it, leaving Celia standing in the entry hall, fastening the clasp of her mantle. When the maid opened the door, Celia wasn't surprised to see who stood on the threshold.

"Is Mrs. Hutchinson at home?" the man asked, looking past Hetty's shoulder into the dim recesses of the house. He caught sight of Celia and frowned.

"Why, good morning, Mr. Greaves."

"What're *you* doing here?" he asked Celia, and stepped forward to get past Hetty.

The maid stood her ground. "You can't come in without me knowing who you are, sir."

Nicholas Greaves reached into an inner coat pocket and pulled out a badge. "Police."

Hetty blanched. "We're in trouble with the police now?"

"Hetty, you should fetch your mistress," said Celia.

The maid looked happy to do so and sprinted off without remembering to shut the door. Mr. Greaves closed it for her. Overhead, Hetty's feet pounded along the carpeted first-floor hallway.

"What are you doing here?" he repeated.

"Jane and Frank Hutchinson are my dearest friends."

His frown deepened. "You could've told me that before. Is there anything else you've decided not to mention?"

Celia held his gaze as guilt twinged. "There is something I should tell you about Frank . . ."

"Oh!" Jane rushed down the stairs, her skirts hiked in one fist. She glanced between Celia and Mr. Greaves. "The police have come already, Celia?"

"Well, that answers what you're doing here, Mrs. Davies," he said. "Interfering with an investigation."

Celia made introductions and removed her mantle again, handing it back to Hetty, who had descended the steps behind her mistress. At the top of the stairs, Grace looked down upon them, unhappiness etched upon her face.

Mr. Greaves was staring at the girl. "My God," he murmured. "It's been that long."

Celia followed his gaze. He knew Grace? The girl turned and fled to her room, and he released a breath.

"Do you know my stepdaughter, Detective Greaves?" Jane asked.

Mr. Greaves didn't answer, instead looking over at Celia. "There's no need for you to stay, Mrs. Davies."

"I expect that Jane would like me with her."

"Please permit her to stay, Detective," said Jane.

"Sure. Why not." He tossed his hat at Hetty, who deftly caught it. "Where can we sit, Mrs. Hutchinson?"

Jane extended a hand in the direction of her parlor. "In here," she said, leading the way.

Celia gave a final look toward where Grace had vanished. Clearly, there were more mysteries than who had buried an unknown man in the cellar of Martin and Company.

*Celia Davies is a damnable pest.*
Nick folded his arms and studied both of the women seated on the parlor sofa facing the fireplace. Mrs. Davies looked back at him without a hint of contrition.

His uncle Asa, who'd been a detective before Nick and had secured his nephew a place on the police force, would never have allowed her to stay during an interview with a witness. Worse, she'd alerted the witness about the crime, taking away

Nick's opportunity to spring the news on the woman and observe her reaction.

*A damnable pest.*

"Are you sure you need to speak with us, Detective Greaves?" asked Mrs. Hutchinson.

She was clutching Mrs. Davies' hand like a lifeline, but her gaze was steady. She was pretty, in a small-boned, delicate sort of way. Not at all like Frank's first wife. Arabella had been spit and fire—rather like Celia Davies, if he wanted to make a comparison—as well as lithe and beautiful. There hadn't been a man in San Francisco who hadn't thought Frank Hutchinson was the luckiest man alive. But all that spirit and life hadn't seen Arabella through the bout of pneumonia that had killed her. After her death, maybe Frank had been looking for somebody peaceful and quiet. Somebody who didn't remind him of what he'd lost.

*Well then, Frank, we might both be running away from memories.*

"Frank has nothing to do with the body that's been discovered at his office," Mrs. Hutchinson added.

"I think I'll decide that for myself, ma'am."

Nick shifted his weight, and something crunched beneath his boot. There was a shard of porcelain on the ground, and he wondered what that was about. The room, in muted shades of blue and gold and scarlet, was otherwise in perfect order. So far as he could see, not a speck of dust marred the surface of the mahogany furniture or sullied the gilt frames of the paintings hanging from the picture rail. The floral wallpaper and the pattern in the carpet were too fussy for Nick's taste, but he knew they were fashionable. Apparently, Frank had done very well since he'd returned to San Francisco after the war. *Very, very well.*

Jane Hutchinson was watching him, a look of concern on

her face. She wasn't as good at concealing her feelings as the woman seated next to her.

"Nice house, ma'am."

The comment caught her off guard. "Why, thank you, Mr. Greaves."

She glanced around her, perhaps trying to see it through his eyes. He'd been at the house before, though. Not long after Frank had bought it and he and Arabella and a young Grace had moved in. Back when they were still friends. Back before he and Frank and Jack had gotten the brilliant idea to join the Fourth Ohio Volunteer Infantry and soldier together.

"Frank, however, insists on our buying a new house. Something larger, finer," she said. "They are building up on the California Street hill, you know. Beautiful homes. He wants us there and not here on Stockton." She turned to Celia Davies. "To impress Papa, of course."

*So, Frank had grander ambitions,* thought Nick.

Celia Davies smiled tightly at Mrs. Hutchinson, but her gaze shifted warily to look at Nick. They'd known each other only a brief while, and it was unsettling how well she'd learned to read his suspicions.

He stored Jane Hutchinson's comment away. "Since you apparently already know about the body," he said as he glanced at Mrs. Davies, who lifted her chin in response, "I think it's pretty clear why I've come to talk to you, Mrs. Hutchinson. I should let you know that we'll be interviewing all of the partners at Martin and Company. Checking on their whereabouts and their relationship to a man named Virgil Nash."

Jane Hutchinson's gaze flickered, and she released her grip on Celia Davies' hand. "Is he the dead man?"

"Do you know him, ma'am?" he asked.

"Yes," she said. "Well, I know *of* him more than I actually know him. He's a very successful importation merchant, from what I understand. He and his wife have a large home on Rincon Hill. You can easily see it from Second Street."

Nick had read something recently in the newspaper about Second Street, but he couldn't remember what.

"The handsome white one with all the columns and the gorgeous gardens?" Mrs. Davies asked. "I do so admire their roses. They are growing some of the new pink-and-cream General Washington roses that are so very lovely."

She sounded wistful, but then Nick knew what her roses looked like.

"That very house, Celia," said Mrs. Hutchinson.

"What was his business with Martin and Company?" asked Nick.

"Mr. Nash engaged their services in certain real estate deals. Seeking locations for new warehouses, was what I'd been told. Frank doesn't talk about the business much, though. Not at home," she explained. "And I can't say exactly what happened, but I think there'd been some sort of a problem with Mr. Nash a while ago. A bit of a row. Didn't Jasper tell you about it?"

No, he hadn't. *So what was it that Jasper Martin didn't want me to know?* "What did your husband think of Virgil Nash?"

"My husband rarely shares his opinions of the men he does business with, Detective," said Mrs. Hutchinson, her hands twisting together in her lap.

"Ma'am, I wouldn't advise keeping the truth from me." At her side, Celia Davies blushed. What did *she* know? "Mrs. Davies? Have something to say?"

She hesitated, stealing glances at her friend before answering. "Owen witnessed an argument between Frank and a man missing part of one arm. Owen did not say which arm, but . . ."

The corpse was missing part of his right arm. Virgil Nash was missing part of his right arm. And now this. It wasn't much of a leap to assume the men were all one and the same. And she'd known, and not told him.

"Do you want me to arrest you for interfering with an investigation?" he asked.

"Mr. Greaves, really—"

"I'm not joking, Mrs. Davies."

Celia Davies glared but pressed her lips together.

"All right. I admit that Frank didn't like Virgil Nash," said Mrs. Hutchinson. "But the dislike arose purely because of the man's resistance to the Second Street cut. Nothing that would lead to violence, if you're telling me that it's Mr. Nash buried in the cellar of my husband's business."

Another cut. That was what he'd read in the newspaper. The men who owned property near the wharves at the foot of Second Street wanted to level the road between the city and the piers, which right now climbed steeply over Rincon Hill, in order to ease movement between the two points. Cuts had happened in numerous locations in town, attempts to tame the hills, and the people who lived alongside them often found their houses stranded twenty, thirty feet in the air above the new road. Rincon Hill, home to the fashionable, would lose its treasured isolation if the cut occurred. *When* the cut occurred, since not much stood in the way of development in San Francisco. Not even Virgil Nash.

Nick eyed Jane Hutchinson, whose composure impressed

him. Not so delicate, after all. "I gather the partners wanted the contract for the cut?"

"Mr. Martin owns several lots near the Pacific Mail Company wharves," she said, revealing how much she actually knew about Frank's business and no longer pretending she didn't. "There is also an expectation that a terminal for the transcontinental railroad will one day be located nearby."

All of which made Martin's property along the southern end of Second Street potentially very valuable. "So, yes about that contract?"

"Yes. Not only was the contract lucrative, but the value of their property was sure to increase."

Nick glanced between the two women, Mrs. Davies' expression turning grim. "Has your husband come home late any evenings in recent weeks, Mrs. Hutchinson, looking disheveled?"

She paled, a crack in that composure. "No later than usual."

"What about last night?"

"I didn't see him come in last evening." She cast a hasty look at the woman seated at her side. *Sharing secrets?* "I was asleep."

"I have learned that Frank arrived home around ten," said Mrs. Davies. "I spoke with Jane's maid, and that is when she recalled hearing him return."

"I only suggested that you ask Hetty what time she brought me my soporific, Celia," said Mrs. Hutchinson. "Not that you interrogate her."

"I apologize, Jane, but I wished to know."

Her answer didn't seem to appease her friend. "Frank was with Abram Russell last evening, Detective," she said, a twitch at the edge of her eye revealing a whole lot about what she thought of Frank's outings with the man. She volunteered the names of their usual haunts, which included some of the finer restaurants and saloons in town. "You should talk to him."

"You can bet I will."

"You might also wish to ask Abram Russell about Mr. Nash."

"I might?" he asked.

He waited for her to go on. He wouldn't need to do any prompting; Jane Hutchinson looked perfectly content to spill all when it came to the man who kept her husband out late.

"I hate to say this," she actually said, "but Abram Russell gambles."

"Isn't anything unusual about that around here, ma'am."

"I know, but he also loses badly."

And that wasn't unusual, either. "Who told you?" Nick hardly thought Russell was sharing his gambling travails with her.

"Frank did. Abram has asked my husband for money to cover debts, in fact. More than once. I suppose he's asked others as well. But he'd never ask Jasper. He wouldn't approve of Abram's behavior. Jasper leads an abstemious life, and he doesn't think well of men who give in to their baser instincts."

"Doesn't Martin encourage his partners to socialize with their clients?" Nick asked. Supper, booze, women—the sorts of things that tied men together. Even wealthy men with families back at their fine homes.

"Not to gamble," said Mrs. Hutchinson. "He was opposed to that. He thought it a weakness, and if Jasper ever discovered that Abram had gambling debts and had been tapping people to cover them, he'd lose his position at the company."

"What's his gambling got to do with Nash?" asked Nick.

"Mr. Nash is wealthy. Abram might have asked him for money

to cover his debts and been rebuffed," Mrs. Hutchinson suggested a little too readily.

"Which makes sense," said Mrs. Davies, looking over at Nick. "When Mr. Nash refused to give Mr. Russell money, he killed the man."

Nick felt his patience stretching thin. "Mrs. Davies, we haven't positively identified the dead man, and I'd prefer that you don't jump to—"

"*Or* Mr. Russell owed Mr. Nash . . . All right, he owed this *dead person* money and was tired of being pressed to pay off his debt. Is Mr. Russell the sort of man who might be violent, Jane?"

"I don't know," said Mrs. Hutchinson. "Maybe."

"Since you've put so much thought into this, Mrs. Davies, maybe you can tell me why Mr. Russell then proceeded to bury a corpse in the basement of the place where he worked?" asked Nick.

That was the question that bothered him most. Why would any of the men, including Frank, have done that?

A tiny crease formed between Mrs. Davies' eyebrows. And then it eased. "It is most obvious, Mr. Greaves."

"It is?"

"Absolutely. Because he could hardly be seen dragging a body through some of the busiest streets in town."

"And now you're going to explain why Abram Russell returned to the cellar last night and tried to dig up the body and remove it," said Mr. Greaves, once Hetty had shut the front door behind them.

"I—," Celia started to reply, and he held up a hand to cut her short.

"And don't forget how Russell might've even learned that

Owen and Matthews had found the body, when Russell was out drinking, gambling, eating—who knows what—with Frank Hutchinson last night," he said. "If I'm supposed to believe Mrs. Hutchinson's story."

"I presume that the killer might have wished to remove the corpse so that he could not be charged with murder," she answered. "Given that it was foggy last evening, he may have believed he could move the body this time without being detected. But how he learned about the discoveryof the corpse . . . I have no idea."

Mr. Greaves settled his hat atop his head, leveling the brim with one sweep of his hand. "Well, thank goodness you don't have all the answers. I was starting to worry about my job."

"Sarcasm is unnecessary, Mr. Greaves."

"Not with you it's not." He scanned the street, looking up Stockton in the direction of Telegraph Hill. The hills of the city were casting off the morning fog, but the buildings crowding the road kept Celia from seeing much more than the traffic and the stir of dust from a crew replacing cobbles. It was a pleasant spot, and Celia wondered at Frank's desire to move to a finer house on California Street. This location would satisfy her, but she didn't have a father to impress like Jane did.

"Mrs. Hutchinson was awfully ready to accuse Russell and clear her husband of any suspicion, wasn't she?" Mr. Greaves asked, cupping Celia's elbow to help her down the front steps.

"Jane is only doing what any loyal wife would." They reached the planked walkway, and she removed her elbow from his grasp. " 'Words are easy, like the wind; faithful friends are hard to find.' Or faithful wives, if you will."

"An interesting choice of quotes, ma'am." He looked down at her, his eyes shaded by his hat. "A really interesting choice."

"It comes from Shakespeare."

"You know an awful lot of Shakespeare."

"Courtesy of my uncle's large library back in England."

His library had been a refuge from her aunt's disfavor, which had seemed limitless to a young girl used to her parents' unconditional love. When they had died, and she and her brother had gone to live with their aunt and uncle, books became a solace. She missed her uncle's library, the aroma of the leather and paper, the whisper of her feet padding across the thick rugs, the tick of the clock on the mantel, the excitement of discovering a new world to escape into. The library was about all she missed of that house, however, what with her brother's grave in the nearby church cemetery, the echo of his voice haunting the hallways.

She banished her morbid thoughts. "Fortunately for me, my uncle did not believe that learning how to embroider was a better use of a young lady's time." In fact, he'd paid her very little attention at all.

"What would he think of your interfering with police business?"

"His opinion would be the same as yours—he would not approve. But Jane is my friend, as is Frank, and my uncle would comprehend my desire to defend my friends," she said.

"Just as loyal as Mrs. Hutchinson."

"I suppose I am," said Celia. "I must ask you something, Mr. Greaves. You believe the man Owen saw fighting with Frank was Virgil Nash, don't you? If the dead body turns out to be Mr. Nash, that is."

"I do."

"A fight does not mean Frank killed him."

"It's a good place to start."

"You *will* speak to Mr. Russell, though, won't you?" asked Celia. "And—although I hate to suggest this—Dan Matthews as well. His comment to Owen suggested he knew the dead man. He might have good information."

"I know what I'm doing, Mrs. Davies," he said curtly.

"My apologies for making you think I believed otherwise."

He lifted an eyebrow. "Don't know why I put up with you, ma'am."

"Neither do I, Mr. Greaves," she said, and was quite certain he chuckled.

"You might be glad to know that Martin isn't going to press charges against either Matthews or Owen. But Matthews has been sacked, and I expect Owen will be next."

"Oh dear." Now where would she find Owen employment? Frank had been reluctant to hire a boy most people considered a street urchin, and had only done so as a favor to her. Owen had let them both down. "He feared that would happen."

"Maybe next time he gets a job, he won't go digging for gold in his boss' cellar."

"I already told that other officer that I don't have anything to say about that dead fellow," insisted Dan Matthews, glowering from where he sat in Nick's office.

He had a broad face, small eyes, and was heavily muscled from carrying hods and working with his hands. There was a scar along his chin, and he favored his right arm as though his shoulder hurt him. If Nick had run into him in an alleyway, he'd have been nervous; Dan Matthews didn't look like the sort of fellow who'd shy away from a fight if given the slightest reason to brawl.

"Cassidy and I was workin' in the cellar like Mr. Martin wanted, and we found that body. That's all we was doin'."

"Let me correct that statement," said Nick, not amused by the man's insistence on repeating himself. "You convinced Cassidy to help you dig for gold, which you thought was buried there. Sounds to me like you were committing burglary."

"He's lyin'."

"Owen Cassidy happens to be somebody I trust."

"That kid? Heck, it was his idea all along. Yep, it was. His idea to dig down there," said Matthews, looking pleased that he'd come up with the notion to finger Owen. "Nope. Weren't my idea at all. You should be questioning him, not me."

"Let's try this. Let's say I believe it was all innocent, what you two were doing in that basement," said Nick. "And your story is simply that you were down in the cellar digging around to level it before laying bricks and then happened to uncover a decaying body. Here's something I find interesting, Mr. Matthews. When that happened, you cried out, 'Why won't he leave me be?' according to Cassidy. What did you mean?"

"Cassidy's lyin' about that, too." Matthews rolled his right shoulder, the movement familiar to Nick. Was there a wound from an old battle on that shoulder? Did it throb when the fog rolled in like it had last night?

"Rotten kid," Matthews added, and reached up to squeeze his shoulder.

"The war?" Nick asked, though the question wasn't relevant to his investigation.

The man looked at him with eyes gone suddenly blank, focused on another time and place.

"Vicksburg," Matthews finally said.

"Bad, that one," said Nick. "The Wilderness."

Matthews returned to the here and now. "You there?"

"I was." And he could feel the air, hear the sounds of the battlefield, smell it still. The damp. The stink of gunpowder and spilled guts. The acrid stench of fear.

"Lost a cousin at that one," Matthews said quietly.

"I lost my closest friend." A rush of anger swept over him. He'd never known a better man than Jack Hutchinson. A much better man than his cousin Frank. It should be Jack who was alive, and his cousin who'd bled out his life on the trampled dirt beneath a canopy of shattered trees. But that wasn't how life worked. And Nick had spent the intervening years learning and relearning the unfairness of it all.

*And you, Meg. To have lost you, too, Meg . . .*

But his sister couldn't be recovered, either, and Nick had become a cop so that he could wrench some justice out of this unforgiving and heartless world.

"Too many men died. Too many good men," said Matthews.

He shook his head somberly and dropped his hand, forming a fist to thump against his leg. At the army hospital, Nick had once seen a soldier, his leg sawed off and his head swathed in so many bandages that only one staring eye was uncovered, do something similar. They all had their tics, the pain and terror seeking a way out of their wounded bodies.

"So how about you tell me the truth, Mr. Matthews, for the sake of all those good men?" Nick asked. "Did you return last night to check if you knew the man you'd unearthed? Take your key, unlock the door, and go down to the cellar for another peek?"

"Heck no!" Matthews reached into the pocket of his coat

and removed a large key. He tossed it to Nick. "It's a key to the offices. You can bet I won't ever be going back there to return it."

"You won't be going back there to return it because you're not working there anymore."

Matthews cursed. "I don't know nothing. And tell John Kelly that."

"Why should *I* tell him that?" asked Nick. "He's your brother-in-law."

"Don't think I'll be talking to him ever again."

Nick thought that was likely true.

He examined the steel skeleton key in his hand. "Who gave you this?"

"John, of course."

So John Kelly had a key. That was one. And apparently Dan Matthews was permitted to borrow it. That made two. "Who else has keys to the offices?" he asked, setting it on his desk.

"The partners, of course. I don't know who else."

*Three, four, and five.* "Does Kelly lend this key"—Nick tapped it—"to you, because you're his brother-in-law and supposedly trustworthy?"

"He'll give it to whoever's working late that night."

Did Martin know? He seemed too prudent to allow any of the workers to have use of a key to his offices. "Seems awfully trusting of him."

The other man shrugged.

"Matthews, I'm going to ask you again." Nick leaned forward. "Did you know the fellow you found?"

He hesitated. "I can't be sure."

"What if I told you it was Virgil Nash?"

A bead of sweat broke on Matthews' upper lip, and his eyes widened. Not with astonishment, though, but with alarm. "Shit."

"That name bother you?"

"Honest to God, I only heard of the fella. Heard rumors around town that he caused all sorts of trouble for some of the miners back in Nevada, but I never did know him myself."

"What sort of trouble?" asked Nick.

"Claim jumping."

*How about that.*

Matthews' small eyes glimmered in the light of the overhead gaslight. "But you know what else, Detective? Jasper Martin wanted him dead. I heard old Martin cussin' him out one day. I did. Yes, I did. Told Mr. Russell he hoped Nash would up and die. Whaddya think of that?"

"I think that's very interesting, Mr. Matthews," said Nick, mildly disappointed that Matthews hadn't overheard Frank making that wish. "Very interesting."

Celia's hand hung suspended in the air, prepared to knock on the Kellys' door. She dreaded this encounter, absolutely dreaded it. A neighbor, out on her front porch thumping a floor cloth with a heart-shaped rug beater, looked over. Celia smiled at the woman and rapped upon the peeling paint of the wood.

A few moments later, a red-faced Maryanne answered.

"Mrs. Davies, you're back already to check on me?" she asked, a hand pressed to the swell of her belly. From somewhere inside the house came the yowl of her young daughter.

"Might I come in, Mrs. Kelly?" she asked. "I need to speak to you about your brother."

Maryanne's gaze narrowed. "Which one?"

"Daniel. He is in trouble with the law."

Maryanne's indrawn breath came in a jagged rush, and she pressed her hand harder to her belly. "Come inside. And don't mind the mess."

The interior of the narrow house—two rooms plus kitchen downstairs, three tiny rooms up—was dark, the proximity of the neighboring homes blocking the sunshine from reaching the few windows. The front room, which served as a parlor, seemed to have accumulated every piece of cast-off furniture and utilitarian item that would not fit in the remainder of the home.

Maryanne stepped around a basket holding a pile of sewing as she led Celia toward the kitchen at the back. "Would you like some coffee? Or tea? I might have some around."

"There is no need, Mrs. Kelly. Thank you."

A pot bubbled on the small iron stove, and Maryanne's young daughter—she was named Clarissa, if Celia recalled correctly—clung to the side of the wood cradle tucked into one corner and bawled.

"There, there, Clary. Stop that," said Maryanne, making to lift the girl from the cradle.

"Here. Let me take her," said Celia, interceding.

"If you're sure."

"I have handled children before," Celia replied, hoisting Clarissa onto her hip. The child, dark hair curling around her tiny face, stared in astonishment at the stranger holding her but didn't protest.

"Thank you. I never have enough help around here." Maryanne searched for a towel and used it to remove the pot of stew from the grate. She turned to look at Celia. "So what's Dan done?"

Celia bounced Clarissa—not all that readily accomplished

in corset and crinoline—and provided a short version of events. "Although Mr. Martin has chosen not to see him charged with attempted theft, he has apparently directed that Dan be released from his position."

Maryanne, who'd been listening in unhappy silence, gasped. "He's lost his job?"

"A better situation than being thrown in jail."

"I'm not so sure about that, what with so many men unemployed." Maryanne gazed at her daughter, who'd taken to fiddling with the tassels suspended from the collar of Celia's mantle. "John will be mad. He never did take to Dan, nagging him always, criticizing him, making Dan miserable. After this . . ." She sighed. "He won't be welcome in this house any longer."

"Even though Mr. Martin is not pressing charges, the police will still interview your brother, because it seems he might have known the dead man."

"Dan doesn't have anything to do with some dead man!"

Maryanne's outburst caused Clarissa to let out a howl, and Maryanne rushed to grab a wood-handled baby rattle from the crib. "Here, now, Clary." She jingled the bell on the end, then handed the rattle to her daughter, who quieted.

"Did he ever mention to you a man who was missing part of an arm? Dan may have seen him at Martin and Company, perhaps having an argument." For if Frank had fought with this person, the other partners may have as well.

Maryanne rested her hand on her belly. "We don't see Dan much," she said. "And the last time I saw my brother, I can't recollect him mentioning anybody like that."

Clary dropped the rattle and began to fuss. "Do you have any idea why your brother thought to dig for gold in Mr. Martin's cellar?" asked Celia, tickling the child with one of the tassels and getting her to squirm.

"Because he wants to get rich quick like everybody else and that man's got oodles of money?" asked Maryanne. "It's that Rob Bartlett. He put Dan up to this sure as I'm standing here."

Another name to mention to Nicholas Greaves. "Who is Rob Bartlett?"

"One of the other fellows who works for John. He and Dan spend a lot of time together. Best of friends," she said. "He's trouble, that one. I warned Dan after I met him once. I can tell by the way he looks at you, I said. Just trouble. John doesn't much like him, either, though he's a good-enough worker. Always trying to get Mr. Hutchinson to promote him." Maryanne shook her head. "But Dan doesn't care for my opinion. Never has. Dan just doesn't listen to anybody."

*C*aptain Eagan reclined in his high-backed chair, the polished top of his massive desk reflecting the light from the tall windows behind him. He ran his fingertips through his thick black whiskers—what had Celia Davies once called them? Magnificent?—and considered Nick. "If this man turns out to be Virgil Nash, you know he's got important friends, Greaves. A stockholder of the Merchants' Exchange and all. Eats dinner with Mr. Levi Strauss, even. Strauss, for God's sake."

*And how do you know all that already?* Nick wondered. But maybe Eagan's ability to rapidly gather information was why the captain was on that side of the desk and Nick was on this side, acting subservient.

Nick shifted his stance on the plush carpet that stretched from one paneled wall to the other. It was an office leaps and bounds nicer than the smelly one Nick shared with his fellow detective, Briggs. "You know I've never let the status of a victim determine how I handle a case, sir."

"Don't I, now," he said, lowering his hand from his whiskers. "Why not arrest that Irish kid who found the body? Cassidy's his name, right?"

Nick's wound took to aching. "He found the body, sir. He didn't kill the man. If he had, he wouldn't have come to the station to inform me."

"Really, Greaves?" Eagan scoffed. "You're a better detective than that. Besides, he's an orphan, that Irish kid, isn't he? Who'd care?"

The captain was Irish himself. Greaves would have expected him to feel kinship with Cassidy. But maybe when a person had achieved a measure of success, made his way in the world, and landed on his feet, he stopped caring about the ones still scrambling for a foothold and constantly sliding backward, the wall they climbed slick beneath their boots.

"I would." *Celia Davies would, too.* "I won't arrest a kid just because it's convenient, sir. Not when one of the partners at Martin and Company was seen arguing with Nash and another was overheard wishing him dead."

Eagan scowled at Nick long enough for one of the nearby clock bells to go through an entire series of chimes. "I'm counting on you to do good work on this one, Greaves, and don't cause any trouble this time."

"If trouble's necessary—"

"Hell you will, Greaves," Eagan barked. "There are only so many spots for detectives on this force."

"I'm aware of that, sir."

"Some days I wonder."

# CHAPTER 4

"They've found Virgil Nash buried in a cellar?" Briggs laughed, dribbling doughnut crumbs onto his beard. "Well, I'll be. So that's where he's been since his wife reported him missing two weeks ago. But I had a witness claim he'd seen the fella heading out of town with his lady friend that night. Huh."

Nick leaned back in his chair and considered his fellow detective. He suspected that once Briggs had found that witness, he hadn't bothered to do any more checking and had quickly closed the case. "We can't be certain it's him until his widow identifies the body, but it's looking likely."

Briggs whistled and shook his head.

"What day was it that Nash disappeared?" Nick asked him.

"Let's see . . ." Briggs stuffed the rest of the doughnut into his mouth and pondered. "Wait, let me get my file."

He rooted around in his desk and pulled out a tattered
folder. He flipped through the papers inside and extracted one.
"May twenty-eight."

A Tuesday, realized Nick, checking the calendar tacked to
the wall opposite his desk. One of the days when the office closed
early, as per Martin's instructions.

"According to his missus, he got a message from Jasper Martin to meet him that night at eight," said Briggs, reading from his
case notes. "But Jasper Martin denied sending Nash a message.
Martin also provided an alibi for the evening Nash disappeared,
which proved he didn't meet with the guy. Seems he was with
the mayor having supper until later than most regular folks take
their meals."

The mayor. It would be hard to refute his testimony. "And the
mayor confirmed that?"

"I didn't go asking him!"

Of course not. "So if Martin didn't send the message, who *did*?"

"At the time, I figured Nash made up the story about a meeting so his wife wouldn't object to him going out. He had a
mistress—a popular actress at the Metropolitan—who a witness
claimed to have seen Nash with that evening. This witness saw
the two of them together at the back door of the theater. The
woman had a bag with her, and she climbed up behind Nash on
his horse and off they went. Said it looked like they were planning a trip out of town."

A reasonable assumption, but clearly wrong.

"When I mentioned the actress to Mrs. Nash, she got all hot
and bothered. Wouldn't even consider that her husband might've
gone off with the woman." Briggs scowled. "Well, shoot, finding

Nash's body explains why that actress has been in town this week. They didn't go anyplace together. Danged lousy witnesses."

Nick rubbed the ache in his arm and wondered how Briggs managed to stay on the force.

"Something else," Briggs added. "I spoke to the local who recalled finding the front door at Martin and Company ajar the evening Nash disappeared. Around ten, he thinks, since he always passes the place on the hour, and it was well after sundown. Took a quick look around, didn't find anything out of place, got it locked up again, and went back to his business."

Which gave Nick a rough timeline of the crime—somewhere between eight and ten in the evening of May 28.

"I've seen the condition of that office, Briggs," he said. "It's a mess of construction debris. How could the local cop claim to know nothing was out of place?"

"You think you're so smart, don't you, Greaves?"

The knock on the door interrupted Nick's response. Taylor poked his head through the opening. "It's Nash all right, sir. His widow's been to see the coroner. Hear she held up pretty well, considering what condition the body's in."

"What else did Harris have to say?"

"Confirmed that Nash died from a deep cut, and he didn't find anything of value on the dead body, sir. Looks like he'd been stripped of his money and the silver watch his widow claims he carried everywhere," said Taylor. "Do you think the fella who was trying to dig up the body took those things?"

"It would've required an awfully strong stomach to steal money and a watch off a rotting corpse."

"Suppose so." Taylor blanched over the thought. "And it

looks like that Jean-Pierre fella's willing to claim Martin was at his restaurant last night 'til all hours." He shook his head. "Just wish we coulda found a clue in that cellar, though, to tell us who did this. I'm having a couple of the men search some more."

"It's been two weeks, Taylor. Any clues are probably gone, but continue the search," said Nick. "And good work."

"Thanks, sir. And there's somebody here to see you—"

The somebody burst through the doorway, shoving Taylor aside.

"Hey!" Taylor shouted at him.

"It's okay, Taylor," said Nick. "Why, hello, Frank."

"What are you doing questioning my wife?" Frank Hutchinson slapped his hands on the edge of Nick's desk. Briggs, happily anticipating trouble, got comfortable in his chair and folded his hands over his thick belly. For once he wasn't the one having it out with Nick.

"She was at your house and you weren't." Nick stood because he didn't want Frank towering over him. Frank was a good head taller than most men, including Nick. "But thanks for coming in. By the way, you've put on some weight."

He had, and it filled out his striped silk vest. His boss might dress like a pauper, but Frank Hutchinson didn't. He'd also decided to grow thick muttonchop whiskers, which made him look even more pompous than he used to when they were both much younger men.

"Very funny, Nick. And you've upset Jane with your questions, so I want an apology."

"I'll apologize if you prove I'm wrong to want to talk to you."

"But you didn't talk to me," said Frank. "You spoke to Jane, and now she's in tears."

Nick didn't like upsetting women; that wasn't what he'd meant to do. "Since you're here now . . ."

Frank's nostrils flared. "I don't know the man who was found in the cellar, certainly didn't put him there, and have nothing more to say."

"Oh, you sure do know him. His name is Virgil Nash."

"Dear God."

"Furthermore, you were seen arguing with him not long before he disappeared. And was killed," said Nick. Frank didn't deny that, which meant the argument Cassidy had witnessed was with Virgil Nash.

"I didn't kill him."

"How about you start by explaining where you were last night, Frank," said Nick.

"I was out with one of the partners. Abram Russell. Dinner."

"Until ten? That's when you returned home, right?"

A muscle ticked in Frank's jaw. "We went drinking afterward. A new place. I don't recall its name."

At least his story was consistent with his wife's. "What about the evening of May twenty-eight?"

"What's that supposed to mean?"

"Seems like a simple-enough question," said Nick.

"I just said I didn't . . ." Frank leaned over Nick's desk, his hands balling into fists. Briggs was eyeing him. If the man decided to throttle Nick, Briggs would never come to his rescue. "Don't think for a moment I don't understand why you want to cast blame on me. It's your fault Jack is dead. Not mine."

"No, you coward, it's your fault."

Frank's hand shot out, and he grabbed Nick's coat lapel, slamming him forward against the desk edge. Briggs chortled.

"It's a crime to assault a police officer," Nick said coolly.

Frank dropped his grip. He had intense eyes, and they stared at Nick with undisguised hatred. "I have nothing to do with Nash's death, and you know it."

"How about this, Mr. Hutchinson." Nick straightened his coat. "I won't charge you with assault if you admit that you killed a man, namely Virgil Nash, and buried him in the cellar of your office. You're known to have argued with the man. Did a fight get out of hand, maybe? It was all an accident?"

Frank's eyes narrowed. "I'll see you rot before I admit to anything as idiotic as that."

He turned and stomped out of the office, bumping into Taylor, who'd been hovering near the door.

Briggs snickered and reached for another doughnut from the supply he kept on his desk. "That was—"

"Not another word, Briggs, if you know what's good for you."

"The lass from Burke's Saloon is here, ma'am," said Addie, taking Celia's things. Her housekeeper schooled her expression to conceal her disappointment in her mistress's choice of patients, having been forced to accept that saloon girls, actresses, and prostitutes would ever make up the bulk of the women who came to the clinic.

"I would have returned sooner, but after leaving Jane's, I decided to visit Maryanne Kelly," explained Celia, stepping out of her half boots and into her leather slippers. "Has Katie been waiting long?"

"Nae, ma'am. And Miss Barbara's next door, tending to that Angelo."

"What has he done now?" Their neighbor's son was forever

falling ill or injuring himself. His mother, however, had several young children to keep watch over, and they were all boisterous.

"The catarrh. Poor wee lad." Addie, who had a soft spot for the boy, tutted before returning to her chores.

Celia entered her examination room, a former parlor she'd converted with Uncle Walford's help. Together they had lined the wallpapered walls with bookcases and supply cabinets, and found an old desk for her use, its surface now covered with files and stacked copies of *The Edinburgh Medical and Surgical Journal*, her most precious possessions. They had filled other spaces with chairs and the padded bench she used as an examining table.

Upon which sat a downcast Katie Lehane.

Celia closed the door, and the girl looked over. "It's my ankle again, ma'am."

"Let me see."

Katie extended her right leg. She hoisted her olive plaid skirt, untied her garter, and rolled down her cotton stocking. "See? My ankle's still as big as a rutabaga! And such a nasty color, too. All greeny purple."

Katie turned her foot from side to side, studying her ankle with a frown. It *was* a nasty color but nothing out of the ordinary.

"Did you tell Mr. Burke that you needed a few evenings off in order to recover?" Gently, Celia felt the girl's ankle. The swelling had actually subsided, and the bruising was less pronounced than when Celia had examined it last, but Katie winced at her touch anyway.

"I can't be takin' a bunch of evenings off, ma'am! Burke would give my job to one of those girls who hang around the back door lookin' for work," she said. "How many of 'em have to keep comin' here, the next one hungrier lookin' than the last?"

"You came here from New York City, Katie," Celia reminded her. "Those girls simply want the same opportunities you've enjoyed."

"I guess." Katie peered at Celia. "So can you set my ankle to rights, though? Wrap it or something?"

"I can wrap your ankle, Katie, but if you keep dancing on it, you will continue to aggravate the sprain."

A blush flared on her cheeks. She was a pretty young woman, with resplendent auburn hair and gray eyes, and the blush made her even prettier. "I wasn't dancin'!"

Celia lifted an eyebrow over Katie's assertion. It was against the law for saloon girls to dance if liquor was being served, and Celia had yet to encounter a saloon that did not serve liquor.

"Honest!" Katie added.

"Let me get my strips of flannel bandaging." Flannel was preferred over cotton when she wished to apply a bandage that would allow movement and yet maintain support of the injured joint.

Celia retrieved a box from the shelving on the far wall of the clinic room. "I have a question for you, Katie." She fetched out flannel, snipped it into a proper length, and returned the rest to the box. "It is about some men who visit Burke's."

Namely Frank Hutchinson and Abram Russell. Burke's was one of the drinking establishments Jane had mentioned to Mr. Greaves as a favorite haunt.

"Burke doesn't like us talkin' about the customers, ma'am," said Katie, looking uncomfortable. "We had one of the police captains in the other night, all liquored up. Burke made all the girls swear we wouldn't breathe a word about it."

"I would not ask if it were not important." Celia tapped Katie's right leg, and she held it aloft again. "My question is about a Mr. Frank Hutchinson and a Mr. Abram Russell. Do you know them?"

"Not sure I know Mr. Russell, but I do know Mr. Hutchinson," she said, her cheeks pinking.

"And?" Celia asked, holding the end of a flannel strip against the sole of Katie's foot and proceeding to wrap the bandage up and around her ankle.

"He likes to drink. Play cards. That's about it."

Drinking. Jane had to know. Perhaps Frank's carousing was why she had taken to using soporifics; if she was asleep when he returned home, she would not have to witness his inebriation. Celia hoped at least that he'd hidden his habit from Grace; no girl needed to realize that the father she adored had faults.

"By any chance, was he in the saloon last evening?" Celia asked.

"I didn't work last night. Because of my injury," said Katie, watching Celia's hands as she worked on her ankle. "So I can't say for sure. But he stops in some Tuesdays and sometimes Thursdays, too."

Her response did not leave Celia any nearer to knowing for certain where either Frank or Mr. Russell was last night.

"What about a man named Virgil Nash—does he frequent Burke's as well?" Celia asked, tearing the end of the flannel strip in half lengthwise in order to form a tie around the bandage.

"He does, but I haven't seen him in a while," said Katie, reaching for her stocking. Her fingers worked it into folds so she could slip it back over her leg. Stocking in place, she retied her embroidered garter and smoothed her skirt flat. "He's a good customer, he is. Likes to flash his money around, though. Not that any of us girls minds that, since some of that money lands in our pockets."

"Does he come in alone or with friends?" asked Celia, considering who else might be an associate of Mr. Nash's and worth adding to the list of suspects.

"The only friend he ever brings with him to Burke's is a woman. And I don't think she's Mrs. Nash, if you know what I mean," she said, winking.

"No friends, then?"

"None that I've noticed, besides the ones who flatter him in order to get a free whiskey out of him," said Katie, climbing down from the bench and gingerly stepping on her right foot, testing her ankle. "He sure didn't care for Mr. Hutchinson. Nearly came to blows one evening."

*Gad. Not another fight.* "Did you overhear what they were arguing about?"

"Some business deal gone bad. Mr. Nash was cursing like the dickens at Mr. Hutchinson. Burke had to kick the both of 'em out that night before somebody sent for the cops."

"When was this?"

"It's been a while. A month or more," Katie answered. "Surprised I haven't seen him since. Maybe he doesn't want to run into Mr. Hutchinson again."

"Mr. Nash hasn't been scared off, Katie," said Celia quietly. "It appears very possible that he has been murdered."

"Mercy sakes alive!" Katie exclaimed, her mouth dropping open.

"Whooee," said Taylor, whistling over the Nashes' house— a mansion by most folks' standards—that dominated the neighborhood of Second Street and Harrison.

"Pretty fine, isn't it?" said Nick.

The building was three stories high, with tall columns propping up the roof of the porch that wrapped around the street-facing sides, and surrounded by gardens crowded with those roses, thick blooms of crimson and peach and yellow, that Mrs. Davies so admired. Who filled up all the house's rooms, Nick wondered, when as far as he knew the Nashes didn't have children? It would feel empty and lonely to him, all that echoing space.

"And the view ain't half-bad, either, sir." Taylor squinted in the sunlight, looking across the rooftops below the hill, down to the masts of ships at dock in the bay, Goat Island in the distance, church towers and smokestacks poking above the houses rolling over the hills to the north and west. The giant brick tower of Selby's lead pipe and shot works down on First and Howard was a bit of an eyesore, disturbing the view across the city.

An eyesore that would be nothing compared to the Second Street cut when it happened, though.

"Let's go see what Mrs. Nash has to say," said Nick.

He pushed open the gate and strolled up to the front steps. A Mexican laborer, trimming bushes, looked over at him and Taylor without much interest.

The knocker was wrapped in black cloth, so Nick pounded on the door with his fist instead, which prompted someone inside to run across the entry hall and fling open the door.

"The missus isn't seeing anybody," said the maid sternly.

Taylor showed his badge. "This here's Detective Greaves. Come to talk to Mrs. Nash about her husband's death."

The maid's hand remained firmly on the door handle. Nick had to admire her for adhering to her employer's orders.

"I think she'll want to see us," he said, and pressed a hand to the door, which she released.

"Come into the front parlor," the maid said, pointing to a room off to their right before rushing off to find Mrs. Nash.

The room was flooded with light from the massive windows. It reflected off the burnished wood floor and marble-topped tables, and it sparkled in the cut-glass lamp shades. Cut roses scented the air. A portrait hanging above the fireplace was covered by a length of black fabric. If Nick lifted a corner, he might find Virgil Nash staring back.

Taylor eyed the amber-colored velvet upholstering of the settee and armchairs arranged around the room. "Don't think I can sit on anything this nice."

"Then keep standing, Taylor," said Nick.

They didn't have long to wait before Mrs. Nash swept into the room, her full ebony skirts swaying. She was younger than he'd been expecting—in her mid-thirties, if he had to make an estimate—and handsome.

"Mrs. Nash," he said, removing his hat. "I am Detective Greaves, and this is my assistant, Mr. Taylor. Thank you for agreeing to see us."

Her gaze was clear, her eyes dry. Nick supposed that meant she hadn't been too shocked by the discovery of her husband's body. Like Briggs had said, she must never have believed the story that her husband had run off with an actress from the Metropolitan.

She settled onto a chair with a rustle of bombazine, the fabric releasing the scent of magnolia water. "I want Virgil's killer found," she said, her voice modulated by a good education. "You can be certain I'd want to see you."

Nick took a chair opposite while Taylor picked a spot out of her line of sight between a pair of potted ferns and another armchair. He dug out his notebook and pencil from the pocket he kept them in and waited.

"First of all, you have my condolences, ma'am," Nick offered, as he'd done too many times to count to too many other family members.

"Poor Virgil. Dumped in a cellar, treated with no more respect than a dog." She drew a lace-trimmed handkerchief from the cuff of her sleeve where she'd tucked it and held it to her mouth. "Where is the pity, I ask you? Where?"

"In my experience, ma'am, pity's a rather scarce commodity."

Alice Nash squeezed her eyes closed for a moment. "Virgil deserved better."

Most folks deserved better. "Now, if you don't mind, I'd like to ask you about the day your husband disappeared."

She inclined her head, letting him know he could proceed.

"Detective Briggs told me that your husband received a message that morning that had supposedly come from Jasper Martin," said Nick. "Who brought it, and why did you think it had come from Martin? Did Mr. Nash share the contents of the message with you?"

"A boy—I don't know his name—brought it. Virgil didn't share the contents, other than to tell me that he'd been summoned by Mr. Martin to his office downtown." She emphasized "summoned" in a tone of disdain.

"Mr. Martin denies sending that note."

Mrs. Nash returned Nick's stare. "I'm not one to trust *his* word."

"Why did your husband agree to the meeting?" asked Nick. Taylor's pencil scratched noisily.

"Virgil thought Jasper had finally changed his mind about his plans for the Second Street cut."

"I gather your husband had been attempting to stop those plans before they started."

"And failing," said Mrs. Nash, occupied with folding her handkerchief into sequentially smaller squares. "Jasper Martin and his partners have been working to convince the city planner to go ahead with the improvement, as they like to call it. A contract they would quickly pursue, since Mr. Martin owns land down near the Pacific Mail Company wharf at the foot of Second Street."

Exactly what Mrs. Hutchinson had told him. "And the easier access given by a flat road meant that land would become more valuable," said Nick.

"Absolutely, Detective," she concurred. "However, Virgil knew he had little chance of stopping the grading of the road. Jasper Martin has friends on the city planning commission."

*No kidding. He took meals with the mayor, too.*

"So you believe your husband nonetheless wanted to meet with Martin, hoping he'd changed his mind about the plans," said Nick. "Seems rather optimistic, given what you've just said."

"I said as much at the time." Mrs. Nash shifted slightly in the chair, and the sunlight coming through the window at Nick's back reflected in her eyes. He noticed they were pale, but not the clear gray-blue of Celia Davies' eyes. He preferred Mrs. Davies'; their light color made her gaze and the thoughts behind them more transparent. "I told him not to go, but Virgil thought it was worth a try."

"On the day he disappeared, what did Mr. Nash do between the time he received that note in the morning and when he left to meet with its author?"

Mrs. Nash proceeded to unfold her handkerchief. "We had

lunch together in the garden. Then Virgil left for an afternoon appointment with Mr. Strauss."

"Mr. Levi Strauss?" asked Taylor. "He's got that big new dry goods place on Battery, right?"

"Yes, that's who I mean," she replied.

"Did your husband head straight to Martin's office after his visit with Mr. Strauss?" Nick asked.

"I do not believe so. He sent me a note saying he intended to stay downtown to attend to some business, so I was not to wait supper and he would return after his eight o'clock meeting with Mr. Martin. Although I suppose he'd actually gone to see that woman," she added under her breath.

Everything so far agreed with Briggs' account, including the bit about Nash's meeting his mistress.

"He'd still be alive if he hadn't gone to Mr. Martin's office, wouldn't he?" She lifted the handkerchief to her mouth again, and Nick was surprised to see tears in her eyes. He'd begun to think her as cold as a wagon tire. "One of these men killed my husband in order to get him out of the way, didn't they? You must bring them to justice, Detective Greaves. You must. They're murderers."

Nick wasn't going to argue her point. Matthews had claimed Martin wanted Nash dead. Frank and Russell might want that, too. "Would anybody else profit from your husband's death, Mrs. Nash?"

"Who else would possibly want to kill Virgil?"

"I don't know," said Nick. "That's why I'm asking."

Mrs. Nash glanced over at Taylor, who was keeping a poker face, then back at Nick. "Are you afraid of the men of Martin and Company? Afraid to accuse them? Is that why you're asking a question like that?"

"I'm trying to pursue all the possibilities, ma'am," he said. Which was what Uncle Asa would've advised. Always keep an open mind. "So if you'd kindly answer my question, I'd appreciate it."

"No one," she answered, staring him in the eyes to make certain he believed her. He wasn't sure he did. "The only men who stand to gain from Virgil's death," she continued, "are Jasper Martin, Frank Hutchinson, and Abram Russell."

If she suspected anybody else, he wasn't prying it out of her. She had an ax to grind with the partners, and so did he.

"Your husband was a very wealthy man," said Nick. "He didn't make all that money from his import business. Maybe there's somebody in his past who's caught up to him. I've been told about disputes during the time he was in Nevada. Maybe he upset some miners there who might have been looking for revenge."

"He and his brother, Silas, had a lucky strike in the Comstock Lode. Any allegations he'd cheated other miners is an absolute lie," Alice Nash said fiercely. "So there's nobody from his past 'looking for revenge,' Detective. He is an honorable man." She caught the error in her statement, and her chin wobbled. "Or rather, he *was* an honorable man."

"Are you his sole beneficiary? Or would his brother inherit?"

Alice Nash turned an unattractive color. "Silas Nash was murdered years ago in Virginia City by a lunatic who fled the country," she said. "Silas was denied justice, Detective, but there had better be justice for Virgil. There simply must be."

"Any other beneficiaries, ma'am?" Nick asked, steering her back to what he wanted to know.

"I am the sole beneficiary. There are no children. But if you think I'd kill my husband—"

"It's been known to happen."

She stood as quickly as heavy bombazine and a stiff corset permitted. "Are we finished, Detective Greaves?"

Taylor hastily stowed his pencil and notebook, but Nick took his time getting to his feet. "Sure, ma'am. But I might come back to ask more questions. If you don't mind," he threw in.

"If they are more questions like that, you can be certain I mind. Good day to you both." With a huff, she spun on the heels of her expensive shoes and marched out of the room.

*L*ook what I found on the front porch, Addie," said Owen, strolling into the kitchen later that day. He held out a bouquet of daisies, a paper tag hanging from the twine tied around the stems. He squinted at the tag. "Says they're for you."

Celia, who had been reviewing the household accounts in the warmth of the room, glanced at Addie. The housekeeper blushed furiously over the vegetables she was chopping.

"Och, what nonsense are you blathering now, Owen Cassidy?" She snatched the flowers from him and read the tag herself. "No name again."

"Again?" asked Celia. "Have you received flowers before?"

Addie, who developed a sudden case of deafness, fetched a glass vase for the daisies and ignored Celia's question.

Owen chuckled. He plopped onto one of the kitchen chairs arranged around the oak table where Addie prepared meals. "I presume your being here means you have been released from employment," said Celia.

He grabbed the last pieces of shortbread sitting on a plate. "Wasn't at work five minutes before Mr. Kelly marched me out the front door."

"I will speak to Mr. Hutchinson," said Celia. "Hopefully I can convince him to give you another chance and tell Mr. Kelly to take you back."

"Thanks, ma'am," Owen mumbled, his mouth full of biscuits. Addie, the flowers properly arranged and finding a home on the windowsill, took the empty plate over to the wet sink. Owen mournfully watched its departure.

He swallowed. "Got any more of those, Addie?"

"You've eaten the lot of them, Owen Cassidy. Do you think we're made of sweets here?" Addie asked.

"Nope, but a body can dream, can't he?"

"Whisht. Get on with you."

Celia stacked the notices and bills into a neat pile and considered the boy. "Since you were forced to leave so quickly, I gather you did not have an opportunity to overhear what the other workers are saying about the murder."

"Nothing more than nobody seemed to be staggered that Dan got in trouble," said Owen. "This ain't . . . isn't gonna be good for Dan, though. He needs money to pay off some fella. That's why we were digging in the cellar to begin with. Said he was gonna finally pay off his debt to some mean old cuss when we found that treasure. Only there weren't any treasure, was there?"

"No, Owen," said Celia. "Who told Dan about Mr. Martin having gold buried in the cellar? Do you know?"

"Rob Bartlett, I think, ma'am," said Owen.

"Rob Bartlett." The person Maryanne had mentioned as being "trouble."

"Och, ma'am," said Addie, wiping her hands on the edge of her apron. "I canna say I like where this is going. You investigating and all again."

"Please do not worry, Addie."

"'Do not worry'? I canna help but worry when it seems you've forgotten what happened last time," Addie responded, grabbing the sack of potatoes waiting nearby along with an empty tin bowl. "If you need me, I'll be on the back porch peeling potatoes and thinking about what I did wrong to merit such a quantity of worries. Maybe I'll see my astrologer about this unchancy event. She'll ken what troubles lie ahead for you, ma'am. And as they say, a man forewarned is forearmed."

With that, Addie stormed outside, the back door slamming behind her.

"Sorry, ma'am," said Owen.

"Addie is concerned, but it is nothing for you to fret over," said Celia. "I have heard of Mr. Bartlett from Mr. Matthews' sister. What can you tell me about him?"

"He's a plasterer. He and Dan are friends, and go to the billiard hall and bowling alley together all the time," he said. "Known each other for a while, I hear. Do other things than just go to the billiard hall and bowling alley, if you catch my meaning."

"I do catch your meaning, Owen." Drinking and possibly also gambling. And other disreputable pursuits. "Do you happen to know whom Dan owed money to? And was it possibly a gambling debt?"

Abram Russell liked to gamble, according to Jane. Was there a connection between the two men? And if so, what did Mr. Russell's or Mr. Matthews' gambling debts have to do with Virgil Nash, if he was indeed the corpse in the cellar?

*Mr. Greaves is much better at this than I am.*

While she was pursuing those thoughts, Owen had answered her question and was staring at her.

"My apologies, Owen. What did you say?"

"I said I think Dan owed money to some fella named Virgil."

"I hope Mr. Greaves shall not mind if I wait for him," said Celia, already regretting the impulse that had brought her to Nicholas Greaves' rooms after her failure to find him at the station. But once she had learned Owen's—and Mary-anne's—information, she'd discovered an urgent need to talk to him about the next steps she intended to take.

Mr. Greaves' landlady, a Mrs. Jewett, looked Celia up and down. "I don't think he'll mind at all, ma'am. However, I insist you leave the door open."

"I—I promise you, my visit is not at all what you think, Mrs. Jewett," Celia insisted, her cheeks warming. She recalled another time and place, another man and an illicit visit to find comfort in his arms. This time, however, she was pursuing justice in a murder case, not the distraction to be found in a moment of passion. And Nicholas Greaves was not Patrick Davies. "This is a business matter, not a social call."

"At least you're not pretending to be his sister, like that other woman does," said the landlady.

*That* other *woman?* An emotion too similar to jealousy swept her blushing embarrassment aside. *What other woman?*

Mrs. Jewett was not about to enlighten her; she was already headed up the flight of steps that hugged the wall on the way to the first floor.

"We'll have to mind that dog of his," she said, unlocking the door. A fierce round of barking ensued. "The bark's worse than the bite, ma'am."

Easing the door open, the landlady pressed a knee against

the floppy-eared speckled dog that stuck its nose through. "Now, Riley, get back."

Riley quieted and obeyed, his tail wagging as he retreated from the door. Celia entered behind Mrs. Jewett and looked around. The door led into a parlor of sorts with a tiny kitchen off to one side and a bedchamber at the back. The space was tidy and comfortable, with deeply cushioned chairs and a recently dusted table, which was topped by a coal-oil lantern already lit to chase away the shadows. A photograph rested atop a short cabinet, and the walls were bare, save for a framed sketch of a farm scene that appeared to have been done by a child. *Homey*, thought Celia with surprise. She expected Mr. Greaves to have no time or concern for such comforts.

Mrs. Jewett grabbed Riley's collar and led the dog to the bedchamber. "I'm putting you in here, you beast, so you don't slobber all over Mrs. Davies' skirt."

She closed the door and turned to face Celia. "Don't be tempted to let him out. Riley might lick you to death before Mr. Greaves gets here to save you," she said. "Can I fetch you some tea while you wait?"

"Thank you, but no. Business, remember."

"I'm leaving the door open, ma'am," Mrs. Jewett said, and departed, her footsteps fading as she reached the ground floor.

Celia wandered over to the cabinet. Mr. Greaves' dog heard the movement and pressed his nose to the gap beneath the bedchamber door, snuffling loudly. The daguerreotype was of a young man and two girls, one about the man's age, posed in a photographer's studio. There was no doubt who the young man was, and she supposed the two girls were his sisters. Celia tilted the image to catch the light from the lantern. His eyes weren't haunted like they were now. In fact, he appeared happy. Content. It was the demeanor of a man who had not yet lost the younger of those sisters nor seen the ravages of war.

"Mrs. Davies!" Mr. Greaves exclaimed, entering the room, his gun drawn. "What in blazes are you doing here?"

Celia hastily returned the daguerreotype to its spot, its frame clattering against the cabinet's top. She'd been so preoccupied with the photograph, she hadn't heard his footsteps on the landing outside the set of rooms.

"Did not Mrs. Jewett tell you I was up here?" she asked, her heart knocking in her chest. "And you may put down your revolver, Mr. Greaves."

"I didn't see my landlady to have her tell me I had company." Easing the hammer closed, he laid the gun on the table. "And that's me and my sisters," he said, nodding at the photograph.

"They are very lovely."

"Yes," he said brusquely. He flipped back his coat and removed his holster, setting it on the table as well. Next, he reached around to remove a bowie knife from a scabbard strapped around his waist.

He noticed her watching. "A policeman has to be prepared for any situation." He set the knife next to the gun, making an orderly row. "Now that I'm disarmed, perhaps you'll explain why you're here at this hour."

"The sun has not yet set." She wasn't certain why she pointed that out.

"So I don't have to worry about my virtue?" he asked. "No wonder the door was open. Mrs. Jewett wants to protect your reputation. Or hear what we're talking about."

"I explained to her that this was a business call."

"Are we engaged in business, Mrs. Davies?"

She frowned at him. "You may cease teasing me, Mr. Greaves. Honestly."

He pulled out one of the chairs arranged around the table. "Have a seat, ma'am. It makes me uncomfortable to leave a lady standing when I have every intention of putting my feet up. It's been a long day."

She perched on the edge of the chair while he took a seat. True to his word, he leaned back, tipping his chair onto its rear two legs, and propped his booted feet on the edge of the table. "Well?"

"I have been thinking over some recent information I have received, Mr. Greaves," she said. "And I wish to tell you of my plans."

# CHAPTER 5

He didn't laugh at her plans. And he didn't yell at her for suggesting she had a role in his investigation. Which, as far as Nick was concerned, meant he was more tired than he'd thought.

"I appreciate that you want to help, Mrs. Davies," he said, "but asking questions at some party Martin's holding at Cliff House only seems like a good way to get yourself in trouble."

If he mentioned to her the bit about Nash's visiting Levi Strauss the day he died, she'd next be offering to haul herself over to the man's house to interrogate him, too.

"What do you expect the luncheon conversation to be, Mr. Greaves?" Mrs. Davies asked.

"Um, let me see. They'll talk about how rich they're going to get when the Second Street cut is approved and they've won the contract to make it happen?"

He had told her all that he'd learned so far and she had done likewise, even revealing that Frank had argued with Nash at Burke's. It was a peace offering, that bit of news, to smooth matters over between them. But as soon as she mentioned that fight, she reminded him that many men argued and didn't proceed to kill the other fellow. She then rushed to tell him about Rob Bartlett, that he'd been behind getting Matthews to dig around and that he resented Frank for not promoting him. She also mentioned that Dan Matthews owed money to a man named Virgil, according to Owen, and what other Virgil was that likely to be besides Virgil Nash? Learning that meant Nick would have to explain to Matthews how bad it looked when a person lied to the police about not personally knowing the dead man he'd dug up.

"They will not likely brag about their imminent wealth, Mr. Greaves, but they will undoubtedly speak about the cut," she said. Despite a stiff corset, she managed to lean down to scratch Riley's ears. The second Nick had let him out of the bedroom, the blasted fickle dog had run up to the woman as if she were his long-lost best friend. He was lying against her skirt, leaving hairs behind as his tail thumped in pleasure. "Furthermore, they will also likely gossip about Virgil Nash. Or I can ensure that they gossip about Virgil Nash."

"Even though you're not a police officer, ma'am, I don't think they're going to be confessing a secret plot to get rid of the fellow."

She gave Riley a final scratch and straightened.

"When men relax among their friends, they are capable of revealing all sorts of intimacies, Mr. Greaves," she said. "I am a friend and a woman. Surely they will not think to guard their tongues in front of me, a mere female."

"The perpetrator could still be somebody other than the men planning to attend that party, Mrs. Davies," he said. "His brother, Silas, was killed in Nevada. According to Dan Matthews, the Nashes had a reputation for jumping claims, and maybe that was what led to Silas Nash's death. Apparently, his killer managed to leave the country. Maybe the fellow has returned, though, and has finally come to San Francisco to murder Virgil, too."

"Very worth considering," she agreed. "But I cannot discover anything about that possibility at this party. I must stick to my primary goal of understanding who all might have lost money to the man, like Dan Matthews, thereby providing a motive for murder. Perhaps Jane was right to suggest Mr. Russell as a possible suspect because he owed Mr. Nash money as well."

"And maybe Frank, Russell's good friend, owed Nash money, too?" Nick couldn't resist adding.

"Must you insist on pursuing him?"

"Seems a good suspect at the moment," he said. "What with all the arguments between them."

"Jane has not invited me to attend in order to prove her husband guilty."

"Can't help it if he is, ma'am," said Nick. "And if one of those men is the killer, your questions are going to put you in danger."

She might be bosom friends with Frank Hutchinson, but that wouldn't stop the man from removing her if she was a threat. The man had no scruples when it came right down to it.

Celia Davies returned his stare without blinking. Or without comment. Which meant she understood the risk she was taking.

Nick sat forward, dropping the chair onto all four of its legs. He might as well agree to her proposition. She'd go ahead and ask questions whether he was happy about it or not.

"Just be careful, Mrs. Davies. And warn Cassidy to lie low, too. My boss wouldn't mind seeing him accused and this case wrapped up in a tidy bundle."

"But Owen would never—"

"I know, ma'am," he assured her. "I just want the pair of you to be careful. That's all."

"I shall do whatever is required for our investigation, Mr. Greaves."

"'Our' investigation?"

"Why pretend otherwise?" she asked. Sensibly.

"Heck if I know."

A short downhill walk from Nicholas Greaves' rooms, Celia caught the horsecar at the corner of Montgomery and Bush, where the awnings of Russ House stretched over the pavement to shield the hotel's large windows from the sun. The North Beach and Mission Railroad would have been more convenient, but she wished to travel along Montgomery, past Martin and Company, and the Omnibus line was the one that accomplished that.

She climbed aboard and paid her fare. The car was filled with workers bound for home after work, but she squeezed between the standing passengers and found a seat on one of the two benches that ran the length of the car.

The horsecar started up with a jolt and rolled along the rails set down in the middle of the road. Celia stared out the window opposite her, watching the grand buildings pass by. They would come across Martin and Company soon, and she leaned as far forward as her corset would permit in order to catch a glimpse. A man seated on the bench across from her gave her a curious glance before returning to his newspaper.

The door she and Owen had rushed through last night came into view. A workman, employed to paint the trim in blinding white, was gathering his supplies, finished for the day. She strained for a better view, not knowing what she searched for. Someone skulking about, looking guilty perhaps? *I am being silly.*

"Gad," she muttered, causing the man with the newspaper to peep at her over its top edge.

Just then, John Kelly came through the front door to speak with the painter, and then, presumably satisfied, he went back inside. How strange it was that Celia knew so many people at Martin and Company—Owen, Frank Hutchinson, John Kelly, and Dan Matthews by virtue of his relationship to Maryanne. She was tied to this murder by more than one thread.

The horsecar clopped along Montgomery, and the offices moved out of sight. But had any of those threads killed Virgil Nash? Obviously, Owen had not, even if Mr. Greaves' supervisor sought to have the boy accused. That was all she could be certain of. That and her conviction that Frank was not a killer.

The car came to a halt and loaded more passengers. There was a fuss occurring at the corner restaurant, and a number of people were gathered around a man wearing a tattered uniform and a tall hat overtopped with feathers, and carrying a knobby walking stick. *The infamous Emperor Norton,* thought Celia. Another eccentric in a city filled to capacity with them. The crowd's cheers roused the man with the newspaper, and he turned to look out the window.

"Dad-blamed fool," the man grumbled. He shook out his paper and resumed reading.

The horsecar resumed its trudge along Montgomery.

Like the Emp, Jasper Martin enjoyed his own form of eccentricity. When she'd met him at Jane's dinner party, he had worn the plainest of clothes and looked a trifle dirty around the edges, even though he'd built a mansion in the hills at the edge of the city. Celia had been eager to hear about his exploits in the gold fields and curious whether he'd known Barbara's father, a fellow forty-niner. However, Mr. Martin had very effectively steered their conversation away from his past, seeking instead to talk trivialities. Though he'd been reasonably polite, she had taken a dislike to him, detecting a ruthlessness in his manner.

But was he ruthless enough to kill?

Celia leaned back, despite the years she had spent listening to her aunt's admonitions about a lady's proper posture, and thought of all the reasons people wished Virgil Nash dead: unpaid gambling debts; disputes with miners when he and his brother worked the Comstock Lode; his stubborn resistance to lowering Second Street, which lay not far from his lovely home, by a gouge through Rincon Hill—a possible explanation for the fight Katie Lehane had witnessed.

The scenery beyond the horsecar windows became the sights and sounds of the Chinese quarter. Next would come the area near Celia's home, where construction pushed the city ever westward and north toward the inlet to the bay. Even in the few years she had lived there, San Francisco had changed so much, and leveling the roads was merely one way to accomplish that change. Celia and Patrick had only recently moved to the city when Broadway had been leveled, and she clearly recalled the ugliness of the exposed rock face, the makeshift staircases—more like ladders—that the property owners had constructed to reach their buildings marooned high above the roadbed. Every time it rained, torrents of mud and rubble broke free to churn along the street. In the years since, the cliffs had been smoothed, but if a cut was planned for the road passing through Rincon Hill, the loveliness of the area would be forever changed. She could not blame Virgil Nash for vehemently resisting.

She could only marvel that *he* was the one who was dead and not one of the partners at Martin and Company.

"*G*race sent me a note asking me to go to Cliff House tomorrow. She thinks it won't be fun otherwise," said Barbara the next morning. She handed Celia a curved needle, a length of silk suturing thread dangling from its eye. "Apparently, her stepmother has barely spoken to anybody since yesterday—she's too upset. And her father is furious with Mr. Greaves."

They were seated by the window in their neighbor's front room, Celia preparing to stitch up a gash in the forehead of Angelo Cascarino, who squirmed in his mother's arms. Mrs. Cascarino, robust, loud, and passionate, was pinning him against her chest.

"First the catarrh and now this! You will sit still for Signora Davies!"

Blood dripped from Angelo's forehead onto the red shawl his mother always wore over her white blouse, the ends tucked neatly into the waist of her skirt. "Mama!" he yowled.

"If you listen to me, you do not get hurt. But you do not listen, Angelo!" she responded. "Be quiet now for the *signora*."

Angelo howled louder.

Two of the other Cascarino children—there were five in total—watched from the doorway. Dark eyed, dark haired, and handsome, they were usually cheerful. Angelo's crying had made them less cheerful, however, and one, the youngest girl, was expending her anxiety by scuffing a toe across the worn floorboards.

"This is not the proper time, Barbara," said Celia, concerned by what Barbara was saying as well as displeased she'd brought it up at this moment.

Celia dipped a cloth into a tin bowl containing a solution of alum and resumed attending to Angelo. She daubed the cloth across his forehead to slow the bleeding. He'd been climbing a stack of crates piled against the back fence in order to tease the dog on the other side of it. The crates had not withstood his scramble up them, however. He was lucky he hadn't broken a bone.

"But is it true the police think Mr. Hutchinson might have killed that man?" Barbara asked.

Celia glanced up at Mrs. Cascarino's face, bent very near hers. The woman looked back with open curiosity, but she was far too polite to ask questions.

"That is quite enough, Barbara," said Celia. "You will need to hold his head very still, Mrs. Cascarino. This shall hurt."

Angelo paused his complaints to goggle at her in fear. Mrs. Cascarino grimly clamped his head between her two strong hands. Celia pinched closed the wound and plunged the needle through the skin, weaving the ligature through the wound as quickly as possible. By the time Angelo registered the pain and cried more loudly than before, she was finished.

Barbara snipped the needle free of the thread, and Celia tied it off. Not her best effort, and the ragged stitching would likely leave a scar, but not bad, considering the situation.

NO PITY *for the* DEAD

Celia daubed blood from the wound. "There, Angelo. You will look quite wonderfully fierce with those stitches. When people ask how you got them, make it a good story, all right?"

He hiccuped a sob, then nodded and scrambled down from his mother's lap. He ran to join his siblings, and they vanished from sight.

"Thank you, Signora," said Mrs. Cascarino, shaking her head over them. "Do I pay?"

"Most certainly not," she answered. For what spare money could the Cascarinos have? As far as Celia knew, they could barely afford the fifty or sixty dollars a month they spent renting this frame house with its paper-thin walls.

"But you have the expenses also."

Mrs. Cascarino slid a glance at Barbara, who was repacking Celia's supplies into her portmanteau. Celia understood why the woman looked at Barbara. The house Celia lived in belonged to her cousin, or it would once Barbara reached her majority, and Celia resided beneath its roof solely in her capacity as guardian. When Patrick had abandoned her, the entirety of her possessions containable within one medium-sized trunk and one carpetbag, she'd had nowhere else to go.

"You know I have never expected my patients to pay me, Mrs. Cascarino."

"*Grazie.*"

Celia rose from the chair. "Watch the wound for inflammation, Mrs. Cascarino. If you keep the site clean, it should heal properly."

Mrs. Cascarino showed Celia and Barbara to the door. "Thank you, Signora. And I tell that Angelo to be good."

"He is simply being a boy," said Celia. "Although you might

wish to have your husband relocate those stacks of crates. They are too tempting."

"You understand the children," the woman said. "You make a good mother, Signora. You are kind and you are calm."

Celia smiled politely, recalling Maryanne's contention that Celia was fortunate to *not* have children. Instead, the love she would have spent on any was given to Barbara and her patients.

Running feet thudded over their heads, accompanied by childish screeching. Mrs. Cascarino scowled at the ceiling. "More calm than I."

Celia and Barbara offered their good-byes and descended the stairs to the street. Celia watched her cousin as she limped down the steps, too proud to ask for assistance.

"I do wish that you had waited until we were alone to talk about the Hutchinsons," Celia said to her. She could not fathom how Mrs. Cascarino thought she would be a good mother when she herself seemed barely able to handle a single cousin.

"How could I be sure I'd have your attention?" Barbara shot back. "You're always too busy with this or that."

"You have my attention now." Celia paused on the pavement. "Jane is upset?" Yesterday, she'd seemed so composed when Mr. Greaves was questioning her. A brave front, apparently.

"Grace thinks her stepmother's afraid her father is going to be arrested."

"If Mr. Greaves intended to do so, he would have told me that last night." Celia hadn't meant to reveal that she had gone to his rooms to speak with him. Her cousin's expression did not change, however; she must have suspected.

"Grace also thinks Detective Greaves hates her father," said Barbara, not taking her eyes off the uneven planking she walked upon. "At least, that's what her father's saying. He's saying that the detective wants to see him hang."

Why was that? What lay in the past between the men? "Detective Greaves is simply questioning all the men connected to the person who died, Barbara. And no matter how much Mr. Greaves supposedly 'hates' Mr. Hutchinson, he will not hang an innocent man. Tell her not to worry."

"Mr. Hutchinson went to the station yesterday and yelled at Detective Greaves to leave Mrs. Hutchinson alone."

*Oh dear.* "*That* was not wise on his part."

"Grace was pretty proud of him," said Barbara, reaching for the railing of the stairs that led to their porch and struggling up them. "I don't like that she's worried, though."

"I do not, either," said Celia, even though she was worried herself.

"Why, look. What's this?" Barbara bent down and picked up a rose resting on the threshold of the front door. A yellow rose with a paper tag tied to its stem. She read the tag. "'To Miss Ferguson.' It looks like Addie has an admirer."

Celia took the rose from her cousin. "Someone left her flowers yesterday as well." She scanned the length of the street. "I wonder who it is?"

Barbara shrugged and opened the front door. "She'll be tickled."

"She was very embarrassed yesterday."

Celia paused to look up and down Vallejo again. The deliveryman from Bateman's Dairy was unloading a milk can from his wagon parked at the curb. Across the street, the Chilean woman who lived there was sweeping the ever-present sand from her steps, the *whisk* of her broom echoing off the clapboard walls of her house. At the corner boardinghouse, two men were loudly arguing on the long balcony that ran the length of the upper floor, their voices carrying to where she stood. They were fighting about the war that had ended more than two years earlier but was still quarreled over. Some of the neighborhood children were playing a rough game of tag in the street. One of the older Cascarino boys was with them. Celia would be stitching him up next.

But no one looked as though they had left a billet-doux for Addie.

"Joaquin," she called to one of the boys, the only son of their Chilean neighbor, who'd gone from playing tag to tussling, kicking up sand and dirt. She gestured for him to come over.

Reluctantly, he left his friends and slouched up the steps. "*Señora?*"

She held out the rose. "Did you notice a man come to our house and drop this here?"

"I leave it. A man from the . . ." Joaquin paused as he searched for the English word and gave up when he couldn't find it. "From the *florería* give me a nickel to put it here." He pointed with the scuffed toe of his right kip boot. "Yesterday, too."

A person with enough money to hire a florist to deliver flowers seemed to limit the potential suitors. "Thank you, Joaquin."

He ran off and Celia went inside, set down her medical bag, and headed for the kitchen. "Addie?"

Barbara was there before her, waiting on a cup of tea. "I've already told her about the flower."

"Another one, Addie." Celia set the rose on the table. "And you said there have been others. When did this start?"

Addie glanced at it and blushed, looking over at the daisies on the windowsill. "Och, I didna tell you? Last week, a note. The week before, a cluster of blooms from a laurel bush," she said. "Oh, and the week before that, sweets. They were verra good, those."

Barbara was grinning. She so rarely did, that it caught Celia off guard. *What an incredible situation.*

"Do you suspect who it is, Addie?" Celia asked.

"I've nae idea. And that would be my sort of luck—I finally have a man interested in me, and he willna leave his name!"

"Addie, you've had other admirers before," said Celia. Somehow, though, she always managed to chase them off. Or run away herself.

"I bet it's Mr. Taylor," said Barbara.

Addie's blush deepened. "What's that? Him?"

"Or the deliveryman from the butcher's. Grace and I were right about him being awfully sweet on you."

"Whisht! Get on with you," said Addie, flapping a corner of her apron at Barbara. "And if those are my choices, I'll stay unwed, thank you verra much. A grinning galoot from the butcher's or a gowk who laughs over my astrologer and is bound to get himself killed by a criminal sure as I'm standing here. What a selection."

"But why not leave his name?" asked Celia.

"Perhaps he's afraid she'll rebuff him, and he wants time to win her over," said Barbara, proving to be insightful for a sixteen-year-old.

"Well, 'faint heart never won fair lady,'" Celia quoted the idiom. In Addie's case, though, a cautious approach might succeed.

"I prefer a saying from the home country, 'They that love most, speak least.'" With a crisp nod of her head, Addie tucked

the rose in among the daisies and turned back to the Good
Samaritan stove, wrapping her apron around the handle of the
kettle to lift it off the rear grate.

"Another mystery, I guess," said Barbara, looking up at Celia.

"A more pleasant one to contemplate than who killed Virgil Nash."

"*L*ook at this, sir." Taylor dropped a newspaper onto Nick's
desk and jabbed a thumb at an article on the second
page. "A story this morning about Virgil Nash and a lawsuit.
Says the fella who'd brought it isn't going to be winning his
case, now that the defendant has been found dead."

Nick pushed aside the file he'd been reviewing, a case Mullahey had wrapped up. "What's this, Taylor?"

"Seems somebody named Enright was suing Virgil Nash for
trying to kick him off the plot of land Enright was renting.
Guess Nash had even gone so far as to try to tear down the man's
cooperage!"

Nick scanned the story. Mr. Horatio Enright had been pro-
testing Nash's efforts to negate the rental contract for the lot
Enright's cooperage was located on. The author of the article
had inserted his opinion of the case by mentioning that Enright
was a regular visitor to the Board of Supervisors meetings, object-
ing to the fees he'd been levied to plank the sidewalks, install
Nicolson pavement in the nearby alley, and put new redwood
cisterns along the road.

"So did Enright merely like to complain, or was our Mr.
Nash busy making enemies of more folks than the ones who
work at Martin and Company?" asked Nick. "I think I'll have a

talk with Enright after I go see Nash's mistress. See what he can tell us about his dispute with Nash."

"Nash's death solves one of Enright's problems, doesn't it, sir?" Taylor grabbed the newspaper, folded it, and tucked it under an arm. "Looks like we've got another suspect."

"Another suspect, Taylor."

"*P*lease follow me, Mr. Greaves." Lydia Templeton led Nick to the hallway behind the Metropolitan Theatre stage. They passed a man carrying a large oil lantern, its glass shade painted with a thin red coating. He nodded to the actress and barely glanced at Nick, uninterested that she was taking a man to her dressing room.

"We're debuting *Mephistopheles Jr* on Monday to open the season," she explained as they evaded ropes tied to scenery-painted cloths suspended from the ceiling and stepped around a man touching up a backdrop. "It's Mr. Howson's creation, and he's trying to evoke the fires of hell. As bad as rehearsals have been going, we're already there."

With long-legged strides, she marched through the chaos, her green dress—the color surely chosen to show off her fine chestnut hair, and the waist pinched to a ridiculously tiny diameter—swaying with each step.

"Here we are." She paused at a door marked PRIVATE and led him inside. Striking a match, she lit the lantern on a small corner table. "Welcome to my home away from home, Detective."

Nick removed his hat as Miss Templeton wended her way between spangled costumes and discarded stockings littering the floor. On one wall, she'd tacked a framed review, the paper turning yellow. The room smelled of her ambergris perfume and of cigar smoke, a reminder of Miss Templeton's most recent male visitor.

She lifted a purple silk robe off a chair, tossed it aside, and dragged the chair over to a table covered with enough lamps to light a city block. The large looking glass hanging above it reflected her pained expression.

"I've read the news. Poor Virgil," she said, sitting down.

"I'm sorry, Miss Templeton."

"Thanks, Detective." She motioned Nick to take a seat on the sofa shoved against the wall. "Just give me a moment, okay?"

She rummaged through the miscellany covering the table—pots of makeup, combs and brushes, feathers and other ornaments for her hair. Once she'd located a handkerchief, she wiped her eyes. Her hand was shaking.

Nick sat back, turning his hat in his hands, and contemplated Miss Templeton as she cried into her handkerchief. Even while sniffling and blowing her nose, she was pretty. She looked to be about the same age as Alice Nash, but the tiny lines around her eyes and lips made Nick think she liked to laugh. Unlike the sober Mrs. Nash. Maybe Virgil had found Miss Templeton a refreshing change. God knew Nick would.

Lydia Templeton blew her nose one more time and tucked the handkerchief away.

"I knew when Virgil didn't meet me at the ferry this past Wednesday that something was wrong. But murder?"

"He was seen with you at the back door of this establishment the evening of May twenty-eight, the day he was killed," said Nick. "You had a bag with you, and you climbed onto his horse and left. Later, a witness saw you and Mr. Nash heading out of town. Any explanation for that?"

"If someone claims to have seen me leaving town with Virgil," she said, "they were mistaken. He did collect me from the theater that evening, though. I was scheduled for a series of theatrical performances in Oakland, and we wanted to have supper together before I left on the last ferry out of San Francisco."

"Did he mention plans to visit with Martin that evening?"

"Virgil went to see him? I wish I'd known. I would've stopped him . . ." Her lips began to tremble, and she paused to regain her composure.

Nick didn't know if he should be buying what she was selling, but she was awfully good at selling.

"He took me to the Davis Street dock and said he would see me on my return. That was the last I saw of him," she continued, her emotions steadied. "I returned this past Wednesday. He was not at the dock to meet me. I was worried, but not worried enough, apparently."

"Did a Detective Briggs ever interview you?"

"No, but then I was out of town. Although everyone here at the theater knew where to find me."

*Good old Briggs. So thorough.* "Who might've wanted to kill Mr. Nash, Miss Templeton?"

She'd left the door open, and she turned to stare at the hallway beyond. Out in the theater, the orchestra was playing, a woman singing along. Miss Templeton winced when the vocalist hit a sour note. The music ground to an abrupt halt, and a man, probably Mr. Howson, started shouting.

"He did have enemies," she admitted. "Men who resented him."

"Because he'd gotten rich mining the Comstock? Or as a successful gambler?" Nick asked.

"Both," she said, without a hint of apology or shame. "He didn't talk much about his time in the Comstock, though. He lost his brother, Silas, there, and it pained him still. Murdered by a knife-wielding madman."

"Mrs. Nash told me about Silas. Did Virgil ever mention to you the name of the man who'd killed him?" Nick asked, making a note to have Mullahey contact the police in Virginia City for details.

"Cuddy Pike. Isn't it funny that I can remember his name? Apparently he thought Virgil and his brother had encroached on his lode, driving their shaft into Pike's ore vein in order to mine it."

A claim jumper, then, like Matthews had said.

"Virgil only mentioned him once or twice. He was furious that the sheriff allowed his brother's killer to get away. He's never been located, as far as I know," she continued. "No, Virgil preferred to talk about his adventures, how wild and carefree it was in those days. Desperate men desperate for wealth and living like hungry wolves. It wasn't easy to pull silver from those stones. Not at all like panning for gold. Virgil was very proud of his success and had little tolerance for the weak and the quitters. He used to say that the injury to his arm was proof of how hard he was willing to work. His forearm was crushed when a hoisting cage cable broke, Detective, and he was nearly thrown to his death at the bottom of the mine. He was awfully proud about surviving the accident, too."

"I've been told men owed Mr. Nash money. Gambling losses. What do you know about that?"

"Virgil was skilled at playing faro—now that he's dead, I suppose we can admit that," she said. "Wouldn't Alice be shocked."

"Where did these faro games take place?" Nick asked.

"Everywhere and anywhere men take wagers—their houses, private rooms in hotels, basement dens beneath saloons. An alleyway, if necessary."

"Any particular hotels or saloons, Miss Templeton?"

"He'd favored the Golden Hare lately. Not much to look at on the outside. Intentionally so," she said. "But his fancy for that place would've eventually passed, I'm sure. Once the cut was decided for or against, he would no longer have a need to go there and would've moved on. Virgil was restless."

"What does the Golden Hare have to do with the cut?" Nick asked, noting how many conversations kept coming around to the Second Street cut.

"The right sort of men have a taste for that place, Detective. Men Virgil thought he could persuade to join his side against the cut."

"Through debts to him."

Miss Templeton tilted her head and looked at him. She had a fine neck, and the pose showed it to advantage. "Whatever it took, but Virgil wasn't naïve. He knew resisting the Second Street cut was like Sisyphus pushing that boulder up a hill, only to watch it roll down again. Progress here is inevitable, especially when you are somebody like Jasper Martin, who has friends on the planning commission."

*Sisyphus?* "So who do you think is responsible for Virgil's death, Miss Templeton?"

The music began again, and the vocalist in the theater picked up the song. It went better this time. "Who else but the partners at Martin and Company, Detective Greaves? They'd sent him threatening notes, and they finally followed through."

"Threats?" Martin had been overheard wishing Mr. Nash were dead.

"They've had it out for Virgil all along, Detective Greaves, and now they've won."

"Would you like lunch now or later?" asked Addie from the doorway that connected the kitchen at the rear of the house to Celia's clinic examination room.

Celia looked up from the piece of paper she'd set atop her corner desk. The paper was blank except for a drip of ink. She hadn't been certain where to start on her efforts to be a detective.

"Lunch can wait until after I return from downtown," Celia answered. "Hopefully I shall have more of an appetite once I have convinced Mr. Hutchinson to take Owen back."

"Weel, I wish you luck with that, then." Addie scowled. "And I ken what you're up to there." She pointed at the paper.

"I am merely making a list in order to collect my thoughts on this affair before I leave."

"This affair is nae your concern, ma'am."

"I have made it my concern."

"Aye, that you have again." The housekeeper harrumphed and returned to the kitchen, banging the connecting door closed.

Celia resumed her contemplation of the piece of paper, dipped the pen in the inkwell, and proceeded to write down her thoughts.

*Frank Hutchinson* . . .

Celia stared at his name. It felt traitorous to list him first, as though she considered him her primary suspect, just as Mr. Greaves did. *You must be unprejudiced, though.*

*Frank Hutchinson. Motive: eliminate the man attempting to keep Martin and Company from pursuing the Second Street cut, a source of future revenue.* Most concerning, Jane was upset, which led Celia to fear her friend thought her husband guilty.

Celia wondered if Frank had an alibi for the night of Mr. Nash's death. Mr. Greaves had not mentioned it, if so. His propensity to stay out late with Mr. Russell, and Jane's inclination to take soporifics to mute her unhappiness, might make it challenging for him to provide one.

She moved on.

*Abram Russell. Motive: avoid paying off a gambling debt owed to Mr. Nash? Also stood to profit from the Second Street cut, although possibly less so than Frank.* However, if he had gambling losses to cover, any money to be obtained by the cut might seem precious. Furthermore, Jane did not like him.

*Jasper Martin. Motive: again, profits from the Second Street cut. As the owner of Martin and Company, he would gain the most. Overheard by Dan Matthews (who might not be telling the truth) that he wished Virgil Nash were dead.* A ruthless and strong-willed man, which suggested he would not tolerate obstacles like Virgil Nash. *Was with the mayor the evening of the murder. Denied setting up meeting with Mr. Nash.*

*Dan Matthews. Motive: avoid paying off a gambling debt owed to Virgil Nash.* Maryanne was not surprised to learn that her brother had become entangled in a crime, suggesting a propensity for running into trouble. But why would Dan dig up the body?

Celia tapped the end of her pen against her teeth. Who else was there?

*Rob Bartlett. Motive: unknown. Gambling debts, also? Might have wished to steal from Mr. Nash, a wealthy man, then killed him. Encouraged Dan to dig up the cellar in search of Jasper Martin's supposed buried gold.*

She lifted the paper and scrutinized Rob Bartlett's name. What if he had murdered Virgil Nash in the cellar of the building where he worked, buried the man there, but then wanted the body discovered in order to implicate someone else at Martin and Company? Someone like Frank, whom Mr. Bartlett resented for not promoting him. But then why bother to bury the man in the first place? Why not simply leave him lying in his own blood for one of the partners or Mr. Kelly to discover in the morning when he came to work with his crew?

Perhaps Mr. Bartlett had wanted time to work on his alibi. Perhaps, panicked, he had acted in haste and over time had developed an idea of how to lay the blame on someone else. As far as she knew, though, he hadn't presented any accusations to the police.

"Also, if the murderer *is* Rob Bartlett, I stand little chance of learning much about him at Mr. Martin's party tomorrow."

She laid the notepaper flat again and wrote another name. *John Kelly. Motive: steal from Mr. Nash to support growing family.*

"I most sincerely hope he can be eliminated, Maryanne," she murmured.

Then, of course, there were all the other workers to consider. The improvements being done on Mr. Martin's business would require several laborers. Did they work on Saturdays? They might, given that the work had fallen behind because of the discovery of Mr. Nash's body. Celia glanced at her watch. It was not yet noon. She might have an opportunity to speak with one or two of them while she was at the offices, pleading Owen's case to Frank. If he was there.

To the bottom of the list she added *Stranger who killed Silas Nash. Motive: Further revenge for a jumped claim in Nevada.* If Dan Matthews' account was to be believed, and if the man had returned from wherever he had fled.

Wiping the pen nib clean, Celia laid it down and closed the inkwell lid. Sadly, making the list had tangled her thoughts more than clarified them.

# CHAPTER 6

"My wife was right that the cops would be coming here, after that article in the newspaper." Horatio Enright straddled a shaving horse, scraping his two-handled drawknife along the edge of an oak stave. Nick noticed that he was missing half of his left forefinger. The damage to his finger didn't interfere with his expert use of the drawknife, though. "More trouble from Nash, even after he's dead."

Enright was difficult to hear over the sound of one of his workers sizing staves with a hand saw and another worker banging iron hoops into place on a keg. Out on the street, a wagon pulled up with a fresh load of cut lumber. A man hopped down to start hauling it into the shop.

"There," Enright said, directing the man. "Put it all there."

The sound of boards plunking into a pile added to the noise.

Nick moved aside as the pile of lumber began to encroach upon the one open spot he'd found among the mounds of buckets and barrels. "I've heard some about your dispute with Nash, but what are the details, Mr. Enright?"

"Nash claimed he hadn't agreed that this lot was to be used for a cooperage." Enright set down the drawknife and released the foot pedal that held the clamp around the piece of wood. "A convenient memory lapse, but I knew what he wanted. He wanted this lot back so he could expand his warehouse next door, but my rental agreement hasn't expired yet."

Enright wiped his thick hands down the leather apron he wore and examined the stave. Satisfied, he picked up another and began shaping it.

"Virgil Nash owned the building next door?" Nick asked. The lumber deliveryman departed, which left only the rasp of sawing and the hammering to contend with.

"Him and his partner," said Enright. "Pretty funny that Nash was the one complaining to the planning commission about the grading proposed for Second Street. Seems he always made sure to rail at me whenever I protested the latest so-called upgrades he supported. All that street work comes at a cost to me, doesn't it, Mr. Greaves? Me and all the rest of the small businesses on this road are going to be levied to death, that's what'll happen. Laying down those wood blocks to pave the alleyway and calling it progress, when everybody knows Nicolson pavement ain't worth a hill of beans. Bah."

"Does this partner of Nash's intend to pursue the suit and get you off this land?" he asked, noticing that the fellow hammering the iron hoops seemed to be enjoying making a lot of noise, since he'd been working the same spot on the keg for the past few minutes and had to have accomplished what he needed to already.

"They had a falling-out a while back," said Enright. "When Nash tried to demolish my shop, he pissed off Hutchinson all right. Had enough of Nash's nonsense. Stopped being partners after that."

That was a name sure to focus Nick's attention. "Did you say Hutchinson?"

"I did."

"Frank Hutchinson?"

"That's who I mean." Enright finished with that stave and grabbed another from the stack alongside the shaving horse. "He was in with Nash when I first started renting this place. But like I said, he didn't care for Nash's treatment of our contract, and that was the end of their partnership."

The fine Frank. Might be the only noble thing he'd ever done. "Did you witness their argument? How violent was it?"

"Didn't see it. Didn't have to. Heard all about it, though." He dragged the drawknife toward him, flakes of wood falling to join the others at the man's feet.

"What about threatening notes that Nash had received?"

Enright sat up and considered Nick's question. "Can't say I recollect hearing about those. But I remember some fellow named Martin coming by not too long ago, and Nash cursing at him to leave. Martin didn't look rattled at all."

Nick regretted that every time he heard Martin mentioned in connection to Nash, he was forced to recall that Martin had an alibi. "You're probably not all that sad that Virgil Nash is dead, are you, Mr. Enright?" And the man was good with a knife. "Do you have somebody who can vouch for where you were the night Nash was murdered, May twenty-eight?"

"I've been in Seattle the past few weeks, Detective. Business matters associated with my lumber supplier. Got back yesterday." He nodded toward the depths of the shop. "And look how far behind we are on orders. Can't leave for one minute."

The young man sawing staves registered that he was being criticized and scowled.

"And there are people who can verify where you were," said Nick.

"Of course there are. And listen, Detective. I wouldn't bother to kill Nash, then bury him in the cellar of some building," said the cooper, setting down his drawknife again. "I'd lay him flat out in the middle of Market Street where everybody driving past could see the bastard's body and have a chance to spit on it."

*Celia* stepped down from the horsecar a block early and hastened along the pavement of Montgomery Street, deftly avoiding a collision with a woman carrying parcels out of a milliner's. She experienced a momentary pang of envy as she watched the woman climb into the carriage waiting at the curb for her; it would be wonderful to purchase a new hat for tomorrow's fete at Cliff House, a notion Celia rarely allowed herself to indulge.

Passing a ladies' fancy goods shop she sometimes visited, she slowed to examine the colorful ribbons on display. Perhaps she could buy a length of embroidered gauze to trim her old bonnet. A small expense.

"Hello, ma'am," said the girl cleaning the front window.

Ginny Simmons was one of Celia's patients. She lived rent free in a room above the shop in exchange for her labors, which the woman who owned the business took full advantage of. "How are you today, Ginny? Better?"

"Well enough. My rash is all cleared up, thanks to you."

"Good," Celia replied, casting a final glance at the ribbon. "I shall return in a short while to buy a length of your cream gauze ribbon there."

"I'll tell the missus," Ginny responded, bobbing a curtsy that seemed utterly out of place on an American street, and resumed polishing the glass.

A few steps farther on, Celia arrived at Martin and Company. The man who had been painting the trim yesterday was outside continuing his efforts, which meant the other workers were possibly there as well. Her first priority, however, was to get Owen rehired.

From his perch on his ladder, the painter tipped his cap, and Celia swept through the front doors that had been propped open to allow the breeze to waft through. The din of saws and hammers greeted her, quite a change from the thorough silence of Thursday night. The room was a beehive of activity, carpenters fabricating a partition nearby, gas-fixture installers hanging elaborate chandeliers, ladders propped against walls so that the plasterers could finish the ceiling work. One of them might be Rob Bartlett, she supposed.

"Mrs. Davies," called out John Kelly, noticing her arrival and striding over to intercept her before she progressed more than a few feet beyond the doorway. "What would be bringing you here?"

He was handsome, but not with Patrick's shimmering brightness, her husband's charm as much a feature as his blue eyes and broad shoulders. Mr. Kelly's accent was also fainter than Patrick's, which Celia had attributed to many years lived in America, the lilt washed out like dyes exposed too long to sunshine.

"Ah, Mr. Kelly. Good day to you," she said, pitching her voice loud enough to be heard over the racket. "I wish to speak with Mr. Hutchinson. Concerning the matter of Owen Cassidy's dismissal."

"I'm afraid Mr. Hutchinson won't be wanting to hear your pleas for a fellow who was trying to rob Mr. Martin," he said, shaking his head in sympathy. "Cassidy's lucky Mr. Martin didn't ask the police to arrest him."

"Likewise your brother-in-law," she said, interested in his reaction. "The police have spoken to him about why he was digging in the cellar, but they did release him."

"I've always said to Maryanne that her brother's trouble." Mr. Kelly's expression darkened. "I wonder what excuse he gave the police to explain why he'd be doing such a thing."

"I can hardly answer that question, Mr. Kelly. I am not a member of the police force and was not privy to the conversation," she replied, even though Mr. Greaves had informed her that Dan Matthews had denied knowing the victim, despite owing the fellow money.

"I should never have taken him on, but Maryanne insisted," he said. "And then he was never appreciative."

Celia regretted her comment; she did not want him to argue with Maryanne. "Your wife's health is fragile, Mr. Kelly. Please do not upset her more than she already is over her brother."

"You can be sure I'll be careful with her, Mrs. Davies," he replied. "I've no more time to talk. We've work to do, as you can see. And I'll not be wantin' either Mr. Martin or Mr. Hutchinson coming down from their offices to wonder why I've let a woman on the premises to distract the men."

"So Mr. Hutchinson *is* here today. We are friends, and I will only require a moment of his time," she said, hurrying off before he could stop her.

A man holding a trowel and a square of wood topped with mortar moved out of her way as she turned the corner into the vestibule. Unsurprisingly, the door to the cellar was closed, but the door to the steps leading to the first floor was open, and she went through.

It was quieter up here, and she slowed to a more leisurely pace. Frank's office was one of two located on the street-facing side of the building—the other belonging to Jasper Martin, whose wavy form she could make out through the frosted glass.

After drawing in a deep breath, she rapped on Frank's door.

"Come," he called out, and she entered.

When Frank noticed it was Celia, he stood from where he'd been seated behind his large walnut desk. He was very tall, and Celia had always thought him handsome, if somewhat restrained.

"Mrs. Davies, what brings you downtown?" He smiled and looked past her. "Is my wife with you?"

"No, I've come on my own."

"You're not here to tell me you don't want to go with us to Cliff House tomorrow, are you?" he asked. "Jane's counting on your joining our party."

"I have no plans to disappoint her, Mr. Hutchinson," Celia answered, certainly speaking the truth. "I am here to beg a favor. I need you to tell Mr. Kelly to take Owen Cassidy back."

The smile slipped from Frank's face, and he gestured for her to take a chair, which she did.

"We need this situation to be resolved before we consider doing that, Mrs. Davies." The light streaming through the large windows at his back cast his face in shadows and made his expression difficult to read.

"Dan Matthews coerced Owen to cooperate. He is innocent of any criminal intent."

Frank spread his hands flat atop his desk. She had interrupted his reviewing maps of the city. A heavy red line was drawn across several of them; if she peered closely at the one beneath his left hand, she expected she would see it was a map of the Rincon Hill area.

"Mr. Hutchinson," she said when he didn't respond, "I realize you took Owen on only because of my friendship with your wife, but I maintain that he is a good lad. He deserves a second chance."

"After this situation is resolved, Mrs. Davies, and the dust has settled."

"Thank you." She twisted the straps of her reticule around her fingers. "It is a dreadful business. What is your opinion on who might have murdered Virgil Nash?"

His gaze narrowed. "I don't have an opinion, Mrs. Davies."

*Ah, but most certainly you do.* "Have you overheard any of the men talking about him? I suspect your workers are very observant."

"The men working on this building aren't paid to gossip, Mrs. Davies."

"Of course not. How silly of me—"

"You're asking questions because you know Detective Greaves, aren't you? Did he put you up to this?"

"He did not. I am asking solely out of personal curiosity."

"Asking questions seems pretty dangerous, Mrs. Davies," he said, "when a man's been murdered."

His tone was ominous, but Frank Hutchinson would never threaten her. "I shall be cautious."

"A good idea," he said. "And since you know Nick Greaves so well, why don't you tell him to leave us alone, too?"

"I do not believe he would listen," she said with a smile, an attempt at lightheartedness that Frank did not reciprocate.

Abruptly, he got to his feet. "Expect our carriage around eleven tomorrow, Mrs. Davies. Until then . . ."

She'd been dismissed. "Yes. Tomorrow. Good day to you."

She exited the room and retreated down the stairs, her plan to speak to the workers thwarted by John Kelly's vigilant gaze. As she stepped out onto the street, her skin tingled with the certainty that she was being watched. She fought the urge to look back at the building. It was best to pretend she had nothing to fear. Even if that might not be the case.

Nick strolled up Post, heading for Abram Russell's house. Two stories of cream-painted brick, the house stood just shy of Union Square. It was close enough, though, that Nick supposed Russell could lean out his window to observe the parades that always seemed to be taking place there. Today the square was empty except for a handful of men in tattered uniforms and grizzled beards, lounging on the benches.

From the far end of Union Square, the bells of Trinity Church, its multitude of skinny spires poking toward the heavens, sounded the top of the hour as Nick climbed the steps to Russell's front door.

A Chinese boy answered the bell. Nick explained who he was, and the boy bowed him into the entry hall. Then, his long black queue swinging over his turquoise silk tunic, the boy ran off toward the back of the house, leaving Nick to wait. He tapped the toe of one boot on the white marble beneath his feet. Here he was again, in yet another fancy house, its rooms stuffed to the rafters with expensive furniture. If Nick poked through the polished rosewood secretary he noticed in the adjacent parlor, would he find stacks of bills demanding payment for the oriental vases and silk curtains? Gambling debts could have pitched Russell over the brink, encouraging him to kill Nash rather than figure out how to produce the money he might've owed the man.

"You come." The boy had returned and gestured for Nick to follow. "Garden."

At the end of the hall, a doorway let out onto a rear porch. It overlooked a garden with a fountain that spurted water into the sky. From the porch, he could also see the sparkle of the bay and the ships and steamers like rolling specks traveling upon blue fabric. A fine view, but not quite as nice as the one from the Nashes' house on Rincon Hill.

Mr. Russell sat at a table alongside a plump woman, her nut-brown hair cascading around her face in a fuss of spirals. Plates of food sat in front of them; Nick had interrupted them at their lunch.

Russell rose from his wicker chair and introduced the woman as his wife, Dorothea. He was short of stature and thin, and didn't look like he'd be able to successfully stab another man to death. Unlike Dan Matthews, who had plenty of muscle, or Frank, tall and strong. Nick would have to ask Harris how powerful he thought the fellow was who'd severed Nash's abdominal artery.

"I'm not sure why you're here, Detective." Russell's voice trembled, but some folks got nervous around cops whether they were guilty of something or not.

"What is this about?" asked his wife.

A small fluffy dog jumped down from her lap and ran over

to Nick. It stopped at the foot of the steps—a safe distance—
and proceeded to yelp.

"Peaches, be quiet," she commanded, and then also stood,
her heavy skirts rustling. "Peaches, come here."

The dog didn't quiet or come to her. Dorothea marched over
and bent to retrieve it. "If your arrival has anything to do with
that wretched business at my husband's office, Detective, I can
assure you he is blameless."

"I prefer to assess that for myself, ma'am," replied Nick, which
caused her to scowl. The dog—Peaches—must have felt her
tense, because it began yapping again. She didn't attempt to stop
it. She might have wanted to yap at Nick, too.

"I'd like to hear whatever you have to say about this affair,
Mr. Russell," said Nick. The man flushed. The day was warming,
but their backyard enjoyed a pleasant breeze sweeping down off
the western hills. It was too cool a midday to have turned such a
bright shade of pink.

His wife spoke for him. "Virgil Nash was born to be a thorn in
good folks' sides, Detective. His efforts to interfere in the plans of
Martin and Company brought him great delight, I do believe. It is
my expectation that he had numerous enemies and few friends. He
and his wife were so often at the opera or theater alone."

"Dottie, you're not helping matters," said Russell.

"How well did you know Nash, Mr. Russell? Beyond any
interactions through your work, that is," said Nick. "Ever drink
with him at Burke's or the Golden Hare, for instance, or maybe
gamble with him?"

"My husband does not gamble!" Peaches squirmed in her
arms, and she released the dog, which ran over to Nick again

and barked more fiercely. It made Nick glad to have Riley, who barked only at reasonable times.

"That's not what I hear," said Nick.

"What you hear is utter scandal, sir," pronounced Dorothea Russell.

"You didn't answer my question, Mr. Russell."

"I did see Mr. Nash at Burke's, the one time I went there. Bought him a drink. Trying to be friendly with the man. That was what Martin wanted from us. Didn't he, dear?"

"You have always been dependable, Abram." Dorothea patted his arm. "Always."

*Hmm.*

"How long have you known Mr. Nash? Since the Comstock?" Nick asked, a shot in the dark.

Russell swallowed. Peaches gave up barking at Nick and scurried back to his mistress. "I've never been to the Comstock, Mr. Greaves."

"Where were you Thursday night, Mr. Russell?" Nick asked.

"I was with Frank," he said. "We usually spend Tuesday and Thursday evenings together."

"That's what Mrs. Hutchinson told me as well," said Nick, and Russell perked up. "About what time did you two part ways?"

"He was home before sunset," answered Mrs. Russell for him.

And Frank was back at his house around ten, according to the Hutchinsons' maid. Which left an unaccounted-for gap of a little more than two hours. If Dottie wasn't lying. "What about the night of May twenty-eight?"

"Is that the night Nash died?" Russell asked, proving reasonably perceptive.

Nick inclined his head.

Mrs. Russell prepared to speak again, but her husband hushed her. "I don't recall. It's been too long."

"It was the Tuesday two weeks ago, if that jogs your memory," said Nick.

Russell ran a finger between his collar and his neck. "Oh yes, I remember. I'd gone out to dine with Frank that particular evening as usual, now that I think back. I'm right, aren't I, Dottie?" Mrs. Russell responded with a slight nod. "We were out late, I hate to admit."

"Both of you?" Nick asked.

"Yes. Both of us."

"Why, of course he was with Mr. Hutchinson, Detective Greaves," said Dorothea Russell. "And believe me, I was ever so unhappy about it, having been quite unwell that entire day."

"So, it's not possible Frank Hutchinson murdered Virgil Nash and buried him in the cellar of Martin and Company?" Nick asked Russell. "Because you were with him that entire evening."

"What reason would Frank have to do something stupid like that?"

"Because he wants to impress his father-in-law with a nice new house, and Mr. Nash stood in the way of his getting the money he needed," Nick replied. "Witnesses have said they'd fought many times. About some business with a Mr. Horatio Enright, for instance."

"And I just told you Frank was with me that night," insisted Russell. "Frank Hutchinson would never murder a man simply to afford a nicer house for Jane, Detective. Or as a way to settle a dispute over the way Mr. Nash liked to conduct his affairs."

"Are you absolutely certain he was with you all evening, Abram?" his wife asked him, suddenly deciding to change her story. "You know how . . . You know how forgetful you can be. Could it be somehow possible he slipped away from you—"

"I won't accuse my closest friend of murder in order to save my own neck, Dottie," he said sharply, which caused her to blanch.

Nick would give the man credit for his staunch support of his friend, if for nothing else.

He stared at the steadfast Abram Russell, and part of Mrs. Davies' Shakespeare quote came to mind: *Faithful friends are hard to find.* Maybe all the partners were involved in getting rid of the annoying Virgil Nash. Every one of them stood to gain from his death, and two of them hated the man. They were certainly doing a bang-up job of covering for one another.

"I'm going to advise you to stick around town, Mr. Russell, like I'm advising everybody connected to this case to do."

"You can't think my husband is a suspect, sir!" Mrs. Russell screeched, sending Peaches into a clamor of barks.

"Until I learn otherwise, I very much can, Mrs. Russell."

The bell of the fancy goods shop tinkled overhead as Celia pushed open the door.

The middle-aged woman who owned the shop, Mrs. Lowers, looked over. She stood at a counter, helping a customer examine a selection of beautifully carved hair combs of tortoiseshell and ivory. "I'll be right with you, Mrs. Davies."

Celia closed the door and glanced around. She had always found the smell of the space—slightly musty from the bolts of wool ranged across the shelves—comforting. And the riot of colors from the many fabrics and lengths of lace that filled nooks and spilled from cubbyholes was a delight. Peeling off her cotton gloves, Celia lifted the corner of a piece of golden pongee silk not yet returned to its place and rubbed the material between her fingers, relishing the sheen and the luxuriously soft feel of the textile against her skin.

"How can I help you?" Mrs. Lowers asked, having bustled to Celia's side as soon as the customer had departed with her purchase.

She released the pongee. "I would like half an ell of your cream gauze ribbon. Ginny knows which one. I spoke to her earlier about it."

The woman perked, pleased that Celia had come in to make a purchase, rather than merely browse as so often occurred.

"I can fetch . . . ," the woman began to say as the shop bell rang out and a matron in expensive silks entered.

"You may assist your other customer, Mrs. Lowers. I shall locate Ginny on my own."

"She's in back," the owner answered, and strode off to attend to her other customer.

The rear room was located behind a curtained archway. A space about the size of Celia's parlor, it was filled with worktables, neatly folded stacks of material, and sewing implements. Ginny, a woman too young for the air of pinched solemnity that hung about her, sat on a low stool by the grimy window, embroidering a pair of cotton gloves. If she had set alight one of the gas lamps suspended overhead, she might be better able to see her work. The relative cleanliness of the ceiling, however, suggested Mrs. Lowers rarely permitted their use.

The girl looked over. "There you are again, Mrs. Davies." Ginny poked the needle into the embroidered section to not lose her place and stood. "You here for that pretty ribbon?"

"I am, but I would also like to ask you some questions," said

Celia, glancing toward the doorway. The sound of voices indicated that Mrs. Lowers remained occupied with her customer. "About something that happened Thursday night."

Ginny's eyes widened. "Is it about that dead man they found at Mr. Martin's?" she whispered. "I saw the police crawling all over the place yesterday and carrying the body off." She crossed herself. "It's got Mrs. Lowers dreadful scared, especially when the cops came around to ask her questions. It's got me scared, too."

"There is no need for you and Mrs. Lowers to be concerned about your safety, Ginny. The circumstances suggest the murderer is not likely to be after other individuals who work and live on Montgomery."

"Did someone at Martin and Company kill the fella?" Ginny's eyes grew wider. "I knew it! I'll never talk to those two again! Trouble, the both of them!"

"Which two?" Celia asked.

"Rob and Dan. Won't leave a girl alone. If they see me outside when they're on their way to the billiard saloon down the street, they can't go by without teasing and saying stuff," she said. "And once they're liquored up, they're worse. Always plotting and scheming, those two. Plotting and scheming."

Another mention of Rob Bartlett. *I must move him up my list of suspects.*

"Did you notice anything unusual a few weeks back?" Celia asked. "Tuesday the twenty-eighth. Did you perhaps hear a commotion?"

"Don't think I did, ma'am."

"What about Thursday night, Ginny? That evening, a man tried to remove the body, but he was chased off," said Celia, hoping Ginny didn't stop to ponder how Celia was in possession of

NO PITY for the DEAD

such information. "I believe he ran past the shop here. Did you happen to notice?"

"Wait . . . Yes, I did!" She lowered her voice again. "I was out in the alley shaking out the rugs at the end of the day. I heard the sound of running feet and was headed back inside, scared of what was going on. He came past quick . . . *They* came past quick, because there were two of them. A man followed by a boy. The boy turned back, though. I thought that was strange."

She meant Owen. "Could you describe the man?"

"Didn't really see him to describe him, ma'am," she said, "but I did notice where he went."

"You did?"

"There was a wagon waiting for him. It was hitched to a strange pale horse with the blackest mane, and it was waiting at the end of the alleyway." Ginny pointed toward the north. "The horse and wagon were lit up by the gas lantern at the business down there, so I could see them pretty well, even with the fog. The man climbed onto the seat next to the driver, and they drove off quick."

"A wagon? Are you positive?"

"No mistaking, ma'am. No mistaking at all."

The proprietor of the restaurant across the street from the Golden Hare made another circuit past Nick's table, giving him an annoyed look. He'd been sitting there for two hours already, drawing suspicious glances not only from the owner but from the barkeep and aproned waiter. He'd sit there for another two hours if that was what it took to ever spot anybody related to the case going into or coming out of that saloon.

"Another beer," Nick said, tapping his empty glass. He'd be

sloppy drunk if he kept this up, though, and unable to do anything about a suspect if he ever did spot one.

The proprietor snagged the glass and walked off. Nick wiped his mouth with his napkin, dropped it on the table, and stared across the road past a wagon parked at the curb. Not much to look at was right, just as Lydia Templeton had claimed. The front facade was about as discreet as the entrance to the meeting rooms of a ladies' society. However, the brawny brute who manned the door wasn't the sort of fellow you'd find greeting guests at a charity organization.

"Here," said the restaurant owner, banging the full glass on the table and grabbing Nick's plate. Even though the place smelled of soured spilled beer and charred meat, at least the food had been decent.

He'd just taken a sip of the beer when a man came strolling down the street, a nearby streetlamp lighting his face. A man Nick recognized, who loped into the Golden Hare, the door guard nodding in recognition and letting him pass.

Nick counted to ten, then jumped up and threw some coins onto the table.

"Hey!" the proprietor shouted after him.

"I paid!" Nick shouted back, sprinting out into the street, evading horses and carriages, and staying clear of the light cast by the streetlamps. In this part of town, close to the warehouses and lodgings that boarded seamen and transients, his furtive movements didn't draw notice. In this part of town, folks knew not to mind other folks' actions.

Nonetheless, he was glad he'd dug out the old battered slouch hat he'd kept from the war and an oversized sack coat that had belonged to Mrs. Jewett's son, given to Nick in a bout of sentimentality. Not his usual outfit, and he hoped it was enough of a disguise, should anybody who knew him be hanging about.

Nick stepped onto the opposite curb and strode up to the man at the door like he belonged.

"Just saw my friend Dan, there. Told me to meet him here." Nick looked around him like he was awed by the very idea of getting to enter the saloon. "Dan always did tell me I oughtta come here, and I'm sure glad I finally got the chance!"

He made to walk past the guard, but the man grabbed Nick's arm. "You got a name, mister?" he asked in a deep rumble of a voice.

"Bartlett," he bluffed, in big trouble if the other man personally knew Bartlett.

The guard, evidently familiar with Bartlett's name but not his face, released Nick's arm. "Have a good night, Mr. Bartlett."

"You can bet I will!"

Inside, the place looked like any other saloon, a long bar on one side with an immense mirror behind it, tables scattered everywhere and crowded with men enjoying their libations. The crowd wasn't the usual sort, though, for an area so near the wharves. There were fewer rough laborers and dockworkers, and more fellows in fine suits of clothes, men with trimmed beards and clean teeth. Nobody was gambling, though; in fact, Nick didn't spot a single card anywhere. Maybe Lydia Templeton had been wrong.

A young woman was making the rounds, talking with the customers who weren't so drunk that they might paw her. She bore a familial resemblance to the man behind the bar, making Nick wonder whether she was the fellow's daughter or sister. She'd been evading a rambunctious fellow's attentions when she noticed Nick.

Ignoring customers' attempts to flag her down, she walked over to him.

"I haven't seen you in here before," she said, greeting him with a welcoming smile, her gaze sharp as a hawk's. On the outside, she looked like a schoolmarm, but Nick was well aware that looks could be deceiving. "Welcome to the Golden Hare. The first drink is always on me."

"Maybe later," he said, spying Matthews as he slipped through a doorway at the end of the hallway, a man who could be the twin of the monster guarding the front door ushering him through. It wasn't much of a stretch to imagine that the doorway opened onto a set of stairs that led to a basement room where men like Nash played faro and men like Dan Matthews lost money to them. "Right now I'm trying to catch up with my friend Dan."

"You're with Mr. Matthews?" she asked, her gaze flicking toward the hallway door. "By all means, join him. I'll see you later."

Nick tapped his hat brim and strolled across the room, nodded at the barkeep, and walked up to the sentry.

"I'm with Dan," he said to the fellow.

Two deep-set eyes stared back at him. "He didn't say to expect nobody else."

"He didn't? Well I'll be danged. How'd he forget? Must be skunked, eh?" Nick laughed.

The man gave him another lookover and rapped on the door. Nick heard a number of bolts being thrown, and the door swung wide to reveal another man as burly and ugly as the sentry.

"I'm with Dan!" Nick repeated, which satisfied him, too.

He barged past, reaching for the stair railing. A series of

lanterns flickered in the dark at the bottom of the steps, casting shadows, and he could hear the faint sound of clinking barware and the murmur of voices.

"Better not be lyin'," the man called after him as Nick reached the hallway and strolled along it.

A number of doors, firmly shut, led off the hallway. At the far end, however, one stood ajar, revealing a large room blazing with gaslight, smoke thickening the air. He could see a good dozen men clustered around a long table covered in glazed cloth, coins glinting on the surface, the gamblers hunched in silent concentration.

"Red wins."

One of the gamblers stalked off, leaving an empty spot at the table through which Nick could see the dealer at the far end, a man in enveloping black robes, a wire mask on his face concealing his features and a large floppy hat covering all of his hair. The getup guaranteed Nick would never be able to identify him again and prosecute him. He didn't see Matthews, though. He'd have to search the other rooms.

Just as Nick turned to leave, a man strode into view to take the empty place at the table. No, not a man, a kid. A scruffy Irish kid who had no business being there. So much for his investigation into whether the goings-on at the Golden Hare had anything to do with Nash's murder. He had a more immediate problem.

"Excuse me, gentlemen," he called out. "That there's my kid brother."

Owen gaped over being caught and took off across the room, looking for another door to escape through. There wasn't one, though.

"C'mon now," said Nick, chasing after him, gamblers shouting complaints and the dealers hastily scraping cards and dice and winnings off the tables.

One of the sentries—Nick didn't know which one; they all were the same amount of burly and ugly—charged into the room, summoned by the uproar.

Nick reached Owen, cowering in the corner, and yanked him to his feet. "I've got you. Ma's gonna whip you to kingdom come." He pulled Owen past the guard, who tried to stop their exit. "It's okay. He's done this before. I'll see he gets the strap."

"What?" screeched Owen. "You ain't!"

"I ought to," said Nick, dragging him down the hallway, which looked far longer than it had a few minutes ago. If they could reach the stairs, they might be safe. "Let's just get out of here first, before somebody decides we both need a whipping."

"But, sir—"

"And stop with the 'sir' stuff." They made it to the bottom of the staircase. "You're my disobedient brother, got it?"

Owen nodded and hung his head. "Aw, now, don't take me back to Ma. She'll tell Pa, and I'll be black and blue come tomorrow!"

*Good job, kid.*

The door at the head of the staircase was standing open, and the upstairs guard was waiting. "Didn't Dan want to see you?"

"He musta slipped out." Nick jerked Owen's arm. "But I did find my kid brother. What're you doin' here, lettin' children in?"

Owen, keeping up the act, struggled in Nick's grip, managing to deliver a kick to the sentry's shin in the process. The man yowled, and Nick and Owen tore past him.

"Thisaway!" cried Owen, headed for the rear of the build-ing. "There's a back door."

"I won't ask how you know," said Nick, running to catch up.

"Hey! Stop there!" The sentry hobbled after them, his shouts raising a ruckus in the main room. Chair legs scraped across the wood floor, and a man hollered for them to stop or he'd shoot.

*Damn,* thought Nick as he followed Owen down the sour-smelling hallway. They reached a steaming kitchen area with a greasy floor, the rear door propped open with a chipped stone-ware crock.

The thick-faced cook looked over from the pork chops he was frying on the cast-iron stove. "How'd you get back here?"

"Just visiting." Nick shoved Owen through the doorway, kicked away the crock, and slammed closed the door behind them.

Owen skidded on a pile of kitchen scraps overspilling a vat out back. "Which way?"

Nick wedged shut the door with a barrel he rolled over. Fists pounded on the other side. "Any way." The barrel scraped against the gravel, and the door opened a crack. "I don't care! Just keep running until I say stop!"

They hurtled through dark alleyways, dodging traffic as they crossed one road and then another. Several blocks distant, Nick finally called for a halt.

"Phew, we made it!" Owen declared. "That was fun. But don't tell Mrs. Davies, okay? She'll wallop me sure as I'm standing here."

"I *should* tell her, and that was *not* fun," said Nick. "What in God's green earth were you doing down there?"

"Looking for Dan," said Owen, his chest heaving as he sucked in air. "It's his favorite place."

"A favorite place you've visited with him before?"

"Uh . . ."

"Which means 'yes.'"

"Sorry, Mr. Greaves," said Owen, shamefaced. "Only Dan weren't down there, was he?"

"No, he wasn't. See anybody you knew, though? Like my boss, for instance?"

"Your boss?"

"Never mind," said Nick, hoping for the day he could catch Eagan breaking the law. "You're going to get yourself killed if you keep on playing detective, Cassidy."

"You're still alive."

"I won't be for long if I have to keep rescuing you."

# CHAPTER 7

Celia yawned into her hand as she extinguished the lamp in her examination room. She'd had a patient waiting for her when she'd returned from Mrs. Lowers' shop, and more paperwork to take care of than she liked. Worrying about who might have murdered Virgil Nash was consuming precious time. She was neglecting her duties, the ones that she had faithfully pursued since she'd left Hertfordshire for the hospital in Scutari during the war in the Crimea, and the realization was unwelcome.

*I should leave the sleuthing to Mr. Greaves.*

She would not examine why she found it so difficult to do so.

Celia went to shut the curtains, pausing to peer through the blinds at the street. *What—or rather, whom—am I searching for? A murderer?*

The rings rattled as she hastily drew the curtain closed.

She headed for the stairs, bound for bed. From the kitchen, Addie called out a good night.

"Good night," Celia answered, pausing to extinguish the lantern her housekeeper had left burning on the upstairs landing's table. As she snuffed the flame, she heard what sounded like Barbara's voice coming from her bedchamber.

"Barbara? Is anything the matter?" she asked through the closed door.

"No. I'm fine. Good night."

Celia opened her cousin's door anyway. Barbara, pink-cheeked, shot bolt upright in her bed, having just tucked something between her mattress and the frame.

"Are you certain you are fine?" Celia asked. "Is your foot hurting you because of the damp?"

Her cousin folded her arms over her high-necked cotton nightgown. "I said I was fine, Cousin."

"Perhaps you are unhappy after all about going to Cliff House tomorrow. I realize that the event might be wearying—"

"I don't care about that. I *have* to go. For Grace. She needs me."

Celia considered Barbara in the light from the bedside lamp, which illuminated her cousin's frown. "Then perhaps this has something to do with what you've hidden beneath your mattress."

Barbara's chin went up, but Celia interrupted her cousin before she could make another denial. "Shall I check for myself?"

Before Celia could make a move, Barbara leaned over and pulled out the item she'd stashed away.

"Here." She held out a sepia-toned salted paper print, the face upon its surface clearly visible across the room. "Here, if you have to know."

"I do not need to take it from you. I can see it is an image of your father."

Barbara set the photograph on her lap and ran a fingertip across its wrinkled surface, the edges of the paper tattered from constant handling. She kept no pictures of her mother, the Chinese woman who'd been employed as a laundress in the gold fields where her father had been a placer miner. Celia remembered the daguerreotype of his wife that Uncle Walford had displayed in his bedchamber, and she wondered where it had gone. Perhaps Barbara had smashed the photograph, wishing to erase the memory of the woman who lived on in Barbara's face and form.

"You're going to think it's silly, but I talk to him," her cousin said. "Almost every night."

Celia sat on the bed next to her, the mattress yielding beneath her weight. "It is not silly at all, Barbara. Sometimes I talk to the miniature I have of my brother, Harry."

There were many nights she'd awoken from her nightmares of Harry as he'd lain dying on a hospital cot in the Crimea, so far from the cool green hills of England, while she'd looked on helplessly, unable to cure him, unable to save him. She had followed her champion, her hero, to war to be near him, only to have her soldier brother die in her arms. So many nights she'd scrambled to find the tiny portrait of Harry and stared at his image until the dream faded and she could sleep again.

"He was my dearest friend in the darkest times," said Celia, recalling Harry's unceasing good humor. "I miss him still. Just as you miss your father."

"I'm sure you do, but it's not the same. If my father were still alive . . ." Barbara stopped and chewed her bottom lip.

Celia could guess where this conversation was headed. "What is it you wish to say? If your father were still alive, I would not be your guardian? You would not have to endure the unsavory women who come to my clinic? You would not have to worry about being in danger again?"

Tears gathered at the corners of Barbara's eyes. "If he were still alive, I might have a normal life!"

"Whatever you view to be a normal life, perhaps the sort Grace enjoys, is not one you might ever have," Celia said as gently as possible. "Given who you are."

"You mean, because I'm half-Chinese," she spat.

"Yes," she said, and saw her cousin flinch.

"You could've lied."

"Would you have believed me if I had? We both understand the situation."

Barbara peered down at her father's face. "I want him back. It was better before. He protected me, and you can't."

"I can only promise to do my best," said Celia, gathering her cousin close as her tears fell.

"*I* collected the post, and you've got a letter, Mr. Greaves." Mrs. Jewett held it out for him to take, which he did.

"You're up late, Mrs. Jewett."

"Somebody's got to worry about you. See that you've come home safe."

"Thank you for your concern," he said, taking in the handwriting on the outside of the envelope, the loops and curls of which he recognized.

"Bad news?" his landlady asked.

"I won't know until I open it. It's not banded in black, though, so nobody's died." Nick headed for the stairs, looking up toward the closed door to his second-floor rooms. Riley was barking happily behind the door, having heard his voice. "I won't find any women in my room tonight, will I?"

"No, Mr. Greaves," she said. "I liked that one, by the way. Very proper and polite with her accent and manners and all. Better than the usual set who come here to see you."

As if he'd had all that many women come to his rooms. "She had information about a case I'm working on. Nothing romantic."

"Which is a downright shame, Mr. Greaves." Mrs. Jewett shook a finger at him. "Settling down is what you need. A wife and kids."

"What woman would want to put up with a detective?" he asked. He'd seen what being a cop had done to his uncle Asa's marriage. Tore it in two as easily as paper shredding in the rain, his wife stalking out a few months before Meg also left Uncle Asa's house, neither of them ever to return. Last Nick had heard, his aunt had remarried after Uncle Asa's death and was living in the Colorado Territory with a clerk for the U.S. Army. She must have figured Indian attacks were less of a fright than the criminals Uncle Asa had dealt with in the Barbary.

"My job's too dangerous, Mrs. Jewett. It's best I save any poor creature the nuisance."

"Don't think we're as weak as you'd like to imagine us, Mr. Greaves," said Mrs. Jewett. "And I think that Mrs. Davies looks like she's got more than enough backbone to deal with you and your job."

Nick thought it wisest not to respond to her observation. He bid her a good night and climbed the steps, Riley's bark increasing in pitch.

Upstairs, he unlocked the door to his rooms and kneed aside a slobbering Riley. "Hold on there, boy. We'll get you outside as soon as I look at this letter."

Nick broke the seal and pulled out the note. Riley dropped to Nick's feet and stared up at him.

"It's a letter from Ellie," he told the dog, who tilted his head to one side. "That's right. You've never met her. She's not quite as pigheaded as I am and a whole lot prettier. You'd probably like her."

His sister had been gone from California since '61, wed and happy in Seattle, only to lose her husband in one of the last battles of the war. She was back in Sacramento now with her young daughter, the two of them sharing the bedroom Ellie had used before she'd gotten married. He wondered how she felt about that. She was practical, though, and in good graces with their parents. Unlike Nick.

The note was short, but Ellie had never been one to waste words.

*Nick—*

*Come home. It's time. Father is ready to forgive you.*

*Love— E.*

As he gazed down at the letter in his hands, he felt the tug of the bond that linked them. They were twins; of course that bond was strong. But it hadn't been strong enough to encourage him to see her in all these years—or to go to see her now.

"I doubt he's ready, Ellie," he said aloud. "And God knows I'm not ready to forgive him."

Riley clambered to his feet as Nick crossed the room and stuffed the note into the drawer of the table against the wall. He slammed the drawer shut, rocking the photograph on the table's surface. The photograph of him and Ellie and Meg in happier times. Nick stilled the frame with a finger and turned away.

"Thank you so much for coming with us," said Jane, leaning across the padded bench in Jasper Martin's hired carriage to whisper to Celia. "I couldn't have managed this event without you along."

Celia patted her friend's gloved hand, which rested atop her lap rug. The midday sun shone brightly, but the wind whipping through the open front of Mr. Martin's carriage carried damp and they both huddled beneath layers of wool. She and Jane had accompanied Mr. Martin while the girls had chosen to go with Frank in the Hutchinsons' rockaway. Celia expected Barbara and Grace were just as cold.

"Most certainly you could have managed, Jane."

"No, I couldn't," she said, her other hand squeezing the railing at her side.

The carriage summited the crest and began the alarming descent to Cliff House, leaving behind the dusty toll road that had climbed the western hills. They had battled for passage amid dozens of Sunday excursionists racing their horses and carriages along Point Lobos Road, one more determined than the next to show off their splendid horseflesh and garner a mention in tomorrow's newspapers. Celia was glad Mr. Martin's driver had not felt compelled to speed along with them. The jouncing pace he'd chosen had been quite fast enough.

Celia stared at Mr. Martin, who was seated up front alongside the driver, his head lolling to one side. She wondered if he was actually dozing or merely feigning sleep, curious about whatever conversation she might have with Frank Hutchinson's wife.

"How are you feeling today, though?" Celia asked Jane. "I'd heard you were unwell."

Jane shot a glance at Jasper Martin's back. "What do you expect, with what is going on? It's awful."

"Has Frank had anything to say about what has happened?"

"He refuses to talk about the matter. And I can't blame him."

The driver slowed the horses to prevent a headlong plunge down the steep lane, and the view opened up to reveal sunlight sparkling off the ocean waves. Seabirds cried overhead as they wheeled in the sky, and sea lions barked noisily on the rocks below the cliff where Mr. Ellis and Captain Foster's establishment took advantage of the stunning views. Celia heard Grace's gleeful squeal and Barbara's more tentative laugh. Her cousin was likely clinging for dear life to the side of the rockaway. She'd slept poorly last night and had been sullen all morning, refusing even to sing at church services though the organist had enthusiastically pounded out "Praise the Lord! Ye Heavens Adore Him," one of Barbara's favorite hymns, the tune shaking the stained-glass windows. Celia wondered if her cousin had paused to remember their murdered Chinese friend as they'd earlier passed Lone Mountain and her grave, located in the cemetery there. Or if Barbara had looked away.

The incline of the road leveled out, and it curved to sweep

wide in front of the low white building before cutting a path to the beach. A great number of horses stood tethered to the fence across from the structure, and several carriages were parked beneath the roof of the shed attached to the building. A beautiful Sunday meant a crowd at Cliff House.

"I want to tell you that I believe Frank is not guilty, Jane," said Celia.

"I hope you're right. He's been acting so strangely lately—"

With a grunt, Mr. Martin roused himself and shifted in his seat to look back at them. "I don't mean to eavesdrop, but are you ladies talking about the unfortunate Mr. Nash's death?"

Jane flushed. "My goodness, no. I don't even want to think about that on such a fine day. Don't you agree, Celia?"

"Why, yes, Jane," Celia replied, calmly holding Jasper Martin's gaze. She did not want him to think she might be spying on him and his guests, hoping to obtain some sort of evidence for the police, but it might already be too late. After yesterday's meeting, Frank would most certainly be on his guard and might have alerted the others to behave likewise.

"And thank you again for allowing me to accompany the party today, Mr. Martin," she added as the carriage driver steered between a buggy and a yellow omnibus, scenes of Cliff House painted upon its sides, that had stopped to unload passengers. "I so rarely enjoy the opportunity to go on excursions."

"Then let's not spoil it, shall we? Let's enjoy our little celebration, rather than talk about such matters," he said firmly, and turned to once again face forward. For having been taken with Celia at Jane's dinner party, he certainly did not appear enamored by her now.

Jane gave her a worried look. All Celia could question,

though, was if he had been the person she'd felt watching her yesterday. Why, though, would Mr. Martin take an interest in her visit? Unless Frank had told him that she had investigated a murder before and Mr. Martin did not care for her presence at his office. But that presumed Mr. Martin was concerned about what she might learn from the workers there, and that it could possibly affect him.

The hostler ran to greet them, and the driver reined in the horses before the front door. Mr. Martin hopped down, more spryly than Celia imagined a man of his age—fifty? sixty?—could do. Frank trotted the Hutchinsons' rockaway over to the railing, and Grace and Barbara clambered down without waiting for help, acting like high-spirited girls instead of young ladies who should be exhibiting more decorum.

Celia accepted the offer of Mr. Martin's hand; he withdrew it as soon as her feet touched the gravel drive. Once he'd finished assisting Jane, he strode over to the front door, where the man at the entrance met him with profuse greetings.

"He is a strange man, isn't he?" asked Jane, her eyes tracking Jasper Martin as he went inside. "I just wish the police would spend some time interrogating him instead of suspecting Frank." She pulled in a shaky breath. "Who could ever have imagined we'd be tangled up in such a situation?"

Her attention shifted to her husband, who was handing the reins of the rockaway to the hostler. A wrinkle of concern tugged on her brows, then was gone.

"Jane, try not to worry," said Celia.

"I simply wish I knew—"

"Are you coming, Jane?" Frank was looking over at his wife.

"Go on in," she called to him. "I need to fetch the girls."

"Simply wish you knew what?" Celia asked her.

"Nothing, Celia." Jane waved her off. "Girls!"

Grace and Barbara had headed for the low rock wall that abutted the road leading from Cliff House down to the beach. Celia could see how sharply the rock face beneath the wall dropped to the churning sea, and the wind whipped the girls' skirts and cloaks around them. Grace was leaning over the wall, pointing at one of the seals, Celia supposed. Though the rocks below slanted into the water, the wall seemed high enough to hold back an exuberant girl.

"Grace!" shouted Jane, drawing a frown from an elderly woman accompanying her husband into Cliff House. Jane hurried over to the girls. "Come away from there! It isn't safe!"

Celia followed. Out of the lee of the building, the wind snagged her mantle, the chill cutting to the bone.

Grace trudged over to Jane, Barbara hobbling across the uneven ground alongside her friend.

"I wasn't going to fall over the edge," Grace said petulantly.

"It's slippery over there from the sea spray. You very well could have," Jane answered, taking her stepdaughter's hand.

"I wish you wouldn't worry so much."

Jane glanced at Celia before answering. "I can't seem to help myself anymore."

Mr. Martin's prominence had secured him a table by the windows overlooking the water. Celia had been surprised that he had not reserved one of the private dining rooms; perhaps he wanted to spare himself the expense, or perhaps he enjoyed the commotion that the presence of wealthy, influential men created among the other diners.

The luncheon itself had been delicious—oysters, crab, chicken in a wine sauce, potatoes and French beans, a dessert of berries—but the conversation had been meager. They had been avoiding the topic Celia was certain everyone wished to discuss. Every time she had attempted to ask the most oblique question related to Mr. Nash's murder, she had been effectively silenced. Instead, the assembled guests had commented repeatedly on the loveliness of the view, the interesting sight of the sea lions and seals lolling on the pyramid-shaped rocks, the majesty of the sea spray as the waves crashed against them.

*I do not know why I thought I could get them to gossip at all.*

"This is dreadful. I can't bear the tension," said Jane, who had contrived to sit next to Celia, though it unbalanced the seating arrangement. Anything to put space between her and the decidedly unfriendly Dorothea Russell, who was at that moment shooting scowls at her husband. After three glasses of claret, Abram Russell was swaying drunkenly, rather like a willow in a stiff breeze.

Celia scanned the others assembled around the table. Mr. Martin had decided to stop noticing his partner's inebriation and was busy speaking to a silver-haired acquaintance at a neighboring table. Frank was giving an order to their waiter, who bowed over his apron and scuttled off.

"The girls are enjoying themselves, at least," said Celia. Just then they walked past on the terrace beyond the windows, Barbara clutching her hat while the ribbons of Grace's bonnet fluttered like streamers. "And they are staying away from the railing."

"Thankfully. Grace can be reckless. I think she forgets Barbara's infirmity at times."

"Actually, I appreciate that she does." The girls strolled out of

NO PITY for the DEAD

their view, though Celia noted the couple walking in the other direction, who turned to stare after them, the man frowning. There had been no recent attacks on the Chinese of the city, but anti-coolie sentiment had caused Barbara to become a target before. The man's wife tugged on his arm, and they continued without incident.

"Do you think Barbara noticed his attention?" Jane whispered to Celia.

"I hope not." Barbara's appearance confounded people, many of whom could not reconcile the quality of her dress and the refinement of her speech with her features. She'd been asked if she hailed from the Sandwich Islands or South America or some other exotic locale. Celia's cousin had learned to simply say no, because to be marked as Chinese caused more trouble than being honest justified.

"He's moved on, so I don't think there's anything to worry about," said Jane. She was in the middle of lifting her final bite of ice cream when she paused, the spoon halfway to her mouth. She set it down. "What's he doing here?"

"Who?" Celia asked, trying to discern whom Jane was looking at. Several men and women clustered along the railing at the edge of the terrace, while others walked by.

"I . . . No, it's not him," said Jane. "I thought I saw one of Frank's workers, but I'm mistaken. It's not him. Of course it wouldn't be."

"Which one did you think you saw?"

"I don't know any of their names. And I don't know why I remarked on it. Especially since I was wrong."

Jane shrugged over her error and finished her ice cream. But she didn't stop staring outside. Celia did not recognize any of the men on the terrace, although she'd never met Maryanne's brother and had only skimmed over the workers at Martin and Company.

The waiter returned with a bottle of Charles Farre champagne, which he proudly showed around to the diners at the table.

"Compliments of Mr. Levi Strauss," he announced, nodding in the direction of a dark-suited man seated across the room.

"That's so generous," Mrs. Russell said tightly. Did she disapprove of gifts from Jewish men, even ones as successful as Mr. Strauss?

"How ironic," whispered Jane. "I'd heard that Mr. Strauss and Mr. Nash were close acquaintances. In fact, Frank once told me they'd known each other for years. All the way back to Nevada, where Mr. Nash began to accrue his wealth at the silver mines."

"Do you think, by sending us champagne, Mr. Strauss is making a comment about Mr. Martin's involvement in Mr. Nash's death?" asked Celia.

"Oh my goodness."

Frank clinked a fork against a glass and stood. The waiter removed the cork, which came free with a loud pop. In a profusion of bubbles, the man poured the wine into Frank's glass, then filled everyone else's save for Jasper Martin's.

"I propose a toast. To ten more years," announced Frank, standing with the glass in his hand. "Or twenty. Or thirty."

It was difficult to discern, based on the others' expressions, if those seated around the table shared his sentiment. They ought, considering how wealthy Martin and Company had made them all. Working with Jasper Martin, however, would not be easy; he was more than strange. He was dour and watchful, assessing everyone's response, everyone's attitude.

Mr. Martin raised his glass of lemonade. "To Martin and Company."

"Hear! Hear!" said Mr. Russell, downing his champagne in one gulp. His wife consumed hers more slowly, but with no less enthusiasm.

Celia had never cared for champagne, which tended to give her a headache, but she took a sip out of politeness. It fizzed against the roof of her mouth.

"I owe the success of our establishment to the diligent work of my partners," said Mr. Martin. To Celia's ears, his praise sounded oddly insincere, though what he said was no doubt the truth.

"And we owe you, Jasper," said Frank. "Without your shrewdness, we would not have achieved what we have."

"You mean without my money financing our investments, don't you?" He smiled affably to take the edge off the words, but a muscle in Frank's cheek twitched anyway.

"Oh dear," Jane muttered.

"I'd never forget that Martin and Company is founded upon your hard work, Mr. Martin," Frank responded, his tone clipped. He must be displeased to be criticized, no matter how blandly, in front of his wife and the Russells. "And the good fortune you have enjoyed in all your endeavors. My father wouldn't have partnered with you ten years ago if he had not thought you a man of wisdom and great foresight."

"That's true. He wouldn't have. And I also know to strike while the iron is hot, Mr. Hutchinson," Mr. Martin replied, "as well as when to leave well enough alone."

Frank set down his glass of champagne so abruptly that the wine sloshed over the edge of the glass and onto the pristine white tablecloth. "What are you suggesting?"

"I think you know. And I don't approve."

Even Abram Russell, in an advanced state of inebriation, noticed the undercurrent of anger. He wobbled to his feet. "Now, now, gentlemen, don't fight."

"It's that awful policeman." Dorothea Russell pouted, an expression that did not sit well on her small mouth. "Nosing around. Putting everybody on edge."

And there it was, thought Celia, grateful that someone other than herself had finally raised the topic.

The girls, windblown and rosy cheeked from the brisk air, chose that moment to return and take the seats they had vacated. Jane signaled to the waiter to pour them each a small amount of champagne. Celia didn't protest. In fact, she believed she could use more herself. She would address the headache later.

"We saw Ben Butler, Cousin. He's out there right now, in fact," said Barbara, her eyes bright with happiness for a change. She gestured toward the seal-covered rocks. "Do you see him? The big fat sea lion on the highest pinnacle. He's quite the lord of the manor!"

"Not now, Barbara," Celia murmured, observing Grace's gaze, fixed on her father's face. Had she heard Mrs. Russell's comment? She had to have done, because the people at a nearby table had heard, if their hasty whisperings to one another were any indication.

"Frank was with me that night, Jasper," said Mr. Russell, leaning across the table and knocking over his glass.

"You don't need to defend me, Abram," said Frank, who had calmly retaken his seat. He returned his daughter's gaze and winked at her.

*Now, that is most odd.*

The champagne had spilled in a golden rivulet across the tablecloth, and the waiter was sopping it up with his apron.

"Go away," Mr. Martin barked at the man, his voice bouncing off the window glass. Mr. Russell, who must have believed Mr. Martin was speaking to him, started to rise. His wife was following suit. "Not you, Russell. Sit down."

The waiter scurried off, bound for a robust man dressed in a vaguely naval uniform over near the door leading to the kitchens. The man with the silver hair at the adjacent table looked discomfited by Mr. Martin's outburst. He grumbled to his wife, and they both stood to leave. Not another soul in the dining room made to depart. Why miss the entertainment? It was nearly as engaging at the sea lions barking on the rocks outside.

"You are a weak link, Mr. Russell, and I don't like weak links," said Mr. Martin. He withdrew his gold watch from his coat pocket and began snapping the watch lid open and shut. "And I don't like it when I can't trust one of my partners to keep his mouth closed."

In front of strangers, he meant. *Me specifically*, thought Celia. Although the remark was hypocritical, given his thinly concealed comment to Frank.

Dorothea Russell gaped like a beached fish, her mouth opening and closing nearly in unison with the snapping of Mr. Martin's watch lid. "Mr. Martin! I must protest this attack upon my husband. He is blameless!"

She risked much, confronting the man who employed her husband as an architect, and whose money had gone to purchase the lovely shell cameo brooch pinned at the lace collar of her expensive delaine gown.

"Dottie." Mr. Russell shushed her with a wave of his hand. "It's all right."

"No, it isn't, Abram. He's impugning your integrity," she said, glaring at Jane even though Mr. Martin had been the man doing the impugning.

Jane did not see; she was clasping her hands together in her lap, her face a mask of composure as she whispered something to Grace. Mr. Martin had turned to look at her, his gaze slowly transferring to Celia. She returned his stare; she found his manner threatening, but she would not be cowed. It was clear he was not a man to cross, however, and she wondered if Mr. Nash had learned that lesson the hard way.

"He was with me that night, Jasper," repeated Mr. Russell in his own act of rebellion, given the conversation that had just passed between them. He might be a weak link, speaking in front of Celia without restraint, but he was loyal to Frank.

"How can you even be sure, Russell?" asked Mr. Martin.

Abram Russell subsided into his chair and gestured for the waiter to come and refill his glass. More rebellion. Celia wondered how long he would continue as a partner at Martin and Company if he could not learn to control his habits.

"Virgil Nash was a terrible man who cheated all sorts of people," said Dorothea Russell, persisting in her defense of her husband. "Any one of them must have wanted to get rid of him. Nobody liked him. A grasping, hateful person. Standing in the way of progress."

Finished with her speech, she fanned her face with her serviette. Silence descended over the table, except for the irritating sound of Mr. Martin's watch lid.

Jane, ashen, had been listening quietly, trying to catch her husband's attention and failing. "How about we all go for a stroll down to the beach?" she suggested. "I could use a walk to digest this wonderful meal."

"A splendid idea, Mrs. Hutchinson," said Mr. Russell, pushing back his chair and standing. He swayed as he assisted his wife. "I think we could all use some fresh air."

"Some more than others," muttered Jane.

The girls jumped up as the rest of the party stood. Celia felt every eye in the room upon them. Mr. Martin went to speak to Captain Foster while they filed out of the dining room. The girls took up the rear.

"Thank you for suggesting we go for a walk, Jane," Celia said quietly to her. "I feared the men were about to come to blows."

"Jasper would never resort to violence," she replied, sounding certain. "But I'm afraid Abram will pay for his behavior today."

"Does he always drink so heavily?" Celia asked, watching him as he passed through the front door. He was leaning more on his wife's arm than she on his.

"Not in front of Jasper."

Celia and Jane paused just outside the door as the rest continued on, heading for the rutted drive that took carriages and promenaders alike to the beach. Grace and Barbara rushed ahead, though they both appeared more subdued than before.

"Grace told Barbara that Detective Greaves hates her father," said Celia. "Why might that be?"

"They've known each other for years, but that's all Frank will tell me."

Bad blood, then. Which did not bode well for Mr. Greaves' objectivity. "Jane, are you certain that Frank was with Mr. Russell

Thursday evening and the night Mr. Nash died, May twenty-eight?"

"You heard Abram." Jane clutched her fringed shawl around her shoulders, tendrils of hair teased free of her bonnet by the sea breeze. "And Frank says he was. I have to believe him." Her green eyes searched Celia's face. "If I do not believe him, what does that say about me as a wife? I have tried so hard, and it hasn't been easy. He and Grace . . ." She paused, tears trembling on her lashes. "He and Grace are very close, and it hasn't been easy to replace Arabella. She's a ghost in our house, a specter that refuses to leave. I try not to see the looks that pass between my husband and Grace, the secret signals, the winks—yes, I saw it, too, Celia—I try to not see them and be hurt. I try to show them both I belong, that my love is worthwhile. So I can't doubt Frank. Even if I do."

Celia reached for Jane's hands and clasped them in hers. They were icy cold. "I am sorry it has been hard."

"You've lost a spouse. Maybe you understand Frank's abiding grief."

*No. I do not.*

Just then, a shout came from their right. Near a curve in the drive wall, a crowd had gathered, blocking carriages of those wanting to make the passage down to the shoreline. They were clustered around someone who was trapped in the middle of the group. A man on horseback had stopped to one side, his view unencumbered by bodies and hats.

"You don't belong here, China girl!" a male voice called out. Celia felt sick.

"Barbara!" she cried, and began running toward the group. *Not again. Not again!*

Through a break in the mob, she could see Barbara and Grace huddled together in the center. A man in a tweed coat shoved her, but she stood firm.

"Leave me alone!" Barbara exclaimed, though she was pale. Her bonnet had been knocked askew.

"Stop!" Celia pushed through the crowd, which parted slightly, then once again merged like water flowing around a stone to fill in the gap she'd created. One or two looked over at her, interested in the source of the voice, clipped and angry, her cultured accent clear. But no matter how hard she tried, she could not seem to forge a path, the press of bodies forcing her to the rock wall lining the roadway. "She is my cousin and has harmed none of you. Shame on you all!"

At that, a few of the bystanders trundled off, looking guilty. Behind Celia, Jane squeezed through the crowd. Frank had heard the shouts and ran to join them, catching up to his wife. Celia didn't notice the Russells, but the gaunt man off to her left who was half-hidden by a rotund fellow in plaid might be Mr. Martin. He did not appear eager to help, however.

Grace wrapped her arms about Barbara and glared at the people clustered around them. "You're all louses!"

Celia's hip bumped hard against the rock wall. A man shifted, blocking her view, and she leaned over the wall to try to see around him. She had to get to Barbara and extract her from this mob.

Then she felt a hand at her side, shoving her. Distracted by her cousin's plight, she lost her balance. She grabbed for the wall, slowing her descent. But her fingers could not maintain their grip on the damp stone, and she tumbled headfirst, her hands outstretched to hold off the sharp rocks rushing ever closer.

# Chapter 8

Celia's descent ended right before her head connected with the boulders. As she hung there with someone's strong hands wrapped around her ankles, a tremendous wave crashed against the cliff, spraying frigid seawater against her face. A sea lion looked up at her, seemingly intrigued by her predicament.

Jane was screeching. "Celia! Are you hurt?"

Celia pressed her hands against the ground and tried to twist around to see who held on to her. Her corset, as ever, prevented her.

"I am unharmed." *Though thoroughly mortified.* The hem of her gown was inching ever closer to her hips, and the air was cold against her exposed stockings. *How bloody embarrassing.* For once, she was grateful for the stiffness of her crinoline, which had, for the most part, remained in place over her legs.

"Frank, I think Mr. Greaves has her," said Jane.

*Nicholas. Thank heavens.*

But what on earth was *he* doing here?

"Mrs. Davies, I'm going to lower you down," said Mr. Greaves. "It's not that steep right where you are. You'll be able to get your footing. Just be ready. Okay?"

"I am ready."

He lowered her until she could support her weight. Mr. Greaves let go, and she collapsed in an undignified heap.

Celia slapped her skirt into place and sat up. The distance from the top of the wall to the ledge of rocks she'd settled on, which had seemed to stretch infinitely far away when she was falling, was in truth seven or eight feet at most. Enough of a height to have broken her neck, however, if she had landed wrong. Had the person who shoved her intended to kill her, or had it merely been an accident?

She studied the faces peering over the wall. Barbara and Grace were gaping back at her alongside Jane, whose color had drained from her cheeks. Frank stood next to Mr. Greaves, who eyed him with suspicion. Dorothea Russell had arrived and smirked behind her hand. Jasper Martin had taken up a post off to one side, apparently unwilling to be associated with the spectacle. The rest of the crowd had thinned considerably, though the sight of a woman hanging upside down over the crashing waves had to have been highly entertaining. Celia could only hope the incident would not be in the newspapers tomorrow.

"Mr. Greaves, I was not expecting you here," said Celia with as much dignity as she could muster under the circumstances.

"Good thing I came along," he said. "Looks like you needed

help. Although it was Mr. Hutchinson who grabbed you first. He seems to have damaged your skirt in the process."

There was indeed a huge rip in her favorite dress. Better a tear in her gown, however, than to have her neck snapped in two.

"Thank you, Mr. Hutchinson." He inclined his head in acknowledgment.

"Pretty convenient he was right there when you fell," said Mr. Greaves.

"What are you implying?" Frank shot back.

"Gentlemen!" Celia called out, interrupting their tiff. "Rather than quarrel, perhaps you could provide some assistance in returning me to the proper side of the wall."

Hand outstretched, Frank leaned down, but Mr. Greaves nudged him aside. "I'll take care of this. Here, ma'am." Mr. Greaves extended his gloved hands. "However, you wouldn't need assistance if you hadn't fallen over in the first place."

"Very amusing, Mr. Greaves."

She grabbed his hands and scrabbled up the rock face, loosened pebbles clattering to fall into the water. In one motion, Mr. Greaves pulled her onto the top of the wall.

"Thank you," she said to him, her breathing steadying, now that she was safe. *Or perhaps I am not truly safe.*

"Don't think you would've come to much harm," he said. "As I said, it's not all that steep right where you fell."

"Nonetheless," she replied. His words might indicate a lack of concern; his gaze told a different story.

Barbara rushed over and clasped Celia around the waist. Celia closed her eyes, hugging her cousin in return. "Are you all right, Barbara?" she murmured against her cousin's silk-covered bonnet.

"I want to go home," Barbara replied.

"So do I."

"What happened?" Jane asked Celia. "One moment, you were just a few feet in front of me. The next, you were tumbling over the wall."

"It felt as though someone pushed me," Celia answered, giving Barbara a tight squeeze and then releasing her.

She avoided looking at anyone in particular; Mr. Greaves was being sufficiently thorough as he examined every face for guilt.

"There was such a crush of people," said Jane. "Frank, you had to have seen what happened, since you were close enough to Celia to grab her."

"I was worried for Grace's safety, and my attention was focused on her," he said. At some point he'd lost his hat, and he squinted in the sunlight. "Though I did, obviously, see Mrs. Davies fall, I didn't notice anyone push her."

"Do you swear to that, Hutchinson?" Mr. Greaves asked him.

"I did *not* push Mrs. Davies," he answered firmly. Frank glanced at his daughter, who intentionally evaded his look. *What does that mean?* Celia wondered.

"My husband would never harm Celia!" said Jane. "What nonsense!"

Celia clambered down from the wall with Mr. Greaves' help. Her right hip ached; she'd likely find a bruise there tomorrow.

"Did anybody see who pushed this woman?" Mr. Greaves queried the remaining gawkers. He pulled out his badge, which did not have the desired effect of encouraging anyone to be forthcoming.

"An accident, Detective. No one pushed her," drawled Mr.

Martin. "The gravel is loose, and she lost her footing in her hurry to get to her cousin's side. That's all. Nothing sinister."

She wouldn't correct him by pointing out that she had distinctly felt a hand on her side.

Mr. Martin extracted his pocket watch and popped open the lid. "It's time to depart," he announced, and signaled for the hostler to fetch his carriage.

The crowd dispersed. Abram Russell, who had arrived to join his wife, took Mrs. Russell's arm and led her away.

"If you didn't push her, Hutchinson, who did?" Mr. Greaves asked Frank.

"An accident, Greaves. As Mr. Martin has said."

They stared like two dogs circling while each assessed the strengths and weaknesses of the other.

"Barbara, go on ahead with Grace," said Celia to her cousin. They did not need to overhear this conversation. The two girls headed quietly for the Hutchinsons' rockaway.

"First, a man you fought with turns up dead, Frank, and now, a woman you were standing near almost falls to her death," Mr. Greaves was saying. "I don't like those sorts of coincidences. Looks bad for you, doesn't it?"

"Why not arrest me, then, Nick?" Frank dared him.

"Maybe I will. Especially since Mr. Russell, your good friend, has contradicted your claim that you two were at some saloon on Thursday night."

*Gad,* thought Celia.

"Frank, what does he mean?" asked Jane.

"He's trying to trick me into an admission, Jane. If he had any proof I'd done something wrong, he'd arrest me, but he isn't going to, because I haven't," he said. "Everyone knows how I felt about

Virgil Nash, Greaves. I didn't like him because he turned out to be a cheat. But I didn't kill him, try to dig him up on Thursday, or attempt to hurt Mrs. Davies. So find someone else to bully."

He stalked off to where the rockaway was tied to the fence.

"Sorry about that, ladies," said Mr. Greaves. He tipped his hat to them and set off to question the few people who'd remained behind to watch the proceedings.

"I thought they were going to come to blows," said Jane, pressing a hand to her throat. "This is awful. What an awful, awful day."

"I shall prove your husband is not guilty, Jane. I promise." But, oh dear, matters did not look good at all.

"Come back in our carriage, Celia," she said. "I don't want to drive back with Mr. Martin, and I don't want you with him, either. Come with us. There's room if we all squeeze in tight together. Grace can sit on the front bench with her father."

"I can return with Mr. Martin, rather than make you all uncomfortable—"

"No! No. I mean . . ." Her gaze slid to where Jasper Martin was climbing into his carriage.

*Mr. Martin?* "Do you not want me to go with Mr. Martin because you thought you saw him push me?"

"But I can't be right, can I?"

*Then why are you suggesting I not ride back into town with him?*

"Or maybe it was that man I noticed earlier. But I was wrong about him, too, wasn't I?" said Jane. She went from looking concerned to looking concerned and confused. "I know I'm being silly, but I'd really prefer that you come with us."

"If you insist, Jane."

"I do. I'll tell Mr. Martin we're taking you home," Jane said, and headed for where Jasper Martin stood near the carriage shed.

"So what did she have to say?" asked Nicholas Greaves, who had returned to Celia's side without her hearing his approach, the crashing waves muffling the sound of his boots on the gravel.

"She thinks Mr. Martin pushed me, but she is unwilling to say as much."

"Because that's a dangerous accusation when your husband works for the man."

"Speaking of Frank, what is this animosity between you two, Mr. Greaves?" she asked. "It is not simply because his account for Thursday night appears to have a hole in it."

The brim of his hat cast shadows over his eyes, concealing any thoughts that might have been revealed in them. He was never easy to read, though, in sunshine or shadows.

"Isn't it?" he asked.

"Now you are being disingenuous," she said. "You think Frank pushed me, don't you?"

"He was the nearest to where you were standing, Mrs. Davies, although Martin wasn't so far away, either."

"But Frank grabbed me and stopped me from falling."

"Hmm," he said, which was an unsatisfying response to her observation. Mr. Greaves might have a good reason to suspect Frank, and that reason might reach back years, underpinning the hatred that crackled between them like sparks off wool. But it was clear he did not wish to share that reason with her.

"Did you see any of the men from Mr. Hutchinson's work crew here?" she asked.

"Why?"

"Jane made a comment while we were finishing our meal

that she had seen one of Frank's men on the terrace outside, but then decided she was in error."

"I didn't recognize anybody in the crowd, but then I'd only just arrived and the excitement with your cousin was already under way."

"And why *were* you here, Mr. Greaves?" Celia asked.

"Maybe I'd developed a sudden hankering to visit Seal Rocks and see Ben Butler."

"Why do I suspect that is not the real reason?" she asked, a smile tugging at her lips even though her entire body had begun to ache and she was feeling light-headed, which made smiling a wearying exercise.

"Maybe I simply know when it's time to worry that you might be about to get yourself into trouble, ma'am," he said.

She let the smile take hold. "I must say I am glad you do."

Owen yawned and adjusted his stance, his back aching from leaning against the wall of the corner grocery while he spied on Dan's lodgings across the way and a few doors down. Dang, but his feet hurt, too. He'd spent the morning staring at Rob Bartlett's boardinghouse and got nothing out of that, either. Other than to have somebody toss the contents of a slop bucket into the gutter near his feet, splattering his boots.

He wanted to be a cop like Mr. Greaves, though, and this was the sorta thing they did, wasn't it? Kept an eye on suspects? Sure, he hadn't succeeded at the Golden Hare last night, but he had to keep trying, didn't he? All he'd seen so far, though, was a ragtag bunch of fellas coming in and out of the front door to Dan's lodgings, looking like they were heading out to raise Cain even though it was Sunday.

He glared at the worn-out old cowboy studying Owen from a chair he'd propped against the wall of the closed saloon across the road. Owen's glares didn't scare the fellow, who calmly tucked his arms beneath his bright-colored Mexican serape. He didn't much like this part of town, not that where he lived with the widow lady who rented him a room for fifteen cents a day was a whole lot better. And since this was where Dan lived, he sort of had to stand here.

"Well, dang it, I don't got to. I'm not learning anything, am I," he muttered to himself.

*And who asked you to keep an eye on Rob Bartlett and Dan Matthews, anyway?*

He'd been twiddling his thumbs since Kelly had marched him out of the offices, spending too much time thinking about how he could help solve the case. All that thinking time had given him this bright idea on top of last night's bright idea. And now his stomach started to growl. He wondered what the widow lady might set out for supper once he got back. Probably soup and stale bread again. Maybe he could stop at Mrs. Davies' instead and see if Addie had anything for him. She never turned him away. Plus, maybe he'd get news about whether Mrs. Davies had gotten his job back for him.

There was a commotion up the road as a kid ran in front of the horsecar clipping along Kearney and the driver shouted at him, joined by a chorus of pedestrians with loud opinions on the stupidity of street urchins.

Commotion over, Owen scratched at an itch on his neck and returned to watching Dan's lodging house. Maybe he was wrong about Dan. People didn't usually go around killing folks just because they owed them money. Though the more Owen thought about Thursday night, the stranger it seemed that Dan had been so all-fired keen to dig around in Mr. Martin's cellar. It'd been a mighty big risk from the start. So why the heck had Owen gone along with the scheme and gotten himself fired? *Shoot, you're dumb, Cassidy.*

On the other hand, maybe Dan did want to kill the guy because he couldn't pay him back. He could've easily buried him in the cellar, too. He always seemed to have Mr. Kelly's key to Martin and Company's front door, so why not be the one who did it? Lure Nash there and kill him. And Dan would've known about the oilcloth scraps the business across the alley always discarded behind their store, the scraps used to wrap the body. Of course, almost everyone working at Martin and Company knew about them.

But why dig the body back up?

*I'll never get the hang of this. Durn it all.*

Owen kicked at the wall behind him. He still hadn't seen hide nor hair of Dan. Just some Chinese scuttling past in their shiny silk tunics and all the wagons and carts rattling along the street. A restaurant down the road looked to be filling up with laborers and sailors. No women among them. It was that kind of place.

Owen shifted his stance again and noticed that the cowboy had gone off somewhere and that shadows were beginning to stretch along the road. What time was it? Owen had stopped paying attention to the church bells a while back. Maybe he should leave.

He was about to turn away, when hands grabbed him from behind, pinioning his arms against his back.

"Yowch!" Owen cried, struggling against his assailant.

The man yanked him backward. "What the hell are you up to, Cassidy?"

"Bartlett, let me go."

Rob spun him around. "You spying on Dan? Is that what you're doing?"

"I'm not." *Durn it. Durn it!* This hadn't worked out at all. Not one dad-blamed bit. "I was just passing by and—"

Rob, who hadn't let go of Owen's left arm, yanked it so hard, Owen thought it would pop clear off his shoulder.

"No you wasn't. You was spying on Dan," Rob said, leaning in. His breath didn't smell all that good. "You think he killed that fella? Is that what you're doing here? You helpin' the police?"

"No, Rob, honest!" Owen had forgotten all about the ache in his back and feet and how cold it was, because he was sweating like a pig and scared to death. Rob had strong hands, and he was hurting him. Didn't Dan once say he'd been given some sorta nickname that showed what a mean cuss he was? If Rob killed him, would anybody notice he was missing? Mrs. Davies would. She cared about him. And Mr. Greaves had warned him to stay outta trouble.

*Durn.*

"Stop shaking, Cassidy."

"Sorry, Rob," he answered, trying to keep his voice from trembling as much as his body.

"You'd better leave well enough alone if you know what's good for you." Rob released him with a rough shove. "Now get outta here."

Owen happily obliged.

*lasted woman. Here we go again.*

"Why can't she stay out of trouble?" The roan he'd rented pricked its ears, and Nick leaned forward to pat the horse's neck. "She's just as bad as Cassidy."

Nick had taken his time returning from Cliff House. He trotted the horse through the city streets, steering the roan around kids playing with a ball made from strips of cloth. A man Nick had arrested last year for cheating gullible tourists strolled out of a restaurant, cleaning his teeth with a silver pick. He saluted as Nick rode by, but hastily turned the other way, slipping into a nearby alley. It might make for a fun evening to chase after him. Nick would if he weren't so angry over what had happened at Cliff House.

He'd been too focused on the mob tormenting Barbara Walford to realize where the real threat lay. Because of that distraction, he hadn't seen who'd given Celia Davies a shove over the wall. And nobody else had, either, apparently. She was lucky not to have suffered more than a tear in her gown and some bruises.

*Blasted woman.*

Nick reined in the horse at the door of the brick stables on Montgomery, a block over from the police station. The liveryman scurried through the tall arched opening that led to the stalls, bringing the smell of manure and straw with him. He took the reins while Nick slid down from the saddle.

"Send the charges to my boss," Nick said to the man, who led the roan inside.

He made for the station, though on a Sunday he could justifiably head to his rooms. But there was nothing more there to entice him back than on any other night of the week, except for a dog. And Mrs. Jewett was happy to attend to Riley while Nick was off doing police work, so not even the dog needed him.

The stink of the basement jail cells, wafting through the barred windows level with the roadbed, greeted Nick long before he reached the side door to the station. His foot had just descended to the first step when a scrawny kid rushed across the road from the direction of Portsmouth Square, weaving between the hacks lined up on its perimeter and almost getting trampled by a cart horse.

"Oy! Detective!" Owen Cassidy hailed him. "There you is! Are!"

What did he want now? "What is it, Cassidy?"

Owen trotted over. "I've got information, sir."

"You don't have to call me 'sir,' either." That was Taylor's habit. Did he look like he needed to be called "sir"?

"Okay, Mr. Greaves," he said, eyeing Nick from beneath the brim of his wool cap as if not sure it had been a good idea to have stopped him.

"Just tell me your information, Cassidy, okay?"

"Well, I ain't seen hide nor hair of Dan Matthews all afternoon, and I'm wondering if he's skipped town," he said.

"Have you been watching him? I thought I told you to be careful!" Why couldn't he listen? Just like Celia Davies. Both of them were deaf.

"I was being careful. Sorta," he said. "But I want to be a cop like you, Mr. Greaves. Plus, I thought that watching Dan's place would help make up for what I did wrong by digging in Mr. Martin's cellar. And that whole mess last night. I was gonna follow him if he went out, see who he met, but he never left the whole time I was standing across the street from his boardinghouse."

Owen peered at him, seeking Nick's approval. But Nick doubted that any praise he'd lavish would be enough to banish the hunger in Owen's eyes, which always made him look as if he were lost and searching for something out of reach. Nick had seen Meg look like that more than once. Adrift. Needy. He should've worried more about what those feelings could mean, but he hadn't. He'd thought his sister would end up strong, like him and Ellie. Instead, she'd ended up dead by her own hand.

"How do you even know Dan was at his lodgings in the first place?" Nick asked.

Owen's face fell. "Guess I didn't think of that. But he must've been, if Rob Bartlett was there," he said. "I ran into him while I was watching. He was going to Dan's, and he'd probably know if Dan had made plans to not be there. They're good friends."

"Dan might not have told him his plans. Even if they are good friends."

Owen's shoulders drooped along with his face. "Durn."

"And you don't want to be a cop, Cassidy."

"Yes, I do!" he insisted. "I want to make things right, like you and Mrs. Davies try to do."

He *would* drag her name into the conversation.

"Come here." Nick sat down on the dirty top step and indicated Owen should do the same. Never mind that people walking past on Kearney were staring at them. "Listen, Cassidy. Go to school. Learn a trade. Do something sensible, because being a cop is not sensible."

That was Nick's father talking. *I thought you were smart, Nicholas. Why do you want to be a policeman?* His father hadn't been persuaded by the argument that his own brother, Asa, was a San Francisco police detective and a good one, the best. *Just proves that Asa's more of a fool than I ever imagined,* his father had replied. Nick had never learned what had driven a wedge between Abraham Greaves and Uncle Asa. He'd never learned what had caused Meg to decide to leave Asa's house and strike out on her own, either, even though Nick had left her in their uncle's charge while he went off to fight in the war, expecting her to stay there. He'd never understood his sister's terrible decision, and he'd never understood his father's hatred for the uncle Nick had always admired. By the time Nick had figured out a wedge even existed between the two men, however, it was as firmly rooted as the one that stood between him and Frank Hutchinson.

Nick blew out a long breath. "Worse, Cassidy, the crimes never seem to end, no matter how hard you try, no matter how many people you send to jail. This job is nothing but frustration."

"But we caught the folks who killed Mrs. Davies' Chinese friend and the girl who worked at that apothecary store, didn't we? That worked out."

*We.* "One success."

Owen was beginning to look worried. "But you've had other successes, right, Mr. Greaves?"

"I have, but not enough to satisfy me," he said.

The number of criminals who'd evaded justice took up more than the fingers on both of Nick's hands. Even the ones he'd managed to get sent to jail sometimes continued to commit crimes once they got back out. A boy not much younger than Owen had died because of a violent drunk who hadn't learned anything from his years spent in prison. And Nick had felt responsible.

"So if you don't want to grow up to be a bitter, disappointed old man like me," Nick said, "don't be a cop."

"Shucks, Mr. Greaves, you ain't old!"

*But I am* bitter *and* disappointed. Maybe he should take his own advice and find a different line of work. He'd make a decent clerk, as much time as he already spent pushing papers around.

"And Mrs. Davies must think you're worth something, else she wouldn't bother with you!" Owen added with a wink.

"*A*re you nae going to sleep, ma'am?" asked Addie, her long braid hanging down over her wrapper. The dining room lantern cast Celia's housekeeper in a pool of dim light, the kitchen at Addie's back hidden in shadows.

"I struck the wall harder than I thought," Celia answered, setting her pencil atop the sheet of paper she'd taken from her clinic office. After a somber meal with her cousin, she had read through patient files, taken a warm bath, and tried to relax with a book. And failed miserably at sleep. She simply had too much to think about.

"I believe I am a singular bruise from my ribs to my knees." Celia pressed a hand to her back and rubbed the ache there, something she was able to do since she was absent the interfering layers of a bodice and corset. "And I scraped my hands rather badly."

"Do you want a poultice for the bruises?"

"I will be all right," she said. "Is Barbara asleep?"

"At last. She's scared, though, poor bairn," said Addie. "And so am I. Miss Barbara confronted again, and you . . . It doesna bear contemplating."

"It was an accident, Addie. I was clumsy and fell."

"If you believed that, you wouldna be making more lists," she said, nodding at the paper at Celia's elbow.

"I was adding new thoughts to my inventory of suspects," she said. "And it does no good to scowl at me, Addie. I am caught up in this investigation whether I like it or not."

"Aye, that may be so, but I dinna have to be happy about it."

"Please join me, though. And help me think," said Celia as the case clock in the entry hall struck the hour. Midnight. It *was* late.

She yawned while Addie pulled out one of the chairs.

"If I am correct to link Mr. Nash's murder to my near collision with a quantity of sharp rocks, I must now consider which of my suspects had access to both the cellar and Cliff House," Celia explained, picking up the pencil and indicating the tick marks she'd made next to the names. "Sadly, I have not eliminated many. The partners were all in attendance, including a new addition, Dorothea Russell. Although the likelihood she could have murdered and buried Virgil Nash seems rather remote. Furthermore, both she and her husband were standing nowhere near me when I fell." *At least, I do not believe they were.*

"Och," said Addie mournfully.

"I cannot, however, account for the movements of Maryanne's brother yesterday," said Celia, telling Addie about Jane's comment that she thought she'd seen one of Frank's workers at Cliff House. "Although, if Dan Matthews was the man she'd seen and he intended to hurt me, I would have to ask why. He does not know me, nor that I am assisting Mr. Greaves' investigation."

"Mrs. Kelly might've mentioned your name to him," suggested Addie.

"I doubt that Mrs. Kelly has spoken to her brother since Mr. Nash's body was discovered, given how upset Mr. Kelly is with his brother-in-law," she said. "However, the other worker whose name has come up, Rob Bartlett, might have observed me at the offices of Martin and Company yesterday. How he also might have connected me to the investigation, though, is unclear." Unless he'd overheard her conversation with Frank.

Addie scooted her chair closer to Celia's and studied her notes. "But Mr. Martin or Mr. Hutchinson or the other partner *would* have noticed those two men, ma'am, if they'd been at Cliff House."

"Unless they are simply not as observant as Jane. However, if any of them did spot one of their workers, they neglected to mention it to Mr. Greaves." Although they might wish to protect their workers or thought their presence irrelevant. Or, neither Dan Matthews nor Mr. Bartlett was there, after all. "The partners also would have noticed John Kelly, as would I have done. But I did not see him."

"Och, to think Mrs. Kelly's husband might be involved."

"He does work at Martin and Company and was at their offices yesterday when I felt someone spying on me."

"Now you've someone spying on you?" Addie tutted. "'Tis just like last time."

Celia reached over and squeezed Addie's hand.

"The last possibility is 'Stranger who killed Silas Nash.' Mr. Nash's killer and my assailant could be the same person and someone we have yet to identify. However, he is supposed to have fled the country."

"Folk come and go all the time, ma'am."

"That is true. But what would be that person's motive to push me over the wall?"

Addie's brow furrowed as she puzzled over Celia's question.

NO PITY for the DEAD

"Perhaps this dreadful person has come to believe you've a clue to his identity."

"But where have I been and what have I learned that he might believe that?" asked Celia. "And how would he know of my involvement in the investigation in the first place? Since my name was not included in the newspaper reports, this would again suggest that the person behind the attack on me is someone at Martin and Company and not a stranger." She frowned at the list. "I do not like that I cannot seem to eliminate Frank Hutchinson from consideration. His claim to have been with his friend Abram Russell all of Thursday evening is apparently untrue."

" 'Tis possible, ma'am, that he is guilty," said Addie.

"Frank and Jane are my friends. He would not hurt me."

"False friends are worse than bitter enemies, as my father would say."

"We have learned that before, have we not, Addie?" she asked. "Nonetheless, I refuse to believe that either of them are false friends."

Celia sat back in the chair. Had she overlooked a vital clue? Perhaps on Thursday night. She thought back to the scene in the cellar. There were two shovels, a lantern teetering on the uneven ground, piles of coal and a scuttle, stacks of bricks, some already put in place, multiple holes. And the body, wrapped in oilcloth. The stench of decay had been so overwhelming she'd not concentrated on searching for clues. And when she had heard the sound of running feet overhead, she had been concerned only for her and Owen's safety.

Was it their visit to Martin and Company's offices that had prompted the attack on her, or had someone observed her going to speak to Ginny, who had noticed an unusual horse and wagon? A recollection flitted through Celia's brain, but she failed to seize it. Perhaps she did know more than she realized.

"Another mystery I feel incapable of solving, Addie," said Celia, rubbing the ache throbbing at the base of her spine. "It might be a more productive use of our time to turn our attention to uncovering the identity of your secret admirer."

Addie blushed. "Whisht, ma'am. There's no need for such nonsense," she said. However, she leaned forward eagerly. "Do you think it could be Mr. Taylor?"

Finally, a question that made Celia smile.

"*T*hank you for coming in so early, Taylor," said Nick, unlocking the door to the detectives' office. The booking sergeant was yawning at his station, and a ruckus was under way in the jail cells, the warden's shouts to shut up loud enough to be heard everywhere.

Nick hung his hat on the rack by the doorway and tossed his keys onto his desk.

"No need to thank me, sir . . . Mr. Greaves," Taylor replied, entering the room behind Nick and taking his usual chair. "Ain't got no wife to mind what I do."

"Did the beat cop have anything to say about the Golden Hare?" Nick asked. He'd told Taylor about what he'd uncovered in the basement of the saloon, leaving out any mention of Owen Cassidy.

Taylor pulled a cigar from his coat pocket along with a friction match, which he struck against the floor. "Said you're lucky you got outta there in one piece. He also claimed to have never heard of Dan Matthews or Virgil Nash, although the way his eyes danced around when I mentioned Nash's name made me wonder if he's been paid to say that."

"The police chief wouldn't be happy to hear your suspicions. He's been trying to clean up the force."

"Good luck with that!" said Taylor. He puffed on the cigar to get it to light. "However, the cop was real familiar with Rob Bartlett. Bartlett and the locals go a long ways back, and not in a friendly sorta way."

"Did you manage to talk to Matthews, though? That Cassidy kid took it on himself to keep an eye on the fellow's boarding-house yesterday and said he never caught sight of the man."

"I talked to his landlord on my way in," said Taylor. "Apparently, Matthews was holed up in his room like a scared rabbit yesterday, which is why Cassidy didn't spot him. But the landlord also said he went to check on Matthews late last night, because he didn't come down at his usual time for Sunday supper, and Matthews wasn't in his room. In fact, it looked like he'd cleared out."

Nick cursed. *See what I mean, Cassidy? This job is nothing but frustration.*

"Matthews was at the Golden Hare Saturday night," said Nick. "I wonder if he met someone there who encouraged him to leave town. Or if Bartlett did. Cassidy saw Bartlett near Matthews' lodgings yesterday."

"That's what his landlord told me, too." Taylor leaned his head back, a stream of smoke issuing from between his lips. "That a visitor had come by to see Matthews, but the landlord only saw the back of the fella and couldn't describe him. Must've been Bartlett."

A fist rapped on the doorframe, and Officer Mullahey

stepped into the room. A big man, he was ornery enough to have once suffered a broken nose from a fist connecting with it. He didn't like to admit that the fist had belonged to another cop. Or that he'd started the fight.

"Have you heard from the police in Virginia City?" Nick asked him.

"Not yet, Mr. Greaves. But you'll want to hear about a message that just came into the station," he answered, glancing over at Taylor puffing away on his cigar. "While you and Officer Taylor were back here in your office."

"I have every right to be in here, Mullahey," Taylor responded touchily. The tiff between the two men was as annoying as the one between Nick and Briggs. "So don't be looking at me like that."

"Well, the policeman who took the message came lookin' for me. This mornin', a body was found in a ditch. The man's neck was broken," Mullahey said. "And my money's on the body belongin' to one Dan Matthews."

# CHAPTER 9

"Guess that explains where Matthews went," said Taylor, flicking a look at the body crumpled in the ditch and turning pasty. This one was in much better shape than old Virgil Nash's corpse, however. Still fresh.

Dr. Harris had arrived and managed to assemble a coroner's jury from out of thin air. A remarkable feat, considering how few houses there were in this area south of the city. The laborers from a tree nursery across the way, its almond trees and evergreens organized into neat rows like mustered soldiers, had stopped their work to stare. A few Mexican vaqueros in sombreros and boots, headed into town from Rancho San Miguel to the southwest, sat astride their horses and gawked. And if those weren't enough spectators, workers building a house on a neighboring lot leaned over the property's picket fence and pointed. It always amazed Nick how curious folks got whenever there was a dead body to be seen, as if a glimpse of the deceased gave them a peek into their own mortality.

"What was Matthews doing on this road, though?" Nick asked.

"Skipping town, of course," said Taylor.

"It would've been easier and quicker to take the train." And possibly safer as well.

The tracks ran a few hundred feet distant. Right then, a train from the San Francisco and San Jose Railroad approached, the locomotive chugging smoke that trailed off in the breeze. It whistled past, disturbing the small number of promenaders strolling through the Willows on a Monday morning, not far from where Nick and Taylor stood.

"Maybe it wasn't until after the last train departed San Francisco for the day that he decided he was in a hurry to vamoose," said Taylor.

"But why leave last night? He could've run off Friday, once he'd figured out he could be a suspect in a murder investigation."

Taylor paused to consider, his gaze following the train as it rumbled south. "He got scared all of a sudden? Thought we'd learned something that would definitely pin the murder on him?"

"Or did somebody else get scared and encourage Matthews to leave?" asked Nick.

"Because Matthews knew who'd killed Nash . . ."

"If he did, I wish he'd shared the name with us before he ended up dead."

"Want me to bring over the fellow who discovered Matthews' body?" Taylor asked. The man in question was standing near the house builders, who were pestering him with questions. Wearing a suit of dark clothes and a bowler hat, he was dressed as though he had been bound for the city until finding a body had changed his plans. Up at the man's clapboard house, a woman had come to stand on the porch along with a small child, the girl clutching her mother's tan checked skirt. "He wasn't much use earlier. Pretty shaken."

Even in rough-and-tumble California, it wasn't every day one found a dead body in a ditch. "Bring him over."

While Taylor went to fetch the man, Dr. Harris finished with his jury and dismissed them.

He spotted Nick and came over. "Looks like Mr. Matthews broke his neck. Died instantly," he said. "Who is he? The name's familiar."

"He's the man who found the decaying body of Virgil Nash in Jasper Martin's cellar," said Nick. "Any signs that it could have been murder?"

"Looks like an accident to me," the coroner answered. "The contusions along his arm and head suggest he fell—probably thrown from a horse, an arm outstretched to break his fall—and landed awkwardly enough in the ditch to snap his neck. I haven't located any other wounds on him. Of course, I'll have his body hauled back to town for an autopsy, but I don't think my conclusions will change. Oh, and here." Harris dug around in the pocket of his coat, pulling out a coin purse. "Fifty dollars or so on him. Didn't have time to count it all. And this, too."

Nick took the purse, the coins clinking against one another, and the engraved silver watch Harris held out. Not what you'd usually find on a man who'd been renting rooms in a run-down lodging house near the Barbary. "Nash's? Didn't his widow say he carried a silver watch?"

"Maybe you have your killer, Greaves."

Nick pocketed the coin purse and the watch. "Maybe."

With a tip of his hat, the coroner strode toward the wagon that had pulled up near the ditch. Taylor brought over the man who'd discovered Matthews' body.

"This here's Mr. Lombardo," said Taylor. He left to help the wagon driver hoist Matthews onto the bed of the buckboard.

Mr. Lombardo's weather-beaten skin and broad shoulders made him look as though he'd be more comfortable at the docks with the whalers and fishermen than living down here on the southern fringe of the city, nestled in among the scrub and sand and cattle.

"Detective?" he asked warily.

"Tell me how you came to find the body, Mr. Lombardo."

"This morning, I go out early and I see a pile in the ditch," he answered, his voice rising and falling in the rhythm of native-born Italians. "I go to look and it was the man. There." He jerked his chin in the direction of the wagon driver, who was busy wrapping Matthews' body in a tarpaulin.

"And when you found him, you didn't touch him or move him?"

"A dead man?" The Italian crossed himself. "No. I see and I tell the police."

Nick should commend the man for not searching Matthews' clothes and coming across the coin purse and watch. Lombardo likely could've used the money, if the condition of his property—weeds cropping up, the unpainted fence, a cracked windowpane—accurately reflected the balance of his bank account. His wife and daughter had gone back inside, but the woman was watching them through the first-floor window.

"Did you hear anything unusual overnight? See anything?" Nick asked him.

"Last night I am in bed and I hear the horse galloping. Then a shout. But then nothing," said Lombardo. "I do not go and see. Very late. My wife, she look through the window. It is so dark and the fog heavy. She sees nothing also."

"There was nobody with him?"

Lombardo raised his shoulder, his hands lifting in unison, palms up. "We cannot see. But when I remember the shout, that is why I think to look for the person this morning. The fog, it is still thick, but I could see him." The man shuddered and made the sign of the cross again. "There is a bad place in the road here. I show you."

Nick followed him over to the dirt road. Matthews' body was gone, carted away on the buckboard that was now lumbering toward the city. Harris climbed onto his horse, saluted Nick with a tap of his hat brim, and trotted off. The vaqueros kneed their mounts and rode off as well. Taylor was speaking to some of the neighbors standing around. Since most of them were shaking their heads, Nick expected his assistant wasn't learning much.

"Here." Lombardo gestured at the ground. A gully stretched across the road, leaving a sizable gap. "Bad for the wagons."

Nick looked from the break to where Matthews had been lying. If he'd been riding fast through here last night, in the fog and the dark, and his horse had stepped into the gully, it would've stumbled. And Matthews would've been thrown clear as easily as water from a duck's back. Nick crouched on his heels and examined the dirt. There were gouges in the packed earth. It was possible they could have been made by the hooves of a horse trying to regain its balance.

He stood. "Thank you, Mr. Lombardo. You've been very helpful."

The man left and Taylor rejoined Nick.

"Well, sir?"

"It seems that Matthews came through here late last night. The horse he was on must have stumbled and thrown him. But Lombardo didn't notice if anybody was with Matthews. Too foggy last night," said Nick. "Also, Harris found a bag of money on Matthews and a fancy silver watch."

Taylor whistled. "So he *did* rob Nash!"

"Not necessarily. We don't yet know that those items came from Nash, and we don't know how Matthews came to have them in his possession." But if the watch *was* Nash's, they had just linked Matthews to the man's death. He either killed Nash himself or knew the person who did.

Nick lifted his hat, ran fingers through his hair, and reseated it. He looked out over the rolling hills, dust swirling and the fog retreating to the north. Over a ways, a windmill turned lazily in the breeze. The carpenters working on the neighboring house had returned to their hammering, and Lombardo was back inside with his wife and kid. Sparrows chattered in nearby shrubs. A peaceful place, with fresher air than what hung over the city some days. Peaceful, if you disregarded a man implicated in another man's murder having been found in a ditch with his neck broken.

"It's sorta nice out here, ain't it?" asked Taylor. "Away from town."

*Maybe I should buy a homestead out here.* Who would he share it with, though? Because the only woman he could see himself sitting with on the porch had a missing husband who hadn't had the common decency to turn up dead.

Still, he could build a house for himself. Give Riley a real yard to roam in. Get some chickens, too. They'd had chickens back on the farm in Ohio. Shiny black Hamburgs that Meg would chase around the farmyard, angering their father. He missed that life, but Nick knew why they'd left. Their cattle had died from anthrax, and his father had lost the desire to start over. So they'd come out west to California looking for . . . what? His father hadn't wanted to pan for gold like everybody else when they'd arrived in '53. Maybe Uncle Asa had convinced him there was something better to be had out near the ocean than what he was trying to wrestle from Ohio's clay soil, from the fields near the stream that flooded too often, from the apple trees that never produced enough to make up for what the birds and the bugs ate. Did his father regret listening to his brother? Meg might still be alive if he hadn't listened, and she—or her children—could right now be chasing her own black Hamburgs.

"Sir?" Taylor was squinting at him. "Should I go talk to Bartlett?"

"I'll go," said Nick, returning his focus to the case and dismissing the thoughts of a homestead and chickens. He was a cop, a life that didn't leave much room for domesticity. And frankly he couldn't imagine Celia Davies wanting to live out here with a bunch of chickens. She needed proper English tea and lace doilies and whatever else it was that women like her required. He wasn't fooled by her plain brown holland skirt and red blouse to think she might be happy changing out straw in a coop.

Even if he wished otherwise.

"The child could come any day now, Mrs. Kelly," said Celia. *Too soon.* The baby had yet to turn head down; the possibility it never would became more likely with each passing day.

Maryanne, her face shiny with sweat, pressed her hands into

the mattress to sit upright. She leaned against the pillows propped at the head of her bed and stared at her belly bulging over her legs. "You're worried, aren't you?"

"No more than I normally am, Mrs. Kelly," said Celia with a comforting smile. It was a lie but a worthwhile one.

Straightening, Celia gave a stifled groan for all her aches from yesterday's adventures, then lifted the bedsheet and covered Maryanne with it. The other woman spread her fingers across the swell. They were trembling.

"The more you rest, the longer we can delay the baby's arrival," said Celia.

"I'm trying, ma'am," she said. "And I did ask the woman who lives next door if she could go to the grocer's for me yesterday. Do you know what, Mrs. Davies? She actually did."

"I told you that your neighbors would help."

There were footsteps in the hallway, and John Kelly stepped into the room. He carried their sleeping infant daughter in his arms. "And how is she, Mrs. Davies?"

"I did not realize you were here today, Mr. Kelly," she said.

"Mr. Hutchinson knows Maryanne's unwell." He looked at his wife. "How are she and the baby, then?"

"She must continue to rest," she said. "The contractions are growing more frequent and increasing in intensity. We do not want the baby to arrive too early, though."

"Don't worry, John," said Maryanne to her husband, seeking to soothe the furrow in his brow. "I won't ask you to stay with me and ignore your work. Our neighbor will help me again, I'm sure." She turned to Celia. "Mr. Martin has hated the delay in repairing his offices so much that he even asked John to meet with him yesterday and review the progress. On a Sunday, of all days. The man's a tyrant."

"Now don't be sayin' that, Maryanne," reprimanded her husband. "His money puts bread and butter on our table."

"Yesterday?" Celia asked him. "After the excitement at Cliff House, I am surprised Mr. Martin wished to meet with you, Mr. Kelly. We all left so shaken."

"Excitement, Mrs. Davies?" he asked, shifting his daughter in his arms and causing her to stir. "What happened?"

"Someone pushed me over the wall above the cliff," Celia answered, watching his face. After all, he *was* one of her suspects.

"So that is why your palm is scraped," said Maryanne.

"Yes." Celia had scratched her hands when she'd clutched at the rock wall; she buffed her fingertips across the tiny scabs on her skin. "Fortunately, Mr. Hutchinson grabbed me and prevented me from falling to my death."

Maryanne gasped. "Mrs. Davies!"

"There is no need to be alarmed, Mrs. Kelly," said Celia. "I did not mean to cause you to worry for me."

"You should be more careful, ma'am," said Mr. Kelly, his expression as unchanging as the expression on a ventriloquist's doll. He did not, however, look guilty.

"I endeavor to try, Mr. Kelly." Celia rose and folded away her stethoscope, then gathered her shawl and medical bag. "I shall return tomorrow."

"If you have the time," said Maryanne.

"I most certainly have the time for any and all of my patients," Celia replied, and bid them both farewell.

She touched the sweet face of the child sleeping in Mr.

Kelly's arms and stepped around him to descend the stairs and exit the house. When she was a few doors distant, something made her turn and look back—just as the curtains in the upstairs window flicked back into place.

"*I*'m looking for Rob Bartlett," Nick said to Frank's workers, the entire bunch lolling about on overturned barrels and empty crates in the enclosure behind the offices.

He'd found the building itself empty, tools discarded, all work stopped. No Kelly. No Martin. No Frank. And all his employees enjoying a break in the sunshine. *When the cat's away . . .*

One of the men spat a stream of tobacco juice into the corner. "Bartlett ain't here."

*I can see that.* "Perhaps you can tell me where he *is*, then."

"Rob was done for the day, and Kelly sent him home," said another, his mouth quirking. "To recline on his divan."

"His divan!" guffawed the tobacco-chewing fellow, a trickle of juice dribbling down his chin. "Yep, that's it. Old Rob's reclining on his *divan* at his place, Officer."

The youngest one of the group, who looked no older than eighteen with his scanty sprouts of chin hair, spoke up. When he did, Nick noticed he was missing a front tooth. "He mighta gone to the restaurant on the corner, Officer. He likes to eat there."

"Obliged," said Nick, turning to leave.

As soon as he was out of sight of the men, Nick heard the sound of a thump followed by a muffled bawl.

"What'd you go and tell him that for?" one of them asked.

" 'Cuz he's a cop!"

"Stupid kid," came the answer. "You get Bartlett in a pucker and you'll live to regret it."

Nick stepped outside and surveyed the busy street. He located the restaurant and headed there. He didn't have to poke around inside it, because a man who looked like the fellow he wanted—Nick realized he'd seen Bartlett the last time he'd been at Martin and Company—came strolling out through the front door.

"Mr. Bartlett!" he called out. The fellow confirmed he was Bartlett by stopping. "I need to speak with you."

Bartlett watched him approach, his right hand resting on his hip where a gun caused a bulge in his dark reefer coat. Didn't he know it was against the law to conceal a deadly weapon? Bartlett, not the handsomest of fellows, had a heavy chin outlined by a scraggly beard and narrow-set eyes. When Nick walked up to him, he caught a whiff of what smelled like almonds. Maybe Bartlett was using bear's grease to fill in a patch of thinning hair hidden by his bowler. Just because a person was plug-ugly didn't mean he couldn't be vain.

"Can I help you, Officer?" he asked, recognizing Nick as well from the last time he'd been at Martin and Company.

"I have some questions about Dan Matthews."

Wariness showed in his eyes. "What about him?"

Two men exited the restaurant at Bartlett's back and slowed to stare at the cop and the fellow he was interviewing. "How about we find someplace more private to talk, Mr. Bartlett?"

Fortunately for all concerned, Bartlett was astute enough to go without complaint.

Nick chose a nearby alleyway, the sole occupant of which appeared to be a flea-bitten mongrel nosing through trash, and stepped into its shadows.

"Ain't this cozy," said Bartlett.

"I want to know why you went to visit Dan Matthews yesterday."

Bartlett folded his arms and leaned against the brick wall of the building behind him. "We're friends. Been friends a long time. And friends visit each other."

"Did you talk to him about his plans to leave town?" asked Nick.

"He wasn't there. I left without talking to him."

The mongrel trotted over, intrigued by the visitors to its alley, and sniffed Nick's trouser legs. "Pfft. Get outta here."

The dog got the message and scooted.

Bartlett raised his brows, which had the effect of lifting his bowler hat. "Don't like dogs, Officer?"

"Not when I'm interviewing suspects."

"Didn't know I was a suspect," said Bartlett. He fished around in the pockets of his reefer coat and found a brass toothpick, which he proceeded to use calmly. Among the many things that amazed Nick, the ability of suspects to act composed was a never-ending wonder. Innocent people tended to shake in their boots.

"And what are you talking about? Dan leaving town?" said Bartlett. "'Cuz if he did, I wanna know. He owes me money."

Nick removed the silver watch from his inner coat pocket. "Recognize this?"

Bartlett eyed it. "Can't say that I do."

"You sure? It was found on Matthews' body."

For a second, the toothpick paused. "His what?"

"Your good friend Dan is dead, Mr. Bartlett, and this watch and a whole lot of money were found on him."

"What do you mean, he's dead? How is he dead?"

Bartlett did look surprised by the news. Nick repocketed the watch. "What I mean, Mr. Bartlett, is that Matthews was found this morning with a broken neck on the road heading south out of town."

"What the . . ." He put away his toothpick with a shaking hand. "He killed him, then."

"Matthews died in an accident."

"All the same . . . ," said Bartlett. He glanced toward the street at the end of the alleyway—maybe hoping a diversion would calm his nerves. Cowboys rode past with their spurs jingling, a cart went in the other direction, and rough laughter echoed nearby, one of the voices that of a woman. Not much to note, actually, and when Bartlett looked back at Nick, he was ready to talk. "Last Friday, Dan was blubbering in his beer that he'd seen somebody suspicious hanging around the offices one night a couple weeks ago. He figured it was the night Nash was murdered. 'He'll kill me.' That's what Dan said to me. 'He knows I saw him and he'll kill me.' I tried to get him to say who, but he wouldn't."

"Why didn't you come to the police with that information?" *If it's even true.*

"Would you have believed me? You sent that kid to spy on Dan. How do I know you're not trying to get information on me so you can accuse *me* of killing Nash?"

"You don't," Nick answered. "Who do you think Matthews might've seen that he thought would kill him for noticing?"

"Somebody he knew and who knew him. Seems obvious," said Bartlett.

"It sure would've been helpful if Matthews had told me what he'd seen so I could be more inclined to believe you."

"And admit that he'd been going by Martin's office every night to figure out when was the best time to dig in the cellar?"

"To look for a treasure you told him about but that didn't exist."

Bartlett shrugged, his expression revealing not one ounce of remorse for having lied to his so-called friend. "Ain't my fault Dan Matthews was a sucker. Never could tell when I was joshing."

Nick stepped up close to Bartlett, who recoiled at the sudden movement. "I don't think you're telling me the half of what you know, Bartlett, and if you've been leading me down a merry path, I can be very unforgiving."

"I ain't lying to you, Officer."

So, it was back to "Officer." And Nick had felt so privileged to have had Rob Bartlett address him as "Detective Greaves."

"I'd be careful if I were you, Mr. Bartlett."

"Oh, I'll be careful, Officer," Bartlett responded, his hand hovering above his waist where his weapon was concealed. "You can bet I will."

*Celia* walked home, lost in her thoughts, and was nearly run over by the horsecar clopping along Powell. Lifting her skirts, she dashed to the safety of the curb, knowing this particular accident would have been solely of her own making. She passed the grocer's, a bustle of activity, and turned up Vallejo.

Angelo Cascarino was perched on the porch step of his house, looking forlorn as he watched the neighborhood children chase a hoop in the street, their feet, some bare, kicking up dust. His mother must have forbidden him to join them until the gash on his head healed.

"How is your cut, Angelo?" Celia called out to him, gesturing at her own forehead so that he understood her.

Angelo touched the stitches and nodded. *"Grazie, Signora,"* he said in his small voice. He resumed watching his friends, propped his chin on his fists, and heaved a dramatic sigh.

Celia entered the house and dropped onto the entry hall chair. Female voices—Barbara's and Grace's—sounded in the parlor. Having heard the door, Addie rushed in from the back of the house. She was wearing her best straw bonnet and had tossed her shawl over her shoulders.

"Are you going somewhere, Addie?" Celia asked as her housekeeper knelt to untie the laces of Celia's half boots.

"We havna enough butter and flour for supper, ma'am."

"Well, you are looking very smart for a visit to the market," Celia observed.

"Am I?" Addie asked evasively, her head bowed over Celia's feet.

Celia leaned to one side to get a better view of Addie's face. Yes, her housekeeper was definitely blushing. "Yes, you are. Are you perhaps intending a visit to someone in particular while you are there?"

"I had the thought that, while I was at the market, I could stop at the butcher's stall and ask that galoot who works there if he's been sending the tokens," she answered, not meeting Celia's gaze.

"And if Mr. Knowles turns out to be your admirer, you wish to look your best."

"It canna hurt," said Addie, Celia's boots sliding free.

"That is so."

Addie looked up at her. "Will you be all right, ma'am? Here, by yourself?"

"I am not alone, Addie. The girls are here with me."

"They'll nae be able to protect you."

"Do I require protecting?"

"I've come to believe you always require protecting these days, ma'am," said Addie. "I didna doubt that becoming involved with that detective would come to grief for you."

"I am hardly 'involved' with that detective, Addie," Celia protested. "And I do not feel that I have come to grief."

"Nae yet, ma'am, though you had a close call at Cliff House," said Addie, rising to her feet. "God has been watching over you, but I canna help but wonder for how long he'll tolerate your foolhardiness."

Addie emphasized the comment by lifting an eyebrow. How many times she'd seen that expression on her housekeeper's face. How many times she'd been glad for it, too.

"Och aye, I see where your thoughts are headed." Addie added pursed lips to the lifted eyebrow. "You've nae mind to be careful."

"I always wish to be careful, Addie. I cannot help that I do not always succeed," Celia said, standing as well and removing her bonnet, which she hung on the hook near the door. "If it eases your mind, I will lock the door behind you."

Addie heaved a sigh nearly as dramatic as Angelo's had been. "If I dinna go, I willna need worry."

"But I thought we required butter and flour," Celia teased, which raised another blush in Addie's cheeks.

"There it is! I willna go." Addie moved to take off her shawl, and Celia stopped her.

"Please. Go on. We will be fine here."

"If you are certain . . ."

"I am," she said, giving her housekeeper a small push toward the front door.

"Well then," said Addie, checking her reflection in the mirror that hung adjacent to the hallway's case clock. "I do wonder, though, that a man like him would keep his admiration a secret. He's e'er so loud with everything else."

Celia laughed, and Addie went out onto the porch. "Lock the door, ma'am."

"Yes, yes, yes," she replied, and did so.

Wrapping her shawl tight around her shoulders, Celia slid open the parlor doors. "Good afternoon, Grace."

Grace stood up from the piano bench and gave a small curtsy. "How are you doing today, Mrs. Davies?"

When Barbara turned her head, Celia could see dark circles beneath her eyes; it had been another sleepless night for her.

"I am quite well, if a trifle bruised, Grace," Celia said. "Were you preparing to practice something on the piano?" An unfamiliar piece of music sat waiting.

"My stepmother wants me to play 'The Battle Hymn of the Republic' for our upcoming Fourth of July celebration," said Grace. "I brought it over for Bee to play, too. I'm trying to cheer her up."

"Grace," said Barbara crossly, turning around to face the piano keys and flipping open the cover of the sheet music.

"Thank you for trying to lift her spirits, Grace. We all had a shock yesterday, I dare say."

"It was awful, wasn't it?" asked Grace. "And we were having such a nice time. Well, up to the point where that man called Bee a bad name while we were walking along the terrace. And then to have that crowd gather around like a pack of rabid dogs. I think I was too angry to be scared of them, though. Cowards."

"Grace," Barbara repeated, more insistently. "Cousin Celia

doesn't need to hear about this. She's familiar with the names people call me and how I'm treated." She rested her fingers on the keyboard and listlessly tapped out the opening measures of the song. "I shouldn't have gone to Cliff House. I shouldn't go anywhere I'm not welcome."

Grace rapped Barbara on the shoulder, a rough gesture for a well-bred young lady. "Don't say that! You know that's what those people want, don't you? They want to scare you into hiding inside your house like a trapped animal!"

Barbara glanced up at her friend standing over her. "You don't understand, Grace. People don't look at you the way they look at me, like I'm a leper."

"You don't think I understand? I remember what it was like when my mother died, and everyone would stare when I went to the market with Hetty or to church with my father." She dropped onto the bench next to Barbara. "The looks and the whispers. 'Poor little Grace Hutchinson. Her sweet, lively mother dead so soon after her father came back from the war. So shocking. And him not the same at all.'"

Grace pressed her lips together and glanced over at Celia.

"No one returns from war the same as when they left," said Celia quietly. *And some do not return at all*, she thought, the memory of her brother pricking as sharply as the spiny stem of a weed.

There was more behind Grace's words than the concern that her father had changed, however.

"My mother died, too, Grace, and my father," said Barbara before Celia could consider what Grace had been trying to say. Her cousin looked over her shoulder at the portrait of Uncle Walford, who grinned at them from above the settee. "And whereas people have stopped whispering about you, now that your father's remarried and nobody likes to think about the soldiers anymore, I'm still half-Chinese. And a leper."

Grace wrapped an arm around Barbara's shoulders and hugged her close. "Not to me. Not to me *ever*. And anybody who thinks differently is a no-account fellow!"

Barbara closed her eyes and let her friend hug her.

*Thank goodness you are here, Grace,* Celia thought. *Thank goodness she lets you comfort her.*

"Would you two like some lemonade?" Celia asked. "I expect Addie has left a pitcher in the kitchen for us."

"Thank you, Mrs. Davies," said Grace, releasing Barbara.

Celia made to walk past them, heading for the kitchen via the dining room.

"Mrs. Davies," said Grace, halting her. "I'm glad you didn't get hurt."

"So am I," she said. The way the girl was looking at her caused Celia to recall the odd interaction between Grace and her father at Cliff House. "Grace, do you have something you wish to tell me about what happened yesterday?"

"Cousin, do you have to?" asked Barbara.

"This is important."

"It always is," she muttered, plunking away at the piano, perhaps hopeful that she could drown out Celia's voice.

"Barbara, please stop," said Celia. Her cousin ceased playing and lowered her hands to her lap. "Grace, you were standing directly across from me, facing my direction when I was trying to push through the crowd to reach my cousin. You had to have noticed who was standing nearest to me." *And who might have pushed me over the wall,* she did not need to add.

"I saw you coming, but I didn't notice anybody else," Grace answered, holding Celia's gaze. "I was so worried about Bee."

Her eyes might not have wavered, but she plucked at the lace banding her left cuff. Celia had been taught by one of her instructors at the Female Medical College that if she wanted to understand a patient's true feelings and thoughts, she must watch for unguarded movements more than observe what was reflected in their eyes. People could learn to control their faces; they found it far more difficult to manage the anxiety that caused them to shuffle their feet or pick at their fingernails.

"Mr. Martin was nearby. Mr. Greaves must have been close. There was a woman, also. Several males," said Celia when Grace maintained her silence. "And your father had to be very near, since he grabbed me."

*What did you see, Grace? Tell me what you saw and are afraid to admit.*

"*Did* you see somebody push my cousin, Grace?" asked Barbara, suddenly interested in Celia's questions.

"Mr. Martin," Grace answered, her fingers closing around the lace band. "I saw Mr. Martin push you, Mrs. Davies."

# CHAPTER 10

"Do you recognize the watch, Mrs. Nash?" Nick asked, holding it out to her.

Her maid glided into the parlor, set tea on the parquetry table between them, and tiptoed off, unnoticed by her employer.

Alice Nash hesitated to take the watch, as if afraid it might bite. When she finally did, she lifted the watch from his hand as gently as she might lift a holy relic.

Her eyes widened. "It's still warm," she said, sounding alarmed.

"That's from me, ma'am."

"Yes. Of course." The hallway case clock chimed the hour as she glanced at the watch, not looking too long at her husband's dried blood still embedded in the fancy scrollwork carved across its surface. Matthews would've received at least thirty dollars for it, a nice sum of money, if he'd lived long enough to get to a pawnshop. "Yes. It's Virgil's."

She brought the watch to her lips, kissing the silver case. It was the most emotion he'd seen her exhibit.

"Oh, Virgil." She handed it over as reluctantly as she'd taken it from him. "Where was it found?"

"In possession of a man found dead this morning," answered Nick, tucking the watch into a pocket. The tea remained untouched on the table.

"Thank heavens that the murderer is dead," she said, pressing a hand to her throat, the rapid motion of her arm wafting the aroma of magnolia water his way. "Who was it?"

"Nobody you know, ma'am," he said. "I'm curious about something, Mrs. Nash. When my assistant and I visited you on Friday, why didn't you tell me about the threatening notes your husband had received?"

"I didn't think it was necessary. Virgil and I both knew who'd sent them, even though they weren't signed. One of Jasper Martin's many ploys to get his way."

"When did they start?"

She paused as she thought back. "More than a month ago. Not long after Virgil learned about Jasper Martin's plans to level Second Street."

The timing made sense. "Since we last spoke, I've learned the name of the man who killed your husband's brother. Cuddy Pike. Sound familiar?"

She shook her head and finally reached for the tea, pouring it out for them both, the fawn-colored stream of liquid catching the sunlight. "As I told you then, Virgil didn't like to talk about Silas' death."

"And he never talked about cheating miners at the Comstock, either," Nick said. "But what about the men he tried to cheat here, like Horatio Enright?"

The lid of the china teapot clinked noisily as she set it down. "Horatio Enright's complaints have no merit, Mr. Greaves. I repeat that my husband was an honorable man. How often do I have to say it?"

"Mr. Enright thinks otherwise about your honorable husband."

"He envies my husband's success, like so many others." She drew out a handkerchief from the sleeve of her ink-dark gown. Above her head, the black-swathed portrait hung in mute testimony to the brutal end of one man's life. "That's all one finds in California—grasping men for whom nothing matters but the acquisition of wealth. I hate it."

He looked around at what Nash's money had bought—a house brimful of luxuries most of the people in San Francisco could only imagine owning. Just like Frank's house. Just like Russell's. "Strong words, ma'am, when you've got plenty of wealth yourself."

"You think I'm a hypocrite."

Nick shrugged. It really didn't matter what he thought about her.

Her tears had dried and she gazed steadily at him, her emotions come full circle, back to the calm of the first time he'd met her. The woman was a wonder.

"Well, none of my lovely, precious possessions will bring Virgil back, will they, Mr. Greaves?"

_Now what, Celia?_
After seeking to confront Mr. Martin at his office and learning he was not there, she had taken the North Beach

# NANCY HERRIMAN

and Mission Railroad line all the way to Union Square. Celia walked the intervening uphill blocks to Jasper Martin's impressive home on Sutter Street, nearly in the shadow of the onion domes of Temple Emanu-el that towered over the neighborhood. A limestone fence with sinuously carved balustrades separated the front yard from the pavement, the building further safeguarded from the passing street traffic by a thick screen of evergreen trees. The shutters behind the many arched bay windows were closed against the midday sunshine, though the fence and the trees were sufficient guards against the unwelcome scrutiny of pedestrians and conveyance drivers.

*Trust me, Mr. Martin, they very adequately relay your desire to remain undisturbed. But what to do next?*

Anticipating that she would speak to Mr. Martin at his offices, where there would be plenty of witnesses should he turn violent, she'd gone out alone. The lack of a protector had not kept her from impulsively visiting his house to speak to him, however.

*You can be rather imprudent, Celia.*

But surely there would be servants inside, and since she was here . . .

Celia pressed her hand to the iron gate leading to the front steps. It swung open as silently as a skate blade gliding on ice. She'd known people who intentionally allowed their gate hinges to go rusty, the squeal an early alert to the presence of guests—or strangers. Celia supposed Mr. Martin must not be concerned about either, confident that he could dispose of anyone unwelcome.

She climbed the limestone steps—seven in total and very steep—and arrived at the front door, which appeared as solidly

{ 210 }

forbidding as the rest of the property. Celia tugged the lever that activated the doorbell, hearing the responding trill echo through the front hallway. Minutes passed without any indication of life within.

Celia leaned over the porch railing and attempted to peer through the shutters covering the nearest window. She couldn't see any movement, or much of anything at all inside. A matron strolling by on the pavement gave Celia an inquiring look before continuing on down the road.

"Hello?" Celia called out, tugging the doorbell lever again. She hadn't come all this way to give up easily. "Any—"

The door was yanked open, interrupting her midword. A thickset man in a frock coat scowled down at her, his expression bracketed by the bushiest mustache she had ever seen. He hadn't released the handle, giving the impression he was quite prepared to slam the door upon whoever had been ringing the bell.

"What do you want?" he asked.

"I need to speak to Mr. Martin," she said, using her most imperious accent, the one that made her sound like the rector at her family's parish in Hertfordshire when he was delivering a Lenten sermon. "Most urgently."

The man did not appear in the least impressed. "And who are you?"

"A friend."

He did not appear impressed with that claim, either. In fact, he appeared utterly dubious. "Mr. Martin is not receiving 'friends' today."

He swung the door to shut it, but Celia inserted her boot in the way, preventing it from closing. The man scowled at her foot and pushed harder on the door, pinching her toes.

"It is most important that I see him," she said. "Tell him Mrs. Davies is here."

"My patient is resting and not seeing anybody." He shoved at her foot with the toe of his shoe.

*Patient?* "What has happened? I am a nurse. You can tell me."

"A nurse."

"Yes. I have a clinic on Vallejo," she said, trying to peep around him into the depths of the entry hall. "Is Mr. Martin all right?"

"He had an attack of angina pectoris, but he's resting now. And *not* seeing anybody."

From within the bowels of the house, a man bellowed, "Johnston!" The physician glanced toward the sound.

"Dr. Johnston," said Celia, "you should probably return to Mr. Martin before he has another attack whilst calling for you."

He flung wide the door and ushered her inside. "Meddlesome woman," he muttered as he hurried off down the hallway, bound for the steps rising from the center of the house.

Celia closed the door. She barely had time to absorb the luxuriousness of her surroundings before she chased after Dr. Johnston, her footfalls muted by the Turkish carpet runner climbing the wide staircase. She felt only momentarily abashed for intruding upon Mr. Martin; he may have suffered an attack of angina but sounded quite recovered, if the volume and tone of his voice were any indication.

"Johnston, what was keeping you?" Jasper Martin was asking the man as Celia located the bedchamber and stepped inside. Mr. Martin was propped up in his tester bed, a mountain of pillows at his back. The windows were shuttered here, too, which made an already dark room darker still. The space felt close and smelled of camphor.

He noticed her arrival. "What are you doing here, Mrs. Davies?"

"Now, now, Mr. Martin," soothed Dr. Johnston. "Don't let her disturb you."

"When did this happen?" she asked Mr. Martin, coming to his bedside.

His color was good for a man whose heart had attempted to fail him. But the nightshirt he wore exposed the bones of his neck and hung awkwardly upon the sharp angles of his shoulders and elbows, making him appear even more gaunt than usual. Very frail, actually.

She tried to feel the pulse in his wrist, but he moved his hand beyond her reach.

"Really, Mrs. Davies," protested Dr. Johnston. "Mr. Martin is my patient, and you're agitating him. Please leave."

"When did this happen, Mr. Martin?" Celia asked again. Had guilt about pushing her contributed to the onset of the angina?

"Last evening, Mrs. Davies. It seems our outing to Cliff House was more than my heart could stand," he said with more than a hint of sarcasm. "But you haven't answered my question. What are you doing here?"

"I've been troubled by my small accident yesterday, Mr. Martin, and you may be able to set my mind at ease."

He elbowed himself into a more upright position and folded his arms in his lap. "Oh? How so?"

"You were very near me, you and Mr. Hutchinson, and you had to have seen who shoved me," she said.

"I didn't see anybody push you, Mrs. Davies. You should just accept that you fell on your own."

"But I am certain I felt a hand at my side. And—you will find this most disturbing—two people have told me they believe the hand belonged to you."

Dr. Johnston gasped. Mr. Martin laughed—perhaps at his physician's response, perhaps at her accusation—then clutched his chest.

"Mr. Martin, remain calm," said his physician, hastily pouring a glass of water from the crystal decanter waiting at Mr. Martin's bedside and dispensing the powdered contents of a packet into it. "Ma'am, I insist you leave. My patient needs his rest."

Mr. Martin exhaled as the pain passed. "It's all right, Johnston. Mrs. Davies is an amusing diversion," he said. "Why would I push you, ma'am?"

"I have no idea. I was hoping you would tell me."

"Don't you think that if I'd been attempting to kill you, coming here and confronting me was rather unwise?"

"With servants in the house, Mr. Martin, you would not harm me. They would overhear my shouts for help."

"But I don't have any live-in servants, Mrs. Davies," he said. "And my hired domestic hasn't returned from an errand I sent her on. If it weren't for Dr. Johnston here, it would've been just you and me."

Her skin prickled. What *had* she been thinking?

Dr. Johnston thrust the glass at Mr. Martin. "Drink this, Mr. Martin. This woman is going to bring on another attack if you're not careful."

"I'm feeling fine, Johnston. It's *you* who's going to give me another attack with your endless pestering." Jasper Martin waved his hand, nearly knocking the glass out of Dr. Johnston's hand. "Who was it who saw me push you, Mrs. Davies?"

"I would prefer not to tell you."

"And I would prefer not to respond to your accusation," he said. "I don't know why you imagined I might confess to such a ridiculous assertion."

"I did not believe you *would* confess, Mr. Martin." She had merely wished to observe his reaction. But his coolness disconcerted her, and she felt rather like an insect trapped within a spider's web. *And here I had imagined myself the spider, expecting to entrap him . . .* "I have a different question now. What has Frank Hutchinson done that you disapprove of?"

The bell rang again downstairs, and Dr. Johnston went off to answer it.

"I'll tell you plainly," said Mr. Martin. "His open feud with Virgil Nash has cast suspicion upon Martin and Company for the man's death. We deal in trust, Mrs. Davies, not merely real estate. Our customers trust our judgment when it comes to recommendations for purchasing property, or securing the best price for property they own or for buildings they would like to construct. And any action that diminishes our customers' trust is an action I can't accept."

"I believe it was the discovery of Mr. Nash's body in your cellar that brought suspicion upon Martin and Company," she answered.

His sudden frown wrinkled his face. "Take my advice, Mrs. Davies, and leave the detective work to the police."

"Who pushed me if not you, Mr. Martin? You must have seen."

"There were a lot of people scuffling for a view of the excitement. If you felt pushed, one of them did it. An accident," he said. He waved the same hand he'd waved at Dr. Johnston. "My doctor insists that I rest, and that's what I plan to do. Good day to you."

He folded his hands over his stomach and closed his eyes.

With a sigh, Celia departed the bedchamber and headed downstairs. Dr. Johnston was in the entry hall with a robust woman whose wiry hair sprung out around her straw bonnet.

"I told him on Saturday that all the recent excitement would make him sick, Doctor," she was saying, her chapped hands undoing the ribbons of her hat.

Undoubtedly she was the housekeeper who did not live in, thought Celia as she descended to the ground floor. The one who was not usually around and would not see whether her employer had ever returned late at night with dirt on his clothes.

"Not surprised he's had an attack," the woman added.

Dr. Johnston murmured an agreement. Hearing Celia's tread, he looked over. "Leaving, Mrs. Davies?"

That he did not clap for joy was something of an astonishment.

"I suggest tincture of belladonna for Mr. Martin's condition, Dr. Johnston," Celia replied. She didn't wait for him to open the front door for her. He did not look as though he intended to extend the politeness anyway.

Celia swept out onto the street as the hack that had brought the housekeeper wheeled away from the curb. She watched it depart, noting the unusual coloring of the horse . . . The horse! She rushed out to the road just as the dapple gray pulling the carriage turned the corner. The horse was very pale, except for its mane, which was dark as coal. Just like the horse Ginny had described.

The one that had been hitched to a wagon at the end of an alleyway the night Celia and Owen had interrupted a man attempting to exhume Virgil Nash's decaying corpse.

Celia hopped down from the horsecar, leaping to avoid a puddle of kitchen wastewater, and hurried toward home. She had to inform Mr. Greaves. Because the more she considered, the more she was convinced that Mr. Martin had been at his offices Thursday night, trying to remove Mr. Nash's body. He had the opportunity and no one at home to notice when he came or went or what condition his clothing was in when he returned. Most important, he had both the motive to murder Mr. Nash, who'd been an obstruction to his plans to increase his wealth, and an understandable desire to dispose of the evidence of his crime, once he'd somehow learned the corpse had been found. Furthermore, that she and Owen had interrupted his scheme explained why he might have wished to shove her over the cliff wall yesterday. In such a public venue, however, he had taken quite a risk to remove a witness.

"There you are at last, Mrs. Davies," a male voice called down to her from the porch.

Mr. Greaves leaned against one of the posts. He turned his flat-crowned hat in his hands, his expression dour. No matter. He would be pleased to learn what she'd uncovered.

"Ah, Mr. Greaves. No wonder you were not at the station." She paused on the stairs to catch her breath, her blasted corset restraining her efforts. "I am glad you are here. I have news."

"Sleuthing, Mrs. Davies?"

"I have just been to Mr. Martin's house. He is our killer!"

He glanced up and down the length of Vallejo. "You feel

the need to announce that to every one of your neighbors, ma'am?"

Right then, Angelo popped up from where he'd been playing on the Cascarinos' porch and peeped at them over the top of the railing. The rest of the street, including the balcony of the boardinghouse on the corner, was empty and quiet. The children who'd earlier been playing in the road were no longer outside. All was deserted save for a twist of windblown dust propelling a piece of straw wrapping paper along the street.

"It is only Angelo to overhear, Mr. Greaves, and his English is poor," she answered, nodding at the boy. She climbed to where the detective stood. "However, if you are concerned, come inside where we can talk without all of my neighbors hearing."

He scrubbed the soles of his boots over the iron scraper near the door and followed her inside. "What has you so convinced Martin's our murderer?"

"Grace Hutchinson saw him push me over the wall at Cliff House."

Mr. Greaves offered a blank stare in response. *He is annoyed that I uncovered a key piece of information before he did.*

"And you went to ask him kindly if he was trying to kill you, too?" he asked.

"I was not in danger," Celia said, hanging her bonnet on its hook by the door. Barbara and Grace had abandoned the parlor and gone off elsewhere. Possibly to Barbara's bedchamber or the back garden. "Mr. Martin was incapacitated, as it turns out. He suffered an attack of angina pectoris last evening and is bedridden under his physician's care."

"You didn't know that before you went to his house," he said.

"Then I am fortunate he was ill, am I not? Please come through to the kitchen and allow me to tell you all my news," Celia said, stepping into the parlor. "I shall endeavor to make us both coffee. It comes from Mr. Folger's company, so at least the beans have been roasted properly. I cannot vouch that I will brew it properly, however."

"Don't worry about the coffee. It'll be better than the sludge I drank during the war."

"Nonetheless, I apologize in advance. Addie is the one who is skilled at brewing coffee, but she is not here."

As they passed the dining room windows that overlooked the rear yard, Celia spotted Barbara and Grace seated on the wicker chairs near the unhappy rosebushes that inhabited the garden. They were so unlike the bushes in Mrs. Nash's garden, their flowers lush and bountiful. Celia wondered if Mrs. Nash would sell the house, and the rose gardens, now that she was widowed and alone. But who would purchase the property, knowing that the Second Street cut was coming?

They entered the kitchen, so quiet without Addie bustling about.

Mr. Greaves pulled out a chair and sat at Addie's worktable while Celia pumped water into a pot and took it to the stove. "So what did Martin have to say about Miss Hutchinson's observation?"

She retrieved the white and blue tin labeled PIONEER STEAM COFFEE AND SPICE MILLS from the pantry. "He denies it, of course, but then, he would," Celia said, and removed a cover from the stove grate. Addie had refreshed the coals early that morning, but they had burned too low to boil the water.

"Were you hoping that he'd have a change of heart and

suddenly be willing to confess?" asked Mr. Greaves. "Because you heard his explanation on Sunday. You had an accident."

"I was hoping to trick him into looking guilty, since Grace's observation proves his so-called explanation is false," she said, collecting the coal scuttle. "Regrettably, he did not look guilty, either."

She bent to open the stove door with the thick towel Addie used to turn the handle.

"Here, let me do that. You'll get dirty." Mr. Greaves jumped up from his chair and took the scuttle from her. He opened the door and tossed in a shovelful of coal.

"Hate to tell you, ma'am, but I don't think Martin's our killer." He closed the stove door and returned the scuttle to its spot.

"Obviously, I do not have definitive proof, but with what Grace observed, his culpability does seem much more likely now." She set the pot of water on the grate and levered off the lid of the tin can, the brisk scent of coffee rising. "Doesn't it?"

"I can't explain what Miss Hutchinson saw, but the reason I came by was to tell you that Dan Matthews was found dead this morning. In a ditch outside town."

"Gad! Does Maryanne Kelly know? I was with her only this morning . . ." And the baby. This news might be all the strain required to speed Maryanne's labor.

"I sent Taylor over to inform her."

Celia hoped Mr. Taylor would be gentle. "What happened?"

"Matthews fell from his horse and broke his neck," he explained. "And he had Virgil Nash's watch and money on him."

Which seemed the sort of evidence a jury would believe proved Dan's guilt.

"But Dan Matthews was not the man who attempted to

disinter Mr. Nash's body." She told him about the horse and wagon Ginny had seen. "And today, while I was at Mr. Martin's house, the same horse was hitched to the hack that delivered his housekeeper."

"There are a lot of horses around, Mrs. Davies. You can't be sure."

"But how many are very pale dapple grays with dark manes?" she asked. "I have seen no other like it in the city."

"Could be a coincidence that the same horse was at that alley and at Martin's today." The water began to boil, and Mr. Greaves moved the pot partway off the grate. He took the tin from her hand and scooped coffee grounds into the water. "Or the explanation is that all the partners hire the same driver, a man who makes use of that particular horse."

And those partners included Frank Hutchinson. "But it is still quite possible that Mr. Martin is connected to Mr. Nash's death."

"Not so quick, ma'am. The man who owns the restaurant where Martin was eating Thursday night is willing to state Martin was there most of the night."

"He would say such a thing, would he not, rather than offend a wealthy customer," she said, bringing over the coffee cups— delicate china ones with flowers painted around each rim. Too delicate for a man's hands. "This restaurateur's first inclination would be to preserve his business. Perhaps if I spoke to him—"

"Mrs. Davies, even though you like to think this is 'our' investigation, you really—"

"I really must stay out of police matters?" she asked. "But I shan't, so long as friends of mine are implicated in a man's murder."

"You might want to get acquainted with folks who don't get tangled up in crimes, ma'am. Just a suggestion."

"Ah, but then, Mr. Greaves, I would not know you."

A look she could not decipher crossed his face, and an awkward moment ticked past. *I only meant to tease. Didn't I?*

Mr. Greaves cleared his throat. "I'll have Taylor talk to the owners of the stables located nearest to Martin's house. There might be a driver he prefers to use. We'll find the man and see what he has to say about Thursday night and who it was who hired him."

"Thank you."

The rear door opened, and Barbara and Grace came into the kitchen.

"Thank goodness you're still here, Mr. Greaves," said Barbara, glancing between them. Grace paused just inside the threshold. "Grace would like to tell you something."

"I've already heard your claim that you saw Mr. Martin push Mrs. Davies, Miss Hutchinson," he said.

"It's not that," said Barbara. "Go on, Grace."

Grace Hutchinson squared her shoulders, an intense look on her young face. "It's time I confess, Detective. Time I confess what else I know. About my father."

*Well, well.*

Nick looked over at Celia Davies, who was staring at Grace as though the power of her gaze might get the girl to take back her words. Miss Walford rolled her lips between her teeth. She knew what was coming, Nick could tell, and he wondered how long she had known.

"How about we go into the parlor and you tell me all about it, Miss Hutchinson," he said.

"Grace, are you certain?" Mrs. Davies asked, taking hold of the girl's arm.

"Yes, ma'am," she murmured.

Nick strolled into the parlor, and the womenfolk followed, taking places on the various seats available. Barbara Walford chose a spot on the settee beneath the painting that Nick guessed was a portrait of her father. Mrs. Davies took a chair opposite her cousin, and Grace sat on the other chair, her face as pale as a skimming of cream off milk.

Nick remained standing; anything else would seem too cozy. Besides, he always thought better on his feet. "Go ahead, Miss Hutchinson. I'm listening."

"It has to do with the night that Mr. Nash died." Her voice trembled, and she swallowed. Mrs. Davies reached across to take the girl's hand. "I saw my father."

Barbara Walford sat perfectly still, her dark eyes wide, as if she were posing for a photograph and waiting for the exposure to complete. How many times would she find herself intertwined with the family of a killer, as had happened when Nick had first met both her and Celia Davies? She must feel cursed.

*Dang it, Nick, not one minute ago you let Celia Davies convince you that Martin was involved.*

"You saw your father do what, Miss Hutchinson?" he prodded.

She blinked to stop the gathering tears from falling. "He was not with Mr. Russell that evening like he and my stepmother said he was. I mean, I'm pretty sure he wasn't."

"How can you recall so clearly, Grace?" asked Mrs. Davies.

"It has been some time since then. Perhaps you are confused about the day in particular."

"That's what I told her!" said Miss Walford. "You're simply confused, Grace, and your father's not involved at all."

"Of course he's involved, Bee," Grace replied. "How many times was he seen fighting with Mr. Nash? Even I saw them arguing once, at a picnic. And the day before Mr. Nash died, my father came back from visiting him, angrier than I've ever seen him. I guess he'd gone to try to convince Mr. Nash one last time—yes, that's exactly what he said: 'One last time'—to stop getting in the way of their plans for the Second Street cut. But Mr. Nash refused and tossed him out of the house." Grace looked at Nick. "My father doesn't like to be bossed around."

"I'm aware of that, Miss Hutchinson," Nick answered, reaching up to rub the ache in his left arm. Getting ordered around made Frank pigheaded. Reckless. Stupid. So different from his cousin Jack, as easygoing a man as ever was born.

"You still have not explained how you can be so clear about the date, Grace," said Mrs. Davies.

"Because the day Mr. Nash died was the twenty-eighth of May, correct?" Grace asked.

Nick nodded.

"That's what I'd heard," said Grace. "We were supposed to go out and have a special dinner on the twenty-ninth. To celebrate my mother's birthday. We'd been planning on it for days and days. That's how I know, Bee. That's why I'm so sure."

"But Jane's birthday is later in the summer, Grace," said Mrs. Davies.

"Miss Hutchinson means Arabella's birthday," said Nick.

"Oh."

"But we didn't go to dinner on the twenty-ninth, even though my stepmother had promised we would. Because she awoke with a headache that Wednesday morning and didn't leave her room all day long." Grace paused, and Mrs. Davies gave the girl's fingers a squeeze. "I assumed her head hurt because she was mad at Father for the night before."

"Why might she be mad?" asked Nick.

"Because of what my father had done," said Grace. "I thought she was asleep. She's been taking her sleeping medications, and I thought she didn't know that Father had come home and then left again. I thought only I'd seen. I was waiting for him—I always do, even though I'm supposed to be in bed, because I want to make sure he gets home safe—watching from my bedroom window. It overlooks the street. I saw a hack arrive and my father step down onto the street. But he wasn't with Mr. Russell, because Mr. Russell always leans through the window to wish him a good night. He's always so drunk. And loud."

Nick caught Mrs. Davies' gaze. She looked worried for Frank.

"Do you remember what color the horse was that pulled the hack, Grace?" Mrs. Davies asked.

Grace's forehead puckered. "I don't."

"So it was not a dapple gray?"

"Mrs. Davies," Nick warned.

"Forgive me, Mr. Greaves."

"Anyway," said Grace, continuing, "my father didn't come in. The hack drove off, but he just stared up at the house. He saw me watching and nodded. I sensed something was wrong, though. I almost lifted the sash so I could call out to him, but he turned away before I could. He just walked off, down the street. He didn't come home again until really late, and all I can think is my stepmother must have seen him walk away, too. Maybe she was watching from one of the other windows and wasn't asleep. Or maybe Hetty told her."

"Do you remember what time it was you saw him, Miss Hutchinson?" Nick asked.

"I usually go to my room around nine, so after that. I'd guess close to nine thirty, since I'd been reading in my bed for a while."

Another discrepancy in Frank's alibi. If he wasn't with Russell at that point, then where had Frank been earlier that evening? The message to Nash had requested a meeting at eight.

"What condition were his clothes in?" asked Mrs. Davies before he could. "Were they dirty? Torn?"

*Bloody?* Nick added to himself.

"I don't think so," Grace answered. "But I wasn't really trying to see if he was dirty or anything. I just thought it was strange that he didn't want to come inside right away. It was like he was trying to avoid us."

"Grace, this doesn't mean he killed Mr. Nash," said Barbara, who'd remained stuck in her pose on the settee, an observer made out of granite. "It just shows that he didn't want to come home."

"But why did he pretend to be with Mr. Russell when he wasn't, Bee?" she asked, her voice catching. "The next day, he told me he had been with him, even though I'd seen that he wasn't. He's never lied to me. Never. It was part of our pact. We'd always be honest with each other. He's never explained, though. He won't."

The tears she'd been holding back fell, and she pinched her eyes closed.

"Why did you not tell us this earlier, Grace?" asked Mrs. Davies, leaning closer to the girl. "Terrible events might have been avoided if you had."

"My father didn't push you yesterday, Mrs. Davies," she said, looking up suddenly. "I know he didn't. It was Mr. Martin. I saw him."

Miss Walford hurried over to her friend, sinking to her knees at Grace's feet. "It'll be okay, Grace. You'll see. It'll be okay. Your father will have an explanation for everything." She glanced at Nick, daring him to say otherwise.

"I'll have to bring Mr. Hutchinson into the station," Nick said, which caused Mrs. Davies to frown.

"You can't!" Miss Walford shouted. "You just can't!"

"It'll have to wait, Mr. Greaves," said Grace Hutchinson. "My father went to Oakland this morning to discuss a project there. He won't be home until tomorrow." She bit her lower lip. "At least that's where he claims he is. This is awful."

"Do you know where he's staying?" Nick asked her.

"You are going to fetch him back now?" Mrs. Davies asked. "Can this not wait until tomorrow? What about your implication that Dan Matthews was responsible? Or that Mr. Martin had a role?"

"I'm not overlooking them, Mrs. Davies, but Frank has to explain his actions and right now."

He'd send Mullahey to track Frank down and haul him to the station. The arrest would probably make the morning papers. Nick tried to feel exultant at the idea of Frank's humiliation, but he couldn't muster the satisfaction. Revenge never was as sweet as advertised.

*Don't let the desire for vengeance color your judgment, Nick, or justify your actions.* Good old Uncle Asa. Always a saying for every situation.

*Well, Uncle Asa, I might be letting you down on this one.*

Grace Hutchinson gave Nick the name of the Oakland hotel. "Much obliged, miss."

"You must be happy at last, Detective, that you have sufficient proof to arrest Frank," said Mrs. Davies, her pale eyes gone as frosty as a January's snow.

Nick knew better than to respond.

# Chapter 11

"How long have you known about what Grace witnessed?" Celia asked her cousin. They stood on the porch together, watching Grace climb into the hack Jane had sent to fetch her. Mr. Greaves had left immediately after he'd finished questioning Grace.

"She told me only today," said Barbara, her arms wrapped about her waist. "I'm worried about what'll happen to Grace if her father's sent to jail."

"I am concerned as well. Deeply concerned. But Grace's account only means that her father was not where he'd claimed to be the evening Mr. Nash was murdered," said Celia. The driver shut the door behind Grace, and she peered through the window, her face wan. She offered a wave, which Barbara limply returned. "It does not mean he was at the offices of Martin and

Company, stabbing the man to death and then burying him in the cellar."

"Mr. Greaves believes that it does."

Celia had also seen the certainty of that belief in his eyes. How much, though, did his old hatred for Frank influence his decision to send a policeman haring off to Oakland to drag Frank back as soon as possible?

"Unfortunately, Mr. Greaves cannot turn a deaf ear to what Grace has told him," said Celia.

However, the question remained—where *was* Frank between the time he parted from Mr. Russell, if they had even been together that evening, and half past nine when Grace saw him? Frank was in desperate need of explaining his whereabouts at the time that Mr. Nash was murdered as well as what he'd been doing Thursday evening.

The hack rolled off, scattering finches pecking among the stones of the road.

"What do we do now?" asked Barbara.

"I have no patients this afternoon, which leaves me time to speak with the shopgirl who may have seen the man who'd been digging up Mr. Nash's body. I want to confirm the fellow was not tall and therefore not likely to be Mr. Hutchinson. We do that first," answered Celia, giving Barbara a squeeze and then reentering the house. She plucked her bonnet from its hook. "Afterward, I shall go and speak to Katie Lehane before the saloon opens. I'm curious if she ever noticed Mr. Nash arguing with any other men at Burke's. Men we have not already considered as suspects."

They needed more names. Because apparently the man's watch and money in the possession of Dan Matthews, along with the horse she'd seen at Jasper Martin's, were now insufficient for one Nicholas Greaves—and Celia very much feared Frank was running out of time to prove his innocence.

$\mathscr{T}$he shop bell jangled as Celia opened the door to the ladies' fancy goods shop.

Mrs. Lowers glanced over from where she stood behind the counter, folding a length of fawn-colored silk. "What can I do for you today, Mrs. Davies?"

"I need to speak with Ginny again." The girl was in the corner with a customer, discussing dress trimmings. "I will not require much of her time."

"Ginny," Mrs. Lowers called.

The owner jerked her head toward Celia. Ginny scurried over, and her employer went to help the customer.

"Ma'am?" Ginny asked.

Celia took the girl's elbow and led her to the front corner of the shop, where the sun streamed through the tall windows, lighting the display of embroidered reticules and shawls, and a parasol dripping with mauve fringe. A woman outside on the pavement peered through the window glass at Celia and Ginny, then returned to examining the ribbons laid out for examination.

"The man on Thursday. Think very, very carefully, Ginny. This is most critical. Was he tall?" Celia asked the girl.

"I don't right recollect, ma'am. I'm sorry."

"Come with me." She was being brusque with Ginny, but she could not help it; time was slipping away if she wished to help Frank's cause.

Celia parted the curtains at the doorway, then strode through the rear of the shop and out the back door into the alleyway. Ginny rushed after her.

"Here, Ginny. You saw him run through the alleyway," said Celia. "How tall was he in relation to your neighbor's fence there?"

She motioned toward the slat fence across the way, the top of which was higher than Celia's head by a half foot. If the quite tall Frank Hutchinson had passed through this alley, the crown of his hat would've been above the uppermost stretch of wood.

"I'm not sure . . . ," said Ginny.

At that moment, an aproned male shop assistant stepped into the alley from the adjoining eyeglass business. He struck a safety match against a stone near his feet, lit a cigarette, and strolled in their direction. Noticing Ginny, he offered her a jaunty hello, which made her blush.

"Taller or shorter than that man?" Celia asked once he'd passed. The shop assistant was of average height, and his uncovered head did not clear the top of the fence.

"The same. About the same, I think," said Ginny, staring after him.

So, not tall. And not Frank Hutchinson, if Ginny was correct in her observation. "You are quite certain? Because you may be asked to testify to that in court."

"What? Mrs. Lowers won't like that at all!"

"Just answer me, please, Ginny."

"I'm sure, ma'am."

*Thank goodness.* Celia could not explain where Frank was Thursday evening, but at least she *could* say he was not in this alleyway after having attempted to disinter Virgil Nash.

"What about the man's size?" Celia asked Ginny. "Was he very thin or portly?"

"He had on a long coat. It flapped around his legs when he

ran down the alley. I really couldn't say, ma'am, but I don't think he was portly."

Perhaps he was gaunt, then. Gaunt and unusually spry.

"Thank you, Ginny." Celia took the girl's hand. Her fingertips were calloused from plying a needle. "You have been of great help."

It was now time to speak to Katie Lehane.

"*C*are to now tell me the truth about what you and Mr. Hutchinson were doing the night Virgil Nash was murdered, Mr. Russell?"

Nick leaned against the windowsill in one of the upstairs offices of Martin and Company. The sound of hammering echoed through the floor. The workers were back at it, since one of the bosses had come in. Their work hadn't stopped them from learning about Matthews' death, though. Unfortunately, none of them had any clever ideas about why he'd been fleeing town like the devil was on his heels. Other than they all agreed that Matthews owed an awful lot of money to an awful lot of folks.

He wasn't up here to talk about Dan Matthews, though. He was here to pin the murder of Virgil Nash on Frank Hutchinson.

"You weren't with Frank that night, were you?" Nick asked Russell, who'd taken one of the chairs around the large table that occupied most of the room. A portrait of Frank's father, one of the company's founders, glowered from where it was displayed at Russell's back. On the wall opposite hung a detailed map of the city, tacks dotting its surface. A metallic trail of previous and planned acquisitions, Nick supposed. One of the tacks had been pushed into the area of Rincon Hill.

Rather than answer, Russell fidgeted in his chair and picked at a cuticle on his left forefinger.

"It's okay, Mr. Russell," Nick assured the man. "You can tell me. I won't be angry."

"We went to supper."

"You sure?"

"We went to Jean-Pierre's like we always do," said Russell. Nick had a stray thought that he should try Jean-Pierre's, since it seemed to be such a popular place. "And yes, I'm sure."

"But then what? You didn't accompany Frank back to his house like usual," said Nick. "I'm not even going to ask why you lied to me about that."

"I guess I don't remember that night all that well. Too much time has passed."

Nick really wished people would cooperate. It would make his life a helluva lot easier.

"A reliable witness saw Mr. Hutchinson returning home in a hired hack, alone. I've heard, though, that you're usually with him," he said. Russell took to chewing the torn cuticle. "Why not that night? What was different?"

"I said I don't remember."

Nick slapped his palm on the table. Russell jumped. "Blast it, Russell, I'm not keen to waste the day waiting for you to get around to the truth. I'm really not," he said. "So make me happy and explain why you weren't with him. Did he have plans to meet with Nash after supper, and you two went your separate ways? Is that what happened?"

Russell's chin sagged to his chest.

"Listen," said Nick. "Tell me what happened that night, and

I won't have you booked as an accessory to murder when my officer hauls Hutchinson into the station."

Russell looked up. "Frank didn't kill Nash. He didn't go to meet him. I swear to God."

"That's an awfully powerful thing to do, Mr. Russell."

"He didn't," he repeated. "I swear."

"You're willing to admit that you and he parted after you'd eaten, though?" Nick asked.

"I may as well, since you know we did."

Nick returned to leaning against the windowsill and rubbed a hand along the ache in his left arm. The sounds of the street sifted through the window, which was thrown open to catch the cool breeze and disperse the eye-watering odor of fresh paint. Down on the sidewalk, a boy shouted out the menu from a nearby restaurant, trying to entice diners. A church bell tolled the hour. The combination of the two made Nick's stomach grumble, reminding him he hadn't eaten since he'd had a quick cup of coffee for breakfast.

"Mr. Hutchinson was seen at home after nine," Nick said to encourage Russell to start talking and stop staring at his cuticles. "And you usually take supper around six thirty or seven, right? Doesn't seem likely to me that you gentlemen lingered over your chicken and sauced vegetables for two hours."

"We might have," Russell said, trying one last time.

"Not amused, Mr. Russell."

Russell's cuticle got another chew. "Frank went to Burke's. Must have been around seven thirty."

Why lie about going to the saloon he regularly visited? It's not like Jane Hutchinson didn't know her husband's habits. "How do you know that's where he went?"

Russell stared at him long and hard. Whatever he had to say, he didn't relish sharing. "Because Frank told me he was going to see one of Burke's girls. Katie Lehane."

"He went to see a saloon girl?" Poor Jane Hutchinson. Living not only in Arabella's shadow but in the shadow of another woman who was very much alive. "How long's this been going on?"

"Oh. Oh, oh! It's not like that! They weren't . . ." Russell's face turned as bright as a beet. "Just company. And cards. But he didn't think Jane would understand, so he didn't want her to know."

Nick was positive Jane Hutchinson wouldn't "understand" one bit. "If Miss Lehane can give Frank an alibi, Mr. Russell, I'm sure Mrs. Hutchinson will want her to speak up."

Russell slumped in his chair.

"Where'd *you* go that evening, Mr. Russell? After you two parted?"

"You can't tell Dottie."

"Where?"

He peered at Nick. "It's just a little place in an alley off Dupont . . ."

The streets of the Chinese quarter. "Do they happen to sell opium at that little place by any chance?"

Russell slumped lower; he looked like he wanted to cry. "Dear God. Dottie will have my head."

"Have you ever noticed Mr. Nash arguing with anyone other than Frank Hutchinson, Katie?" asked Celia.

Celia had interrupted Katie, who was washing her hair in the chipped tin basin in her boardinghouse room, and a trickle of water dribbled down the girl's cheek. The room smelled of rectified spirits and rosemary. A more pleasing aroma than what had arisen from the clogged sewer Celia had passed on her way there.

"Maybe, but I'm not sure, ma'am." Katie scrubbed at the errant drip with the edge of her coarse linen towel, then wrapped it around her hair.

"Please think back. It is most critical."

"I'll try." She tugged her wrapper closed over her underthings and dropped onto a nearby chair, positioned alongside a wobbly table. Katie's room was small, really not much more than a bed-chamber with an area to wash up and an even smaller area to sit and eat, but it was tidy and clean. "I hope you don't mind if I sit a spell. I'll spend all evening on my feet, and they get to hurting. Plus, my ankle's still bothering me a bit. You should sit, too, Mrs. Davies."

"I am fine standing. Thank you."

Katie unwound the towel and retrieved a wide-toothed horn comb from where she'd left it on the table. Bending over, she began to run the comb in steady sweeps through her long hair. "As I said before, Mr. Nash didn't seem to have friends, but as for enemies . . ."

"I should not be telling you this," said Celia, aiming to encourage Katie's memories, "but Mr. Hutchinson is going to be arrested for the murder of Virgil Nash."

Katie straightened, her damp hair swinging. "Frank? But he didn't. He can't have."

"Why do you say that?"

"Because—because he wouldn't. That's why," she said. A blush rose, and she lowered her head again, her damp hair forming an effective screen. "He and Mr. Nash fought, but not like that. And Mr. Hutchinson's a good man. I see enough of the kind who aren't to know the difference."

"I am aware that Mr. Hutchinson is a good man, Katie," said Celia. "But you know more than that, don't you? What is it you are not revealing?"

Katie yanked the comb through her hair, wincing when she hit a knot. "Nothing, ma'am."

"A reliable witness has come forward to repudiate the alibi he has provided," said Celia. "If he cannot explain himself, given that everyone in San Francisco seems to know of the animosity between the two men, he will likely be indicted for murder."

Katie's hand began to shake. She let out a sob and threw the comb across the room. It clattered across the wood floor. "It's *my* fault." She sat up and shoved her hair off her face. "It's all my fault."

*Gad.*

A shadow crossed Katie's eyes, normally so bright and lively. "We were together the night that Mr. Nash died. But we didn't . . . He *never* would. Just playing cards and having a drink. Honest. Don't think bad of me, ma'am. I don't ever bring men up here from the saloon. Honest, I don't."

No wonder Frank's explanation for where he'd been that evening had always been so vague. "Are you certain you mean the night of May twenty-eight?"

"I am. It's the last Tuesday he's been in the saloon, and I remember that night because he was so miserable." Water plopped from a curl of hair onto the floor. "The saloon had only been open a short while when Frank . . . Mr. Hutchinson came in. I could tell right away that something was the matter, especially when he asked straight off that I come sit with him. He likes when I do that." She smiled a little. "Says it cheers him up."

Had Patrick done similarly, Celia wondered, all those evenings after he'd stormed out of the house, another argument sending him out into the night? Found solace with a woman who did not disappoint him? And did it matter any longer, now that she could not repair the damage she had caused? Now that he might never return.

Celia exhaled, wishing away the guilt that clung like tendrils of ivy. "Go on, Katie."

"Mr. Hutchinson started drinking whiskey, which he doesn't usually do. He kept muttering about a birthday," Katie said.

"I see." His first wife's birthday. The celebration that had been cancelled on the twenty-ninth because of Jane's headache. Or heartache.

"After a while, he suggested we leave. I didn't want to, because Mr. Burke don't like us girls to leave with the men, but Mr. Hutchinson insisted."

"Then what?" asked Celia.

"I told Mr. Burke I wasn't feeling well, and Frank . . . Mr. Hutchinson met me here. Must've been around eight or so because the sun had set," she said. "My landlady was out for the evening, and he snuck up the back stairs. We played cards for a while. I beat him lots of rounds, which just shows how awful sauced he was. I did start to worry he meant for something else to happen . . ." Katie glanced toward her bed, the cheery blue and yellow Irish chain quilt covering the thin mattress looking as wholesome as a church picnic. "But then all of a sudden he said he needed to get home and left."

"When?" asked Celia.

"Nine, maybe? Had to have been, because the woman who sings in the saloon across the street was warbling 'Aura Lea,' which she always does halfway through her evening and makes all the fellows without gals cry," Katie explained. "On my nights off when I'm here, I get treated to that song. Just wish she sang better."

Around nine allowed Frank the proper amount of time to reach home when Grace had seen him. Katie might have just provided the alibi he required.

"Did Mr. Hutchinson tell you to say nothing about his visit?" asked Celia. "Is that why you kept it from me?"

"I'm sorry, ma'am. He made me promise not to breathe a word. And of course, I didn't want to." Katie pulled a worn handkerchief from the pocket of her wrapper and blew her nose. Finished, she peered at Celia. "Tell his wife I'm sorry. I didn't mean to hurt her."

"I wonder what I *shall* say to Jane."

The girl tucked away her handkerchief and rose to fetch her comb.

"Wait." Katie stopped in the center of the room. "There *was* somebody else." She rushed over to Celia, her eyes wide. "A fellow I've never seen before. He came into Burke's a few weeks before Mr. Nash died. Can't remember the exact day."

"What was it about him that you recall?"

"He was drinking whiskey at the bar and Mr. Nash come in. The fellow looked over—everybody looks at the door when somebody new comes in—and turned as white as a ghost. He spilled his whiskey and almost fell off his stool. Asked me if there was a back door out of the saloon."

A man scared of being spotted by Virgil Nash . . . Celia supposed there was any number of reasons a person might not wish to be seen by the argumentative Mr. Nash. To presume the man was the fellow who had killed Mr. Nash's brother in Virginia City seemed a conceivable conclusion, albeit a rash one.

But his agitation could reflect emotions strong enough to have led him to murder.

"Did Mr. Nash notice this man?" Celia asked.

Katie furrowed her brow as she considered the possibility. "He might've, but I don't know because I was busy taking the fella out through the back room and into the alley."

"Do you recall what he looked like?"

"Plain sort," said Katie. "Average size and height. Nothing unusual in particular . . . oh, except once he was done looking like a ghost, his cheeks flamed a funny red when he got worked up about Mr. Nash. Ain't never seen that before, not all dark and splotchy like he got, which is why I remember," she added.

Sadly, the description did not match any of Celia's suspects. "Might you recognize this fellow if you saw him again?"

"I might."

But where to have her look? One place, Celia supposed, was among the laborers working at Martin and Company. She kept returning to her belief that the man she and Nicholas Greaves sought was in some way connected to Mr. Martin's business.

"There is a coffee shop across the street from Martin and Company," said Celia, providing the address. She should tell Mr. Greaves of her intentions, but he undoubtedly would scoff at her. *Where ignorance is bliss, / 'Tis folly to be wise.* And if he did not learn of her plans, he could not criticize them. "Can we meet there tomorrow, around eleven in the morning?"

"I don't know, ma'am. I'm awful busy—"

"Katie, it is critical that we find this man. He might not have killed Virgil Nash, but he may have important information that will lead us to the killer," Celia explained. "However, I cannot find him without your help."

"Okay," Katie said, though her reluctance was clear. "I'll be there."

Katie Lehane hadn't come to work yet—Burke's wouldn't open for another hour—but Nick had found somebody who knew where she lived. He turned the corner just as Celia Davies exited a boardinghouse a few yards distant, the sunlight catching the wisp of golden hair that had escaped her straw bonnet.

*Well, well.*

She turned to look in his direction as though she'd heard his thoughts. "Mr. Greaves."

He tapped his fingertips to the brim of his hat. "We meet again, ma'am."

"Have you already sent your officer to retrieve Mr. Hutchinson?" she asked, waiting on the sidewalk for him to join her. She didn't look as mad at him as she had when he was questioning Grace Hutchinson. In fact, she was looking smug.

"Afraid I have," he said.

"He is not guilty," she stated. Yep. Smug.

"You've come from talking to Katie Lehane, haven't you?"

"How did you know?" she asked.

"I was just on my way to see her myself," he answered, taking her elbow and leading her away. "But maybe I don't need to now."

"Katie was with Frank the evening of Virgil Nash's murder," said Mrs. Davies. "But who told you about her?"

"Abram Russell." He guided her across the road in the wake of a lumbering coal wagon. "Looks like everybody's finally willing to confess what Frank Hutchinson was doing the night Virgil Nash was murdered."

"It vexes you that they were willing to protect him this long, does it not, Mr. Greaves?" she asked.

"Does it show?"

"To me, it does," she replied, admitting to a dangerous occupation—observing his moods. "However, not only did Katie provide Frank with an alibi; she told me about a man who had been in the saloon a few weeks before Mr. Nash died. This man seemed very alarmed to spot Mr. Nash and snuck out of the saloon to avoid him. Curious reaction, would you not agree, Mr. Greaves?"

"Curious reaction, Mrs. Davies."

"The thought struck me that perhaps he was the man who killed Silas Nash in Virginia City. I am aware the likelihood seems remote, but it could explain his alarm at spotting Virgil Nash at Burke's," she said, shooing off a persistent newspaper boy with a flick of her hand.

"The man's name is Cuddy Pike, by the way. In all the recent excitement, I forgot to tell you," he said. "And now all I have to do is locate a stranger in a city of more than one hundred thousand people. Sort of like trying to find a needle in an uncooperative haystack."

"Most daunting," said Mrs. Davies. A gust of wind flung dust along the road, and she drew her wrap closer around her. "At least we can exonerate Frank of murder and the attempt to disinter Mr. Nash's body. The shopgirl who noticed the man hurrying down the alleyway is convinced that he was short in stature. Much shorter than Frank. And possibly very thin, like—"

"Like Jasper Martin. I got it. But Mrs. Davies, I really wish you'd let me do the investigating and you stick to keeping out of trouble," said Nick. "What do you think of that?"

"I think we are running out of time, Mr. Greaves," she said. "And we are likely both in danger."

"That may be so, ma'am, but I'm betting you're the one more likely to find it first."

"You make me sound quite reckless."

"Ma'am, I don't have to make you sound like that at all for it to be true."

"You've come home at last, I see," said Addie. She leveled a frown at Celia, who was in the entry hall stripping off her bonnet and wrap. "You didna think I might be fretting? Canna help but think next you'll be pushed in front of a horse-car or pummeled in one of those alleyways you're e'er so fond of visiting. Och. You're making me old before my time, ma'am."

"I am unharmed, Addie. A visit to a shop on Montgomery, then to see Katie Lehane," she replied, omitting her visit to Mr. Martin while Addie was at the market. She patted her hair to make certain all was in place. "On a Monday afternoon, there is nothing to worry over."

"I'll worry if I wish, ma'am!"

"Cousin Celia, you're back!" Barbara leaned over the upstairs banister. "What did you learn?"

"That Mr. Hutchinson has a solid alibi for the evening of Mr. Nash's murder," Celia replied. She would never tell Barbara the details of that alibi, however. "Furthermore, he is not likely to be the man Owen chased through the alleyway last Thursday. We have thus cleared him of all responsibility, Barbara."

"Thank goodness."

"Making me old," muttered Addie, taking Celia's wrap and brushing a hand over the hem, dusty from the street.

"What did you learn at the market today?" Celia asked her, seeking a more pleasant conversation.

"That Michael Knowles remains a grinning galoot," Addie said. "And he didna send me any flowers."

"Perhaps your admirer is Mr. Taylor, after all," said Barbara.

"Whisht, what a thought."

"I know it's him. I just know it!" said Barbara in a burst of high spirits, before hurrying back to her bedchamber.

Celia smiled at her cousin's unexpected exuberance. "She wants you to be happy, Addie."

"Does she now?" Her housekeeper stared at the spot where Barbara had been standing. "Och, ma'am, I near forgot about the telegram we received when I returned home from the market." Addie fished among her pockets and withdrew the item in question. "From that Mr. Smith, I think."

Celia took the telegram from her, tore open the envelope, and read.

"Weel? Out with it!"

Her gaze met her housekeeper's. "It has indeed come from Mr. Smith. From Mexico," she replied, the contents making her tremble. "He claims to have proof that Patrick is dead, and he will be shortly returning to the United States with the evidence."

"It's about time Mr. Davies has done you the favor of being verifiably deceased," she said, giving a brisk nod. She had never cared for Patrick. "Now you dinna have to file for divorce on grounds of abandonment."

Celia folded the telegram and tucked it into her skirt pocket. "Tell no one, Addie. Not even Barbara."

"Mr. Greaves might like to know," said Addie.

"I shall absolutely not tell him," she answered quickly. "I want to be positive, Addie. Utterly positive."

"So I'm not to bring out your mourning?"

What a question. "Not yet."

Because, knowing Patrick, being confirmed dead was no guarantee of the permanence of the condition.

After having supper and briefly reviewing the records of the next day's patients, Celia retreated to the quiet of her bedchamber. She sat at her dressing table, removed the telegram from her pocket, and unfolded it, spreading it flat upon the table's surface.

*Ah, Patrick. Could it be true?*

She opened the drawer and withdrew the small sandalwood box tucked in the far reaches. Brushing a finger over the pattern carved upon its surface, she recalled when her brother had gifted it to her upon her sixteenth birthday. The box had seemed such a grown-up present, the sort of item one would see on a lady's writing desk, and she had been thrilled. Celia turned the key that undid the lock and opened the box, releasing its spicy aroma. Inside were Patrick's letters. The ones he had sent when she was a nurse in Scutari, after he had been cleared to return to duty and released from the hospital. When he had been trying to woo her, her heart still raw from Harry's death. She caressed the plum-colored ribbon she had wound around the stack. There were others from when he'd served with the Irish Brigade in the Americans' civil war, and she had been studying at the Female Medical College of Pennsylvania and then volunteering at Satterlee Hospital. Halcyon days, when she had come to realize that she had chosen the right path in wanting to become a nurse. In the Crimea, she had done little more than feed soldiers or read them letters or wipe their fever-soaked foreheads. At Satterlee, however, she had discovered that there could be more to her chosen profession than merely providing companionship to patients.

And Patrick had encouraged her, his own miseries upon the battlefields of Fredericksburg and Chancellorsville only briefly mentioned. He had tried to understand her. For a while, at least.

Had he been jealous that she had been so happy? Had he suspected even as he trudged through mud and filth, lived with camp diseases and poor rations, saw compatriots die horrible deaths while he survived unscathed, that she was not going to be content to be a mere wife when they were reunited? He must have, for when he came home to Philadelphia, he was not the same man who had gone off to fight three years earlier, and the flashes of anger he'd only occasionally exhibited in England became regular outbursts. Addie had grown apprehensive of him, and Celia had retreated more and more to her work, where there was safety and sanity and predictability. Her friends claimed many of the soldiers returned from the war behaving similarly—somber, angry, reliving the fighting in their dreams, sometimes not truly waking from their nightmares though they moved among the living. Those same friends had insisted Patrick would get better. Celia knew he would not.

Because between them lay the bitter truth—Patrick Davies, he of the sparkling eyes and ready wit, had married a woman with a heart of stone. Perhaps if she had conceived a child, life would have been different. Perhaps she would have tried better to love him. But she had not conceived a child, and she did not try better to love him, though for so long she had feigned affection in hopes the emotion would take hold. But seedlings do not sprout on stone, and affection cannot readily be feigned. She had never blamed him for wanting to leave her.

But there was no joy in realizing she was finally free.

"Ma'am?"

Celia looked over her shoulder. How long had Addie been standing there, calling to her?

She stuffed the telegram into the box. "Yes, Addie?"

Addie's gaze flicked to the box, then back to Celia. She must be desperate to read the telegram herself, but Addie was too respectful to pry.

"The young woman down the road, the one who's newly wed, has scalded herself while cooking. Her husband's come to fetch you there and says hurry."

"I shall require my elm bark poultice, some strips of linen, the bottle of spirits, and my medical bag, Addie," she said.

With a nod Addie left, and Celia locked the box, tucking it into the drawer, out of sight and where the memories the box held could not chastise her.

The young woman, who'd recently come from some Eastern European country and spoke a limited amount of English, had bit her lip so hard while Celia tended to her burns that she'd made it bleed. The poultice would help the inflammation only so much, but the woman had been brave. Her husband had watched from the corner of their kitchen while Celia had labored in the light of a lone oil lamp, his scrutiny skeptical of Celia's abilities.

"Aiyee," his wife groaned between clenched teeth as Celia finished wrapping the scalds with clean linen. The boiling hot soup the woman had splashed on her arm had splattered all over the floor. Chunks of potatoes and stringy meat remained where they'd fallen, the scent of garlic and other spices heavy in the air, strong enough to mask smells of mold and bad plumbing. Work for the young woman once she'd stopped crying over her burns.

"I will leave you the poultice. Change the bandage in twelve hours and apply more at that time," Celia instructed the husband, who grunted a reply. *Please*, Celia thought, because she would not plead with a man who would not listen. "And send a message if the burns begin to suppurate."

"Thank you," the young woman murmured in her small voice, resting her bandaged arm atop the stained beige dress that covered the swell of her belly. Soon there would be a child who would probably be as dark eyed and dark haired as both of his parents. Another mouth to compete for the stew.

"You are most welcome," said Celia, who packed her supplies and made to depart.

The husband barked at his wife in their language, and the woman clambered to her feet.

"Please do not go to any trouble," Celia said to her. She did not want the injured—and very pregnant—young woman to feel obligated to formalities. "I shall find my way out."

It had grown dark by the time Celia descended the rickety stairs to the street, and fog blanketed the city again.

Gathering her skirts, she rushed along, her footfalls echoing dully off the buildings. Celia turned the corner at Vallejo and began the steep climb up the road. She scanned her surroundings. This section of the road was the darkest of all, the corner house currently uninhabited and the drapery of the next house always closed so tightly that not even the faintest light leaked through. To make matters worse, the grocer's on the opposite corner was also dark, the lantern that the owner's wife usually placed by the upstairs room's window unlit.

*Could I be more unfortunate?*

Her rapid exhalations clouded in the night air, and she hurried as best as she could, her portmanteau banging against her right knee. Not far. She really had not far to go. In fact, she was certain she could see the welcoming flare of the oil lamp in their parlor from here.

At first, she dismissed the footsteps she heard scurrying behind her. They came from a rat rooting in the trash someone had discarded, or a neighbor's dog on the loose. Or the cat she had seen the other evening. That was all. The furtiveness of the noise was nothing to fret over. Nonetheless, she increased her pace. The footsteps—they were footsteps, not the padding of paws—matched her tempo. *I should not have gone out alone. Not after Cliff House.* Celia glanced over her shoulder, hoping to see who was following her. But the fog was dense and becoming more so. She hoisted her skirts and began to run, turning for another look back. Just as she did, the toe of her boot caught on an uneven plank in the pavement.

She stumbled, lost her balance completely. As she fell, a gunshot shattered the quiet, and she screamed.

# Chapter 12

"Might not have even been trying to shoot you, ma'am," said Mr. Taylor, clutching his notebook and looking uncomfortable to be standing in Celia's entry hall with Addie scrutinizing him. "All sorts of unsavory types up here shooting off guns."

"I am aware of the character of my neighborhood, Mr. Taylor," said Celia.

She was grateful that Mr. Greaves' assistant had arrived so quickly upon receiving the message to come to the house. He apparently often worked late at the station and had been there to receive it. But Celia could not help wishing it had been Mr. Greaves, not Mr. Taylor, who had answered the summons. *He would scold me about wandering the streets at night with that concerned look in his eyes, and I would know that all would be right with the world.* Instead, Mr. Taylor appeared to be anticipating how angry his superior would become once he learned that someone had shot at Celia, and the anticipation was making him fidget.

"And even if he was firing at you, the bullet went mighty wide for thinking he meant to kill you, ma'am," the officer added, a notion that was not as comforting as he'd intended. "The railing it hit was a good five, six feet from where you'd been standing."

Mr. Taylor hadn't had any difficulty locating the bullet; the owner of the house whose banister it had splintered was happy to point out the damage once he'd noticed the police officer wandering around on the street near the man's home.

"Maybe he's merely a dreadful poor shot, Mr. Taylor," said Addie. "Just like the last time, ma'am. You getting shot at and all."

"I was not shot at last time, Addie," said Celia. Attacked in their kitchen by a knife-wielding killer, yes. Shot at, no. *I have come up in the world, it seems.*

"Dinna quibble, ma'am."

"Would you care for some tea, Mr. Taylor? It is never too late in the day for tea." Celia extended a hand toward the parlor. Addie had lit every lantern on the ground floor, and the parlor blazed with light. "You can come through to the dining room and sit with us for a while before you return to the station."

A blush spread across his cheeks. Addie took to noticing a spot of dirt on the hallway wallpaper.

"Wouldn't you prefer I go and catch the fellow who shot at you?" he asked.

"Do you honestly believe he is still loitering in the vicinity, Mr. Taylor? No, neither do I. So let us enjoy some tea, and perhaps some shortbread. Addie makes excellent shortbread." Besides, if she did not sit, she would soon collapse, the way her knees were shaking.

"Och, shortbread after some loony's attempted to kill you," muttered Addie. She bustled off toward the kitchen, likely happy to have an activity to take her mind off her mistress' troubles.

Mr. Taylor watched her depart. "The sooner I get to work looking for the fellow, the sooner we'll find him, ma'am, and get him off the street. So I probably shouldn't be staying for cookies and tea."

Celia glanced toward the parlor; Addie was out of earshot. "Which of our suspects do you think it was, Mr. Taylor?" she asked. "Not Mr. Martin, who is bedridden and recovering from his attack of angina."

"He coulda paid somebody to take a shot at you, ma'am."

"A distinct possibility," she said. "But the shooter was also not Mr. Hutchinson, who is still in Oakland, I presume."

"Should still be. Mr. Greaves telegraphed the Oakland police to let Officer Mullahey know he didn't need to bring Mr. Hutchinson in, after all."

Thank goodness Grace and Jane no longer had to worry about Frank being arrested.

"But we both gotta remember, ma'am, that we don't know if this incident has anything to do with our investigation of Mr. Nash's murder," added Mr. Taylor.

"You're suggesting that one of my neighbors has taken a sudden, strong dislike to me?"

She was feeling short-tempered and allowing it to show. Her aunt would be most displeased with her. *It is ill-bred for ladies to be peevish, Cecilia. One must remain serene in all circumstances . . .*

Celia wondered if not maintaining her serenity could be excused in this situation.

Looking uncertain, Mr. Taylor scratched his neck with the

edge of his notebook. "I'll find out what all of our suspects were doing tonight."

"Thank you, Mr. Taylor. And please forgive my churlishness."

"Um . . . sure. Not a problem." He glanced longingly toward the parlor and sighed.

"Shall I tell Addie you regret not being able to stay and enjoy her wonderful shortbread?" Celia asked.

"Um . . ." His cheeks turned pinker. "If you would, ma'am."

Did his discomfort imply he *was* Addie's admirer or was *not*? "Mr. Taylor, have you been sending flowers to my housekeeper, by any chance?"

He blinked at her. "What's that?"

"Flowers. Notes. Left on the doorstep for Addie."

"I . . . Somebody's courting Ad . . . Miss Ferguson?"

*And apparently that someone is not you.* "Indeed. Another mystery, Mr. Taylor."

"I guess so," he said, looking as though he did not care for this mystery, either. *Hope yet, Addie.* "I'll be going, then. Oh, and I'm pretty sure Mr. Greaves would like you to stay in your house until this fellow's caught."

Which she might do, if not for the small problem of the meeting she had arranged with Katie Lehane tomorrow. She felt a trifle guilty over keeping her plans from Mr. Greaves, but not enough to let him know, even after what had just occurred. If she was honest with herself, she was looking forward to besting his efforts to find the killer.

"If a patient of mine sends for me," she said, "I will have to go."

"I thought you'd say that." He gave his good-byes, tucked away his notebook, and bolted for the door.

As Celia shut it behind him, she heard a rustling at the top of the stairs. Barbara, her long black braid hanging down over her robe, stood on the landing.

"Are they coming here next? To take another shot at you, and maybe me?" she asked. "I'd hoped you'd be finished with this, since Mr. Hutchinson has been cleared. Jane Hutchinson hasn't asked you to do more."

"I must not be finished, since someone elected to fire a gun at me, Barbara."

Her cousin clattered down the stairs, her robe and nightgown held high above her feet. "I want this to stop, Cousin. I'm tired of being afraid. I want to be safe."

Her voice broke, and Celia gathered her cousin in her arms, letting her cry upon her shoulder. Where, though, was safe for a half-Chinese girl and her husbandless guardian?

"This will all be over soon, sweetheart." She stroked a hand down her cousin's thick, soft hair to where the braid twined at the nape of her neck. "I promise."

"But you can't promise." Barbara pulled out of Celia's grasp. The severe set of her expression should have been the first warning of the salvo that was immediately to follow. "Maybe you should move."

*I am not hearing this . . .* "Excuse me, Barbara?"

"I said, you should move."

"I cannot. I am your guardian. Your father left you in my care until you come of age."

"I'm going to talk to my father's lawyer. He'll straighten this out and you'll see."

"Barbara . . ." Celia reached for her, but she jerked away and stormed up the stairs. The slam of her bedchamber door reverberated through the house.

"Weel," said Addie from the parlor doorway, the lacquered tea tray in her hands. "Where will we go now?"

"She will be fine in the morning and full of apologies, mark my words."

Addie's only reply was an expressive roll of her eyes.

"How close did the bullet come to striking her?" Nick asked Taylor as they walked along Dupont Street the next morning.

Nick was always amazed by his assistant's ability to find him, especially considering how vague he'd been about his destination when Mrs. Jewett had tried to pry it out of him a half hour earlier. Given the news Taylor had brought, Nick might've preferred he'd been less successful.

"Five or six feet, if I had to guess," Taylor answered, dodging the broom of a storekeeper out sweeping the sidewalk before his business opened. "She's lucky she tripped and fell. But I let her believe he didn't mean to hit her."

"Maybe he didn't."

Taylor looked over at him as they waited at the intersection. "D'you think so, sir?"

"No, Taylor. I don't think so. That woman . . . I told Mrs. Davies she'd get in trouble," Nick said, dashing across the street. He didn't like being right.

*Danger finds her like a bloodhound tracks a scent.*

"Maybe it *was* a random shot, sir . . . Mr. Greaves," said Taylor, looking hopeful he'd agree.

"And maybe Norton really is the emperor of the United States," Nick replied. "Did you tell her not to leave the house?"

"Um . . ." Taylor gave him a sideways glance. "I tried."

"And let me guess, she gave some reason why she wouldn't comply."

"She's mighty stubborn, sir."

Wasn't that the truth. "Go talk to the folks in her neighborhood and find out if anybody saw anything. We need to find who it was who shot at her." Before there was a next time and the person didn't miss.

"I'm headed there to do that," said Taylor. "Hey, what's this business I hear about some fella sending love notes to that housekeeper of hers?"

Nick lifted an eyebrow. "I thought you weren't interested in Addie Ferguson, Taylor. Something about the fact she likes to visit astrologers?"

Taylor cleared his throat and changed the subject. "By the way, sir, the captain's heard about Nash's watch being found on Matthews' body. Says he's glad we're near to wrapping up the case."

"Glad he thinks we are." At least Eagan was no longer interested in seeing Cassidy accused of the crime. "I'll see you later at the station, Taylor. I'm off to talk to the owner of that dapple gray horse."

One of the beat cops had told Taylor about a horse fitting the description Mrs. Davies had provided. It belonged to a driver who usually waited at the hack stands around Union Square. Not far at all from where Martin—and Russell—lived.

Nick set out for Union Square. It was a short walk and a pleasant one on a morning like this. The day had dawned sunny, last night's fog lifting earlier than usual, and a crisp breeze blew down off the western hills. A seagull swirled above the buildings, enjoying the view below as the city sprung to life. Somewhere distant, a manufactory whistle sounded the day's work shift, and the Central Railroad horsecar clattered along the rails, laborers clinging to the railings. Across the way, a jeweler unrolled the awning above his store windows and tipped his hat to a woman who'd paused to admire his goods. All the trappings of civility and prosperity. But Nick was always aware that outer appearances could hide any number of vices. Just like a bespoke suit and a gold watch could conceal a criminal beneath.

Nick arrived to find Union Square quiet and empty, except for an elderly man feeding pigeons. A quick search of the encircling roads located the horse he was looking for. Luck was with him today, it appeared.

He strolled over to the waiting carriage, the black-maned dapple gray nosing its feed bag and the driver slouched on his seat, reading a newspaper.

The man perked when he heard Nick approach, and he dropped the newspaper to the floorboard. "Where you need to go?"

Nick showed his badge, which caused the fellow to scan the other nearby drivers. There weren't many—Union Square never had the same number of hacks as the streets surrounding the Plaza—and the few there were had their noses in their newspapers, too, not even noticing Nick.

"I didn't do anything wrong!" he protested. "He's lying if he says I did!"

*Well, that's an interesting comment,* thought Nick, eyeing the fellow. "I just want to ask you some questions. First off, do you own this carriage?"

"I rent it."

"What about a wagon?"

The other man cursed. "I told you he's lying! I had every

right to borrow that wagon, and I even returned it earlier than I said I was goin' to, so he ain't got no complaints."

"This was last Thursday night, correct? The night you made use of the wagon?"

The driver narrowed his eyes. "Wait. You're not here because the runt at the livery complained about me?"

"Not today," answered Nick. "I want to know about a man you picked up last week at an alleyway off Pine. With that wagon you borrowed. Who was he?"

A tremor started on one eyelid. "I don't know what you're talking about, Officer."

"I think you do. I know somebody who saw you." Nick reached out to scratch the horse between its ears, straightening the gray's forelock over the harness browband. "Listen, if you tell me the truth, I won't think up what I might have to charge you with, okay? So . . . Thursday night. The time would have been between nine and ten in the evening."

The driver licked his lips. "Let's see . . ." As if tempted to grab them and drive off, he glanced toward the reins, which were tied around the rail. Nick seized the harness cheekpiece to ward off the idea. "Okay. Okay. I'll tell you. The stable boy got a note from a customer looking for a wagon and driver for the evening. Urgent-like. And there would be five dollars in it for the man who got to the corner of Montgomery and Pine the soonest. I knew where to find a wagon, and I put the licks on and got there first. Didn't know who I was looking for, but I figured he'd find me. And he did."

"Then what?"

"I was to wait for him along Pine. He said until nine thirty. If I didn't see him by then, I was to leave. I argued with him about the five dollars he'd promised, and he gave me two to keep me quiet until later," the driver said. "I wasn't waiting there long, though, when he come down the alleyway, makin' tracks."

"Did you get his name?" Nick asked.

"I don't usually have such polite conversation with my fares as to get around to learnin' their names."

"Where did you take him?"

"Sutter and Powell," the driver said. "He told me to leave him there. He gave me the rest of the money, so what did I care where he wanted to be left off? For five dollars, I woulda taken him to the Mission and back if he'd asked."

Sutter and Powell was near enough to Martin's house. "And yesterday you dropped off a woman near that same location?" Celia Davies had told him she'd seen the dapple gray and this hack pulling away after bringing Martin's housekeeper.

The driver considered the sky. "Think so."

"Can you describe the man for me?"

He shook his head. "Didn't get much of a look. It was awful foggy that night, and he kept covered up. Like he didn't want to be recognized."

"Anything. General impression."

"Bony. Educated voice. Used to giving orders."

Which sounded precisely like Jasper Martin.

*C*elia leaned against the balustrade surrounding the porch, the chill of the morning's crisp breeze seeping through her shawl. The half-remembered perfume her mother used to wear lifted from its threads, and Celia longed for a woman she could barely recall. A shadow. A scent.

She had no family left, save for Barbara and Addie. *Plus*

*Owen*, she mentally added with a weary smile. And now Barbara, who had remained barricaded behind her bedchamber door since last night, wanted to have Celia removed as her guardian. Celia doubted her cousin would succeed, but their relationship had been rocky from the start. *She would forgive me if I would not insist upon inserting myself in Mr. Greaves' investigations.* But Celia could not stop now; she would see this inquiry through to its end.

Celia noticed Joaquin's mother out on her porch darning, a scowl on her face. And at the house a few doors down, the owner shot Celia a black look as he patched the bullet hole in his stair railing. If she had not screamed last night and drawn his attention—as well as the attention of nearly the entire street—he might not have known she'd been the cause of the damage.

Soon it would be more than merely Barbara who wished she would remove herself from this house.

The bells of Saint Francis rang out the top of the hour, and Celia had started to turn to go back into the house, when she spotted a boy trotting up the road.

"There you are, ma'am!" Owen called out. He scrambled up the front steps with a grin.

"Owen, my goodness. How have you been?" she asked.

She'd never had a chance to warn him about Captain Eagan's threat to have Owen accused of killing Mr. Nash. However, it seemed he'd kept out of trouble.

"Bored. Ain't got much to do," he said, plopping onto one of the cane-seated porch chairs.

"I do wish I had better news about your employment with Mr. Hutchinson's crew. He will not consider reinstating you until this fuss has subsided."

"That's what I heard, ma'am," he said. "Just got back from there. All kinds of excitement over Mr. Martin's angy. . . . anga . . ."

"Angina," she supplied. "Many folks refer to it as 'disease of the heart.'"

"Yep. That," said Owen. "You sure do know a bunch, don't you, ma'am?"

"I have been fortunate to enjoy an excellent education, Owen." She slid him a glance. "Speaking of an education, how are you coming with that book I lent you?"

"That Mr. Dickens is sorta hard to understand."

"Good effort is eventually rewarded, Owen."

"I s'pose."

Celia smiled and let her gaze wander along the street again. Joaquin's mother finished darning the socks, frowned at Celia, and stomped back into her house.

"What's that about, ma'am?" Owen asked. "Don't she like you now?"

"I caused a bit of a fuss last evening, Owen. Someone shot at me."

He let out a long whistle. "One of your neighbors? That woman over there looks mad enough!"

"I do not believe so." She had spent the early morning hours considering each of her neighbors in turn, selecting and then discarding every one as the person who had shot at her last evening. The gunman *had* to be someone involved in Mr. Nash's murder. It was all that made sense.

"Ma'am?" Owen asked, squinting at her.

"I am merely contemplating how excessively exciting my life can be, Owen. I would not mind being bored myself for a change

NO PITY for the DEAD

of pace," she said. "Since you are here, would you like a quick bite to eat?"

"I've always got time for Addie's cooking," he said, grinning. "But I gotta tell you why I came by. It's about something that happened this morning. At work."

"And what is that?"

He glanced around, searching for eavesdroppers. For once, Angelo was not playing on the Cascarinos' porch. The fact that Celia could hear Mrs. Cascarino shouting inside the house suggested her youngest son's location. "Something that happened with Eddie."

"Eddie?"

"He's the kid who works at the stationer's next door," he explained. "He came 'round the office this morning, slinking near the back door. Asking where the bosses were 'cuz he needed to talk to one of them about 'the note he delivered.'"

"'The note he delivered'?"

Owen eyed her as though wondering how she could have forgotten such an important item. "That one that Nash got," he said. "The one telling him to meet his killer. Remember?"

"I do remember quite well, Owen, but how do you know about that note?" She thought Mr. Greaves had attempted to suppress that piece of information.

"Heard about it from one of the fellas," Owen explained. "After Dan and I found the body, somebody claiming to be from a newspaper came asking questions about the note the killer sent to his victim, of course."

*Of course.* "And this Eddie specifically told you that he had delivered that particular note to Mr. Nash."

"Not exactly." Owen crinkled his nose and scuffed the toe of one dirty boot across the planks of the porch, his surety deflating like a soufflé too long out of the oven. "I did ask him this morning what he meant. I said, 'What note?' but he wouldn't tell me. All he said was 'Wouldn't you like to know,' like a smart aleck. He does that all the time."

For a moment, Owen seemed prepared to spit to show his disgust, but he glanced at Celia and stopped himself. "But it's got to be the note Mr. Nash was sent the day he was killed. Don't you think, ma'am?"

"I am not certain what I think, Owen." Except that if someone at Martin and Company had asked Eddie to deliver that particular note, Celia's request that Katie observe the men working there seemed all the more justified. "Although I do think you would make a good detective."

Owen perked up, looking pleased. "You do?" he asked. "Mr. Greaves says it's a rotten job, though."

"Mr. Greaves likely only thinks that when events are going badly," said Celia. "But you do not know who gave Eddie that note to deliver?"

"Sorry, ma'am. He wouldn't tell me that, either."

"Then what happened?" she asked.

"I told Eddie that Mr. Martin was poorly and hadn't come to the office and that Mr. Russell wasn't in yet and Mr. Hutchinson was away, too," he said. "Eddie got hopping mad about that, and he stomped off. But he didn't get far before Rob spotted him and came running out into the yard, wanting to pick a fight over something. Them two are always fighting, so it wasn't the first time. Mr. Kelly had to break it up."

"Does Eddie or Rob get extremely red faced when they're angry, Owen?"

"Can't say I've ever noticed."

Neither of them was likely to be the fellow at Burke's, then. "Anything else?"

Owen cast around another glance and leaned over his knees to whisper conspiratorially. "Anyways, it was when Mr. Kelly dragged Eddie away that I overheard Eddie mentioning Mr. Nash to him. Clear as could be. And Mr. Kelly told Eddie to keep his nose out of other fellas' business. Not that Eddie'll ever stop doing that," said Owen. "So I'll bet you anything Eddie took that note to Mr. Nash! Don't you think, Mrs. Davies?"

"I do think so, Owen," she said. "You have done very well, and I shall inform Mr. Greaves. I presume he or Mr. Taylor can find Eddie at his place of employment today?"

"He sure can," said Owen. His gaze slid toward the front door, and he licked his lips.

"Tell Addie to make you some breakfast."

He hopped up from the chair. "Thanks again, ma'am," he said, and ran inside without any further prodding.

Celia followed him inside and went into her office to hastily compose a message for Mr. Greaves.

*I have learned who delivered the note to Virgil Nash that summoned him to meet his killer.*

Her pen hovered over the sheet of paper. Even if they learned that Eddie had delivered a message to Mr. Nash, there remained no certainty it was *the* note. She inserted "may have" between "who" and "delivered." However, it appeared that Eddie had become convinced of the message's importance. Perhaps he had opened it and read it, although he had waited a long time to act upon his knowledge. It was not always easy to understand people's behavior.

She gave the location of the shop where Eddie could be found and sealed the note. Mr. Greaves might learn everything they needed to know from the boy or nothing at all. But she felt they were drawing much closer to finally learning the identity of Virgil Nash's killer.

Celia wiped the pen nib and returned it to its holder, then closed the lid on the glass inkwell. Or *were* they any closer? After all, what had she learned from Owen? Only that someone at Martin and Company had given Eddie a note to deliver to Virgil Nash the day he died. And that Owen had never seen Eddie or Rob get red faced.

Celia considered her appointment book, open to the day's list of patients. She had so much work to do once she returned from meeting Katie. She should simply attend to her patients rather than continue to pry.

*But I cannot give up.* After all, someone had tried to shoot her last night. But who?

"Gad!"

"Ma'am?" Addie asked from the doorway where she stood. "There's been a message from Mrs. Hutchinson. She'd like you to visit her today."

"Oh, Addie, I am knotted up in a murder investigation when I should be taking care of my patients and comforting my friends. *They* are my priority, not racking my brains over who might have killed Virgil Nash and getting nowhere."

"But, ma'am, some loony tried to kill you last night. 'Tis sadly understandable you wish to find him and stop him."

{ 266 }

"Yet every piece of information I receive confuses me all the more as to who that loony might be," Celia said, considering the note to Mr. Greaves that sat folded upon her desk.

"You ken it must be the man who killed that Mr. Nash. And now he's after you!"

"What was it Officer Taylor once told us? That sometimes killers like to spy on their victim's funeral? Maybe this man will be at Mr. Nash's funeral." And if she attended, she might spot him, because he would be guilty-looking upon seeing her. Or red faced, perhaps. "Addie, I believe I need the black ribbons for my bonnet."

"What's that?"

"The black ribbons," she repeated.

If Katie failed to identify any of the men at Martin and Company, Celia should still be able to arrive at Virgil Nash's church service long before it got under way. As she recalled from the mention in yesterday's newspaper, it was scheduled for noon at the Church of the Advent. Surprisingly, the article had also mentioned that his remains had been lying there all of this morning for friends and acquaintances from far and near to pay their respects. There would be no visage to gaze upon, given the condition of the corpse, however. As it was, if the coffin was not well sealed, the stench would be unbearable.

"You mean to go to the man's funeral, ma'am?" asked Addie, aghast. "To investigate?"

"Indeed, because everyone who was closely acquainted with Virgil Nash should be in attendance. It is possible some might have known Mr. Nash and his brother in Virginia City. Some might even recall the man who killed Silas Nash and be able to provide a description." One that matched Katie's.

"You canna take to interrogating mourners. 'Tisn't right!"

"There is a risk my actions will eliminate any chance Mrs. Nash shall invite me for tea in the future, is there not, Addie?" Celia asked teasingly.

"Och, get on with you! And if they toss you onto the street, I'll nae be surprised!"

*I shall not be surprised, either.*

She handed Addie the folded piece of paper. "Give this to Owen. I need him to take it to either Mr. Greaves or Mr. Taylor. It contains information about a note sent to Mr. Nash the day he was killed."

Addie tucked the message into her skirt pocket.

"I also need you to send a message to Jane that I will come to her house as soon as I'm able." Celia closed her appointment book and stood. "And please tell the patient I am expecting at twelve that I cannot see her today after all. Hopefully she will not lose her temper with you this time as she did before. And have Barbara speak with my patient expected at one, should I not return by then. It is a simple follow-up evaluation, which she can handle."

"'Tis unchancy to go to that funeral, ma'am. The killer might be there."

Which was the very reason she was going. "If I discover his identity, I shall inform the police immediately," she said. "Oh, and Addie, perhaps you should say nothing to Barbara about my specific plans for the day. Merely say that I have gone out. Agreed?"

"Aye. You can be certain I'll nae tell Miss Barbara you've gone to your doom!"

The coffeehouse across from the offices of Martin and Company had large windows that permitted sunlight to stream into the main room and glint off silverware and the polished wood floor. When Celia stepped through the door, the hum of conversation dipped. The reason was plain—she was the only woman among the handful of men slurping coffee and catching up on news. It was not improper for a woman to enter a coffee-house, but those who did were unlikely to be wearing mourning attire.

The proprietor, a broad-faced man with a gleaming white apron tied over his clothing, rushed up to her. "Can I help you, ma'am?"

"I was expecting to meet a friend here." Celia scanned the coffeehouse again, even though the space was not so large that she would have missed seeing Katie, not with the girl's vibrant red hair and boisterous nature to mark her out. Perhaps she had decided not to wait, although Celia was not that tardy, and Katie was not the sort to be impatient. However, it was possible the proprietor had deduced the girl's occupation and tossed her onto the street. "She has red hair and is quite lovely. Has she already departed?"

"Nobody who looks like that has been here, ma'am. But you're welcome to sit and wait for her," he said, raising a hand to whisper behind it. "Don't worry about the men in here. It's the usual crowd and they're no more dangerous than a pit of fangless snakes."

*An interesting comparison,* she thought. "While I am wait-ing, I would like a cup of coffee, if you will."

"Absolutely, ma'am."

Celia took a seat at a window-side table, feeling the eyes of every male customer upon her. She half turned her head and caught one of them staring at her; when she met his gaze, he grinned, revealing teeth stained by tobacco.

The proprietor delivered her coffee, and Celia clutched the

warm cup while she looked out the window. What she supposed was the typical traffic rumbled past, accompanied by a host of pedestrians—laborers, businessmen, matrons, servants, Chinese laundry boys. She did have a good view of Martin and Company from this vantage point, along with the stationer's next door. A customer emerged, attended by a lad toting wrapped purchases. As she watched them walk off down the street, Celia wondered if the boy was Eddie. If so, she'd missed the opportunity to question him herself.

Her fellow patrons eventually lost interest in her, and the coffee cooled until she did not wish to drink it any longer. It was now half past eleven, according to her Ellery watch, and Celia concluded that Katie would not be coming. She could think of several possible explanations, most of which she did not like.

*Please merely have forgotten that you had agreed to meet me here, Katie.*

Celia rose and left payment upon the table. "Thank you," she said to the proprietor, and swept out onto the street. She surveyed the length of the road one last time before rushing to catch the streetcar heading south toward the church.

Most likely, Katie had simply changed her mind. When Celia had suggested the meeting yesterday, she had not looked keen on the idea. Perhaps she had decided it was not in her best interest to endanger herself by identifying murderers. Celia was beginning to think she was right.

# Chapter 13

The woman who answered Jasper Martin's door showed Nick to a room at the rear of the house. Besides the sweet aroma of pipe tobacco, Nick could smell linseed oil and turpentine, and the scent of roses through the open window currently providing a sunny view of the back garden.

"Policeman to see you, Mr. Martin," the woman droned to her employer. Martin was reading a newspaper—the *Mercantile Gazette*, it looked like—as he sat in a chair with his legs stretched out on an ottoman, a rug tossed over them.

The thick carpeting underfoot had muffled their footsteps, and Martin looked over, startled from his concentration on his newspaper. His domestic hoofed it before Martin had a chance to tell her to take Nick back to where she'd found him.

"Ah, Mr. Greaves. Seems early in the day for a visit by a

detective." He folded his paper and tossed it onto a nearby table. "I also suspect my doctor would not approve of my entertaining a police officer. But I find myself curious. Has another of Mr. Hutchinson's workers been found dead?"

Nick dragged his hat from his head. "The night Nash's body was found in the cellar, you were observed running down an alley behind your offices, Mr. Martin."

"Now I definitely know Johnston wouldn't want me to talk to you about something like that."

Johnston must be his doctor. "Can you explain your actions that night?"

"I don't think I can, Detective, because I don't recall such an event." He turned to smile at a yellow songbird that trilled in an ornate cage nearby. When he turned back to Nick, he was still smiling, but there wasn't any way the expression was genuine. "It doesn't sound like something I would do. There's clearly been a mistake."

"The driver of the wagon waiting for you thinks otherwise."

"The man's wrong."

"Furthermore," Nick continued, "just a few minutes earlier, other witnesses encountered a man who'd been attempting to remove Mr. Nash's body from your office basement. They chased him out of the building and down the alleyway. This man climbed into the wagon I've mentioned and was left off at the corner just a couple dozen yards from your house here."

The bird stopped singing. Maybe it could sense the tension in the room, which would make it a very intelligent bird.

If Martin had broken even a drop of sweat, Nick couldn't tell. "I went by that evening to make sure the offices had been locked. I don't trust Mr. Hutchinson's workers when they've been left with the key."

*He's going to confess,* thought Nick. He wished Taylor were with him to take notes.

"When I went around to the back, I found the rear door wide-open. Furious, I went inside to see if anything had been stolen. Good thing I did. The carpenters had left a pile of wood scraps behind, when they know they're supposed to remove all their rubbish. I had one of the neighborhood boys take a message to the stable to bring a wagon to haul the refuse away. The one that was waiting for me at the end of the alley."

"At that hour?" asked Nick. Martin's story sounded like bunkum to him.

"Why wait until the morning?"

"Most folks would."

"That's not how my business operates," said Martin. "So you see, there was an innocent explanation for the wagon, Detective Greaves."

"Then what's your innocent explanation for why you were seen running down the alleyway and jumping on board it?"

"I found a body," Martin quipped, pausing to remove his watch from its pocket. After checking the time, he started to snap the lid open and shut repeatedly. As if in response, the little bird in the cage hopped from one perch to another, a flitting blur of yellow. "While I waited for the wagon to arrive, I went back inside the building and noticed light coming from the cellar. A lantern had been left burning. And the stink down there was overwhelming; just about knocked me backward. That was when I saw what remained of Virgil Nash. I didn't at first realize it was Virgil, of course."

"And you decided to dig him up to get rid of the evidence."

"No, Detective. Despite the smell, I wanted to know who it was. That's not a crime, is it?"

Nick didn't respond; he'd only cuss at Martin if he did.

"So I began digging," Martin continued. "Conveniently, the men who'd been working down there had left their shovels behind. It wasn't easy work, let me tell you. And then I heard voices and footsteps coming from upstairs. I didn't know who they were or what they wanted, but I knew I didn't want them to find me, so I left what I was doing and took the back stairs to the second-floor offices. I hoped they'd go away, and I could leave without being detected. Interestingly, I discovered it was simply a boy and Mrs. Davies—I'd met her at a party Mrs. Hutchinson hosted some time ago—and they had no intention of going away. They heard me, and I had no choice but to flee. In hindsight, I realized that was stupid, since I had every right to be there and *they* were the interlopers. I should've had them arrested for trespassing."

The clicking of the watch lid was setting Nick's teeth on edge.

"Did you kill Virgil Nash, Mr. Martin?" Nick asked. "Or maybe you had him killed? You were overheard saying you wished he were dead. And you sent him threatening notes."

Martin chuckled. "Those weren't my idea."

"One of your partners?"

"Why assign blame when the subject is deceased?"

*Just some fellows having fun. How amusing.* "Did you kill Nash?"

"No, Detective. As much as I wished Nash would go away permanently, I would never kill him—or have him killed—then bury him in my place of business and risk having him found there," he replied, his words as smooth as old bourbon. "Haven't you considered that my partners and I were well aware that men were scheduled to work in the cellar? How can you possibly think any of us are responsible? Only a fool would bury a body on his own premises when he knows others would soon discover it."

A fool or a very clever man who wanted to seem innocent.

"By the way, corroborating the story you told me earlier, Jean-Pierre has claimed you were eating at his restaurant until late Thursday evening. Guess you weren't."

"He said that, did he?" Martin asked. "Then I suppose I regret my impulse to own up to my role in this escapade."

Nick contemplated Jasper Martin. He didn't care for men like him, men whose success made them confident that the rules didn't apply to them. In this city, they were as thick as a blanket of cottonwood fluff on a June day; everywhere you walked, you stepped on one.

"How about this question," said Nick. "Did you push Mrs. Davies over the wall at Cliff House, afraid she'd spotted you running off on Thursday night?"

"I had no reason to be worried about what she'd seen. Although thanks to her visit yesterday, I know she has also come to the same, wrong conclusion as you have. Poor woman. You should tell her to keep out of police business."

Nick had lost track of how many times he'd tried to tell her just that.

"I've got one more question for you, Mr. Martin. Then I'll leave you to your recovery." Nick ran the brim of his hat through his fingers. "Where were you last night?"

"And why are you asking me that?"

"Somebody shot at Mrs. Davies." It wasn't news; the story was already in the papers.

"Looks like someone's trying to kill her. She should be more careful." Martin returned his watch to its pocket. "I was here, of course, Detective. Enjoying my bed rest, my dutiful housekeeper paid to stay by my side all night. You can ask her all about it. On your way out."

Jasper Martin retrieved his newspaper and, with a jerk of his wrists, snapped it open and resumed reading.

The Church of the Advent stood south of Market, near manufactories and working men's lodgings, close enough to the gas works that the stench might reach the pews, should the wind shift. A neighborhood that residents of the Nashes' status would normally seek to avoid. Celia could not decide if the choice marked them as more tolerant of the rougher classes or merely less willing to take a carriage across town to a church in the more genteel areas along Stockton or near Union Square.

The tall steeple, overtopped by the lantern that brought to mind a crown, came into view. A hearse from the undertaker's stood arrayed in black at the foot of the steps, the horses' heads weighed down beneath elaborate trappings. Several carriages formed a line along Howard Street, liveried drivers waiting their turn to move forward. A steady stream of mourners climbed the church's front steps, many greeting one another, a convivial sea of dark clothing, black ribbons flapping in the wind.

It was an even greater crowd than she'd expected for a man who, according to Katie, had few friends.

"Stop here," cried Celia, pounding on the roof of the hack.

She needed to get out now if she was to scrutinize the remaining arrivals and observe any guilty looks on guilty faces.

The hack came to such a sudden halt, she was nearly thrown from her seat. The driver opened the door, and she scrambled down.

"There is no need to wait for me," she told him, handing him his fare. "I shall fetch a horsecar for my return."

"Suit yourself," he said, shutting the door and climbing back onto his bench.

Celia hurried across the road and found a spot near the front of the crowd where she could easily see and be seen by those disembarking from conveyances. She attempted to make eye contact with every man as he arrived. Some smiled—one fellow even winked—but others hustled forward, disliking the bold attention of a strange woman that caused them to glance at their wives to see if they'd taken note. None of the men, however, looked remotely guilt-ridden.

"Is that it, then?" someone in the crowd asked his companion as the arrivals thinned and finally dwindled to nothing. "I was expecting somebody important."

"The Emp's here," the companion said.

"I meant somebody *really* important. Not a crackbrain who's convinced he's the emperor of the United States."

Celia glanced back to see if she could spot the people having the conversation.

"Who important liked Nash? My brother knows a fella who knew him in Virginia City," said the one man. "According to him, Nash was a real swindler."

"Aren't they all?" his friend asked, and they walked off.

*Aren't they all.*

Celia looked up at the church. The rightmost of the double front doors remained open; perhaps she could find a seat and continue her observation of the attendees.

She climbed the short flight of front steps and entered the narthex. A distinguished-looking man halted her before she could charge through the vestibule doors and into the nave.

"The service is about to begin," he said to her, shifting to block her entrance. As though to underscore his statement, the church bells began to ring.

Celia peered around his shoulder. He was taller than she by half a head, which made the attempt difficult. Beneath the peaked ceiling painted light blue, well-dressed mourners chatted in hushed whispers, and Mr. Nash's casket waited at the head of the aisle. Off to one side, she thought she spotted the feathered top hat and tattered uniform of Emperor Norton. To the other side, a massive bouquet of white flowers filled a corner.

The man noted the direction of her gaze. "Those came from Levi Strauss," he said with some pride. "But you still can't go in. I don't want my sister disturbed by a late arrival."

An usher came down the aisle and shut the doors in Celia's face, deepening the shadows in the narthex.

"I am so terribly sorry for arriving late." Celia smiled her apologies at the man, who was handsome, with his even features. She wondered if his sister, Mrs. Nash, was also handsome. Celia was familiar with the woman's beautiful roses, but she had never seen Mrs. Nash in person. "Perhaps you will not mind if I stand here and wait for the service to conclude, in order to extend my condolences to your sister at that time."

He squinted at her. "I don't believe I've seen you before. Do I know you?"

"Mrs. Nash and I are . . . distant acquaintances." *Lying in the house of God, Cecilia.* Whatever would her aunt think? *Sinful.* That would be her response. "But I held her husband in high regard and wished to show my respects."

"I'll let Alice know."

"Thank you so much." Celia smiled again. A man would not be rude to a woman who was smiling at him, would he? "Your sister must be very distressed that the police have failed to identify her husband's murderer. I had heard it suggested that the person who had killed his brother in Virginia City is also responsible for his death. How dreadful!"

"Where did you hear that?"

"Oh my. I do not precisely recall." Celia rested her fingertips on his forearm with a bit of coy forwardness. Jane would laugh to see Celia practicing feminine wiles, were she here to observe her actions. However, between Frank's open feud with Virgil Nash and Jane's request that Celia visit today, she knew the Hutchinsons would not be among the mourners. "But do you think it could be so? Did your brother-in-law ever tell you or Mrs. Nash that he had seen that man in town?"

"Virgil was always claiming—" He clapped shut his mouth and scowled at her.

"Claiming what?" she asked. "Claiming that he had seen the man, but you no longer believed him?"

"You know what, ma'am? I think it's time for you to go." Mrs. Nash's brother grabbed Celia's elbow and tugged her toward the front doors.

"Unhand me! This is outrageous!"

Disregarding her protests, he maneuvered her all the way outside onto the porch, raising a murmur among the folks lingering

on the pavement. "And I suggest you send my sister a note express-
ing your sympathy."

His grip pinched her skin, and she shook him off. "I shall
do that."

She looked back at the dark recesses of the narthex and
the closed church doors beyond. And had a sudden recollection
of the comment Jane had made at Cliff House.

*They'd known each other for years. All the way back to Nevada . . .*

"May I ask if Mr. Strauss happens to be in attendance along
with his flowers?" she asked.

Mrs. Nash's brother—who had not offered his name, as
would have been proper—looked astonished by the suggestion.
"Him inside an Episcopal church?"

A revealing comment.

And all the answer she required.


"*H*er note says that this kid delivered the message to Nash.
The one that set up the meeting the night he died," said
Taylor, trailing Nick into the detectives' office. He scouted for a
cigar among his pockets, found one along with a match.

"No, Taylor, it says he 'may have.' Not exactly the same thing."
He tossed the note from Mrs. Davies onto his desk. "Any update
on who it was that shot at Mrs. Davies last night?"

"Nobody around Mrs. Davies' place wants to talk. Seems
they don't like cops." His assistant struck the match against the
floor and lit the cigar. "A Mexican fella down on the corner
claims it isn't uncommon for drunks to fire their guns around
there. Not that long ago somebody had a window shot out. Of
course, some of the folks I tried to talk to don't speak much

English, so I'm not positive they understood what I was asking."

Nick rolled his chair back from the desk, the casters squealing, and sat. "I'm not too surprised they don't want to talk."

"It's also plain as day Mrs. Davies' neighbors aren't too happy with her. Don't like the patients she attracts to her clinic. Fallen women and all that, sir."

"Although I suspect their unhappiness doesn't stop them from making use of her free services when the need arises."

"Suppose not," said Taylor. "What'd you learn at Martin's this morning, sir?"

Nick related Martin's explanation for running through that alleyway. "A tidy little story, Taylor."

"He's a pretty smart man, sir . . . Mr. Greaves. He's had time to think up an account that we'd swallow."

"It's always possible, though, that his account is true," said Nick. He scowled at an ant crawling across his desk and crushed it with his thumb. "You sure about Frank's workers? Could've been one of them who had Eddie take that note to Virgil Nash. Bartlett has a record. And no good explanation for his actions the night Nash was killed."

"What about Russell, sir? Just because he claims he was at some opium den the night Nash was killed don't mean he was."

"He's still on the list of suspects, Taylor. But back to Bartlett . . . The guard at the Golden Hare recognized his name. Which means he's a customer, if not a regular enough one for the guard to know I wasn't him," said Nick. "And if he's a customer, he very likely knew Nash."

"But how could the killer be Bartlett?" asked Taylor, gesticulating with his cigar and causing ash to fall onto the floor. "Matthews knew who killed Nash. If it was Bartlett, Matthews wouldn't have gone drinking with him and told him he was afraid he was next!"

"And who told us that story that Matthews knew the killer?"

"Bart—shoot. I see what you're getting at."

"Bartlett could've invented the whole tale to deflect suspicion," said Nick. "Maybe Martin hired Bartlett to kill Nash, but Bartlett got scared once he learned the cellar was scheduled to be worked on. So he decided to convince Matthews to search the cellar for gold. Murderers don't usually arrange for someone to dig up their victims."

Taylor tilted his head and blew a stream of smoke toward the ceiling. "That does make sense, sir."

Nick sat forward in his chair. "Get that Eddie kid to tell you who gave him the note for Nash. It could be the break we need. And have Mullahey bring Bartlett in here."

"Yes, sir." Taylor tucked the cigar in his mouth and rushed from the office.

Nick sucked in air and wrapped a hand around the ache in his arm. He frowned at the paperwork scattered across his desk from other cases he'd let languish. He'd get to work on them once he concluded another bit of unfinished business. Frank Hutchinson business.

Levi Strauss' office was located on the top floor of his new building on Battery Street, the front a colonnade of arches, their contours echoed in the tall windows above. Wagons and crates and men in aprons clogged the roadway and pavement out front, forcing Celia to step around the jumble in order to enter the building. A young man with the accent of the East Coast—New York, perhaps—stopped her from proceeding much beyond the door. She must not be the sort of person, usually male, who wished to review the contents of their showroom. Nonetheless, he agreed to take her to see Mr. Strauss, proving to Celia that a soft voice and mourning attire could produce the most unexpected reactions in people.

The man tapped gently on the office door but opened it before receiving an invitation to do so.

"A Mrs. Davies to see you," he said, showing her inside. The young man noiselessly retreated to the far corner of the room, safeguarding the propriety of the situation.

Levi Strauss' office was sparingly decorated. It contained little more than a mahogany desk, two chairs, a shelf of books in English and Hebrew, and a narrow table piled with paperwork placed in orderly stacks.

The man himself, his hands folded behind his back, turned away from his contemplation of the view beyond his office window. Mr. Strauss was a robust man in his late thirties or perhaps forty years of age, dressed in a well-tailored black suit, with thick dark whiskers that went from ear to ear around his chin.

He executed a small, stiff-kneed bow. "Mrs. Davies," he said, the accent of his German homeland less pronounced than she had anticipated. With a sweep of his right hand, he indicated she should take the chair waiting in front of his desk.

"Thank you for seeing me, Mr. Strauss," Celia said, taking a seat. "I realize you are a busy man."

"Five minutes, Mrs. Davies. I have a meeting." He took a seat in his leather chair and glanced at the clock hanging on the wall to his left. "Tell me what it is your husband wants to sell me."

She had fabricated this small mistruth to increase the chance she would be allowed to speak with Levi Strauss. Not all of the young man's willingness to bring her here had been because of a soft voice and mourning attire.

"In truth, Mr. Strauss, I do not have a husband who wishes to sell you anything," she said, and the young man in the corner muttered beneath his breath. "As it is, I do not have a husband at all. I have come here to ask you about Virgil Nash. I have been told you knew him in Virginia City."

Mr. Strauss drummed his fingers against his desk. "I do not talk to people who lie to me."

"I regret the mistruth, but I needed to urgently speak with you, and I suspected you would not see me unless I pretended to have a husband with a business proposition." She leaned forward as much as her corset permitted. "I shall take up as little of your time as possible, so permit me to get to the point. I am attempting to discover whether Mr. Nash was murdered by the same man who killed his brother in Virginia City. I am wondering what you might know about this person."

"Am I to suppose you are a member of the police force, Mrs. Davies?"

A blush heated her cheeks. "No. But a dear friend's husband was accused of the crime, and though he has since been cleared, I remain eager to see proper justice done," she explained. "In addition, I was shot at last evening, and it is possible this person is now after me."

"Which shows that it is dangerous to become involved in the investigation of a crime."

"I am not afraid of pursuing the truth. I suspect you would feel the same in my situation."

The comment brought a faint smile to his mouth. "You do this because you do not have a husband to stop you."

Patrick would most definitely have never permitted her to become involved.

"My husband was lost at sea." Or killed in a brawl in a Mazatlán saloon. She was not here to dwell upon whichever version of the story was the truth, however.

The man seated across from her bowed his head. "My sympathy."

"There is no need," she answered, evoking a look of surprise from him. She continued with her questions. "Can you tell me anything about the man who murdered Silas Nash? You did know the Nash brothers at that time, did you not?"

Mr. Strauss relaxed in his chair and contemplated Celia. The smile returned to hang on his lips.

*I amuse him.*

"I had dealings with Mr. Virgil Nash," he said. "He pursued many ways to become wealthy, and at one time wanted to supply clothing to the silver miners as my Virginia City partner. He was ambitious and knew many people in the territory. But I already had dealings with a store there and did not need to work with him," he explained. "He did, however, convince me to buy shares in his mine. Our interactions have been few since then. We were reacquainted recently when he became a fellow stockholder in the Merchants' Exchange Company. A difficult man, but certainly ambitious."

This was a description far more generous than others Celia had heard. "What can you tell me about Silas Nash's killer?" she asked. "A Mr. Cuddy Pike."

There was a brisk rap of knuckles upon the doorframe, and

another young man—this one with whiskers that bristled more fiercely than Mr. Strauss'—entered. He glanced at Celia with ill-concealed impatience.

"*Di sokhrim zenen do, Levi*," the man said.

"*Eyn minut.*" Mr. Strauss shooed him away.

"The merchants are here for my meeting, Mrs. Davies," he said by way of explanation. "The police must know all there is to know about Mr. Pike, yes?"

"However, they do not know if he is in San Francisco," said Celia. "But I believe it possible that Mr. Nash spotted him not long before he was killed. Did he ever mention this to you, as a longtime friend?"

"Friend?" Mr. Strauss chuckled. "We were business associates, Mrs. Davies, nothing more. However, I did see Silas Nash's killer."

"Here or in Virginia City?"

"Virginia City. I was dining with Silas and Virgil when he came into the restaurant. He saw the Nashes and became very angry. He accused Silas Nash of illegally mining his claim, and said his partner was dead because of Silas. He threatened to kill him." Mr. Strauss shook his head. "And so he did, right then and there. Stabbed him. But, in the disorder that followed, the man got away."

"Can you recall any detail about his appearance?"

Mr. Strauss formed a bridge with his fingertips and tapped them together. "He was a stout man, dark hair, with a big beard. And his face. It turned red as an apple when he shouted."

Just like the man Katie had described, the man in Burke's who'd been afraid of Virgil Nash. Silas Nash's killer and that man had to be one and the same. She had no proof the red-faced man—Cuddy Pike—had murdered Virgil Nash as well, but it felt right.

*You could be pursuing a false lead, Celia. Do not presume you have the answer.*

Mr. Greaves would know what to make of the information.

"But you have not happened to have seen this man in San Francisco," said Celia.

"I do not think so, no. But it is possible he no longer looks the same," he observed. "Weight can be shed, and a beard is easy to remove." He mimed shaving.

"However, the fellow would not be able to hide the unusual redness of his face when agitated, would he, Mr. Strauss?"

He inclined his head, acknowledging her observation. "No, Mrs. Davies. He would not."

"Mr. Greaves. You are back." Mrs. Hutchinson's smile looked strained, as though somebody were standing behind her and tugging on her cheeks in order to get her lips to curve up. She turned to the domestic waiting near the front door. "Thank you, Hetty. You may return to your duties."

Jane Hutchinson waited to continue until the young woman was out of earshot. "Have you discovered who killed Mr. Nash?"

Nick gripped the brim of his hat. "Not yet, ma'am. But I think we're close."

"Then why have you come?"

"I would like to speak with your husband," he said. "Has he returned from Oakland?"

"About an hour ago. He's in the garden at the moment," she answered. "Shall I show you back?"

"That's why I'm here, ma'am."

"Of course. This way, please."

He followed her through the house and out into the rear yard. Frank was seated on a white-painted iron chair near their flower garden, reading a book, the proper gentleman at his leisure. The bastard.

"Darling, Mr. Greaves is here." She smiled at her husband, and it made Nick's chest hurt to see the desperate affection on her face. *He's not worth it, Mrs. Hutchinson. Not worth it at all.*

Frank glanced up from his reading. "Can't say I've missed seeing you, Nick." He set an ivory bookmark inside his book and closed it. He looked over at his wife, waiting near the garden door. "I can entertain Mr. Greaves, Jane. You don't need to stay."

"Should I have Hetty serve lemonade?" she asked, her gaze darting between the men. She was anticipating trouble.

"Somehow I suspect Mr. Greaves isn't in the mood for lemonade. Am I right, Nick?"

"Thank you, Mrs. Hutchinson, but not this time."

"All right. Please excuse me, Mr. Greaves." A rustle of floral-printed skirts, she swept off, glancing back before she reentered the house.

"Why are you here, Nick?" Frank asked. "Come to arrest me after all? Grace told me what you had intended."

"You're a bastard, Frank."

"As if I've never heard that from you before." He set the book on the iron table at his side and stretched out his legs, pausing to flick a piece of grass off one knee of his pants. "But maybe you'll explain why you've decided to make this announcement today. Is Virgil Nash's murder not keeping you busy enough, and you're so bored, you need to bully me?"

"I know about Katie Lehane."

Frank shot a look toward the house. "Keep your voice down. She doesn't need to hear."

Nick strode over, and Frank stood. "How long, Frank? How long have you been visiting her?"

"Don't make it sound like I've slept with her, Greaves. We just spend time together, talking. Playing cards."

Now he'd heard it all. "How delightful. Playing cards and making small talk every Tuesday and Thursday night." *When you should be here, with your family.*

"I stopped visiting her regularly weeks ago."

"What, moved on already?"

"You *would* think the worst." Frank glanced toward the house again. "Listen, Katie's funny and sweet and plays a mean game of beggar my neighbor. That's all that happened."

"I've got to hand it to you—the timing was perfect on your part," said Nick, wishing Frank looked more remorseful than he did. "You got the alibi you've needed for the night Nash was killed." Nick stepped nearer. He clenched his fist, unclenched it again. "But a saloon girl, Frank? You couldn't be more original than that?"

"Like all of a sudden you're so righteous, Nick?" He scoffed. "Don't claim to be better than me. You, whose stupidity killed my cousin."

"Don't bring Jack into this."

"Why not? Jack is what it's always been about between us. Your guilt that Jack died because you disobeyed an order. My order." Frank punched Nick's shoulder, hard enough to dislodge his hat. "I should've seen you court-martialed. It's what you deserved."

Nick swung at him, his fist connecting with Frank's face and shooting pain through his hand.

Frank staggered backward and fell to the ground. He wiped a hand over his split lip; there was blood on his fingers. "I'll see you reprimanded for this."

"And make sure everybody knows why I hit you? You think anybody would blame me?" Nick reached down and grabbed Frank's coat lapels, hauling him to his feet. "Did you do this to Arabella, too? Huh? Sleep with other women?"

"Oh, now we're talking about Ara—"

"Did you?" Nick shook him. "Did you, Frank?"

"Don't be absurd. You think I'd bother with other women when I had Arabella?" Frank wrapped his fingers around Nick's hands and pried loose his grip. "I know you loved her, Nick. Mooning after her like a lovesick schoolboy. But she was mine. Mine!"

Nick felt his face go hot. "She was too good for you. You didn't deserve her, and you don't deserve Jane, either." He bent down to retrieve his hat. "You're an idiot," he said as he brushed the grass from it and set it on his head. "A damned idiot."

He turned his back to Frank. A stupid move, because in moments he was flat on the ground, seeing stars.

# CHAPTER 14

Celia tugged the Hutchinsons' front door bell again and waited for a response. Jane had to be home; she had asked Celia to visit. Furthermore, someone was there, because she could hear shouts emanating from the rear of the house.

Suddenly the door swung open to reveal a wide-eyed Hetty. "You've got to get them to stop, ma'am! Mrs. Hutchinson is back there, trying to pry them apart, and I'm afraid she's going to get hurt!" she cried. "It's just a good thing Miss Grace has gone out and isn't here to see this!"

"What?" Celia asked, confused.

"Mr. Hutchinson and that detective fellow."

*Gad.*

Celia gathered her skirts in her fists and ran down the hall-way to the rear of the house, Hetty pounding after her. She burst through the garden door to see Nicholas and Frank wrestling in the grass. Not wrestling—beating each other. And Jane futilely attempting to intervene.

"What in heaven's name!" Celia cried. "Mr. Greaves!"

"Stop!" screeched Jane, giving up on her efforts to pry the men apart and resorting to pummeling her husband's back. She grabbed the collar of Frank's coat but lost her grip and tumbled to the ground.

"Jane, what on earth is going on?" Celia asked, helping Jane to her feet and dragging her friend away from the melee.

"They're punching each other," Jane replied unhelpfully.

"You *are* a bastard," shouted Nicholas Greaves before landing a fist on Frank's midsection.

One of Jane's neighbors had come to her upper-floor window to stare down at the fight. At any moment, Celia expected to hear a policeman banging on the Hutchinsons' front door.

"Mr. Greaves! Frank! Cease this at once!" Celia kicked Nicholas' boot, which had the hoped-for effect of getting him to pause and glare at her. Unfortunately, Frank took advantage of the break and delivered a blow to the detective's face.

"Frank!" Jane wrested herself free from Celia's clasp and grabbed her husband's shoulders, successfully wrenching him off Mr. Greaves. "Quit this now!"

Frank, breathing hard, rolled away. His face was bleeding in several places, and what wasn't bleeding was covered in dirt. "Jane, go back into the house."

"I won't. I intend to stay here until you stop this nonsense."

Frank glared at Nick. "Tell *him* to stop this nonsense."

"You son—" Nick glanced over at Celia and held his tongue. "I'm only stopping because there are ladies present."

"Thank goodness, then." Jane dropped to her knees at her husband's side. She retrieved a handkerchief from a pocket and blotted it over his face. "I would now like somebody to tell me what this was all about."

Celia exchanged a look with Mr. Greaves. She was positive the fight had been over Katie Lehane. *How horrid.*

"I had a brother, Jane. Men always fight about the silliest things," said Celia, entering into the conspiracy of silence to save Jane's feelings. Her friend already felt inadequate in the shadow of Arabella's memory. There was no need to add to her misery. "Perhaps this little scuffle is best forgotten. Don't you agree, gentlemen?"

"Sure," said Mr. Greaves. "Don't you agree, Frank?"

"Go to hades, Greaves," said Frank, brushing off his wife's efforts to clean his face. "Please, Jane, that's enough."

Mr. Greaves lurched unsteadily to his feet. He tried to frown at Celia, but his lips were swollen and cut, and she suspected that the effort hurt. "Thanks for your help."

"As it appears I facilitated the conclusion of this brawl, you are most welcome for my help," she responded, holding her hands stiff at her sides to keep from running them over his wounds. The one on his left cheek would likely leave a scar. "It seems most fortunate I arrived when I did and was able to get you two to cease your ridiculous quarrel. Unless you wanted it known that you were exchanging fisticuffs with a person connected to one of your investigations?"

He narrowed his eyes. "You're enjoying this, aren't you?"

"Not in the least, Mr. Greaves."

"Oh, I think you are." He retrieved his hat, lost during the scuffle, and dusted it off. "I'll be taking my leave, Mrs. Hutchinson. Good day to you."

"Please stay, Celia," said Jane. "I do want to talk to you."

"Given this . . . altercation, I believe it best that I leave as well," she said, observing the miserable look on Frank's face. Maybe he would explain the cause of the fight to his wife and prove to be the man Celia had come to believe him to be. She sincerely hoped so. "Shall I come by tomorrow instead?"

Jane nodded. "Thank you."

Celia caught up to Mr. Greaves in the hallway.

"I was wrong about that woman being a delicate flower," he said. "She's got backbone."

"Jane?" Celia asked. "Yes, she does. As for you, you should come to the clinic. That cut on your cheekbone requires stitching. Unless you prefer to bleed everywhere."

"I knew you were enjoying this," he said, not waiting for Hetty to materialize in order to open the front door for them. He ushered Celia through, banging it shut behind them. "And you don't need to take care of me, ma'am."

"Apparently I do, which makes me wonder who tended to you before we were acquainted."

"Don't think I ever got into scrapes before we were acquainted, Mrs. Davies."

"Ah yes. The sedate life of the San Francisco police detective," she said, allowing him to take her elbow as they descended the front steps.

"It *was* pretty boring."

Despite her upset, she laughed.

"Be that as it may, your cuts do require attention," she said as they reached the pavement and turned up the road. His left eye was swelling, but at least the cut beneath it had ceased dripping. She rooted through her reticule for a handkerchief and gave it to him. "And please do wipe your face. You shall alarm the citizenry if you walk about looking like that."

He did as she ordered and rubbed off the drying blood. "Here." He handed back her thoroughly stained handkerchief. "I'll have Mrs. Jewett sew up the cut. She's pretty good with a needle."

"You shall do no such thing, Mr. Greaves. I insist on stitching it myself," said Celia, tucking away the handkerchief. "Furthermore, you will want to hear all that I learned from Mr. Levi Strauss about the man who killed Silas Nash. He witnessed the crime."

"You went to talk to Levi Strauss?"

"I did," she said. "He described a man who had a distinctive characteristic in common with the man Katie encountered at Burke's. A man whose cheeks turned unusually red when agitated."

"So Pike *is* in San Francisco," he said. "Does that describe any of our suspects, though?"

"Not that I am aware, Mr. Greaves. But more worryingly," said Celia, "I had an appointment with Katie this morning to see if any of the men at Martin and Company could possibly be the man she encountered at Burke's. But she never arrived for the meeting."

"Do you think she forgot?" he asked.

"I am wondering if she changed her mind. She was not keen to help identify a man who could be a killer, which I completely understand."

"Or she didn't change her mind, but was prevented from coming."

Fear fluttered in her stomach. "I was hoping to avoid that conclusion, Mr. Greaves."

"Not thinking the worst doesn't make it go away, ma'am,"

he answered, looking grim, which worried her more than her own fears.

"Then we must try to find her, and quickly," said Celia, increasing her pace.

Mr. Greaves matched her stride. "I thought you wanted to stitch my cut first."

"I suggest we do not waste time, then."

"Mr. Greaves, you look awful!" Grace Hutchinson announced from where she stood in the center of Celia Davies' parlor, her expression somewhere between horror and amusement. Her mother, Arabella, would've given him the exact same look before laughter won out. Mrs. Davies' cousin, standing next to her friend, wasn't horrified or amused. She was clearly furious.

"Thanks, Miss Hutchinson," he answered, which cracked open the cut on his bottom lip that had healed shut on the way here. Maybe he just shouldn't talk. Since his wounds had come from trying to beat her father to a pulp, he didn't have much good to say, anyway.

"Grace, I did not realize you planned to visit us today," said Celia Davies, discarding her bonnet.

"Bee sent for me," she said, her gaze never leaving Nick's face. "Golly, Detective Greaves."

"Indeed," responded Mrs. Davies. "Come into the clinic, Detective. And before you let loose your temper, Barbara, please inform Addie that I am in need of hot water. Quickly, please."

Miss Walford stomped off in the direction of the kitchen. He expected Grace to go with her, but she didn't, choosing instead to trail after Nick and Mrs. Davies. "What happened, Mr. Greaves? Were you assaulted by a criminal?"

Nick choked back a response and dropped onto one of the chairs situated inside Celia Davies' examination room. He was starting to hurt nearly everywhere, which he realized when his behind met the hard wood of the seat and the impact jolted through his body.

"He and your father had a small disagreement," said Mrs. Davies as she rounded up supplies and set them out upon the compact table at his side.

"My father did this?" asked Grace, amazed by the possibility. "Does he look this bad, too?"

Mrs. Davies glanced over at Nick and then at the girl. "Yes, Grace. He does."

"Man alive! This didn't happen because of what I said, did it?"

"You should discuss that with your father," Mrs. Davies said evasively, and snipped a length of silk suture. Lighting the oil lamp on the table, she turned its flame high and drew it closer to Nick. She propped a cool fingertip beneath his chin and tilted his head. He could smell the lavender that always scented her clothes, and he wondered if she noticed him take a deep breath of it. "Not too many stitches. Three or four only, perhaps. The cut is not as bad as I feared."

"Glad to hear it."

Her cousin came in with the pot of hot water wrapped in a towel, which she set near Mrs. Davies. She was still frowning, which made Nick wonder what was bothering her. It wasn't like she was mad that Frank Hutchinson had roughed him up. No, he suspected her mood had everything to do with her guardian's propensity for bringing home trouble.

"Addie said she'd like to come in here herself and see what's happened to Mr. Greaves, but she can't leave her cooking,"

Barbara Walford said. "She's also curious about what you learned at Mr. Nash's funeral, which explains where you were while I had to take care of your clinic for you."

"You went *there*, too?" Nick asked. She'd had a busy day. Getting pushed over a wall and then shot at wasn't enough to slow her down, apparently.

Mrs. Davies' response was to go on as if he hadn't spoken. "I will tell her later," she said, and poured a quantity of the water into a waiting bowl. She opened a glass vial labeled TINCTURE OF CALENDULA and counted out drops into the water. "And Mr. Greaves has enough spectators as it is."

"Addie also says your patient yelled at her."

Lines of tension creased the skin around Mrs. Davies' mouth. "I am sorry for that, but I had matters to attend."

"Don't be cross, Bee," said Grace, taking her friend's hand and squeezing. "She's trying to help my father so he isn't blamed for killing that man."

"Why not resume whatever you two girls were doing earlier?" Mrs. Davies asked, dipping a cloth into the water and dabbing Nick's cuts. "Perhaps you should practice your music for your Independence Day fete, Grace."

"Come on, Grace. We've been dismissed," said Miss Walford.

The two girls tromped off toward the parlor, leaving them alone. In no time, the sound of the piano drifted across the intervening hallway.

"Your cousin doesn't like your being associated with me, does she?" he asked.

She gazed down at him, her face close enough that it wouldn't take much effort at all to reach up and touch it. Not much effort at all. "Since you usually end up in this condition, can you blame her?"

"Nope. But *you* do."

Finished with cleaning his wounds, she dropped the cloth into the bowl. "What do you mean?"

"I mean you want her to understand why working to get justice is so important to you," he said, watching her thread the silk suture through the eye of a curved needle. Her palms were scabbed from where she'd scraped them on the rocks at Cliff House, and the need to protect her almost swamped him. "More important even than your patients and this clinic."

She paused, the threaded needle dangling from her fingers, and glanced over. The look in her eyes meant he'd read the situation correctly. "Am I merely being arrogant to think these crimes are any of my affair, Mr. Greaves? Am I nothing more than utterly selfish to be so heedless of others' justifiable concerns for my well-being?"

"It's a disease, ma'am," he answered. "And we've both caught it."

"Then you do not think I am wrong to be involved?"

"Now, I didn't say that."

"No, you did not," she replied. "But I am grateful you did not demand that I keep out of your way as you used."

"I've learned there's no point to telling you that," he replied.

A smile danced over her mouth. "Hold still. I will endeavor to be quick."

He tried not to flinch as the needle punctured his skin. True to her word, she was quick. Quicker than the doctors who'd stitched him up during the war.

"There. All finished," she announced, tying off the thread. "I shall put a small plaster or two over the cut for protection."

"Thank you, ma'am."

"So what do we do with the information that Cuddy Pike is very likely in San Francisco and Katie encountered him at Burke's?" she asked, crossing the room to fetch a strip of adhesive plaster.

"Still a needle in an uncooperative haystack, ma'am. I expect he's changed his appearance and his name."

"But he could not change the way his face flushes."

"Then we need to get some men angry," he said. "Maybe Mr. Pike is masquerading as Rob Bartlett, Dan Matthews' friend. The one who convinced Matthews—and Cassidy—to dig up Nash in the first place. I'd been thinking Martin had hired Bartlett to kill Nash, but maybe Bartlett had an entirely different reason to murder the man."

"I did suggest Mr. Bartlett was worth considering, did I not, Mr. Greaves?" she asked. "Yet why would he encourage Dan Matthews to dig in the cellar if he knew Mr. Nash's body was there? I keep returning to that question."

He explained the theory he'd mentioned to Taylor—that Bartlett, if he was the murderer, got scared when he learned work on the cellar was planned. Who'd suspect the fellow who told his friend to dig around?

"Mr. Bartlett also knows Eddie and could have asked him to deliver the note to Virgil," Mrs. Davies said, finishing with the plasters and straightening. "But why arrange a meeting at the offices where you worked? Why not another, unrelated location?"

"He figured Nash wouldn't be suspicious. Remember, Nash

thought the note had come from Martin. His office was a logical place to meet."

"And Mr. Nash had gone willingly, unsuspecting it was a trap," she mused.

"I've already asked Mullahey to bring Bartlett into the station," he said. "We can have Miss Lehane come in to see if she can identify him."

"*If* we can find her in order to do so, Mr. Greaves."

They agreed that while Mr. Greaves checked Burke's Saloon, Celia would go to Katie's boardinghouse.

"She didn't come home last night," said the landlady, tall and broad of shoulder as so many of them seemed to be. Petiteness, Celia supposed, would not be a desirable characteristic if one wished to maintain discipline over a house full of young women. "Ought to toss that one out. Sneaking men up to her room in the evening, and she thinks I don't know. I don't run that sort of establishment. But what can you expect from a saloon girl?"

"You are certain Katie did not return last evening?"

"You can check her room if you don't believe me."

"May I?" Celia asked, making the woman frown; obviously, she had not actually meant to allow Celia to visit Katie's rooms.

"Come on."

Celia followed the landlady up the steps to the topmost floor, the ceiling dipping low beneath the roofline, the air warm and stuffy. There were only three rooms up here where the rent would be a trifle higher than for the dark and noisy rooms overshadowed by the neighboring buildings. Celia did not care to consider where a girl who worked at Burke's obtained the extra means.

The trill of a woman's singing echoed along the short hallway.

The landlady glanced toward the sound, which was emanating from behind the closed door at the end. "That one's always chirping a tune. She saw some Italian lady singing at the Academy of Music, and now she wants to be famous, too. When pigs fly and snails gallop is what I say." Her keys jingled as she unlocked the door to Katie's room. "See? Empty."

Celia could see that for herself as she stepped inside, the colorful quilt in place atop the bed, the blinds drawn, the room quiet and still and somehow larger without Katie's vigorous personality to fill it. Dresses hung from nails pounded into the far wall, and Katie's comb sat on the washstand next to the white enameled basin. Their presence led Celia to conclude the girl had not meant to leave for any length of time.

"Did Katie mention to any of the other boarders that she did not intend to return to the boardinghouse last night?" she asked.

"If she did, I ain't heard," said the woman, her gaze lighting upon a pretty Wedgwood blue shawl tossed over one of the two chairs Katie owned, a speculative look in her eyes. "If she doesn't come back, I wonder what'll happen to all her things."

"Katie *will* come back," said Celia. She would not see another innocent woman die, as had happened the last time she and Mr. Greaves had worked on a case together. She simply would not. "I promise you."

"Is that so?" asked the landlady. "Well, tell her when you find her that she's got until the end of the week to move all her stuff outta here. I'm gonna find a respectable girl to rent this room. One who doesn't work in a saloon or bring men home."

NO PITY for the DEAD

Or long to sing in theaters?

"I shall inform her," Celia answered, sweeping past the woman and back into the hallway.

"You do that!" the landlady shouted after her.

Out on the sunlit street, Celia was greeted by the stink of sewage, a scattering of dust swirling over the cobbles that made her hold her breath, and the din of the blacksmith's shop across the road. The saloon where a woman sang "Aura Lea" had yet to open.

"Where are you, Katie?" she asked aloud once the gust of wind had subsided, the tiny lump of fear that had taken hold in her stomach turning into a full-fledged stone.

"*D*on't know why you're here, Detective. I haven't done anything wrong," said the owner of Burke's, sneaking a look at Nick's cuts and bruises. By this point, his face must be every color of the rainbow.

"I have some questions for you," said Nick, wishing his mouth didn't hurt every time he opened it.

"About the saloon?" They were out on the sidewalk, and Burke jabbed a thumb in the direction of the front door. "It's closed. I know the law."

"I'm not here to see if you're opening before seven, Mr. Burke," said Nick, moving aside to let a shop boy wheeling a cart pass. "I'm here to ask about one of your girls. Katie Lehane."

"She was *not* dancing the other night. I know the rules about that, too, and I told the officer as much. Can't you fellas believe a man?" Burke shook his head. "I'm gonna get rid of the girls. They're just not worth all the trouble they bring. Men fighting over them. And police coming around, wondering what they're up to."

Nick exhaled, which made him realize how much his ribs were hurting on top of everything else. When did Frank get to be such a good pugilist? "How about this? How about you just tell me if Katie came into work last night?"

The saloonkeeper peered up at him. "That's all you want to ask me about?"

"That and if she seemed bothered. Left early, maybe?"

"Didn't seem bothered to me." Burke cast a look toward the sky, where all memories were apparently located. "Not much, at least. Maybe a bit more quiet, and she didn't sit with any of the men like she often does. She stayed until closing like usual. Walked home by herself like usual, too, because her place isn't far from here." His eyes widened as understanding finally dawned. "Has something happened to her?"

"Did she mention anything about leaving town?" Nick asked.

"I told her she should always walk home with one of the other girls or my barkeep," said Burke. "You don't think one of my customers had something to do with her disappearance, do you?"

"I didn't say she disappeared, Mr. Burke. So just answer my question."

"She didn't say anything to me about leaving town. In fact, when she left last night, she said she'd see me tomorrow," he said, wiping his palms down the apron tied around his waist. "Is she dead? Is that what's happened, Officer?"

"If you're a praying man, Mr. Burke, I'd start now."

Taylor was waiting for Nick inside the detectives' office. Unfortunately, Briggs was in there, too, his heels up on his desk, a stance that showed off the worn spots on the bottoms of his boots. The crumbs from one of his molasses doughnuts littered a piece of brown paper, and he was licking his fingers with a smacking noise.

When Briggs saw Nick entering the room, his brows jigged up his forehead, and he let out a long whistle. "Whooee, look at you, Greaves!"

Taylor's brows did likewise. "Sir?"

Nick tossed his hat atop his desk and took a seat. "Frank Hutchinson lands a mean punch."

"Ha!" Briggs guffawed, and slapped his thigh. "Don't that beat all!"

"Did Mullahey bring Bartlett in, Taylor?" Nick asked, following his policy of ignoring Briggs whenever possible.

Taylor recovered from the shock of seeing his boss with plasters stuck to his face—wasn't the first time, wouldn't be the last—and ceased to gawk. "Yep. He's had a visit to the booking sergeant and is cooling his heels in our fine accommodations as we speak. As wrathy as thunder, though. Swears he had nothing to do with Nash's death, and we can't prove otherwise."

"They always say that," said Briggs, trying to sound authoritative.

"Dad blame it, I know that, Briggs!"

Nick checked the clock hanging on the wall. Almost time for Mrs. Davies to show up. "I'm expecting Mrs. Davies, Taylor—"

"Mr. Greaves," she announced, abruptly appearing at the doorway like the dove a magician would conjure from an empty sack. She greeted Taylor and Briggs, who'd scrambled to his feet. At least the man knew how to show respect to a lady. "She did not return to her rooms last night. Did you speak with Mr. Burke?"

Nick rose as well. "According to him, she came to work and left at her regular time, said she'd be at work today as usual."

Mrs. Davies twisted the straps of her reticule around her hand. Behind her in the main office of the station, one of the policemen was leaning over in his chair to get a better look at her. Nick really wished they'd learn to mind their own business.

"Gad," she said. "So she has disappeared."

"Is somebody missing, sir?" asked Taylor.

"It seems so, Taylor," said Nick. "Her name's Katie Lehane. A witness who might be able to tie Rob Bartlett to Virgil Nash's murder. Alert the men that we're looking for a saloon girl—"

"She has red hair and is very pretty," added Mrs. Davies. "And was likely wearing an orange checked dress. It is her favorite, and I did not observe it hanging in her room."

"We're looking for a girl who works at Burke's Saloon matching that description," Nick continued. "And put a notice in the newspapers looking for information on her whereabouts. Who knows? Maybe we're concerned for no reason, and all she's done is gotten scared and gone to stay with a friend for a day or two."

"She did not take any of her dresses or even her hair comb with her," said Mrs. Davies. "A woman never goes anywhere for any length of time without her brush or comb."

So maybe Katie *hadn't* gone to stay with a friend. "I'll take your word on that, ma'am. Go on, Taylor."

"Want me to take care of this before I go talk to that Eddie kid?" he asked, rummaging through his coat to fetch out his notebook. "I was just headed over to Montgomery, but if this is more important—"

"Yes. It's more urgent we find her," said Nick. "Shall I have one of the policemen see you home, Mrs. Davies?"

"I'll take you, ma'am," Briggs offered, his eyes twinkling in a way Nick didn't care for.

"Thank you, but I shall be fine. It is not far," she said, her eyes never leaving Nick's face. "I merely want Katie found. That is all I am worried about."

"We'll find her, ma'am," he replied.

But when they did, would she be alive . . . or dead?

"Okay, okay, Bartlett," said Nick. "So you're sticking with your story that you set Dan Matthews to digging in Martin's cellar as a joke."

"It ain't a story. It's the truth."

Rob Bartlett was pacing his cell. It took about two seconds to shuffle through the filthy sawdust covering the stone floor before having to turn and go back in the other direction. At the end of the aisle, the warden rolled his eyes at Nick and lit a cigarette, which prompted one of the inmates to decry the injustice of being denied his own smokes.

"And that you didn't give him Nash's watch and money as encouragement to leave town because *you* were the man he'd seen the night Nash was killed," Nick continued, trying to get Bartlett as angry as possible.

"I didn't!" Bartlett shouted. He marched up to the iron grating separating him from Nick. "How many times have I got to tell you?"

"And that Martin didn't pay you to kill Nash," persisted Nick. "Or that maybe your real name is Cuddy Pike."

"What? No!" he shouted, a spray of spittle hitting Nick's chest. His face, however, didn't turn any redder than any other fellow's, even though he was riled. Not Cuddy Pike, then. He still could be a murderer, though. "My name's Rob Bartlett, and if I'm gonna hang for Nash's death, I sure wish Martin had paid me to do it. I woulda used the money to get out of town."

"But you did know Virgil Nash. From the Golden Hare," said Nick, wishing he had something to wipe off Bartlett's saliva other than his lone clean handkerchief. "What did you fellows do there?"

"What do you think we do there? Play tiddlywinks?" asked Bartlett. "We gambled. And Nash won. So often he had to have been cheating. I told Dan to steer clear of Nash, but he wouldn't listen."

"Did you lose a lot of money to Nash?"

"I didn't kill him! I didn't!"

Nick pulled in a deep breath and instantly regretted it, given how putrid the air was. Didn't they ever clean the cells? As if the cockroaches scuttling through the sawdust didn't answer that question.

"I presume you're also going to tell me that you're not responsible for Katie Lehane's disappearance," said Nick.

"Who?" Bartlett asked.

"A redheaded girl who works at Burke's."

"I don't ever go to Burke's. And I don't know a Katie Lehane," insisted Bartlett. "So if you're also tryin' to accuse me of making her disappear, then you're barking up the wrong tree."

He *was* barking up the wrong tree.

And it made him furious.

Addie met Celia at the front door. "It's that Mr. Smith. He is in the parlor." She cast a glance in the direction of the room. "I told him to nae sit on the furniture, though. Grubby creature."

"He has come today?" How was it possible the man always managed to show up at the worst possible time?

"Aye, ma'am," said Addie. "Miss Grace left not long ago, by the by, and Miss Barbara is in her room."

"I am glad they are not around to hear, because I have dreadful news." Celia removed her bonnet, and Addie took it from her. "Not only does it seem that the man who killed Virgil Nash's brother is in San Francisco, but Katie Lehane has gone missing."

"Merciful heavens!"

"Mr. Greaves has alerted the police force to search for her. I expect that is all that can be done for now."

"Poor lass. Poor, poor lass."

"We must hope that she has merely chosen to go into hiding." Celia pressed her hands to her waist. "Wish me luck with Mr. Smith, Addie."

"He says he's brought the proof about Mr. Davies."

"Which is why I would rather run back out the front door than speak with him."

"But you willna do such a thing."

"No."

Celia strode into the parlor, where Mr. Smith was examining the porcelain figurines and silver candlesticks on the mantel. He had failed to remove his bowler hat, which looked more battered than the last time she'd seen him wearing it, and the cuffs of his ill-fitting trousers were dusty. But despite his appearance, his services had come highly recommended, and if he had truly found proof of Patrick's death, then he had earned all the money she had ever paid him.

"Mr. Smith," she said, causing him to guiltily spin to face her.

"Ma'am." He grabbed his hat and swept it off, making a bow that revealed the bald patch on the crown of his head.

"You have returned rapidly from Mexico," she said. "I received your telegram only yesterday."

"Sent that right before I hopped the steamer, ma'am." His eyes darted a glance around at the parlor. They lingered on the portrait of Uncle Walford; Celia fancied her uncle's painted grin slipped a trifle in response to Mr. Smith's perusal. "Mighty fine place you got here."

"Yes, but you have not come to admire the furnishings." She held out her hand. "My housekeeper tells me that you have brought with you the item that proves my husband is deceased."

He dug in his coat pocket and located a piece of paper that was nearly as grimy as the fingers holding it. "It's a copy of a doctor's certificate stating he attended to one Patrick Davies in his final hours, someplace in the city of Mazatlán. It's in Spanish, but I went and got it translated. It says right here . . ." He unfolded the paper and pointed to a line at the top. "*Nombre*. That means 'name' and shows your husband's name and that he was a seaman off a merchant ship and from California. And here . . ." His finger moved down. "Right next to *Causas de la Muerte*, it says he died from knife wounds. And this here's the signature of the doc that attended to him. So it looks like he didn't die when that boat went down but got killed in a saloon like I'd heard. Sorry, ma'am."

Hand shaking, Celia took the paper. It was dated *10 de agosto de 1866*. The day Patrick's soul had left this earth.

"How could the attending physician be certain the man was my husband?" she asked, unready to believe what her eyes showed her.

"I'd guess one of his friends told the doctor who he was. Oh, and I got this, too." Back into his pocket went his hand, and he pulled out a square of linen. He unfolded it slightly, trying to hide the rusty brown stains, but it was enough that she could see the "P D" embroidered in emerald green thread on one corner. "I was wonderin' if you might recognize it."

The death certificate was forgotten. For in Mr. Smith's fist was all the proof she would ever require that the man who had perished in a knife fight in Mexico had been Patrick. "I do. I gave it to my husband as a wedding present."

She took the handkerchief from him and ran a thumb over the initials she had embroidered. The linen was still soft, except for where the blood had dried upon it and turned the material stiff.

*A token to remember me by*, she had told Patrick when she'd given it to him after their wedding luncheon, all of the guests departed and the two of them alone in the small room they had rented at the inn. She'd had a lump in her throat, already uncertain that they had made the right decision to wed. But he had been kind, then, and happy for the gift. Claimed it was a treasure, the green thread a reminder of the green of home, and had kissed her so gently. And he had kept it with him all these years, though he had long ago come to doubt that she had ever loved him.

*He was good to me, as good as he was capable of being, and now he is gone and I cannot apologize.*

Celia looked up at Mr. Smith. "I believe I owe you some money for your efforts. Let me fetch it."

She turned aside before he could see the tears welling in her eyes, and ran from the room.

―――――――

"The handkerchief," said Addie, standing in Celia's bedchamber that evening. "There's nae mistaking now, is there, ma'am?"

"No, Addie. No mistaking." Celia, seated at her dressing table, took out the sandalwood box containing Patrick's letters and unlocked it. For no reason she could comprehend, she kissed the handkerchief and tucked it beneath the letters, then closed the lid. "Do you think we should hold a service, or buy a plot at Laurel Hill Cemetery for him?"

"And then what, ma'am? Put an empty coffin inside?"

Celia looked up at Addie's reflection in the dressing table looking glass. "We must do something to mark his passing, Addie. It is only right."

Addie made a noise in her throat that signaled she did not agree but would no longer argue.

"I suppose I should wear mourning, now that we know," Celia said. "Half mourning. Full seems hypocritical."

"I'll fetch your gray dress down from the attic," said Addie. "And I've told Miss Barbara about Mr. Davies. She sends her condolences."

*She could come to my room and tell me that herself.* But Barbara was still punishing Celia with silence, and Celia had been hiding in her room, uncertain of what to say to her cousin about Patrick's passing when they both knew Celia's grief was born as much—if not more—of guilt than of wifely affection.

*I have a cold, cold heart.*

"Tell her I do not expect much in the way of mourning attire from her. That should please her."

"Aye," said Addie, turning her head as the sound of pounding echoed up from the ground floor. "Who's at the door at this hour?"

The pounding repeated, followed by someone calling Celia's name. A woman's voice.

"She needs help." Celia stood and rushed to the staircase, noticing as she passed through the hallway that Barbara had come to the door of her bedchamber and was peeking out to see about the latest commotion.

"I may need your assistance, Barbara," said Celia, rapidly descending the stairs, Addie on her heels.

Celia threw open the front door to the woman, silhouetted against the purpling sky. With a cry, she collapsed across the threshold, the wound on her shoulder a stain of rusty red against her orange checked dress.

Redder than the color of her hair.

# CHAPTER 15

"Thankfully, the bullet passed cleanly through your shoulder, Katie," said Celia, securing the cotton bandage over the girl's wound. Katie was ashen and exhausted but alive. And unless the wound festered despite Celia's best efforts to clean it, she should continue to remain alive and recover without any long-term damage.

"I can't thank you enough, ma'am." Katie looked down at her shoulder, her gaze flicking rapidly over the rust-colored stain on her chemise, before turning to her discarded dress, crumpled on the floor. "I was so scared. I just knew I had to get here and you would help me."

"I am glad that you thought to do so," replied Celia.

"Where else would I go?" Katie asked, as if the very idea of seeking assistance elsewhere were absurd.

Celia turned to Barbara, who'd been placing the bloody

linens Celia had discarded into a waiting wicker basket. "Has Addie returned from sending Joaquin to the police with my message?" She'd wanted Mr. Greaves to know immediately that Katie had been found safe.

"A few minutes ago," said Barbara.

"Good." Celia nodded at the basket. "Take those linens to her, if you would."

Barbara pressed her lips together, shot a narrow-eyed glance at Katie, and collected the basket, marching out of the room with it.

"I'm sorry to cause you such trouble, ma'am," said Katie, who'd seen Barbara's sullen glance. She attempted to sit up on the examining table, wobbling unsteadily from blood loss. Celia caught her before she tumbled to the floor.

"Lie back down for a little while. You have had quite a shock." Celia lowered Katie onto the bench. "And you are not causing me trouble. I run a clinic to help people, not to drive them away."

Katie pulled in a shaky breath. "I just wish I'd spotted him. If I had, I would've run before he had a chance to get a shot off."

"Do not blame yourself. He might have chased after you and shot you anyway," said Celia, unsettled by her own calm assessment of the situation. Histrionics would not be of any use, however, so she continued with the tasks that would help her maintain her composure, carefully rolling the clean bandaging into a tight coil and returning it to her supply cabinet.

"Do you think it's the same man who shot at you last night, Cousin Celia?" asked Barbara, who had returned to stand in the doorway with a scowl.

"Somebody shot at you, too, Mrs. Davies?" Katie asked, her eyes gone wide. "It's got to be that man from the saloon. The one I was going to identify. He must have known you'd come to talk to me."

*He must have*, thought Celia, firmly closing the door to the cabinet and causing the inset glass to rattle.

"Do you think he's the fellow who killed Mr. Nash? He was dreadful scared of him." Katie shuddered. "I knew that man was trouble. Got me so scared thinking about him, I simply had to find someplace to hide. Sorry I didn't meet you this morning at that coffeehouse, ma'am. I didn't mean to worry you."

"All that matters is that you are safe."

"But it was that man who shot me, wasn't it?" she asked, glancing at Barbara for confirmation of her theory. Barbara returned only the faintest of shrugs, which was sufficient to confirm what Katie had asked. "By gosh!"

Addie bustled into the room, a simple white nightgown in her hand.

"Here you are, Miss Lehane. One of my old nightgowns, since you'll be staying the night with us." She glanced at Celia. "Is it all right, ma'am, to help her up?"

"Yes. Let me know if you get dizzy, Katie."

"'Tisn't much to look at, but you'll nae have to lay about with only a ruined chemise to cover you." Addie helped her change into the gown, larger and likely plainer than Katie ever would choose to wear, covering the sight of the bandages. "There, now, you look right proper." She patted Katie's knee and turned to Celia. "And you, ma'am, look dreadful tired. I'll make tea."

Out she went again, and Katie rested her hands atop the nightgown, pinching the soft cotton between her forefingers and thumbs.

"If I hadn't gone back to the boardinghouse, none of this

would've happened," Katie said. "I should've just borrowed some clothes from my friend and stayed put at her house. Instead, I got the stupid idea to fetch my shawl and some underthings. And now look . . ." Katie tapped her shoulder, the bandaging making a lump beneath Addie's nightgown. "I've got a bullet hole that'll leave a scar, and all the blood has ruined my favorite dress!"

Suddenly, she burst into tears.

Barbara hurried to her side and took her hand—a mature response that surprised Celia. "There's no need to get upset, Miss Lehane. These things happen."

"Have *you* been shot before?" Katie asked pettishly.

Barbara looked on the verge of tears herself. "No, but I've been attacked—"

"Barbara," Celia interrupted before her cousin became overwrought, "please go upstairs and prepare your father's bedchamber for Miss Lehane."

"I didn't come here expecting you to put me up, ma'am," Katie protested.

"I understand," said Celia, "but if you stay with us, I shall be able to assess your recovery in the morning. So, Barbara, if you will."

As soon as Barbara left, the door between Celia's examination room and the kitchen swung open.

"Ma'am," said Addie, peering around the door, "a lad from over by the Kellys' came to the back door. It seems her time's come, her husband's nae with her, and she's asking for you."

Did all bad things have to happen on the same day?

"I was afraid the baby would come early." Celia glanced at Katie and then back at Addie. "Please fetch some tea for Miss Lehane and a bite for her to eat. When she feels strong enough, take her up to Mr. Walford's old bedchamber." Celia stripped off the apron she'd tied over her dress. "Also, tell Miss Barbara that I need her to keep Miss Lehane company while I go to the Kellys'."

"Alone, ma'am?" asked Addie unhappily. "Who's to help get clean linens and towels and fetch the hot water for you at their house? You ken the Kellys have nae female relations to give you aid."

"If it appears I cannot manage matters on my own, I shall send for you." Celia checked her portmanteau for the supplies she would require—her umbilical cord scissors and straight scissors, a scarifying lancet, bandaging, and her midwifery forceps, which would likely go unused if the child had not turned head down. She stared balefully at the crotchet, the hook used to extract the baby if it died in utero, and hoped it would remain in her medical bag.

"I don't like thinking about you out there by yourself, without anybody to protect you," Katie was saying. "What if that person tries to shoot you again?"

"I shall be fine, Katie; truly I shall." Celia closed her medical bag and looked over at Addie. "I do not know how long I shall be. Do not wait up."

"I'll nae sleep with you wandering the streets."

She was grateful that she had someone to fuss over her as her housekeeper did, but they were both well aware that Celia had no choice but to go; her patients came first. "Then have tea ready for me when I return."

"But it's not safe for you, Mrs. Davies!" exclaimed Katie.

"Och, dinna try to talk sense into her head, Miss Lehane," said Addie. "She'll nae mind either of us."

$\mathcal{N}$ick pushed around the papers crowding his desk. No news yet on Katie Lehane. Nothing useful out of Bartlett. A red-faced man who killed Silas Nash somewhere in the city. Eagan pressing him to close the case and declare Dan Matthews the murderer. And here he was, scribbling on forms and scratching his itchy skin where he'd pulled off Mrs. Davies' plasters.

Nick waited for the ink to dry before stuffing all the paperwork into the proper folders. The damp breeze coming through the open street window fluttered the papers and carried noises from outside. He could hear somebody shouting for a hack and a woman's tinkling laughter echoing nearby. A horse whinnying and a drunk shouting in a language Nick didn't recognize. A typical night. Including all the forms.

Ah, the glamorous life of a cop.

"Sir?" asked Taylor, leaning around the door Nick had left ajar.

Nick opened the drawer to his desk and slid the folders in among all the others filed there. "What is it, Taylor?"

"You're gonna like this!"

Nick rubbed his temples—his head still ached from his encounter with Frank—and looked up at his assistant. The overhead gas lamp flickered, making the shadows in the room jump and showing the grin on Taylor's face. He looked like the neighborhood kid who'd learned the location of the best fishing hole around and was hoping you'd ask just so he could prove how clever he was.

"You've found Katie Lehane?" asked Nick.

"Not yet, but I did finally track down that Eddie kid and

talked to him," he said, consulting his ever-present notebook. "He took that note to Nash, all right."

"Did he tell you who gave it to him?"

"Yep," said Taylor, pausing to spin out the suspense. *I could always hand him his walking papers. But who else would work as hard? Nobody.* "John Kelly."

"Kelly? The fellow who supervises Frank Hutchinson's work crew?" Just thinking about Frank made the stitched cut on Nick's cheek throb. He only hoped Frank was in as much pain.

"The same," said Taylor.

"What's his link to Nash, though?" asked Nick.

"Not sure, sir," said Taylor. "I checked on Kelly like I did on everybody working there. I searched our records, and he's never caused any trouble during the time he's been in San Francisco. Came from Los Angeles in 'sixty-four with his wife and has kept his nose clean ever since."

"How long had he lived in Los Angeles? And what was he up to during the years before? Could he have been in Virginia City when Silas Nash was killed?" *Could he be the red-faced man?*

"But I thought Silas Nash's killer was named Cuddy Pike. Doesn't sound like an Irishman to me."

"I'd change my name and pretend I was somebody else, too, if I were wanted for murder." Nick stood and kicked his chair out of his way, sending it squeaking across the floor to bang into the wall behind him.

"Even if Kelly had Eddie deliver the note, how do we prove he wrote it?" Taylor said. "Maybe Kelly got it from Bartlett. Or Martin."

"One way to find out is to ask Kelly ourselves." Nick checked the number of bullets in his revolver. "Where does he live?"

"The Kellys aren't at the address listed in the city directory, sir. Mullahey's been trying to find their house for me, but it seems he and his family move around a lot."

"Mrs. Davies should know. Kelly's wife is one of her patients." Nick took his coat from the hook by the door. "Let's stop by her place and ask her."

Just as they strode into the main office, a boy with hair flapping over his eyes came running in, yelling in Spanish.

"Hey, whoa, there!" Taylor grabbed the kid by the arms before he could hurtle into him. "Wait, don't I know you?" Taylor crouched down. "You live across the street from Mrs. Davies, don't you?"

"*Sí!* She give me this." From deep within a trouser pocket he dug out a crumpled scrap of paper. "For police."

He shoved the wad into Taylor's fist, took one look at the hulking booking sergeant standing at his desk, followed by a look at the barred door that led to the jail cells, and took off in the direction he'd come from. The alleyway door slammed behind him.

"What's it say?" asked Nick.

"Katie Lehane is at Mrs. Davies'. Seems she was shot, but she should be okay."

"Thank God." For once, a missing woman hadn't turned up dead. "Does it say if she saw her assailant?"

Taylor reread the note, though Nick could see from where he stood that Mrs. Davies had written very little. "Nope. But it's gotta be the man she met in Burke's, don't you think, sir . . . Mr. Greaves? 'Cuz who else would shoot at her?"

"I don't know. A disgruntled customer?"

"Oh."

"No, Taylor, I think it's probably him. The man at Burke's

who we now think is Cuddy Pike." And possibly John Kelly as well. "And he got scared we were on to him."

Since Mrs. Davies was shot at last night, Nick had a good idea how the man might've come to suspect that. *Danged woman. Asking questions, drawing attention to both Katie Lehane and herself.*

"Let's see what Miss Lehane has to say and find Mr. Kelly." Nick checked his Colt again. If it was Kelly who'd shot at Celia Davies and Katie Lehane, it meant the man had a gun.

A gun he clearly wasn't reluctant to use.

"*P*lease do try to compose yourself, Mrs. Kelly. Please," coaxed Celia, running a hand over the woman's taut belly. Maryanne Kelly had discharged her fluids already, and the baby *was* coming. Bottom first.

"I can't be calm! He's stuck. I can tell . . . unh." Maryanne grimaced as another contraction swept over her.

"Breathe deeply. It will help."

"I can't do that, either," she panted as sweat trickled down her face and stuck her chemise to her skin wherever it touched. "The baby's going to die!"

"Not if I have anything to say about that." Celia swiped the cuff of her sleeve over her forehead, even though the room's lone window was cracked open and the evening air was cool against the back of her neck. She should have brought Barbara. This delivery was going to be dangerously difficult.

"Oh, John . . ." Maryanne Kelly sucked in a breath. "John will be so unhappy with me. And after Dan . . ."

For some reason, Mr. Taylor had never delivered the message that Dan had been found dead, but Mr. Kelly had learned of his brother-in-law's accident from his employees and informed his wife. The woman's intense labor pains had given her little time to grieve her brother, though.

The possibility of losing a child as well would be even more devastating. "Please try to remain calm, Mrs. Kelly. As best you can."

"But John . . . I need him here."

Celia wished John Kelly were here, too. Anybody other than the sniffling neighbor girl who'd answered Celia's knock, then crept up the stairs behind her. A bony child with greasy hair, she stood off to one side, her eyes as wide as bottle bottoms. At least she had been able to find clean linens to spread beneath Maryanne and drape across her body.

*So I should not complain overmuch.*

Celia shifted her position on the stool she'd found in the kitchen and felt for the baby's buttocks, finding them presenting. She'd read that doctors were now recommending wrapping a silk band around the hips and tugging, but the child's head might shift and jam. This infant was tiny, the legs fully extended; her instincts told her forcible pulling was ill-advised. And she always trusted her instincts.

"It is time to push, Mrs. Kelly," said Celia calmly.

"But—"

"Please."

Her face scrunching, Maryanne pushed. If all went well, the force of her muscles would tilt the head into the proper position, chin to chest, which would help the baby slide through her pelvis, but only if the infant's shoulders weren't too wide or the head too large.

"Oh God, it hurts!" Maryanne cried out. "He's stuck! I told you! I'm going to lose him, too!"

The girl sniffled and drew a fist across her face beneath her nose. "Is she gonna die?"

*Not what's needed at this moment.* "Can you refresh the hot water, sweetheart?" Celia asked her. "The stove is likely still warm enough to heat more."

"I s'pose."

"And do check on Clary while you're down there," Celia added, for she could hear Maryanne's daughter crying.

Suddenly, the front door banged, and the girl jumped. "Who's that?"

"John," Maryanne squeezed out. "John!"

The girl bolted as if the devil himself had just been announced. She must have passed John Kelly on the stairs, because Celia heard his Irish brogue, followed by rapid footsteps on the treads.

John Kelly strode into the room. "That fool girl left the front door wide-open! And what's she doing up here, anyway? She's supposed to be watching Clary, not mooning about in here."

"The baby, John." Maryanne grimaced again. "He's come early."

A look of alarm crossed his face. "Help her," he begged Celia. "You've got to help her!"

"That is my goal," she said. She was unused to the presence of a husband at childbirth, and his fear and helplessness unsettled her. "I will do all I can."

Celia turned back to Maryanne, encouraging her as a fresh thin wash of bloody fluid emerged, followed by hips, then legs and torso. "You have a son, Mrs. Kelly, just as you expected."

"John, do you hear?" Maryanne tried to smile through the pain, but her lips twisted with agony. "Daniel. We'll call him Daniel."

"Yes, Maryanne," he said soothingly. "After your recently departed brother. God rest his soul."

Celia pulled gently on the baby's hips, helping him turn. Most of the torso was free. If she could just deliver the shoulders . . . They were so close. But then . . .

*No! Do not get stuck!*

"Oh dear God!" Maryanne cried out.

Her husband sank to his knees alongside the cot and reached for his wife's hand, squeezing. "Please, Mrs. Davies, help her! Why is she in so much pain?"

"It is natural, Mr. Kelly, I assure you," Celia said, concentrating on trying to ease the infant through the final stage.

"They have to live!" John shouted. "My boy has to live!"

At his outburst, Celia turned to glance at him and was startled to see his cheeks flushed a darker red than she had ever seen on anyone's face. The color of ripest cherries.

*His cheeks flamed a funny red when he got agitated* . . . She recalled Katie describing the saloon customer who had been so afraid of Virgil Nash that he'd run from Burke's.

*Oh dear Lord. Let me be wrong* . . .

"You just hold on, Maryanne," he said. "Don't leave me."

His voice. There was also something about his voice, something different.

*He has lost his Irish accent.* The one that had never sounded much at all like Patrick's or the other Irishmen Celia had known. Perhaps he was not who he had always claimed to be, as false a creation as Emperor Norton.

She could not think about what it all meant now. Not when the baby was so close to entering this world—or departing it.

Sweat dripped into Celia's eyes as she worked her fingers

around the baby's shoulders and neck. There were but precious moments before the umbilical cord, crushed by the head, would stop providing life-giving blood.

"Soon. Soon," she said. "Do not give up now, Mrs. Kelly."

The infant's extremities tinged blue. *No. No! He must come free.*

Celia renewed her efforts, and Maryanne bore down. Suddenly, the baby slipped, and his head, topped with a smattering of hair, broke clear. He let out a wail, and Celia rocked back on her heels, relieved. Aside from bruising on the boy's hips and bottom, he was pink and shuddering with rage. Healthy.

"Ah!" cried Maryanne, relief and pleasure washing over her face. "Our boy, John. Our boy! And such a shout!"

Celia gathered him into a clean towel, wiping him off with tepid water from the waiting basin, the neighbor girl not having returned with fresh. Once the cord had stopped pulsing blood, Celia tied it off and cut it.

"Indeed," said Mr. Kelly. "We shall call him Daniel William. After your brother and me father."

*He's recovered his accent again,* Celia noted, a chill sweeping over her.

Beaming, he bent over his newborn son. But then what father would not be proud of the birth of his first son? Even a killer.

*Oh dearest Lord, I must be wrong.*

Celia dressed the child's navel, bandaging the cord to his stomach, and handed him to Maryanne, who cooed, all of her pains forgotten. Celia stood, her legs cramped from sitting on the short stool she had placed at the foot of the bed.

"Since the neighbor girl is busy tending to Clary, can you fetch clean water for me to wash your son?" Celia asked Mr.

Kelly, feigning calm. Did he see through the pretense, though? Notice how her knees knocked? Was he the man who had shot Katie? The man who had shot at her?

Her hands trembled as she slid the soiled sheet from beneath Maryanne's hips.

"That I will," he answered, giving Celia a sideways glance before heading for the kitchen.

Maryanne began to nurse the child, gently smoothing his hair with her fingertips. Once the afterbirth had cleared—and it appeared Maryanne would not hemorrhage—Celia bundled the dirty linens.

"Isn't he beautiful? Daniel William," Maryanne murmured. "Daniel William."

"He is very beautiful. He looks so much like your husband," said Celia, listening for the sound of Mr. Kelly's return. She hadn't much time to ask questions.

"Do you think so?" asked the other woman, considering the child.

"I do," said Celia. "Tell me again, because I have forgotten and I love to know about my patients' lives—how did you and Mr. Kelly meet?"

"It was in Los Angeles." The baby whimpered, and Maryanne moved her fingertips to stroke his back. "At a fair. Such a lovely day." Her expression turned dreamy. "We had a very short courtship. My father wasn't pleased by that, but my mother could see how happy I was. We were married not long after meeting at that fair. Just over three years ago. Then we moved here."

Three years. When had Silas Nash been murdered in Virginia City? Earlier than that. She wished she could remember precisely.

"Was your husband from Los Angeles?" Celia asked, washing off her scissors and returning them to her medical bag.

"Oh no. He'd only been in Los Angeles a short time. Which was why my father wasn't pleased. He didn't like me running off . . ." She giggled, then winced as a delayed contraction squeezed. "That's what my pa called it. Running off! He didn't like me marrying a fellow whose family he didn't know."

"Parents and guardians can be quite protective, can they not? My uncle felt much the same about my husband." But for all of Patrick's sins, at least he had not been a murderer. What would she do if it became apparent that John Kelly had killed Silas Nash and possibly his brother as well?

*Do not panic, Celia. Stay calm, get out of the house, and inform Mr. Greaves.*

"Why had he come to Los Angeles?" she asked Maryanne. "Do you know?"

"He was looking for work, like so many who'd had trouble in the silver mines."

Celia's pulse fluttered, gained speed. "How could I have forgotten? Now I recall your telling me he had worked the Comstock Lode."

Maryanne's forehead creased. "Did I?"

"Yeah, did she?" asked Mr. Kelly from the doorway.

Celia spun to face him. "Mr. Kelly! You gave me a fright!"

"What's wrong, Mrs. Davies?" he asked, setting down the kettle of hot water he'd brought with him. "You look unwell."

"Oh!" Celia raised her hands to her cheeks. "I've been most concerned for your wife and child. It has taken its toll on my appearance, I fear." She retrieved her bonnet, mantle, and bag. "But I see that she and the baby are healthy, and I should leave."

John Kelly shifted to block her departure. "Why are you asking my wife so many questions?"

She held his gaze. *I must convince him I am harmless.* Although if he was the person who'd attempted to shoot her last night, he already believed otherwise. "I enjoy getting to know my patients; that is all."

"John, what's the matter with you?" asked Maryanne. Downstairs, their young daughter let out a howl, which was hastily stifled.

"I don't care for Mrs. Davies' prying." His eyes bored into Celia's, and she tightened her grip on her medical bag. The portmanteau made a meager weapon, but it was all she had.

"She's not prying." Maryanne must have taken her attention off her newborn, for the baby whimpered.

Sweat trickled along Celia's neck beneath her collar. "No, of course, I—"

"You are!" He grabbed her left elbow and dragged her close. "Did that girl tell ya I knew Nash? Did she?"

Behind Celia, there was a rustling of bedclothes. "John, let her go at once! What's wrong with you, treating Mrs. Davies like this? And what girl are you talking about?"

"Stay in bed, Maryanne." He shook Celia. "Did she?"

"What are you speaking of, Mr. Kelly?" Celia asked.

"Don't play coy with me. I saw you coming out of her boardinghouse. That redheaded saloon girl."

Celia returned his stare, so cold, so alarming. "She never connected you to Virgil Nash. So you did not need to shoot her or try to shoot me, Mr. Kelly. Or should I call you Mr. Pike?"

He flinched, and Celia no longer doubted she was facing a murderer. But with two witnesses in the house, surely he would not attempt to hurt her. Although the girl would make a poor witness and Maryanne might lie to protect her husband.

"Mrs. Davies, what do you mean?" asked Maryanne. "John, what is she talking about?"

"The Nash brothers mined on your claim, did they not?" Celia asked him, recalling what Mr. Strauss had told her. "The claim you and a partner had staked. I cannot blame you for being angry about what they had done. I would have been angry as well."

His grip tightened, cutting off her circulation, and Celia's fingertips began to tingle. "That partner was my brother, Mrs. Davies, and the Nashes' lawyers were able to convince the judge we didn't have a case. That our claim was an offshoot of theirs and they had a right to it. We had nothing left. Nothing. Drove my brother to drink." A shadow fell over his eyes. "And then one night he got himself trampled by a runaway horse. An accident, the cops said. Only it wasn't an accident. It was those Nash brothers, trying to get rid of trouble."

"John, stop this nonsense," said Maryanne, her voice wobbling. "Mrs. Davies, don't listen."

John kept talking. "I didn't go looking for them, but when I went into that restaurant and saw them Nashes yucking it up while my own brother was dead and buried . . ." He released Celia's elbow. "I lost my head. I said some things, showed my knife. I only wanted to scare him, I swear. But you can't scare a Nash. Silas stood there and laughed at me. Laughed. And I saw red and lunged. Cut him deeper than I expected to. There was blood . . . Don't think I've ever seen a man leak so much blood before. Did he ever look surprised."

Maryanne had started to sob. "John, don't talk crazy like

this. Mrs. Davies, don't listen to him, please. He's been working too hard."

"That's enough, Maryanne," he replied gruffly, his attempt at sounding Irish long forgotten. No wonder they lived here and not in the Irish neighborhood of South Beach where the residents would have detected his deception straightaway.

"You might have expected to encounter Virgil Nash in San Francisco, when so many of the men who became rich in Nevada have come here," said Celia, her brain whirling. How could she escape? If she managed to flee, would he harm Maryanne or the neighbor girl instead? "Nonetheless, you were surprised to see him at Burke's."

"I'd seen him once before at Martin and Company," he answered, "but I wasn't sure it was him. Being rich had made him soft, and he'd lost part of his arm. But the second time, I knew it was him for sure."

"You could have left San Francisco." *Rather than kill him.*

"I thought about leaving. I might've, except for the baby." He jerked a chin in Maryanne's direction, whose sobbing had turned to hiccups. "She couldn't travel in her condition, and I wasn't going to leave her. Besides, I was tired of running. Colorado. Indian country. Texas. Mexico. So many places, always scared I'd get caught. I thought I could stay out of Nash's way, but Hutchinson asked him to come to Martin and Company one more time to talk about the work on Second Street, and he wanted me there, too."

"Oh, John," moaned Maryanne.

Her husband continued to explain without any prompting from Celia. In fact, he seemed relieved to finally admit the truth. "So I figured I'd arrange a meeting first and propose a deal. Tell him that, in exchange for keeping quiet about me, I'd convince Russell and Hutchinson to oppose Martin's plans for the cut."

"How did you plan to do that?" she asked, part of her mind engrossed in his story, the other part wondering where the neighbor girl was and what might happen if she came upstairs and interrupted them.

"I'd heard Hutchinson was friendly with that saloon girl. I'd seen them together at her place. He'd sure want that kept quiet," he said, and Celia wondered how long John Kelly had been spying on Katie. "And Russell was an opium eater. I spotted him once. In Chinatown. Old Martin would've been mad as a hornet if he'd found out. Russell even owed Dan money."

"What's that about Dan, John?" asked Maryanne.

"So you had Eddie take a note to Virgil Nash, pretending it was from Jasper Martin to ensure he would show up at that meeting," said Celia.

"He came, all right. Didn't recognize me straightaway, not without my beard, but, boy, once he figured it out, was he shocked to come across me again," he said. "I made my proposal. I should've figured he wouldn't agree. Instead, he laughed. Just like Silas had laughed. It wasn't my fault, see?"

"I'm sure you never meant to kill him," said Celia.

"No, I didn't. I swear I didn't."

"John!" Maryanne shouted, causing the baby to yowl. "What did you do? What are you saying? What's any of this got to do with my brother?"

"I'm sorry, Maryanne, I am," he said, the blush of red subsiding from his cheeks. "But when Nash laughed at me, I got out my knife . . . It was over before I could think."

Maryanne hugged her infant close, his cries muffled against her chemise. "No. No. This can't be."

"I took his watch and money to make it look like a robbery. Wrapped him in some oilcloth left in the alley. Cleaned up. Got lucky that the coals in the box stove were still hot enough to burn the rags I used," Mr. Kelly continued while Celia ticked through the list of possible ways she could escape. He was blocking the only way out, though, and she would never be capable of shoving him aside; he was a good three or four stone heavier than she. "Might've worked, too, if Dan hadn't run into me outside the offices when I wasn't supposed to be there. When he found Nash's body, I knew he'd think I'd killed him and put him in the cellar."

*Why won't he leave me be?* . . . Dan hadn't meant Nash; he had meant the brother-in-law who'd constantly criticized him and made him miserable.

"How could you, John?" Maryanne cried out. "How could you? You killed my brother!"

This time, he looked away from Celia. "I didn't, Maryanne. I didn't, I swear. I went to see him, tried to explain, gave him the money I took off Nash in order to get him to leave town and forget what he saw; that's all. He had an accident."

"Oh, John."

With no time for a second thought, Celia swung her portmanteau and struck him in the face, surprise as much as the blow itself staggering him to his knees. She bolted past him into the hallway, running for the stairs. She heard him shout as she plunged down the steps, stumbling over her skirts.

The bottom of the staircase looked so very distant, and she could hear his feet pounding on the steps above her. She was halfway down. Her pulse thudded in her head. The neighbor girl had come from the back of the house to stare up at them, her mouth agape. Just a few more steps. Then to the door. Maryanne screeched from the bedchamber. Two more steps. Celia tripped, tumbling to the ground, her portmanteau flying from her grasp.

She landed in a heap on the floor. Above her, John Kelly's body was outlined by the shaft of light coming from the upstairs bedchamber.

He had a pistol in his hand, the faint lamplight glinting off the barrel aimed at her. Slowly, he descended the narrow staircase until he stood on the bottom step. "I hate to do this, ma'am," he said, looking down at her. "You've been good to my wife and me."

Her portmanteau was within reach if she simply slid her hand over to it; but she couldn't risk betraying her intentions by taking her eyes off his face in order to determine where her medical bag lay.

"You do not wish to shoot me, Mr. Kelly," she said, quivering so greatly that her teeth clacked against one another. "I trust you did not mean to last night, and you do not mean to now." She scrambled to her knees, the motion inching her nearer to her bag. But her crinoline and her skirts were a terrible hindrance. "I also believe you did not mean to kill either of the Nashes. But if you shoot me now, it shall be murder and you shall hang."

His answer to her logic was to pull back the hammer, the click seeming to echo in Celia's head.

The neighbor girl had crept into the hallway, her thin-soled boots whispering across the raggedy carpet. She stared at them both, her mouth agape.

"I'll say I thought you were an intruder," Mr. Kelly responded to Celia. "This one here won't say different, will you, girl?"

The girl shook her head.

Celia had shifted enough to reach the portmanteau, and she wrapped her fingers around the handles. "But think of your wife. How upset she shall be. And after losing her brother . . ."

"You gonna shoot her?" the neighbor girl asked.

John Kelly turned the gun on her, and she screamed. "Shut up!" he yelled.

She screamed louder, a piercing wail, and he shot at her, the sound deafening in the confined space. The girl fell to the floor, clutching her arm, her blood a rapidly spreading bloom of crimson across her sleeve.

"I'm murdered!" the girl keened.

Mr. Kelly lowered his gun. "I'm sorry," he stammered, gaping at what he'd done. "I didn't mean . . ."

*Now, Celia. Now.*

Muttering a hasty prayer, Celia clambered to her feet and swung her bag at him with all her strength.

# CHAPTER 16

The front door burst open and a man shouted, "Get down!"

But there was no need for Celia to drop to the ground, as Mr. Kelly lay unconscious at her feet. Her portmanteau had connected with the left side of the man's head, rendering him momentarily senseless.

She turned to face the door. "You may lower your weapon, Mr. Greaves."

The detective exhaled and carefully returned the hammer to a safe position. "In one piece, Mrs. Davies?"

Though the entry hall was nearly dark as night, she could see the relieved expression on his face.

"In one piece, Mr. Greaves," she replied as Mr. Taylor hurried around his supervisor. He carried a pair of handcuffs, which he quickly secured around John Kelly's wrists.

"What's happened?" called Maryanne from the top of the stairs, leaning against the balustrade, her swaddled newborn clutched in her arms. "John? John!"

"He shall recover, Mrs. Kelly," said Celia. "Return to bed before you do yourself harm."

"But what are you doing? Where are you taking him?" Mrs. Kelly asked Mr. Taylor, who'd roused her husband and was lifting him to his feet. "John!"

"He is going to the police station to be charged, Mrs. Kelly," answered Mr. Greaves, holstering his gun. "And please go to bed as Mrs. Davies suggests."

Crying, Maryanne returned to her bedchamber.

Celia collected her medical bag and knelt next to the neighbor girl, who had struggled into a seated position against the hallway wall, the blood from her wound smeared along the peeling wallpaper. There was a coin-sized tear in the sleeve of her dress. Celia grasped the fabric and ripped a larger hole, searching for an exit wound. And thankfully finding one.

"My dress!" the girl howled.

"It's already ruined. I could use some light, Mr. Greaves," said Celia while Mr. Taylor escorted John Kelly outside. "There is a lantern in the kitchen. And water as well. I must clean her arm to see if cloth has become embedded in the wound."

He headed for the kitchen, and Celia took out the supplies she needed, starting with her fine-tipped forceps.

"What're you gonna do with those?"

"Remove debris from the wound."

"It's gonna hurt, ain't it?" she asked, recoiling even though Celia had yet to touch the wound.

"Only if you move."

Obediently, the girl went rigid.

Mr. Greaves returned with a basin of water and the lantern, setting them at Celia's side. From the rear of the house came the sound of Clary Kelly's cries. "Somebody needs to tend to that baby back there," he said.

"Perhaps you could assist in that regard until I finish seeing to . . ." Celia glanced at the girl. "To?" she asked.

The girl stared blankly at her. "Oh. My name's Lissy."

"While I see to Miss Lissy here. What do you think, Mr. Greaves?" Celia asked.

He looked alarmed by her suggestion. "I think I'd rather wrestle a bear than try to quiet that kid."

"It is not so difficult," said Celia, gently cleaning Lissy's wounds, which renewed the bleeding. Lissy whimpered. Clary let out a lengthy wail.

"It is for me," he answered, retreating up the stairs.

*Men.*

Celia quickly removed dress fibers from the wounds. "I will not stitch the holes closed, Lissy. Wash them with clean water and try to keep them dry so they heal properly. Here. Hold these in place while I wrap bandaging around your arm," she said, handing the girl two squares of linen to press to the wounds.

"All this time we've been livin' next to a killer," said the girl, watching Celia's hands as they worked. "My ma never did like him none," she added with a sniffle.

"There. All finished." She tied off the bandage and stood. "How do you feel? Are you too light-headed to tend to Clary?"

"I'm not takin' care of some killer's kid!"

"Clary is innocent, my dear. As is Mrs. Kelly."

Grumbling her discontent, the girl allowed Celia to help

her to her feet. As she shuffled off to tend to the Kellys' daughter, Celia heard the girl mutter something about lousy Micks. An ironic bit of prejudice, since none of the Kellys were actually Irish.

Clary's distant cries subsided, and Celia closed her medical bag, setting it on a wobbly three-legged table shoved against the wall.

Mr. Greaves returned. "I think Mrs. Kelly could make use of your services, ma'am."

"By the way, I am glad to see the swelling on your face has subsided, Mr. Greaves. You look far better than you did earlier today." Heavens, it was hard to fathom that his brawl with Frank had occurred only that morning. "I shall need to remove those stitches in a few days, so do not forget to come by the clinic."

He grinned, a crooked lift of his lips. "Is there ever a time when you're not a nurse, Mrs. Davies?"

"Is there ever a time when you're not a detective, Mr. Greaves?"

"Not one minute of the day, ma'am."

She smiled. "It is all over, is it not?"

"Yep, it is." He looked over at her bag. "And good work with that portmanteau. I had no idea it could make such an effective weapon."

"A blow delivered directly to a man's temple has salutary effects, Mr. Greaves," she replied.

"You're fortunate it does," he said. "Because if it didn't, you'd be lying dead on this floor in a pool of blood."

"You do not trust your ability to shoot a man menacing a female?" she asked.

"Not when that female is standing between me and the man we're talking about."

As she looked at him, she realized how close she'd come to serious harm. She pressed a hand to his sleeve. "Thank you."

"Thank your housekeeper for insisting that Taylor and I get over here right away," he said, folding his hand over hers, his skin warm. "Besides, it looks like you managed just fine on your own."

"With only a meager portmanteau."

"You're a mighty resourceful woman, ma'am."

"I will remember that you said that, Mr. Greaves," she replied, slipping her hand from beneath his and keenly feeling the absence of his touch.

"I want to hear everything Kelly said to you."

"And I shall tell you as soon as I've seen how his wife is doing. I do wonder how she shall manage. She loved him dearly, you know," Celia added, not knowing why she told him that, as though one woman's love for a man meant he was worthy of leniency.

He did not comment, and Celia went upstairs, her steps heavy. She found Maryanne seated upright in her bed, her newborn asleep in her arms, a faraway look in her eyes.

"Mrs. Kelly?" asked Celia. "Would you care for a sedative?"

"It's a mistake," she said, clutching her baby closer. "It's got to be a mistake, Mrs. Davies. John's not a killer. He's not like that."

"I am sorry."

"No, you're not!" the other woman shrieked, going from numb to hysterical in a heartbeat.

Celia went to her side and laid a hand upon Maryanne's arm. Her skin felt warm. "Mrs. Kelly, keep calm. You shall wake the baby."

"I don't care! This is a mistake. John wouldn't hurt anybody!" she declared. "I don't care what that detective has to say."

The baby's face pinched, and he woke with a shuddering cry.

"Oh, shh, shh," said Maryanne, dissolving into tears as she tried to soothe the child. "Quiet there, little one. I just wish I understood. My John would never hurt anybody. He just wouldn't."

"He was frightened. Frightened that he might be caught at last," said Celia, clasping Maryanne's hand in hers. "He wanted to protect you and the children from what he'd done in Virginia City. It made him desperate."

"Desperate enough to have killed some man?" she asked. Celia mentally corrected her statement—*two men.* "How could my John have done that? And to shoot that saloon girl." Maryanne's fingers tightened around Celia's. "And you. He shot at you!"

"I trust he did not mean to hurt me. The shot went very wide."

A tear traced a path down Maryanne's cheek, and she swiped it away. "He didn't miss her, though, did he? Or the neighbor's girl, Lissy."

How could she reply? Celia chose silence.

"I knew there was something the matter," said Maryanne. "These past few weeks, he's been so short-tempered with me and Clary. Shouting over nothing. And then there was that night when he came home so late, all dirty and not letting me wash his clothes, saying he'd take care of them himself and I wasn't to worry, what with the baby coming so soon. And buying a pistol the other day when he'd never had use for one before . . ." Her chest heaved with a sob. "I should've suspected. And now I don't even know who I am. Who I'm married to. I've always thought he was a good man, despite his tempers and the way he treated Dan. But I was wrong."

"You wished to believe the best of him," said Celia. "Besides,

NO PITY for the DEAD

what would you have done if you *had* known? Turn your husband over to the authorities? It is just as well."

*But love is blind and lovers cannot see the pretty follies that themselves commit.* Except that these events were hardly pretty follies, Mr. Shakespeare.

"What am I to do now, Mrs. Davies, with two children and no husband? I've got nobody here to help me. Nobody at all." Her tears began to fall faster. "My father was right to tell me I was marrying in haste and would regret it. I should've listened to him, instead of being headstrong."

"We *all* make mistakes. All of us." Celia's thoughts ventured to her own hasty wedding, her own rashness. She vowed she would be cautious from now on.

*I am sorry, Nicholas, but I must protect my heart.*

"We all make mistakes, Mrs. Kelly. And all we can do is hope to learn from them."

"Thank you for discovering the man who killed my husband, Detective Greaves." Mrs. Nash clutched a handkerchief trimmed in black lace, but her eyes were dry.

They stood in the woman's parlor the next morning, he and Taylor, where they'd first spoken to her about Virgil Nash's murder, among the marble-topped tables and potted ferns, the air heavily scented by cut roses. Taylor looked uncomfortable again, crushing his hat in his hand, his boots too dirty to be standing on fancy rugs. Nick had been convinced, back then, that Nash's death had everything to do with the Second Street cut, and that the men of Martin and Company had a role in the murder. Instead, it had come down to one man's desire to save himself from the consequences of a years-old crime.

Kelly had almost gotten away with it, experiencing the greatest stroke of good fortune when a witness had mistakenly thought he'd spotted Nash leaving town with his mistress. But Kelly's luck ran out when his brother-in-law became convinced there was gold in that cellar, and dug up a body instead . . .

"I'm sorry, though, that I can't return your husband's watch yet," said Nick. "We'll need it for the trial."

"I understand," she said, stealing another quick look at Nick's black eye. Again she resisted asking him who'd caused it. Maybe she presumed he'd suffered the injury in the pursuit of justice. "Will this man hang?"

"John Kelly . . . Cuddy Pike has a lot to answer for—the deaths of your husband and Silas Nash. Attempts on two witnesses' lives. Which means a trial here and another in Virginia City." That morning, a telegram had finally arrived from the police in Nevada, who were mighty interested in getting ahold of Cuddy Pike.

"So he *will* hang," said Mrs. Nash, seeking assurances.

Nick glanced at Taylor, who was inspecting the dried mud that had fallen from his boots onto the carpet rather than offering an opinion on the outcome of the trials. Anything could happen, but Nick felt that Kelly's prospects for avoiding the noose were dim.

"We'll have to wait and see," he said.

"Thank you anyway." This time, there were tears in Mrs. Nash's eyes. "I shall speak approvingly of you to Police Chief Crowley."

Well, that'd be a first from a victim's family member.

"We'll be taking our leave now, ma'am," said Nick, reseating his hat on his head and heading for the door, where the Nashes' domestic showed him and Taylor out.

On the sidewalk, Taylor rooted in his pockets for a cigar and his friction matches. "Wonder if she'll sell this place," he said, gazing around and out at the beautiful view toward the bay and the distant hills, the damage caused by leveling Second Street still in the future.

"Doubt she could without taking a huge loss. Nobody's going to want to buy up here, with the cut coming." Even if Martin and Company didn't win the contract for the work, somebody would eventually. Progress, if that was what it was rightly called, was inevitable.

Cigar located, Taylor lit it and took a puff, the smoke streaming from his lips in a satisfied exhalation into the wind that flapped the bottom of his knee-length coat. "Suppose not."

They headed toward Market where they could catch the Omnibus Railroad.

"The only question I have left, sir, is who pushed Mrs. Davies over the wall at Cliff House?" asked Taylor. "And where was Frank Hutchinson the night Martin was digging up Nash's body? Out until ten that evening, right? Did he ever explain?"

"I think he was numbing his woes in a saloon someplace other than Burke's, finally feeling guilty about his dalliance with Miss Lehane," answered Nick. "And as for your first question, Martin won't admit to pushing Mrs. Davies, but I think he did. Just to teach her a lesson."

"If she'd tumbled all the way to the shore, she might've broken her neck," said Taylor. "That's a danged harsh lesson, sir."

"There wasn't much chance of her falling that far, but I wonder if Martin would've even cared."

"You would've cared, sir."

Nick looked over at his assistant. "I would've, and more than I like to admit."

Taylor winked. "She's a fine woman, Mr. Greaves."

"I know, and that's what has me worried." Celia Davies was refined, beautiful, and intelligent, too fine for a man whose only liaisons were with actresses and saloon girls, and who'd fallen in love with a friend's wife.

He stuck his hand into his coat pocket, and his fingers touched the piece of paper inside—a telegram from Ellie saying that, since he'd decided not to reply to her last letter, she was making plans to get on a paddle wheeler bound for San Francisco as soon as she could manage. Another woman to deal with.

But maybe it was time to talk to this one. Dang but he missed his sister. She might be able to make sense of his life for him.

"Mrs. Davies is fond of you, sir," said Taylor after another deep puff on his cigar. "I wouldn't worry about her being too good for a rough old policeman like you or me."

Nick released his grip on the telegram and looked over at his assistant. "Are you saying I'm rough and old, Taylor?"

Taylor laughed loudly. "Not at all, sir. Not at all."

"You're telling me you two girls were the ones who left those notes for me?" Addie's outrage grew with each fresh giggle that came from Grace and Barbara, seated together on the piano bench. "And the flowers? And the sweets? *You're* my admirer?"

Celia, seated by the parlor window, lifted her teacup to her lips and hid a smile behind it. Another mystery solved.

"We wanted to cheer you up, Miss Ferguson," said Grace. "Honest, that was all. You deserve an admirer. We didn't mean to hurt your feelings."

Addie blushed, and she turned toward Celia. "I'll nae be teased so. I'll be leaving your employ, ma'am, if this is what I'm to endure. I would appreciate a character, if you'll be so kind."

"Now, Addie, surely you do not mean you would leave us," said Celia. *Heavens, I dearly* hope *she does not mean that!* "Barbara, apologize at once to Addie for engaging in such a prank."

Barbara hesitated, and Grace reached over to pinch the top of her friend's hand.

"Ouch!" she said, but she was smiling. After all that had happened, Celia was grateful that their friendship had survived. Her own relationship with Barbara, strained by her involvement in another murder investigation, was proving slightly more difficult to patch. At least her cousin had not repeated her threat that she wanted Celia to move out of the house.

*I will give us time. And perhaps Barbara shall come to understand.*

"I'm sorry, Addie," said Barbara. "Truly. We meant well. You were so blue about Mr. Taylor ignoring you—"

"I dinna ken what you're saying, Miss Barbara!" Addie blushed again. "I dinna care if the man takes note of me." She lifted her chin. "'Tis his loss."

"We should've realized, though, you might think the notes were coming from that Mr. Knowles," said Grace. "We didn't want you to think that, because we don't much like him, do we, Bee?"

"Weel, I dinna care for his grinning, either," said Addie. "And I've sent him a note saying I'll nae be going to the pyrotechnics with him for the Fourth of July."

"Wait. When did these plans happen?" asked Celia, setting down her cup of tea.

"I didna tell you?"

"No, you did not," said Celia. "And there is no need to change your plans with Mr. Knowles."

"Aye, weel, 'tis too late. I've gone and told him I'm verra busy."

"Then come with us," said Celia. She had made plans to accompany the Hutchinsons, presuming the contusions Mr. Greaves had given Frank would be thoroughly healed and permit him to appear in public without causing gossip. "You would not wish to miss the Fourth of July celebrations, and Jane will not mind. You can help us chaperone the girls; I am certain they would enjoy having you along."

Addie cast a skeptical glance at Grace and Barbara.

"Please do come, Miss Ferguson," said Grace. "I'll tell Stepmama that you'll be joining us, okay?"

"If you insist, I'll nae disagree. Let me warm your tea, ma'am," she said to Celia, and departed for the kitchen, her shoulders straighter and a bounce in her step.

"Thank you, Grace," said Celia. "That was most kind."

"After the excitement of the last few days, we all could use some kindness, I guess," the girl responded. "At least Papa's forgiven me for talking to that detective about what I'd seen. I wasn't sure he would."

"Your father is a good man, Grace. Of course he would understand that you wished to do the right thing."

"In fact, he's so pleased that you helped clear his name, he's told Stepmama to talk to you about how we can help you expand your clinic," said Grace. "Maybe find a dedicated building for it."

"My goodness," said Celia, overwhelmed. She heard the front door open, and Owen strode into the hallway.

"Guess I shoulda knocked, ma'am," he said, noticing the

girls in the parlor and sweeping his cap from his head, leaving his hair sticking up in its wake.

"Good morning, Owen," said Barbara.

"Owen, I do not believe you and Grace were properly introduced the last time you met," said Celia. Had it only been this past Thursday when he'd burst into the house with news of a dead body? "Grace, this is Owen Cassidy. Owen, Miss Grace Hutchinson."

"Pleased to meet you," he stammered as Grace offered him a teasingly winsome smile. *She is well out of your grasp, Owen. Do not dream of reaching so high.*

Barbara, noticing the looks exchanged by the two, frowned and tapped her friend on the shoulder. "Let's go see if Addie has anything good to eat and go outside. The sun's finally out."

The girls trooped out, and Owen's shoulders sagged as he watched them go.

"Mr. Hutchinson, by the way, had his daughter bring me a note today. He has agreed to take you back on," said Celia, "once he finds a supervisor to replace Mr. Kelly."

"Can't believe Mr. Kelly was the killer, ma'am. Plum awful."

"Very awful. How did you find his wife when you went to her house?" Celia asked him. When he'd popped in before Grace had arrived, Celia had sent him with a small hamper of food to check on Maryanne and the baby.

He went back into the entryway and returned with the wicker hamper. "She weren't there, ma'am," he said, holding it out as proof. "That loony girl next door with the bandage on her arm was hopping around and saying they was . . . were gone. Left this morning. Early. She looked as happy as a tick about to burst to tell me, too!"

"Oh dear." Maryanne, likely eager to get away from the gossiping and unkind neighbors, must have found somewhere to take her children after all. Hopefully not anywhere too far, though; she would want to be close by when her husband was put on trial. "You can keep the food," she said, nodding at the hamper.

"I can?" Owen peeked beneath the checked cloth covering the food. "But the widow I room with is gonna think I stole it!"

"Then let me put a note inside that will reassure her."

"Don't think she can read, ma'am."

Addie returned with a fresh pot of tea, setting it on the table in the center of the parlor. "Have you come now for a meal, Owen Cassidy? Always eating, you are."

He held up the hamper for Addie to see. "Mrs. Davies said I could keep this."

"Then you'll nae need me to feed you, will you?" said Addie, turning on her heel and marching off.

"Never sure she likes me, ma'am."

"Addie adores you, Owen. I think you remind her of one of her brothers." She shooed a hand at him. "Take the hamper into the kitchen and have a bite to eat. And do not be too rambunctious around the young woman you will find there." Katie had risen that morning to take a meal in the kitchen rather than have a tray sent up to her room, which she claimed she found to be too "high heeled" for a mere saloon girl. "Miss Lehane is still recovering from a bullet wound."

"Whoa! Ain't never boring around here, ma'am!" Grinning, he dashed off, the hamper swinging from his hand.

Celia rose, her hips and back aching in protest, sore from yesterday's tumble down the stairs. She was fortunate that a few aches and bruises were all she suffered from, she supposed. Taking two tumbles in the span of a few days was not a practice she wished to continue.

Wrapping her mother's cashmere shawl around her shoulders, she poured herself a fresh cup of tea and went outside to the front porch.

She leaned against the railing as the bells of Saint Francis tolled the hour. At Vallejo's intersection with Stockton, the Omnibus Railroad horsecar clopped by on its way north to Meiggs' Wharf. The wagon from Winkle's Bakery had come from the shop on Battery to make a delivery to the nicest house on the street, the stately brick one a few doors up from them. The grocers on the corner must have received a fresh shipment of vegetables, because a crowd was clustered around the señora in her bright skirts who was monitoring the crates of goods. The neighborhood boys, including Angelo, played a boisterous game of tag in the street, and across the way, Joaquin's mother was once again sweeping her porch and frowning at Celia. *Ah well,* thought Celia as she sipped from her cup, *what can I expect when trouble seems to find me on a regular basis?*

But how ordinary it all was that day. How satisfyingly ordinary.

"Mrs. Davies," called out Nicholas Greaves, striding down the road.

"Good morning, Mr. Greaves. You have come too soon for me to remove those stitches, I'm afraid."

"This isn't a medical visit, ma'am," he said, climbing the stairs.

"Would you care for some tea, then?" she asked.

"No need to bother. I won't stay long." He joined her at the railing and stared out at the street. "I like it up here. Above the city."

"It no longer feels so much above the city. Every day, there are more houses, springing up like weeds," she said. "Soon there will be nothing but buildings between us and the shoreline of North Beach." Even then, the city would no doubt continue to grow wildly; there were even plans to extend that shoreline farther into the bay.

"I've heard that Martin and Company won't be getting the contract for the Second Street cut. The Board of Supervisors decided this morning that nobody will, for a while at least," he said. "Looks like Nash's protests have won out, in the end."

"Small consolation to him or his widow. And oh how Frank shall be disappointed." The house he hoped to build on California Street to impress Jane's father might have to wait. "You were mistaken about him, though, Mr. Greaves. His relationship with Katie was ill-advised, but in other regards . . ."

"I was wrong about his complicity in murder, ma'am, but I'm not wrong about him."

"What did he do to you?"

His hat turned through his hands. "If you want to remain friends with him, I'd rather not say."

"I shall coax the story out of you one day, you know."

"I don't doubt that you will."

She watched the wagon from the bakery pull away from the curb and turn the corner, the driver tipping his hat to a young woman crossing the road. She heard the laughter of the boys as they chased one another. She breathed in the aroma of Mr. Greaves' shaving soap, carried on the breeze, and felt her will to protect her heart weaken. *I should tell him. I should tell him about Patrick.*

"Mr. Greaves, there is something you should know."

"What's that?"

"I . . ." The urge faded. *Don't be impulsive again, Celia. He ignored you for more than three months. Do not forget that.* "Never mind," she said. "It is nothing."

"Okay," he said, the brim of his hat turning around and around. "I didn't come here just to tell you about Martin and Company, ma'am. I came because I wanted to ask you a favor."

"Oh?"

"The fireworks in two weeks . . . Would you . . . I mean . . . ," he stammered.

"Would I like to attend with you?" she asked, aware she had never seen him so discomfited. "Well, I do already have plans . . ."

"Then never mind," he blurted. "I don't know why I asked. Danged Taylor."

Grumbling, he slapped his hat back onto his head, nearly crushing the crown.

*Honestly, Celia, what harm would there be in saying yes to a pyrotechnics display?*

"It would be rude of me to back out of my plans to go with the Hutchinsons, but perhaps you could come with us," she said.

"With Frank?" he asked, sounding as though a bare-legged run through a field of nettles would be preferable to an evening spent with Frank Hutchinson.

"That, I fear, is the price of attending the pyrotechnics with me, Mr. Greaves."

The breath he released came out as a groan. "You drive a hard bargain, ma'am."

"I take it you have just agreed?"

"Yes, Mrs. Davies."

"Good. Very good indeed," she said, smiling as she entwined her arm with his.

Deciding that she would protect her heart some other day.

AUTHOR'S NOTE

On January 8, 1863, San Francisco's *Alta* newspaper ran an editorial decrying twelve years of hill flattening, the efforts to ease transit across town destroying much of San Francisco's natural beauty in the process. The paper's complaints had little effect. Rincon Hill was next in the developers' sights, their plans driven by a desire for easy access to the Pacific Mail Wharves at the south end of Second Street. It didn't hurt that the man most responsible for demanding the cut happened to own property near the city end of the road and expected to profit from the increased worth of his land. The wealthy homeowners atop the hill weren't happy at all, expecting—as the Nashes did in this book—that the value of their property would plummet once Second Street turned into an ugly gouge. The homeowners' complaints had no more effect on the eventual outcome than the *Alta*'s editorial; their opponents would prove to be more politically and socially connected, and unstoppable. In 1869, two years after the events in *No Pity for the Dead* take place, the Second Street Cut was completed. True to the hilltop owners' fears, their property values plunged and the move to what would become known as Nob Hill was on. In 1873, the installation of the first cable car line would thankfully act as a disincentive to future grading projects.

Most of my characters in this series are fictional, but in *No Pity for the Dead*, I have included two very real individuals—Levi Strauss and Joshua Norton, who was also known as Emperor Norton. In 1867, Levi Strauss was already a successful purveyor of dry goods, having taken advantage of the needs of Gold Rush miners by supplying clothing and other items. Despite his position as a prominent businessman, he reportedly asked his employees to simply call him "Levi," a charmingly humble request in such a formal time period. The invention of the riveted denim pant, which would garner him great wealth, was still a few years in the future. Joshua Norton was a very different character. An English immigrant from South Africa, he had arrived with a modest fortune that he soon lost speculating on the rice market. By 1859, he had reinvented himself as the Emperor of the United States, regularly issuing edicts on the proper running of the country. The eccentric fellow became wildly popular with San Franciscans, feted by business owners eager to profit from the Emp's fame, his attendance at the openings of everything from rail lines to stores to musical entertainments a requirement. In 1880 he collapsed and died on a street, penniless but not forgotten.

My thanks to Sarah Bar-Hillel for her assistance with Yiddish, and to the folks behind the California Digital Newspaper Collection, a fabulous trove of knowledge if ever there was one. And thanks as ever to Candace Calvert and to my agent, Natasha Kern—without your support, I would have given up on this crazy writing business years ago! Lastly, to my family, I extend my love and gratitude.

**Nancy Herriman** received a bachelor's degree in chemical engineering from the University of Cincinnati, where she also took courses in history and archaeology. She's a past winner of RWA's Daphne du Maurier Award for Best Unpublished Mystery/Romantic Suspense, and when she isn't writing, she enjoys performing with various choral groups. She lives in central Ohio with her husband and their two teenage sons.